DAW Books presents the finest in urban fantasy from Seanan McGuire:

InCryptid Novels

DISCOUNT ARMAGEDDON
MIDNIGHT BLUE-LIGHT SPECIAL
HALF-OFF RAGNAROK
POCKET APOCALYPSE
CHAOS CHOREOGRAPHY
MAGIC FOR NOTHING
TRICKS FOR FREE
THAT AIN'T WITCHCRAFT
IMAGINARY NUMBERS
CALCULATED RISKS*

SPARROW HILL ROAD
THE GIRL IN THE GREEN SILK GOWN

October Daye Novels

ROSEMARY AND RUE
A LOCAL HABITATION
AN ARTIFICIAL NIGHT
LATE ECLIPSES
ONE SALT SEA
ASHES OF HONOR
CHIMES AT MIDNIGHT
THE WINTER LONG
A RED ROSE CHAIN
ONCE BROKEN FAITH
THE BRIGHTEST FELL
NIGHT AND SILENCE
THE UNKINDEST TIDE
A KILLING FROST*

Coming soon from DAW Books

IMAGINARY NUMBERS

An *InCryptid* Novel

SEANAN McGUIRE

DAW BOOKS, INC.

DONALD A. WOLLHEIM, FOUNDER

1745 Broadway, New York, NY 10019

ELIZABETH R. WOLLHEIM

SHEILA E. GILBERT

PUBLISHERS

www.dawbooks.com

Published by DAW Books, Inc.
1745 Broadway, New York, NY 10019.

First Printing, February 2020
1 2 3 4 5 6 7 8 9

For Alexis.

I got some math in your math.

Price Family Tree

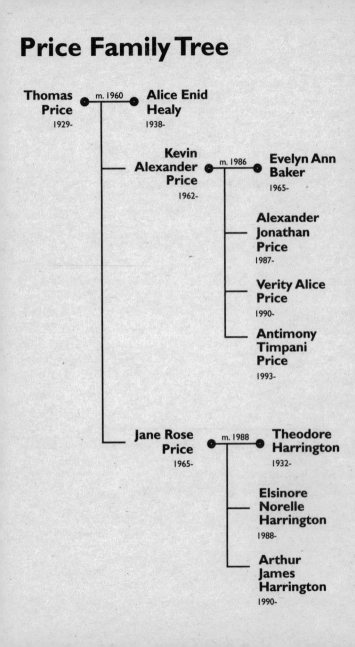

Baker Family Tree

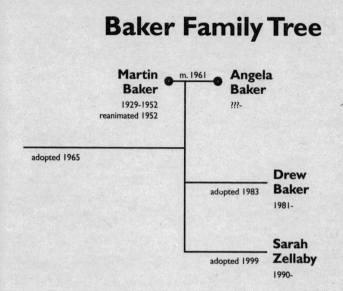

Illusion, noun:

1. A false or misleading image or perception of reality; a sham.

Mimicry, noun:

1. A close resemblance to another organism.

2. Intentional imitation of another person.

3. See also "ambush predator."

Prologue

$$\pi_2(n) \sim 2C_2 \frac{n}{(\ln n)^2} \sim 2C_2 \int_2^n \frac{dt}{(\ln t)^2}$$

"No one deserves to be the only living example of their own kind. No one should be that alone in the world."

—Angela Baker

On the road from Florida to Ohio, passing through the Virginias

Twenty years ago

IT HAD SEEMED LIKE such a good idea at the time.

Take the grandchildren and go to Lowryland. Sure, it was a thirteen-hour drive, but what was the point of having an RV if you didn't use it to go on an adventure every once in a while? Martin loved to drive—one of the men he'd been before he died had been a long-haul trucker, and some of the old instincts and habits still lingered in the long muscles of his legs and the subtle cant of his spine. Angela wasn't as fond of sitting behind the wheel, but her presence caused the worst of the folks they shared the road with to decide to go and drive like fools in someone else's lane; the traffic police could probably have charted their route by looking for the odd reduction in accidents.

The trip down *to* Florida had been as perfect as a two-day road trip with a six-year-old, a nine-year-old, and a twelve-year-old could possibly have been. They'd lost Verity up a tree at one of the rest stops, and had needed to give Alex permission to shoot her with a slingshot in order to get her down; they'd had to dissuade Antimony from following the bright lights of a traveling carnival across the highway and onto private property.

(Angela understood *why* the girl had been lured. Like her father before her, Annie had already spent a summer with the Campbell Family Carnival, and probably assumed anyone who owned a Ferris wheel was a friend of the family. Not being interested in explaining why she'd allowed one of her human grandchildren to run away to join the literal circus, Angela had been forced to lure Annie back to the RV with promises of candy, soda, and another play-through of her favorite Raffi CD. They were all going to have "Baby Beluga" stuck in their heads for the rest of their lives.)

Lowryland had been, as expected, wonderful. Verity had scaled the geodesic wall before any of the security guards on duty had realized what was about to happen; Alex had managed to catch sixteen different species of frog, snake, and lizard, all within the Park proper; Antimony had been able to take her picture with several princesses and a very confused Goblin King, all while consuming her weight in cotton candy. Thirteen hours each way was a small price to pay for five days of grandchild bliss.

Well, thirteen hours each way and a fairly substantial amount of money. The wonders of Lowryland didn't come cheap, and that was before souvenirs, food, and all the other little pins and needles that accompanied a theme park stay. But it was worth it.

Angela looked approvingly at her grandchildren, who were sleeping peacefully on the RV couch. The three of them were tangled together in a rare moment of sibling peace, Alex at one end with Verity's head on his shoulder, Annie curled up with her own head in Verity's lap. All three were sunburned, wearing Lowryland T-shirts, and completely at ease with the world, trusting their grandparents to keep them safe no matter what happened next.

Angela knew they would lose that peace soon enough. They were being trained as soldiers in a war they'd never asked for any part of, and while their parents would never force them to fight, she already knew they would never walk away of their own volition. They had too much family involved in the conflict. She could never leave. Neither could Martin, or Drew, or their Uncle Ted, or their cousins. As long as humans hated cryptids, cryptids would have to fight. As long as cryptids fought, the Prices wouldn't be able to get away.

She was considering going to fetch her camera when the pain began.

It lanced through her head like a bolt of lightning, sudden and intense and agonizing enough that she gripped the nearest piece of furniture to keep herself from falling to the floor. It pulsed, rising and falling like a wave, filling the inside of her skull with static, making it almost impossible to keep her balance.

Slowly, the pulse began to resolve into words. *Help. Help me. Help. Help me.*

Angela's expression hardened. Another cuckoo. One who was broadcasting so loudly that they'd been able to break through her natural barriers against telepathy. She couldn't pick up simple thoughts the way most of her kind could—it was all out and no in, for her—but if someone really wanted to scream, she could occasionally hear them.

The pain would pass. Even the most powerful telepath in the world didn't have an infinite broadcast range, and there was no way she was lingering here, not in another cuckoo's hunting grounds.

Angela was all too aware that she was an aberration among her own kind, a freak of nature. She'd been reminded of that fact every time she'd been forced to interact with another cuckoo. It was a miracle she'd survived—something must have had her mother run-ning scared when it came time to select a nest for her defective offspring, something big enough that she hadn't noticed when Angela failed to acknowledge her telepathic commands. In a species of people who could bend others to their wills, Angela was weak, and cuck-oos didn't tolerate weakness.

The girl—she thought it was a girl—screaming in her head certainly wasn't weak. She was loud enough to make Angela's teeth ache, to make every muscle in her neck lock up in sympathetic agony. They needed to drive faster. They needed to get away from here before the psychic screaming attracted something dangerous.

Please, please help me, wailed the girl, and Angela went cold.

Cuckoos didn't say "please."

Oh, they understood the meaning of the word—they heard it often enough. They just didn't believe in it. "Please" was something victims said. "Please" meant the fun was just beginning. But this girl, this cuckoo-child who sounded no older than Verity, also sounded like she *meant* it. Like she was in trouble, and terrified, and reaching out in the only way she knew how.

Angela Baker was a defective cuckoo who had spent her entire life running away from the species of her birth, putting as many miles as she possibly could be-tween herself and the rest of her species. Her desire for isolation had landed her in a sleepy neighborhood in Ohio, where no cuckoo could hope to find anything to benefit from, had led her to keep herself even further below the radar than her natural inclination. And now there was a cuckoo girl, a *child*, screaming for help in-side her head, in the place that had always been hers, and hers alone.

She had tried to be a good person. She had tried to rise above the inclinations of her species, to choose the better way. She had tried so hard to put her family above herself, to measure her desires against her needs, to get along with the world. And now there was a child screaming in her skull.

Angela Baker was many things. Cuckoo, accountant, monster . . . mother. Mother, and grandmother, and when she heard a little girl crying, it didn't matter where they came from or what they were. She needed to comfort them.

Head still pounding, she pulled herself up straight and turned toward the cab of the RV, opening the small door between herself and the driver. Martin was still focused on the road, humming along with a classic rock CD he had slipped into the player as soon as the children had gone down for their nap. He didn't seem to realize that anything was wrong. Well, of course, he didn't. He wasn't a telepath.

Angela tried to speak. Nothing came out. She licked her lips to moisten them, and finally managed to croak, "We need to take a detour."

Dowsing for a terrified child when the driver couldn't hear her screams and Angela couldn't focus enough to be safe to drive was terrifying. She sat in the passenger seat clutching her temples and occasionally whimpering out an instruction, all of which Martin dutifully followed as soon as he was able. Sometimes she wanted him to turn in places where there was no road, following the telepathic signal as the crow flies, rather than as the highway administration drew the maps.

They'd been driving for an hour and half (including one brief stop for McDonalds when the kids woke up and started whining for fries), leaving the highway far behind. They were cruising along a small backroad just outside Roanoke, Virginia, when Angela abruptly sat bolt upright, throwing one arm out and across Martin's barreled chest, like she thought she could stop the entire RV by pushing the driver deeper into his seat.

"We're here," she whispered. Then, louder, she repeated, "We're *here*. Stop the RV, Martin! *Stop the goddamn RV!*"

Profanity was unusual, where Angela was concerned. Martin slammed one meaty foot on the brake, bringing the whole RV to a shuddering halt. Voices were raised in the back as the children protested this unusual stop. Angela barely noticed. She was already slamming the door open and leaping down, not even bothering to check for traffic as she darted across the road and began slogging through the tall grass on the other side.

"Angela, wait!" Martin turned off the ignition and lumbered after his wife.

He was almost across the road when he heard the back door of the RV slam. He winced. It had been too much to hope that the kids would stay inside when no one had explicitly told them to. It was even more unlikely to hope they'd listen if they were told to turn around.

"Try not to get hit by a car. Your mother would kill me," he called.

"Yes, Grandpa," they chorused dutifully, and kept following him.

By the time their motley little procession reached Angela, she was on her knees in front of a large, muddy storm drain, not seeming to either notice or care about what it was doing to her jeans.

"It's all right," she said, holding out both hands in a beseeching gesture. "You're safe now. I promise, you're safe now."

"You're not my mother!" shouted a thin, terrified voice from inside the drain. It sounded like a little girl; it sounded like she'd been crying. "Don't you try to say that you're her!"

"No, I'm not your mother," Angela agreed. "I heard you calling for help."

There was a long pause. "I didn't say anything," whispered the girl.

"You didn't have to," said Angela. "I'm the same as you are. I'm the same kind of person. I could hear you, even though you didn't make a sound. I'm not your mother. We're still family."

There was another pause, even longer than the first. Then, very slowly, a child crawled out of the storm drain and into the light.

She was very pale, with a milky complexion that should have been flushed, with as hard as she'd clearly been crying, but was washed-out and waxen instead, like something had stolen all the blood from her body. Her eyes were blue, and her cheeks were clean, all the mud having been washed away by the tears. She had twigs and leaves tangled in her long black hair, which was almost identical to Angela's. Everything about her was almost identical to Angela, like she was a carbon copy of the woman, cast in miniature and dressed in a muddy velvet dress that had probably been quite nice before she'd dragged it through an ocean of muck.

There was a tear in the knee of her muddy tights, and she was missing one of her sensible black flats.

"Who died?" blurted Alex. At twelve, he was the best of the trio at picking up on small details, and the worst at keeping his mouth shut about their implications.

The little girl turned wide blue eyes on him, and said gravely, "My parents."

"Oh," said Alex. There was an itching sensation at the edge of his mind, insisting the girl was his sister, his best and *favorite* sister, and he should take care of her. He shoved it aside. It was a stupid thought. Verity was his sister. Antimony was his sister. This girl was a stranger. He'd take care of her anyway, because that was the right thing to do, but that didn't make her family.

Although from the way Grandma was looking at her, maybe she was going to be family soon after all.

The girl sniffled and wiped one eye with the back of her hand, leaving a smear of mud across her cheek. "I w-was sleeping over at Amy's house and then the police were there, saying my parents were dead and did I have anywhere to stay. Amy's mom let me sleep there until the funeral. And then . . . and then one of the cops tried to take me home. He said I was his daughter. But I wasn't his daughter. I'm *not*. My parents died. So I ran from him, only everyone I see says I'm theirs and tries to steal me. It's kidnapping. I wanna go *home*."

The last word was virtually a wail. Angela sighed.

"I'm so sorry, sweetheart," she said. "I'm sorry your parents died, and I'm sorry your home is gone. You're not ours. We can't replace what you've lost. But we'll take care of you, if you'll let us. We'll do the best we can. All right?"

Tired and wet and cold and miserable, the girl sniffled, hard, and nodded.

"All right," repeated Angela. "What's your name?"

"Sarah," said the girl, and the world was different, and everything began.

One

$$\pi_2(n) \sim 2C_2 \frac{n}{(\ln n)^2} \sim 2C_2 \int_2^n \frac{dt}{(\ln t)^2}$$

"There's no such thing as 'normal.' Whoever came up with that idea was probably
selling something nobody wanted to buy."
                                    —Jane Harrington-Price

*Cleveland Hopkins International Airport, outside
security*

Now

Y OU DON'T HAVE TO do this." Angela held me by the
shoulders, keeping her eyes locked on mine, like
she could somehow overcome her own inability to receive projected thoughts and understand exactly what
I was thinking. "No one's going to think less of you if
you need more time to heal. You know that."

"Mom, I'm fine." I put my left hand over hers,
squeezing firmly, hoping the skin-on-skin connection
would let her at least pick up some of my certainty. She
might get my anxiety in the bargain, but she knew I was
anxious. Everyone knew I was anxious. "I've had years.
I need to do this. I can't hide in my room forever."

"You're still recovering. What happened to you—"

"Is part of why I need to get back out there. You
don't know what happened to me. I don't know what
happened to me. Evie has a better chance of helping

me find a doctor who understands my situation than anyone we've got in Ohio."

Uncertainty rolled off her in a wave. I forced myself not to flinch.

Evie is my oldest sibling, adopted by Mom and Dad when she was just a baby. She's also my only *human* sibling, which sort of makes her the white sheep of the family. Mom and I are both Johrlac, colloquially known as cuckoos: telepathic ambush predators who ruin lives for fun. Dad's a Revenant, assembled from somewhere between four and six human corpses— we're honestly not sure. And my brother Drew is a bogeyman. Our family reunions are *awesome*.

Being the only human in a cryptid family got Evie interested in cryptid biology and medicine long before I entered the picture. She's not a doctor, more of a combat medic and herbalist, but it seems like she always knows a guy who knows a guy. None of her assorted guys had been able to help me when I got hurt. That didn't mean she might not be able to find someone who understood the theory, and who could help make sure it would never happen again.

Mom took her right hand off my shoulder, running her thumb across my cheek. "I wish you'd let me come with you to Oregon. Or at least let me tell Evie you're coming so she can meet you at the airport."

"Both of those things sort of go against the point of what I'm trying to do here." I mustered up a wavering smile. Mom's better at reading facial expressions than I am. She has to be. Without telepathy to lean on, she'd had no choice but to learn. "I promise that I will call you as soon as I touch down in Portland. I have to do this. If I can't, if I start to panic, I'll come right home."

"Try not to do it by diverting an entire plane, all right? People notice that sort of thing."

My smile strengthened. I took a step back, reaching up to adjust the strap of my backpack. "I promise that I won't bring an entire plane home with me."

"All right. All right." Impulsively, she reached out and placed her hands against the sides of my face, pulling me closer in order to kiss my forehead. "You are my beloved girl, and I am so proud of you. You know that, right?"

"You never let me forget." I hugged her, quick as I could, and turned away, heading for the security line. I could feel her watching me go, the sweet, familiar edge of her anxiety, of her hope for me. It used to be more bitter than it is now, tinged with the unwanted belief that I was never going to be anything but a cuckoo, never anything but a parasitic predator waiting for the chance to break free of all these silly morals and rules that she worked so hard to teach me. But I fought the world and my nature both, and I won, and now when she looks at me, it's only fear *for* me, never fear *of* me.

I didn't realize how much it ached to have my mother—adoptive or not—living in fear of me until the day it stopped. The day when I realized I could do anything I wanted, because I didn't have to be afraid of myself.

I walked and Angela watched until I turned the corner and she was gone, leaving me surrounded by the press of bodies and the low, constant roar of the minds inside them. I took a deep breath and checked the straps of my backpack again. This was where the test began. This was where I would find out whether I was actually *recovered,* and not just in recovery.

My name is Sarah Zellaby, and my ancestors came from a different dimension.

It's the only way to explain my biology. Earth contains more complicated organisms and bionomies than most people realize. For everything we think we know, every rule of nature we think is unbreakable, there are a hundred things we don't understand yet, a hundred exceptions to that unbreakable rule. There are cold-blooded mammals and hot-blooded fish, butterflies

that drink blood and tears and snakes that give birth
to live young. And then there's me.

According to my Uncle Kevin, who finds my species
endlessly fascinating, I'm more closely related to wasps
than I am to primates, despite my internal skeletal system and mammary glands. I look externally human. I
can move through a crowd without attracting any attention that a human woman wouldn't attract. Technically, I'm a mammal—I have three small bones in my
inner ear, I have hair, and I have the potential to lactate. Not that I'm ever intending to have children. That
would require spending time with a male of my own
species, and I'd rather spend time with the wasps we
apparently evolved from. Because see, that's how you
get a Johrlac. You start with telepathic wasps—not a
great plan—and then you put them through millennia
of evolutionary pressures that somehow force them to
become more and more like what people think of
when they say the word "human." You give them internal skeletons and flat faces with squared-off teeth and
the right jaw structure for vocal communication. You
give them complex hands and the ability to feed their
offspring from their own bodies. Century after century after century of if/then decisions that add up to
something like me.

We are not of this Earth. We're not the only outsiders living here—the Madhura also came from outside,
probably from a world a lot like the one where the
cuckoos originated. The Apraxis wasps, too. Basically,
any kind of insect that tells the square/cube law to go
piss up a rope stands a decent chance of having come
through a dimensional rift at one point or another.
Sorry, Earth. Didn't mean to crash your party.

A man in TSA blue bumped into me. I took a step
back as he whirled around, radiating both irritation
and a smug, bullying sort of satisfaction. He liked the
power of his job, the ability to make travelers scared of
him and what he could do to their carefully laid plans.

Unpleasant fellow. There are unpleasant fellows everywhere—unpleasant women, too—but there's a certain kind of bully who tends to be drawn to positions of authority. Security guards and police and, yes, TSA agents.

He'd do.

I looked at him pleadingly. His face went slack. I'm not good at reading human facial expressions, not even after a lifetime spent living among and beside them, but there are a few I've learned to reliably spot. This one was what Verity liked to call the "I put a spell on you" look, and the fact that he was wearing it meant things were working the way they were supposed to.

"I'm sorry," I said. "I didn't mean to get lost."

His entire psychic profile changed, bullying and irritation melting into solicitous relief. "You know Mom told me to watch out for you," he said, and took my arm in a proprietary way. There was nothing romantic or unsettling about it: everything about him was radiating "brother," and so I didn't fight. "Come on, Sarah. She'll kill me if you miss your plane."

"I still need to pick up my boarding pass," I bluffed.

"Leave that to me." He waved my concern away and whisked me forward, past the throng waiting in line for the security checkpoint, carrying me along with him without waiting to see whether I was willing to go.

This is the primary power, and the primary threat, of the adult cuckoo. Somewhere around puberty, we acquire control over the ability that takes us from being a nuisance and transforms us into apex predators. When we want you to, you know us. You love us. We're your friends and your family and your children. We are whatever the situation needs us to be, whatever we can take advantage of, and we fill the gaps in your life without so much as batting an eye. Did this man have a sister? I didn't know. I didn't want to know. Finding out would mean digging deeper into his nasty little mind, and right now that would be a strain.

If I'd wanted to make him a target, to twist him around my fingers until he broke, I would have taken his hand. Skin contact makes things easier, and faster, and allows us to forge bonds that can't be easily broken. So I would have held his hand until the fragile barriers keeping his mind away from mine wore down, and then I would have plundered him for everything I needed to know. I could have replaced everything important in his life with me, only me, always me, and it would have been nothing. I could have *destroyed* him.

He led me to a checkpoint at the far end, gestured for me to shrug out of my backpack and toss it on the belt, and swiped his badge before waving me through the simple metal detector. It didn't alarm. No one was behind the scanner to check the contents of my pack. I picked it up on the other side, sliding it over my shoulders, feeling the familiar weight settle against the small of my back. One challenge down.

"Now you be careful out there; it's scary for a woman traveling alone." The TSA man pulled his wallet out, opened it, and offered me eighty dollars in wrinkled bills.

I let my fingertips brush against his as I took them, checking for any sign that he needed to be concerned about his finances. I didn't find anything. There was guilt that he was *only* giving me eighty dollars, since he had a lot more than that on him, and frustration that paying his little sister's way had "once again" fallen on his shoulders. It was a toxic mix, and I withdrew quickly. He wouldn't miss the money. That was the important part.

Cuckoos bend our environment to suit our own needs, like ticks burrowing into the skin of the world. What makes me different from most of my species—what I hope makes me different, pray makes me different, remind myself every day makes me different—is that I try to do as little harm as I possibly can. There's no such thing as doing absolutely *no* harm. Human, cuckoo, it doesn't matter. Everybody hurts and is hurt, in a grand cycle of being alive. But minimizing the damage . . . that matters.

Minimizing the damage will never make me human. It'll keep me worthy of walking among them.

"I'll be careful," I said, meeting his eyes. A flash of light reflected there, brief and bright and invisible to any of the cameras I knew were watching us. Bangs are old-fashioned, but they help me hide the way my eyes sometimes go white from top to bottom, reflecting a chemical response to my using my telepathic abilities. I shoved the compulsion to forget me actively against the structures of his mind, breaking through his defenses.

The man stopped moving, his thoughts shifting from ordinary human chaos into a sort of blanked-out static. I smiled again and patted his hand, careful to make skin contact as I said, "Thank you so much for helping me. Airports can be so confusing." Then I turned and walked away, losing myself in the crowd before he could shake off the shock.

I didn't look back—looking back attracts attention— but I knew if I did, I'd eventually see him stagger, looking profoundly confused, and scowl at everything around himself before he went back to whatever he'd been doing before he ran into me. He'd be annoyed at himself when he discovered the missing eighty dollars, but he'd assume he spent it and forgot. There wasn't going to be any lasting damage from this encounter.

To either of us. To my delight, my thoughts were still clear, and my head didn't hurt, not even a little bit. I proceeded to the food court, where I used some of the TSA man's eighty dollars to buy a burger, fries, and a vanilla milkshake before claiming a table with a clear view of the departures board. There were five flights to Portland leaving in the next two hours. I could have my pick of airlines. I settled back to mix ketchup into my milkshake and skim the minds around me, looking for opinions on my options.

I didn't have luggage, so it didn't matter that the people three tables over had strong opinions about one airline's tendency to lose their bags; the fact that they served hot chocolate chip cookies in first class *did* matter, since chocolate makes my throat itch. Another airline apparently had a reputation for poor customer service. They wouldn't be rude to *me*, of course, but I was selecting the people whose minds I'd be trapped in a metal tube with for between four and six hours. No, thank you.

I finished mixing ketchup into my milkshake and went to insert my straw, pausing when I saw a small child staring at me. Facial expressions are hard, but even I can tell when someone's eyes go wide, and the child was radiating confusion and curiosity. I pointed to my milkshake, trying to look quizzical. The child nodded. I took a sip.

The child's wave of awe was so vast that it felt like even the non-telepaths around me should have noticed. I grinned a little and went back to studying the departure board. The milkshake looked like strawberry now that it was properly blended; except for the kid, no one was going to realize there was anything odd about it. People in airports are allowed to be weird. They're liminal spaces. They don't count the way the real world does.

Case in point: about one in ten of the minds around me wasn't human. Traveler or airport employee, it didn't matter. This was a place where people came and went and didn't stop to make friends, which made it safe for cryptid traffic. None of them seemed to have made any special note of me. That was good. That was part of the test. If I'd been too noticeable, I would have needed to call Mom and tell her I was coming home, that I wasn't ready. And I wanted to be ready. I *needed* to be ready.

This had all been going on for too long.

Five years ago—five years! How had it been five *years*? How had so much time been able to slip by while I was too lost in the spirals inside my head to pay proper attention?—Verity and I had been in Manhattan. She'd been going out with a Covenant man, working on her dance career, and trying to decide what she wanted to do with her life. I'd been . . .

I'd been doing what I always did. Math. Math, and flirting with my cousin Artie and pretending I wasn't flirting with my cousin Artie, because he deserves better than me, he honestly does. He deserves a girl who has a heart, and I mean that literally: I don't have one. Remember that whole "I'm not from around here" thing? Well, whatever weirdo world my kind evolved on, it wasn't really invested in the idea of a centralized circulatory system. I don't have a pulse because I don't have a heart, and if I don't have a heart, it doesn't matter how much like a mammal I look from the outside, it doesn't matter if I have three bones in my inner ear and hair and the ability to lactate. I'm something else, something *other*, and Artie is human enough to deserve better.

Not like he thinks of me that way, anyway. Artie and his sister, Elsie, are half-Lilu, courtesy of my Uncle Ted, making them an incubus and a succubus, respectively. Elsie likes girls, always has, and has had a long string of significant others, dating all the way back to middle school. Artie . . .

No one's sure what Artie likes. I think he likes girls, since he avoids them like the plague. I just know he's too smart to like me. I'm Cousin Sarah, everyday and ordinary and dependable. Or I was, until Verity and I went to Manhattan.

For cuckoos, a lot of things come naturally. I can warp the world to suit my needs without stopping to think twice about it; I know what I need and so the universe delivers. I can disappear in a crowd, pulling the curtain of my own fear up around myself until even people who know I'm there may not notice me. I can read a room, literally, picking up on the little currents of fear and confusion and joy that run through the minds around me. Deeper thoughts take more work, and skin contact if it's not someone I know well. It's still part of what I'm designed by nature to do.

Intentionally changing someone's mind, though . . . that's hard. That takes *work*. It used to be the most I could do was shove someone into believing they didn't want to sit at my table at the coffee shop. Changing someone's memories, rewiring them enough to provide them with an alternative story of what had happened, that's beyond the standard cuckoo toolset, and I had always been secretly glad of that fact, because I *should* have limits. I'm a telepath in a world that wasn't built for them, and I'm way too aware that my species trends toward the horrifyingly destructive. Cuckoos aren't friends, or neighbors, or cousins. We're the hunger that consumes everything in our paths, and we *should* have limits.

Only the Covenant of St. George doesn't care about our limits. They care about making sure only humans, and only the *right* humans, are in control of this world. Verity, her siblings, our entire family, we're on the wrong side of the fight as far as the Covenant is concerned. They'd kill me or Artie or my parents on sight for the crime of not being human. They tried to kill Verity for the crime of caring about what happened to us.

Of course, they would have taken her away first. They'd been planning to haul her off to England, where all our secrets could be spilled, and used to wipe the Prices, Bakers, and Harringtons off the face of the planet. There hadn't been any choice. I'm not mad at her for what happened to me, because she didn't ask me to do it, and there hadn't been any other way. I've spent the last five years clawing my way back to lucidity and going over what happened that night over and over again, and there wasn't any other way.

The Covenant operatives who'd come for Verity had been vulnerable. They didn't have the right kind of charms to keep me out of their heads, and so I plunged myself into them like the predator my nature wants me to be. I ripped and I ransacked and I rewrote until they only remembered what I wanted them to remember. They thought Dominic was dead. They thought Verity was an actress he'd hired to impersonate a member of the Price family. My people were safe. The Covenant no longer knew they existed, and they were safe.

That was the thought I had carried down with me into the dark, as I felt something in my mind rip loose of its moorings and crumble into nothingness. My people were safe. I might not survive, I might never see them again, but they were safe. I had done it. I had been better than my nature wanted me to be.

I'm selfish enough to say that I don't know for sure whether I'd have done what I did if I'd realized what the consequences would be. Changing those memories had strained something in my brain, something connected to my telepathy. Since it wasn't like we could exactly take me to the hospital for an MRI, I've spent the last five years putting myself back together one tiny piece at a time, living with my parents in Ohio, leaning on Alex and his fiancée, Shelby, as I tried to figure out who I was and who I wanted to be and how to reconcile the difference between the two.

Five years lost. It's hard to even think about it. The airport was the first time I'd been outside unsupervised since my injury, and here I was trying to cross the country on my own—go big or go home, I guess.

I think whoever said that really, really underestimated how much I wanted to go home.

I finished the last few swallows of my milkshake in

Two

$$\pi_2(n) \sim 2C_2 \frac{n}{(\ln n)^2} \sim 2C_2 \int_2^n \frac{dt}{(\ln t)^2}$$

"A lie's a lie, even when it's wearing Sunday clothes. That doesn't mean a lie is necessarily the wrong choice. Just that you shouldn't pretend it's something that it's not."

—Alice Healy

Heading for the customer service desk of a major airline

THE THREE WOMEN BEHIND the customer service desk were all doing their best to look alert, engaged, and available, all while paying absolutely no attention to the throngs of people passing by in front of them. If they made eye contact, they risked triggering a complaint, or sometimes worse, a long, involved story from a weary traveler who was just looking for a moment of human connection. Great in its place, not so much fun for the person who was bound by professional obligations to sit and listen to every little twist and turn.

Their distraction was a gift for me. I stopped a few feet away, patting my pockets and allowing an expression of bewildered distress to grow on my face. I can't read most human expressions, but I can mimic them: telepathy means that I know what they feel like from the inside.

While I was going through my acceptable airport behavior pantomime, I dipped as far as I dared into each of their minds, checking to see who felt the most pliable, and who was thus the most likely to do what I wanted without either making a fuss or declaring me their long-lost sister. The TSA man with the eighty dollars had been more than enough found family for one day.

The one on the end. She was the youngest, the least experienced, and most importantly, the most offended by the inequalities she saw on a daily basis. I stopped patting my pockets and approached her station, putting a waver into my voice as I asked, "Excuse me? Is this where I go if I need help?"

Her head snapped up and her posture shifted to one of helpful attentiveness. If I hadn't known better, I would never have known she'd been reading fanfic on her phone half a second previously. "How can I help you today?"

"I can't find my boarding pass," I said. "Please, can you help me?" I let my thoughts push forward, just a little. Not enough to qualify as a full compulsion, but enough to make it clear what I wanted to have happen. *You know me,* I thought. *You don't need to ask for ID.*

"Really, Bridget, again?" she asked, fond exasperation in her tone, and began typing rapidly. "This needs to stop happening, honey. You need to buy yourself a purse or something."

"I guess I do," I said, feeling suddenly uneasy. It's not common for people to come up with their own names for me. It's not unheard of, but . . .

It usually means those people have come into contact with another cuckoo, someone who's already taken the time to push and pull and reshape their neurological pathways into something easier for telepathy to work with. I could be in another cuckoo's hunting grounds *right now*. It's not an unreasonable idea. As I said before, airports are liminal spaces. People come and go and if they sometimes seem to forget things or act in unusual ways, as long as those changes don't make them appear dangerous to a casual onlooker, no one's going to notice.

No. I'd know if there were another cuckoo this close to home. There's a sort of feedback that happens when we get too close to each other, a telepathic static that washes over everything and makes it jittery and strange. Mom doesn't notice it, since she's not a receptive telepath, but I do, and the silence when I walk away from her is sometimes the loudest thing in the world. That roaring silence was still there. I could hear it. There was no one else.

The woman behind the desk was waiting, hands raised, radiating expectation. I missed something. I'd been looking for cuckoos, and I missed something.

Damn, I thought, and said sheepishly, "I'm sorry. You know I don't mean to."

"I know," said the woman, relaxing slightly. The other two customer service employees didn't appear to have noticed me, which only reinforced the idea that another cuckoo had come to visit, probably more than once. They didn't see me because they didn't care, because I wasn't unusual. They'd seen me before, or someone who looked so much like me that they couldn't tell the difference.

Humans have an incredible diversity of appearances. Different face shapes, eye shapes, eye colors, all sorts of little variations that people consider more or less appealing. It's part of the way mammalian life in this dimension works. Everything looks different from everything else. Cuckoos . . . don't. We come from another evolutionary path, and like most insects, we're all virtually identical to one another. My face is my adoptive mother's face is my biological mother's face, all the way back to the beginning. We don't vary, except in age and personal grooming choices. We are, in many ways, a hive.

Cuckoos are pale. Cuckoos are black-haired and blue-eyed and delicate, with features some humans see as "doll-like," and some see as "creepy." The humans who find us unnerving are the lucky ones. They might walk the other way when they see us coming. They might get away. Not usually, though. We can pick up on feelings of unease, and too many of my relatives view those people as a challenge, something to be pursued and overcome.

The woman started to type. "Where are you heading today?"

"Portland. The one in Oregon, not the one in Maine."

"That's good—we don't have any flights left to Maine today." She frowned at something on her screen. "That's odd. I don't have you listed on the manifest. Are you flying stand-by again?"

Bridget, whoever she is, must be connected to the airline somehow. "I am," I ventured.

"That explains it. These systems need an upgrade in the worst way." She resumed typing, faster now, plugging in the details of my supposed ID without once asking to verify it. "All right, honey, I've got you back on the correct plane—and since first class didn't check in full, I've managed to upgrade you a couple of levels." Her printer spat out a boarding pass. She handed it to me, eyes twinkling, radiating satisfaction at having done a favor for a friend. "Now *don't* lose this one, all right? I can only save your bacon so many times."

"I won't, I promise," I said, taking the boarding pass and holding it close to my chest, like it was the most precious thing in the world—which, in many ways, it was. It was one more piece of proof that I was recovered enough to leave the safety of Ohio. All I needed to do after this was get on the plane and make it to Oregon without accidentally diverting us to Prague, and I'd be free.

The woman's eyes widened. A moment later, she

was offering me a tissue. "Honey, your nose is running."

My nose . . . oh, no. I took the tissue with a mumbled, "Thank you," and took off, not saying goodbye. Let the woman assume I was booking it for the bathroom because I was embarrassed to have been caught with a runny nose in public.

Human blood is red. Human nosebleeds are obvious.

Cuckoo blood is almost clear, made up of hemolymph and plasma. It looks, to human eyes, like slightly blue-tinged mucus. When set against something as pale as my skin, the blue blends into the background, and a nosebleed looks more like I need a good decongestant.

I waited until I was far enough from the desk to not be observed by anyone who might know "Bridget" before I ducked into the alcove next to a pair of vending machines and wiped my upper lip. A trace of blue shimmered on the tissue. I was bleeding. *Damn*. Damn, damn, *damn*.

I needed to call home. I needed to tell Mom I couldn't do this yet and ask her to come get me. I needed—

I lowered my other hand and looked at the boarding pass I was still clutching. One first class ticket to Portland, Oregon, leaving in under an hour. They'd be boarding soon.

One tissue, lightly streaked with blue.

I had two choices, and I couldn't make them both. Go home and keep hiding and hoping that one day I'd be exactly the girl I'd been before I hurt myself or get on that plane and go to where people who loved me were waiting for some sign that I was truly going to recover. Go where *Artie* was waiting. I hadn't seen him in five years. I hadn't touched his hand in *five years*. Would the telepathic channel we'd opened between ourselves even work anymore? I'd never gone that long without reinforcing it. Maybe we'd be strangers again.

Go home or keep going. I couldn't have it both ways.

I closed my eyes, taking a deep breath, before I crumpled the tissue and shoved it into my pocket. I had a plane to catch.

First class is nice. For one thing, there's never any fighting over the overhead bins. For another, the seats are large enough that there's no chance of accidental contact with the person next to you. I curled my legs underneath me, stockinged feet pressed against the hard side of the armrest—designed to maximize my personal space as much as possible, thank you, human veneration of the wealthy—and sipped my tomato juice as I stared out the window at the receding shape of Cleveland, Ohio.

Back in Dublin, my parents were probably watching the airport departures list, waiting for the last plane to Portland to take off. If I didn't call them a half hour after that, they'd know I was on my way, finally taking my first real step toward rejoining the world. Mom wouldn't sleep until I landed in Oregon and texted her to let her know I was all right. That was fine. She usually had some snarly accounting problem to keep her distracted. Or maybe she and Dad would take advantage of having the house to themselves for five minutes. Alex and Shelby were in Australia, Drew was in California, and I was on a plane. They could—

Ew. No. I didn't want to think about that. We're all adults, but there are some thoughts that send me hurtling right back into easily horrified childhood.

The man who was sitting next to me had been trying to get my attention since takeoff. The fact that I was wearing headphones and staring fixedly out the window didn't appear to be doing anything to dissuade him. If anything, it was just making him try harder. I did my resolute best to ignore the increasing waves of irritation and impatience rolling off him, focusing instead on my recording of the latest lecture series from the American Mathematical Association. They were doing some fascinating things with intuitive primes, and I wanted to see how far they could take the theory before things either resolved or fell apart.

In math, something is either true or it's not. Something either works or it doesn't. If something works and it feels like that shouldn't be possible, it's not the math that's wrong: it's your model of the universe. Mathematics is the art of refining our understanding of reality itself, like a sculptor trimming down a brick of marble until it frees the beautiful image inside.

Math is also distracting for me, like it is for any cuckoo. Something about the calm march of numbers and theory and equations is utterly enthralling to us. We're an entire species of mathematicians, and that fact is the only thing that keeps me believing we can't be all bad. How can anyone who truly loves numbers be irredeemable?

I was so wrapped up in the equations that I didn't realize the man was planning to move until he hooked a finger around the cord of my right headphone and popped it out of my ear. The drone of the plane's engine came roaring back, drowning out the lecture still playing in my left ear, followed by the sound of his smug, faintly nasal voice.

"I *said*, will you let me buy you a drink? Pretty lady like you shouldn't have to fly alone." He laughed, amused by his own feeble attempt at humor. "Of course, this is first class, so the drinks are free . . . unless you want to go someplace nicer with me after we land. I could show you a good time."

Of course. Of *course*. There are days when I wish whatever evolutionary path had decided I should pass for human could have settled on something a little less eye-catching. Not that being pretty by human standards doesn't smooth a lot of rough edges out for me, but it can create a few, too.

I turned to face him, offering a thin, glossy smile. "No, thank you," I said. "I'm sorry. I just want to listen to my book and get some rest." I could have tried to shove "you're not interested in me" at him, but at our current proximity, that was likely to result in him deciding I didn't exist and trying to claim my armrest.

"Book?" He grabbed the headphone before I could protest, bringing it to his own ear. A wave of confusion and disgust rolled off him an instant later. "This isn't a book. This is a lecture."

"It's a lecture taken from a book on mathematics." I tweaked the cord nimbly out of his fingers, pulling it protectively closer to myself. "I don't want any trouble."

"I think you need a little trouble," he said, and grabbed my wrist.

Big mistake.

Maybe once, I could have kept myself pulled back enough not to touch his mind even while he was touching my body. Maybe. But that was before my injury, and before I'd been forced to relearn the little tricks and techniques that made it safe for me to move through the human world. My agitation boiled over, and I saw the flash of white reflected in his eyes before he let go of me, withdrawing into his own seat.

"I'm so sorry," he said. His tone had completely changed, becoming contrite, even guilty. "That was entirely inappropriate of me. I can't believe . . . I'm so sorry. I'll make this right."

He hit his flight attendant call button. I put my headphone back in and returned my attention to the window, trying to radiate "I'm not involved with this" while I watched the clouds and he spoke in a low, urgent voice to the flight attendant who answered his call. I could feel his self-recrimination prickling against my skin like steel wool, but if I didn't reach for details, I wouldn't find them, and that suited me just fine. Not everything can be my problem. There isn't room in my head.

There was a flurry of motion as the man got up and moved away. A few moments later, the flight attendant was waving her hand for my attention. I straightened, removing both headphones, and turned to face her.

There was a woman behind her in the aisle, no more than twenty-five years old, with a baby grasped against her chest and a massive diaper bag in her free hand. The woman was looking around, radiating awe. The baby was sleeping. All I got from it was a pure, unalloyed contentment. It was with its mother, it was fed and safe and content, and it wanted for nothing else in the world.

Lucky baby. "Yes?" I asked.

"The gentleman who was seated next to you has requested a transfer to coach class, and that we credit the value of his ticket to another passenger who looks as if they'd enjoy the opportunity to experience our first-class cabin." Her eyes gleamed. I picked up a combination of genuine joy and malicious anticipation, aimed not at me in specific, but at the rest of the cabin.

Apparently, my former traveling companion wasn't the only one who'd felt entitled to be a little too pushy about his own desires. I couldn't get details without digging deeper, but I felt fairly confident that the woman behind the flight attendant had been chosen at least partially to annoy the rest of first class as much as possible.

Well, that was fine. I smiled broadly, and said, "That sounds great. One of my cousins is expecting a baby soon, so I should probably be spending more time around infants anyway. Getting in practice, right?"

The flight attendant's smile was mostly relief, and only a sliver of disappointment, as she waved the woman to her seat and tucked the diaper bag into the overhead compartment. In only a few seconds, we were alone—or as alone as you can ever get on a plane—the woman radiating wonder, the baby still comfortably asleep.

I smiled at her, dazzlingly bright, an expression I learned from sliding myself into my cousin Verity's head during her dance competitions. Verity learned to smile like she was being graded on it, because she was, and thanks to her, I share the skill. Not bad for someone who can't always recognize a smile when she sees one.

"I'm Sarah," I said. "First time in first class?"

"Yes," said the woman. "I . . . yes. I'm Christina. This is Susie." She gave the baby a little bounce, not enough to wake it up.

She was thinking "my little girl" so loudly that I could actually hear the words, so I turned my smile on the baby and said, "She's beautiful. Let me know if you need me to hold her so you can use the bathroom."

Her astonishment was, briefly, louder than the plane's engines. I gave her another smile and returned my attention to the window. We were on our way to Portland, and I didn't have a jerk sitting next to me anymore.

Things were looking up.

The plane touched down with a thump hard enough to set us all rocking for a moment, stirring the infant next to me back into fussy wakefulness. I smiled encouragingly at her mother, offering a little wiggle of my fingers as distraction. The mother radiated relief. Apparently, flying with an infant was a horror—I could have guessed that—and people were frequently resistant to the idea of flying next to one—I had observed that. Being moved up from coach to first class and seated next to someone who didn't mind babies had been like winning the lottery on multiple axes at once.

I like babies. They're simple. Their thoughts are simple, their needs and desires are simple, and if I need something soothing, I can watch their synapses making lasting connections, a process most adults have long since finished. Plus, babies have such basic inner lives that I don't really feel like I'm eavesdropping when I listen in on them. This baby had such a limited set of experiences that she didn't yet know her name, or have preferred pronouns, or really understand that her toes were always there, even when she was wearing shoes. She was like a tiny, occasionally smelly meditation trigger.

"It was nice to meet you," said Christina. "Is someone picking you up from the airport?"

She wasn't angling for a ride, I realized; she was preparing to offer me one. Oh, that wasn't good. If we got into a private car, after the amount of time we'd spent together, I'd be a member of her family before we could get on the freeway. She was too nice to spend the rest of her life feeling wistfully like she'd somehow misplaced her favorite sister.

"I'm good," I said. "This was sort of a spontaneous trip, and I have family here. I'll be fine. But thank you for asking."

Both statements were true, even if neither of them answered her question. I was planning to head down to the taxi stand and invite myself along on a ride that was heading toward the family compound. It would be safer, since whoever actually paid for the cab wouldn't have been sitting next to me for the last several hours.

"No problem at all," said Christina. Susie fussed. Christina turned her attention to the baby.

That was my cue. Fishing my phone out of my jeans pocket, I turned it back on, and winced as it began buzzing frantically in my hand. Almost thirty text messages had come through while it was shut down for the flight, which seemed a tiny bit excessive.

The first ten were from Mom, wanting to let me know that she was thinking about me, she was worrying about me, she was pretty sure I was on the plane by now, but if I wasn't, I could come home and she wouldn't be angry, it was okay if I needed more time. The next five were *also* from Mom, and were a little closer to flipping out—in one of them, she suggested I make it a round trip, get off the plane in Portland, and get immediately back onto a flight heading for Cleveland. Ugh. No thank you. I'd had my fill of being crammed into a flying metal tube of human minds and human fears, and I wanted to rest.

After that came a series of texts from Dad, detailing the steps he was taking to try and calm Mom down, and reminding me how important it was that I text her as soon as we landed if I didn't want her to come to Oregon and shake me vigorously back and forth. I smiled at that, and switched back to Mom's messages, intending to do as he'd suggested. It was better not to put this off.

Then my phone buzzed again, and I nearly dropped it. Artie. I had a text from Artie.

Trying to be nonchalant, I finished my text to Mom—"Safe on the ground. Made it to Portland. No headache. Think I'm okay."—before taking a deep breath and opening my latest message.

Just had weirdest feeling, it read. Like you were almost in the room. Miss you.

For the second time in under a minute, I nearly dropped my phone.

Wow, I replied. Weird. Where r u?

Text grammar makes my teeth ache a little. When I was in school, part of my job was learning to blend into the human population. Don't stand out, don't make waves, don't attract attention. Do what everybody else does, because the wisdom of the herd is the best possible camouflage. That's spilled over into my adult life, meaning, among other things, that I have to text like I don't care if anyone's judging my spelling.

I care. I care a *lot*. But we do what we have to do to survive in this world.

Home, Artie replied. Face-chat tonight? We can watch a movie.

Can't. Will explain soon. I added several emoji— two snakes, a smiling girl, a rainbow, a bee—and shoved the phone back into my pocket before I could see any reply. I wasn't there yet. I needed to make it all the way to a safe house if I wanted to pass the test Mom had set for me.

The plane finished taxiing to the gate, and the flight attendants turned off the fasten seatbelt sign. I bounced out of my seat, sliding past Christina and the once-again sleeping Susie, and grabbed my backpack out of the overhead compartment, slipping my arms through the straps before the cabin door was even open. It unsealed with a hiss and I was out, not running, but walking very quickly away from the rest of the passengers.

I knew too much about them. I didn't know what they looked like, and it didn't matter, because I knew what they *thought* like. I knew who was cruel and who was kind and who probably needed to be hit with a baseball bat for the things they believed were okay to do to their fellow humans. I was just glad the entire plane had *been* human. Being stuck with too many kinds of minds would have been even worse.

I strode my way along the jet bridge to the terminal, sucking in great breaths of fresh airport air, which might be processed, but hadn't been circulated through the cabin for the last several hours. I wanted a bathroom and a salad and a ride home. I wanted—

I stepped into the terminal and stopped dead in my tracks, suddenly feeling like I'd been punched in the gut. People streamed out behind me, shooting sour thoughts about people who stopped in walkways in my direction. I didn't move. I was struggling to breathe. The thoughts stopped, replaced by weary irritation at the need to step around some inanimate but unavoidable obstacle. I was cloaking myself. I wasn't trying to, but I was, and I couldn't stop, because I couldn't breathe. I couldn't move.

The static roar was drowning out everything else, filling my mind from end to end, so that even the thoughts of the people behind me were muffled, becoming little more than background noise. They were inconsequential in the face of something so much bigger.

There was another cuckoo in the airport.

Three

$$\pi_2(n) \sim 2C_2 \frac{n}{(\ln n)^2} \sim 2C_2 \int_2^n \frac{dt}{(\ln t)^2}$$

"Anyone who tells you that you only die once hasn't actually died. They wouldn't be so cavalier about it if they had."
—Mary Dunlavy

Portland International Airport, trying really hard not to panic

CUCKOOS ARE TERRITORIAL.
I think it has something to do with the static we create when we get too close to each other. It can get so loud that it becomes almost paralyzing, and when the shock of having someone shouting inside your brain passes, it's usually replaced by rage. The sound grates on every nerve we have, making killing whatever's causing it seem like the best idea anyone has ever had. Ever. Which is bad enough, except that most cuckoos won't do their own dirty work. They use the resources they have available to them.

Which means they use humans. They dig into the minds of the humans around them, and they make murder seem like a totally awesome plan. Like it's something that was always on the docket for today, but just got moved up a little bit. You know, between the dry cleaning and getting dinner into the oven. Every person around me had suddenly become a potential weapon, and unless I was willing to do the same—

unless I was willing to force my own will on another sapient being for my own benefit, and force them to risk their skins to save mine—I was completely unprotected.

This was what Mom had been afraid of. That I'd go back out into the world, run into a threat, and freeze up, unable to decide on a course of action that would actually protect me. I tightened my hands on my backpack straps and started walking again, angling as quickly as I could for the nearest bathroom. Bathrooms tend to be safe places. It's hard to seize control of someone when all they want to do is pee. I could catch my breath, try to figure out where the static was coming from, and make a new plan for getting out of the airport.

One thing was sure: I couldn't go to the house. I'd know if another cuckoo was digging deeply enough into my mind to uncover an address, but I couldn't protect that information once I gave it to my driver. If the cuckoo wanted to follow me, all they'd need to do is follow the person who dropped me off. Then they could crack the driver's mind open like an egg, pull out whatever they needed, and attack at their leisure. I couldn't risk my family's security like that.

This wasn't what I'd wanted when I'd said I was ready to go back into the world. This wasn't what I'd wanted at all.

At least I knew that Mom would eventually call Evie and tell her I was in Portland, and why hadn't she called yet with an update on my condition, did she want to worry her poor old mother. They'd come looking for me, and they'd start at my last known location. The airport.

Of course, I could be dead by then. Cuckoos don't have many natural predators. We have to prey on each other. That's how we keep our numbers in check.

The bathroom was empty. I made for the farthest stall and shut myself inside, climbing onto the toilet and crouching in on myself until I took up as little space as possible. Then I closed my eyes and began the slow, painful process of shutting off my awareness of the world around me.

For a non-telepath, the idea of going dark probably seems trivial. Why would bringing myself down to the level of the majority of the people around me be a problem? Humans get by just fine without psychic powers, and the media loves showing telepaths as monsters or martyrs, unable to block out the world around them, eventually consumed by the thoughts they just can't. Stop. Hearing.

And I guess there's some truth to that. Moving through a crowd is like walking through a living YouTube comments section. Even when people have the manners and good sense to keep their mouths shut, their minds are wide open, and in a non-telepathic society, no one bothers to learn how to control their thoughts. Why should they? I've heard things that make me really understand why most of my species thinks it's more fun on the Dark Side. Sometimes I've felt half-convinced to go that way myself. I don't, because it would hurt my family, and it would let my mother down, but wow, do I get the urge.

But at the same time . . . I don't see faces the way humans do. I can't tell people apart except by the very broadest of physical traits, hair color and skin color and height and weight. Even gender can be confusing, and I've learned never to use a pronoun for someone until I've heard them use it for themselves, out loud. I can usually tell what gender someone *is* by the way they think about themselves, but that doesn't necessarily mean I know what gender someone has to pretend to be for social reasons. The world is complicated, and humans are judgmental, and I know more secrets than I should, just by virtue of being what I am.

Shut all that down, take all that away, and what do I have? I have eyes that don't know how to process some of what they see. I have ears and a nose that work exactly as well as their human equivalents, which isn't well enough to keep me safe from danger. I have two legs to run with and two lungs to scream with and those weren't going to be enough if the cuckoo whose presence I could feel pushing down all around me decided to press the issue. I was unarmed. I was alone.

If I died in the process of trying to prove that I was well enough to rejoin the world, I was going to spend whatever afterlife waits for cuckoos laughing until I cried, because otherwise I was going to scream eternity down on my own head.

The static faded, like a radio being tuned, until everything was as close to silent as an airport could ever be. A sink dripped; the air-conditioning whirred; outside the bathroom, a distorted announcement was made over the intercom.

And footsteps, calm and precise, walked into the bathroom.

"I know you're in here." The voice sounded exactly like my mother's, even down to the faint New England accent. "You're hiding very well, but I still know you're in here. I watched you disappear."

I held my breath and didn't move, grateful for my lack of a heart. If I'd been human, she would probably have been able to hear it racing.

"It's cute how you think you can get away from me."

The footsteps came closer. I shrugged out of my backpack as quietly as I could, preparing to swing. If there's one weakness shared by virtually all cuckoos, it's overconfidence. I could only hear one set of footsteps. She was alone, and she probably didn't have a gun, or a knife, or any of the other things that would have guaranteed her victory in direct combat. She'd picked up on my fear—not hard—and decided that it meant I was easy prey. Amateur.

"You should really have done your homework before you decided to fly into Portland, little chick. I understand the impulse to flee the nest, but this is *my* place, and I don't share."

Of course she didn't. Cuckoos are incredibly destructive, as a rule, and when you combine that with our natural dislike for each other, you come up with an equation that says one cuckoo for every million humans is about right. Portland couldn't support two of us. Portland could probably only support one happily because of the airport, and its daily offerings of incoming and outgoing travelers from other places. There was no way she'd be willing to let me settle here.

The footsteps came closer still. She was right outside the door to my stall. If I was going to move, it needed to be now.

I moved.

I'm not a fighter: I leave that to my cousins whenever I possibly can. But I'm a Baker by adoption, and a Price by association, and that means I was expected to learn how to defend myself, whether I wanted to or not. I kicked the stall door open as hard as I could, hearing the dull smack of metal hitting flesh, simultaneous with the cuckoo outside's cry of startled surprise. She probably wasn't *hurt*, but that didn't matter; all I'd really intended to do was throw her off balance.

Jumping down from the toilet, I hit the stall door with my shoulder and slammed it open even harder, hitting her again. She yelped, and I danced out of the way of the door, swinging my backpack for her middle. One nice thing about coming from a species with virtually no phenotype diversity: she and I were precisely the same height, and I didn't have to calculate where my blows were going to land. I just swung on a straight line, and they connected.

My bag hit her squarely in the stomach. I grimaced, hoping the clothes I had wrapped around my laptop would be enough to soften the blow where it was concerned. Artie could fix it if not—Artie could fix anything—but that didn't mean I wanted my machine out of commission because some stupid cuckoo had decided to attack me.

This time she squealed, pained and indignant, falling backward. Bad luck for her, since her trajectory slammed her into one of the automated hand drying machines. It kicked on with a loud rush of hot air. She tried to shout something. I hit her with my bag again. At the same time, I released my hold on my telepathy, beginning to broadcast *nothing to see here, stay away* as loudly as I could. I could dimly hear her mental commands laced under my own, trying to summon her minions, but she was hurt and off-guard, and I was scared and substantially louder. Whatever she'd been trying to ask for dissolved back into the static.

"Wait," she began.

I didn't wait. I hit her in the head with my backpack. She staggered, so I hit her again, and she hit her knees on the tile floor of the bathroom, catching herself before she could topple over face-first.

"You started it," I said, and hit her in the head again.

This time, she didn't catch herself.

I kicked her a few times to be sure she was really out of the fight. Either she was down for the count, or she was a much better actress than she had any reason to be. It didn't much matter, as long as she wasn't following me. I prodded her with my foot, pushing hard enough to roll her over so that her face pointed toward the ceiling. Her eyes were closed, and when I felt for her mind, it was the confused jumble of memories and vague impressions that I associated with unconsciousness. Growing up around my cousins, who've been in combat training almost since they could walk, has left me with a keen appreciation of the various stages of "knocked out cold." This woman was *gone*.

Good. I slipped my backpack on and crouched, rifling through her pockets. She had an airport security badge, my own face staring back at me from the postage stamp picture, a wallet bulging with cash—probably stolen—and fake IDs under a dozen different names. The modern age has forced even cuckoos to adapt, since telepathy can't fool a point of sale system or a security camera.

She clearly knew this airport: it was part of her territory, and she'd been here long enough to bother getting herself a way in and out of secured areas. She might have moved in the day I left for New York. That was good. It meant she wouldn't have attacked me in this bathroom if there weren't something about it that made it safe. Maybe the cameras were down, or maybe the acoustics somehow kept people outside from hearing when someone was beat to shit inside. Either way, I was in the clear, as long as I got out of the airport quickly.

I clipped her badge to the collar of my sweater, took the money from her wallet, and left her there, unconscious on the tile, wallet on the floor next to her. I felt a little weird about the theft, since she'd just turn around and steal back everything she'd lost, if not more, from the humans in the airport, but it was necessary for several reasons. I needed to get a ride without changing anyone's mind, to make it harder for her to follow me; that meant payment. I also needed to make her understand that I'd been calm enough after defeating her to loot the body. Anyone can panic and punch somebody. The fact that I hadn't run immediately after I was done would show that I was a worthy adversary. Someone she shouldn't mess with. Not immediately, anyway.

Turning and walking away from her made my stomach ache because I knew what was going to happen from here. Portland is too small for two cuckoos. That's the way the math works out. When I'd been living with Evie and Uncle Kevin, my presence alone had been enough to keep any other cuckoo from coming to settle there. The city is nice, but it's not big or metropolitan or culturally significant enough to be worth fighting over. Not like, say, New York, which can sustain half a dozen cuckoos at any given time, and where territory battles between them are common enough to be an everyday occurrence. Cuckoos passed through Portland and went on to become someone else's problem.

Assuming they went on at all. Part of why it hurt to walk away from the woman with my face was knowing what would happen when I got home and told Evie there was a cuckoo in the airport. Hunting in a place this public wouldn't be easy, but she'd figure out a way. She always did. And when she was finished doing her job, there would be one less cuckoo in the world, and the population of Portland would be just a little safer, even if they were never going to understand why.

Cuckoos are apex predators. We're not from around here, we don't belong here, and we belong to the only species that my conservationist family believes needs to be killed on sight. We do too much damage. Even Mom agrees that ordinary cuckoos can't be allowed to hunt the way they do, because it's too destructive, and when it goes too far, it triggers Covenant purges, which could get a lot of innocent cryptids killed.

Life is complicated. The equations balance, in the end, but they can be so damn cold on the way to getting there.

No one gave me a second look as I walked through the airport with the cuckoo's badge clipped to my sweater and my head held high. I had nothing to be ashamed of. She was the one who'd attacked me. I knew that. I had to *keep* knowing that, as the guilt began gnawing at me from the inside, whispering that I was just like her, that if I were really the good person I pretended to be, I would have found another way. I would have talked to her, negotiated, found a way to make myself heard through the overwhelming static of our telepathy clashing.

I knew none of that was possible. I knew Mom and I were reasonable people by human standards and freaks by cuckoo standards, because we had silly things like "ethics" and "morality" that got in the way of doing whatever the hell we wanted. I knew the woman in the bathroom wouldn't have stopped with beating me unconscious. If I'd tried to negotiate with her, my body would be hidden somewhere in the depths of the airport by now, ready to be fed into a furnace or mulched and slipped into someone's garden. My biology is different enough from the human norm that no forensic scientist would ever have been able to tell that I'd been a murder victim. I'd just be gone.

It didn't make me feel any better about hitting a woman in the face with my backpack. Or about the fact that I was honestly more worried about my laptop than I was about having done her permanent damage.

I walked a little faster. I needed to get out of this airport.

The cabbie looked at me over his shoulder as I shoved a wad of bills in his direction, enough to pay my fare six times over. "I still think you should go to the police," he said. "It's not right, a young woman like you being this afraid."

"I'll be all right," I said. "I'm so sorry to have involved you in this. I just want to make sure you're safe. So please, promise me, no more airport trips today."

Confusion and concern radiated from him, almost perfectly balanced. "You can't honestly think I'd be in danger because I gave you a ride. I give lots of people rides."

"Probably not," I said, and pushed against his mind, just slightly. Not enough to change him or make him forget me entirely. Enough to blur his memories of me and make him think that maybe a paid vacation day wouldn't be such a bad idea. *You have so much to do at home, and you've already got more money than you would normally have made,* I whispered, directly into his subconscious. *The night is almost over anyway.* "I'd still feel so much better if I knew you weren't taking the risk."

I'd feel so much better if I knew he wasn't going back into the other cuckoo's range. She'd be awake by now, and furious. If she caught any trace of me, she'd pounce on it.

The cabbie looked out the window, concern melting into uncertainty. The sun was slipping down the line of the horizon, painting everything in shades of red and gold. "I suppose my shift was almost over anyway," he said finally. He took the money from my hand, making it disappear. "I still hope you'll change your mind and involve the authorities. A girl like you shouldn't be running scared."

"I'll take care of everything," I said, and flashed him a smile before opening the door and getting out onto the Portland street. I walked a few steps, turned, and waved to him. He waved back and pulled away from the curb. I stayed exactly where I was, watching him go, waiting to be sure that he didn't suddenly realize, as he got away from my meticulous influence, that he'd dropped me in a bad part of the city. His concern was sweet and born largely from the distress that I was radiating.

My upper lip was wet. I touched it and grimaced as the sunset reflected off the clear liquid on my fingers. I was bleeding again. That last push, on top of everything else, must have been too much for my system to handle. I could feel the endless loops of recursive numbers trying to intrude on my thoughts, to pull me down into the comforting safety of pure mathematics, where I could be safe and comfortable and—most of all— protected. The numbers would protect me even as the world ate me alive. And the world *would* eat me alive if I let myself go into a fugue. A cuckoo who can't defend herself is a dead cuckoo.

I pushed the numbers aside and wiped my fingers on my jeans before dragging my sleeve across my face, wiping the rest of the blood away. Most humans wouldn't recognize it for what it was, but I didn't need to walk around Portland looking like I had a runny nose. The cabbie wasn't coming back. He'd taken his money and forgotten me already, and now I just had to hope he was going to decide not to return to the airport, where that other cuckoo was probably waiting to crack his skull open like an egg looking for a map to where I'd gone.

Poor man. He didn't ask to be a part of this, and with any luck at all, he wasn't going to be. Not for long, anyway. I started walking down the street, watching the houses around me for signs that someone was home and moving around. Waking people up can be useful, but only if I want to get something done quick and clean and without actually making them get dressed. I usually only do it when I need a Wi-Fi password.

I'd gone about a block and a half before I saw a house that fit my needs. There was a big dog chained in the yard. He whined at the sight of me, retreating to the corner and growling softly, like he hoped he could frighten me off without getting anywhere near me. I offered him a sheepish smile, hoping he could read the expression better than I could, and climbed the somewhat rickety steps to the front porch. I rang the bell.

Five minutes later, I was comfortably buckled into the passenger seat of a late-model sedan, the woman behind the wheel chattering merrily on about her plans for the weekend, which included a trip to Costco and some really inventive couponing. She drove with the casual disregard for speed limits that only comes from living in a neighborhood for a long, long time, and while she was definitely aware that we weren't old friends or anything, the relationship she had constructed for us was warm and comfortable enough to fill the car with contentment. I was a cousin's girlfriend's sister's niece, or something like that, and it was good enough for her.

It's nice, how quickly some people find their way from "strangers" to "family." Nice, and maybe a little dangerous, but I wasn't complaining. There was nothing to connect me to her. I'd be forgotten as soon as I got out of her car, and the cuckoo from the airport would never be able to track her down. She was safe, or as safe as anyone living in a city with a normal, hunting, hungry cuckoo could be.

"Now, are you sure this is where you want me to drop you?" The woman pulled to a stop in front of an old warehouse, a brief stab of disapproval shooting through her general air of contentment. "I could take you someplace much nicer. Or you could come back to the house and wait for your friends to meet you there. I don't mind."

"Duke might." Duke was the dog. He had been almost pathetically grateful when I left, even as he'd warred with his fear of me and his desire to protect his human. He was going to be clingy and paranoid for days. His human wouldn't understand why, and there was no way I could tell her, and I was sorry for that.

"Duke loves you."

That was a lie. I dug the last of the cuckoo's money out of my pocket and offered it to the woman. "Here. For the ride."

She started to object. Then her own self-interest kicked in, and she took the money from my hand, saying, "It's great of Carol to pay back what she owes me. Sometimes people surprise you."

"Yeah," I agreed. "Sometimes people do." I got out of the car before she could make another attempt to convince me not to. As soon as she was clear of my immediate presence, she drove away, faster than was strictly necessary. Some part of her knew that she'd just had an encounter with a predator bigger than she was, and she wanted to get the hell out of the way.

I touched my upper lip. Dry. Then I turned toward the warehouse, noting the lights in the windows with relieved satisfaction, and started walking.

My family tree can get confusing sometimes. I get that. When you're dealing with multiple generations, including some people whose lifespans aren't limited to the human norm, the names and connections and complications pile up fast. So here's the short and simple, or as simple as it's possible for me to make things:

My adoptive mother, Angela, was born somewhere in New England and raised by a family in Maine who had been chosen without their consent by her biological mother. Cuckoos pick the nests where they abandon their children carefully, according to a set of standards I don't fully understand, and never will, unless I decide to have children of my own. Infants are abandoned in homes that have the space and resources to raise them properly, and where there are no other children to get in the way of dedicating those resources to the new cuckoo-child. Her husband, Martin Baker, was originally several human men. They were killed, only to be brought back to life by a scientist with more ambition than sense. I don't mind, though. I love my father, and he is who he is because of someone with a shovel and a dream.

Mom and Dad couldn't have children of their own—they're not biologically compatible—so they decided to adopt. Evie came first, left on their doorstep by one of the scientist's apprentices as she ran into the night. Drew was next, adopted from the bogeyman community after an accident claimed his birth family. And I came last, dredged out of a storm drain after my instinctive telepathic distress call led them to my location.

By the time I came along, Evie was already a married adult with three children. Alex, who's three years older than I am, Verity, who's basically my age, and Antimony, who's a couple of years younger. And that's all pretty straightforward, I guess. Big age gaps exist in families. Evie's husband, Uncle Kevin—and yeah, he's technically my brother-in-law, but I call him uncle, the same way I call Evie's kids my cousins, since thinking of Verity as my niece would be way too weird—has a sister, Aunt Jane, who married Uncle Ted. They have two kids: Artie, who's pretty close to my age, and Elsie, who's a couple of years older than I am. It's not the biggest family tree ever, but that doesn't mean it can't be confusing.

Elsie likes a lot of things. Shopping, and dyeing her hair to match her nails, and veterinary medicine. And roller derby. She likes roller derby so much, in fact, that when Antimony graduated high school and couldn't cheerlead anymore, Elsie talked her into trying out for the local league. Annie's been skating ever since, while Elsie sits in the bleachers and cheers for her cousin. It's about the closest they've ever come to a nonviolent family activity.

The big rolling warehouse doors were closed, but the smaller door intended for humans rather than trucks was propped slightly open. A sign was taped to the outside—"CLOSED PRACTICE. DELIVERIES TO OFFICE." I ignored it, and let myself in.

Inside the warehouse it was bright and warm. Floodlights overhead illuminated the entire track, making the flat oval look bigger and more dramatic. And on the track, the skaters circled, more than a dozen girls in differently colored gear pushing, shoving, and skating their way to roller derby glory.

None of them looked my way. Neither did the coaches who stood by the sidelines and called encouragement, or the women who weren't currently on the track for whatever reason. They were skating around the edges of the practice, adjusting gym mats, pushing brooms, doing all the little tasks required to keep an amateur athletic league up and functioning.

There were a few people seated in the bleachers. I scanned them until I settled on a woman with short, blueberry-colored hair, wearing the black-and-red gear of a Slasher Chicks supporter. That's Annie's team. I walked closer, reaching out mentally until my thoughts brushed against the familiar, reassuring edges of Elsie's mind.

She turned instantly, eyes searching the floor until they landed on me. Her consciousness immediately narrowed into a single point of wary suspicion. I nodded, satisfied with her response, and kept walking toward her.

Because see, here's a fun thing about Uncle Kevin and Aunt Jane: for some reason, they aren't as vulnerable to cuckoo influence as most humans. Their mother, my Grandma Alice, is even more resistant, and to hear her tell it, *her* mother, Fran, was basically immune. Someone, somewhere back in the family line, wasn't human, and whatever genetic gifts they gave their offspring have resulted in generations of people who aren't at nearly as much risk where cuckoos are concerned. Genetic descendants of Frances Brown *notice* cuckoos. They can pick us out of a crowd. They remember us when we're not directly visible. It's terrifying, and awesome, and I wish to whatever gods watch over my messed-up species that I knew what their inhuman ancestor had been, so I could meet more of them.

Elsie slipped one hand into her purse as I approached, no doubt preparing to draw some sort of weapon if I turned out to be any other cuckoo in the world. She's not much of a fighter as our family goes—I think I'm the only one who's worse—but she was still willing to make the effort in order to protect her people. I appreciated that, too.

"Hi, Else," I said, once I was close enough to make myself heard without needing to raise my voice. The rattle of wheels on the track continued in the background, a smooth, staccato white noise underscoring everything I said. "Long time no see, huh?"

I was trying to sound cool. I was probably failing. But I felt Elsie's suspicion melt into surprise, and finally into awe, as she sent a single, virtually shouted thought in my direction: *Sarah?*

Yeah, I thought back, nodding for good measure. *It's me.*

Elsie stood, withdrawing her hand from her purse. "Are you really?" she asked. "I mean, you're really-really Sarah?"

"I'm really-really Sarah," I said.

"Prove it." Her voice was low, in deference to the derby girls circling the track below us—although one of those girls, dressed in black and red, with a long red-brown braid trailing out the back of her helmet, had slowed to a stop just beside the track itself.

A rush of almost startling joy washed over me. Antimony. I'd been hoping I might be lucky enough to catch the league during practice, and to find one of my cousins in residence. Finding two of them was almost unreasonable.

"You were super double bonus mad when Alex and his sisters came back from Lowryland with a new cousin as a souvenir, until Mom explained that even if she wasn't your grandmother, I was going to be your cousin, too; you think it's unfair that I have such good eyelashes without mascara; you also think it's unfair that I'd rather do math than let you practice your makeup techniques on me. You once accidentally made chlorine gas in the front hall and we had to try to convince Artie to come out of his basement before he choked to death, all without saying anything that would alert the mice. Not that it mattered, because they tattled on us anyway, and we all got sent to bed without dessert for practicing our chemical weaponry without an adult present. Your favorite color is this weird shade of maroon that you insist is pink even though it isn't, you like cocoa without marshmallows, partially as a form of self-defense against Annie, and you had a crush on me for like a year when we were teenagers, which we all pretended wasn't happening."

"How can you know all that and still insist Artie isn't in love with you?" asked Elsie. If I'd had any doubts about *her* identity, that would have lain them to rest; she and my other cousins had been trying to convince me that Artie had nonfamilial feelings for me basically since we'd all hit puberty. They couldn't seem to understand that my being a cuckoo made a difference, and so I'd stopped trying to argue with them when the subject came up. There was a hitch in her voice that could have been laughter and could have been the beginning of a sob. Based on the chaotic thoughts sparking in the air around her, as tangled as a ball of yarn, it was probably both. I braced myself. I'd seen that tangle of thoughts before.

Sure enough, she flung herself at me a second later, locking her arms around my torso and pulling me crushingly close, her chin resting on my left shoulder while her entire body shook with sobs. I stood rigidly still, aware that she didn't need or want anything else from me. She was reassuring herself that I was really here, really real, and that was all that mattered.

The tip of a knife pressed against the back of my neck, positioned so that one quick thrust would slide it into the gap between my vertebrae and sever my spinal

Four

$$\pi_2(n) \sim 2C_2 \frac{n}{(\ln n)^2} \sim 2C_2 \int_2^n \frac{dt}{(\ln t)^2}$$

"There's a special sort of egotism that comes with being a member of the human race. We call compassion, kindness, love, all part of 'showing humanity.' That's not what they are at all. They're part of being a good person. Humanity barely counts."
—Evelyn Baker

In a semi-abandoned warehouse, sitting on the bleachers, waiting for the last of the derby girls to go home

ANNIE PASSED ME A bag of air-popped popcorn, rich with the scents of butter and tomato powder. I sniffed appreciatively before shoving a greasy handful into my mouth. It tasted better than anything had any right to taste. I barely chewed before shoving another handful in after the first. My stomach grumbled at how slowly I was going. The food in first class had been tolerable, as airline food went, but the portions had been nothing to get excited about, and I'd had a busy, physically taxing day.

"I don't know how you can eat that stuff," said Annie, settling beside me and bumping her shoulder against mine. She was back in her street clothes, although she was still wearing a Slasher Chicks T-shirt along with her jeans and flannel overshirt. She was radiating a degree of contentment that I'd never felt from her before. Contentment, and something else, like the faintest hint of ashes in the air.

I gave her a sidelong glance, trying to figure out why she was making the inside of my mind taste like charcoal. "It's easy," I said. "I put it in my mouth, then I chew it up, and then I swallow. See?" I shoved more popcorn in my mouth, gave it a few good chomps, and stuck my tongue out at her.

"Ew, gross." She shoved me, laughing. "Remind me why I missed you?"

"I'd rather she tell us why she carries tomato powder in her *backpack*," said Elsie. "That's weird, Sarah. Grade-A weird."

"Says the succubus," I shot back. "I like tomato powder. It tastes the way you feel when you eat chocolate. Since I don't eat chocolate, I make do."

The warehouse seemed much larger, and much quieter, without the rest of the derby girls. Every word we spoke rose into the rafters, becoming a distorted echo of itself. It would have been unnerving, if I hadn't felt so utterly, blissfully safe. I had my cousins back. I was in Oregon again, and I'd made the trip all by myself. I was healing.

Thinking of the trip made my smile fade. I needed to tell Evie and Kevin about the cuckoo in the airport, so they could figure out what to do about her. I needed to *not* tell Annie and Elsie, because Annie would be all for grabbing a field kit and charging straight at the problem. She was the most level-headed of my cousins in many ways, but not when she felt like she might be able to do something to show up her siblings. Having Verity and Alex in different states had probably helped that tendency somewhat—it's easier to shine on your own when you don't have anyone to measure yourself against—but I couldn't count on that.

Resistant or not, two Price girls wouldn't be enough to take out a cuckoo, and I couldn't do it. I couldn't stand that static again, not so soon on the heels of the first time. Especially not when she was likely to have an active grudge against me for that whole "hitting her" thing.

Annie laughed abruptly. I looked at her again. She had her phone out, attention focused on the screen, radiating smug contentment.

"Something funny?" I asked.

"It's her *boy*friend," said Elsie, in that familiar, hectoring tone of hers. "Didn't anyone tell you? Our Annie's in *love*. With a person, not a siege engine. I never thought I'd live to see the day."

I blinked. That didn't seem like a big enough reaction, and so I blinked again, more slowly, before saying, "*What*?"

Annie's cheeks flushed red, a vascular response I've sometimes envied. People with visible blood don't know how lucky they are. "Both of you shut up," she mumbled.

"Um, no, not going to shut up, don't tell me to shut up, and *what*?" I poked her with my elbow. "I have popcorn, which makes this the perfect time for gossip. You have a boyfriend? As in, a person you're dating, not a boy who happens to be your friend?"

"As in a person I'm dating," said Annie, cheeks still burning. The taste of char grew stronger at the back of my throat. "It's been a weird few years while you've been off recovering. I'm really glad you're back."

"This is so weird," I said.

"Hey, Alex is the one who's having a baby," objected Annie. "I think I'm still in the normal band for the youngest sibling."

Elsie's phone buzzed. She checked the screen. A sudden burst of smug satisfaction radiated off of her. "I hate to cut this short—"

"I don't," muttered Annie.

"—but I'm afraid I'm going to have to. Sarah, you might want to wipe the butter off your cheek. It's red. That's disgusting. It looks like bloody snot."

I frowned at her, perplexed.

The warehouse door banged open. The quality of the air changed, going from the soft hum created by my proximity to Annie and Elsie—two people I'd known for years but had never been particularly physical with—to something louder and more electric, like sparks racing along my skin. I lowered my popcorn, frown becoming an open-mouthed stare.

"You *didn't*," I accused.

Elsie shrugged, reaching over to rub her thumb in a quick arc across my cheek, presumably wiping away the smear of butter. "I did," she said. "I know you. You were going to put it off and put it off and maybe fly back to Ohio without ever telling him you were here. You don't get to be afraid anymore, Sarah-baby. You scared us too much for that. Now stop fucking around and go tell my brother that you're back."

I shook my head, fighting the urge to pull a psychic blanket over me like a shield. Annie and Elsie wouldn't lose sight of me if I did that—they were sitting too close, they could see me too clearly—but they weren't the ones I was trying to hide from. "I'm not ready. You shouldn't have done this. I'm not . . . I don't know that I'm better. I'm not *ready*."

"Sarah?"

Artie's voice came from somewhere back by the front door, pitched loud enough to reach us without becoming an echoing smear in the aural landscape. He sounded . . . he sounded scared, almost, as scared as I felt. He sounded hopeful, too, and resigned, like he knew, somewhere deep down, that this was a cruel joke. It didn't matter that his sister had never been the kind to play this sort of prank; it was easier to believe that she had turned suddenly brutally thoughtless than it was to let himself think she was telling the truth.

I'd been broken, but Artie . . . I'd left Artie alone. I closed my eyes, letting my chin drop toward my chest, and reached for his thoughts.

They were a whirling maelstrom of fear and hope and anger and blame, almost all of it directed squarely at himself. He shouldn't have let me go to New York with Verity; he knew I'd gone because I wanted to challenge myself, and he hadn't been willing to do more things that would be challenging, hadn't wanted to stray outside the comforts of his familiar basement, where he never needed to worry about running into people who might be affected by his pheromones. He was worried he'd driven me away, and terrified that even if Elsie wasn't playing a nasty trick for some reason, that I hadn't called him myself because I didn't actually want to see him. He thought I was done with him. Artie. The person I would call my best friend without a moment's hesitation, thought I was done with him.

Artie, come on, *you know better,* I thought.

His response was silent joy and silent sorrow, both blended together. The connection intensified, drawing me deeper whether I wanted to go or not. I could suddenly see again, despite my closed eyes: I was looking at the back of the bleachers, at the shape of three women barely visible through the slats between the rows. He couldn't quite see us well enough to tell us apart, but he knew we were there.

And I could see through his eyes. I could still slide myself into his thoughts as easily as sliding a book back onto a shelf, because the connection between us wasn't broken. Maybe it was a little less stable than it had been before and maybe it wasn't. I couldn't tell, and it didn't matter. I was here now. *We* were here now. I opened my eyes and stood. Elsie and Annie exchanged a look I couldn't read and didn't need to; the air around them crackled with smugness. I ignored them and ran down the bleachers, almost stumbling on the last step. I grabbed one of the rails, using it to whip myself around the corner of the bleachers, out into the open.

For a moment—only a moment, but long enough—my connection to Artie's mind was still active, and I saw myself, pale, black-haired girl in yoga pants and an oversized teal sweater that hung to cover my hands and almost obscure my figure. It was designed to keep me from accidentally touching anyone, not to be flattering. That didn't stop a feeling of intense joy from welling up and filling Artie's thoughts, almost overwhelming me before it snapped closed, shutting me out.

Artie has always thought of me as a sister, something I remember all too well from when we were kids and I still thought it was okay for me to read his mind. Cross-species relationships are hard enough even when both participants are mammals. But when he looked at me like that, sometimes I could almost let myself forget how impossible anything more than friendship was for the two of us.

"Hi," I said, like none of this was a big deal. Like I came home every day. "I would have called. I just got into town."

Artie stared at me, the expression exaggerated enough that I could pick it up even with the distance between us and the limitations in the way my mind interprets human faces. Then he broke into a run. I didn't move, at first because I was too puzzled to understand what was happening, and then because I didn't want to. Instead, I braced myself and spread my arms a little wider and let him run right into them.

According to Annie and Elsie, who look at Artie the way humans do, he's pretty good looking, for all that he checks a lot of boxes on the "average" side of the sheet: average height, neither fat nor thin, with the build of someone who works out because he has to, not because he wants to. He's a noncombatant with natural abilities that will mostly keep him safe if he ever winds up in the middle of a fight. Natural abilities, and a really vicious family. He has brown hair and brown eyes and a smile that the minds of everyone around me say is sweet and kind, even if it's rare.

He has one of the most soothing minds I've ever touched. Spending time with Artie is better than meditating, or napping, or almost anything else. It's not the only reason I've been in love with him since I was a kid, but it certainly doesn't hurt.

And now he was holding onto me like he never, ever wanted to let go of me again.

I pressed my face into his shoulder, breathing in the bright, faintly spicy smell of his skin. It was largely drowned out by the horrifying quantities of body spray he was wearing, as always when he needed to leave his basement. Normally, I wouldn't have been able to smell it at all. He was usually better about getting even coverage—sometimes spread out across six or seven applications—before he left the house.

"How many speed laws did you break?" I asked, without lifting my head.

"All of them," said Artie, and pulled away.

Regretfully, I let him go. Our big reunion was over, and odds were good he wouldn't let me touch him again for days. Being half-incubus means his skin secretes pheromones that can cloud the minds of anyone who might be sexually attracted to him or genetically suited to making adorable part-Lilu babies. Women and gay men, mostly, and his own species, mostly, but not one hundred percent on either of those counts. Family members—*blood* family—are immune. I'm not blood family, which means I'm not covered in the catch-all immunity, so Artie has been reluctant to touch me ever since puberty first came stalking up and whacked him with its mighty hammer o' suck.

I'm not blood family. I'm also not a mammal, strictly speaking; his pheromones don't work on me, and never have. Even Uncle Ted's pheromones don't work on me, and Uncle Ted's a full incubus, with none of that pesky humanity to get in the way and weaken the effects of his natural weaponry. And Lilu pheromones *are* a weapon. Incubus, succubus, it doesn't matter. They attract mates to make breeding easier and less dangerous, and make it possible for them to get in and out without getting hurt. But they evolved in *this* dimension, not in mine, and their biology doesn't know how to deal with a Johrlac. We're a mystery to them.

Not that this matters to Artie, who figured out fast that touching non-family girls was not okay and filed me in the "not family" bucket shortly thereafter.

Artie took a big step backward. That still left us in arm's reach, so he took another one before he lifted his chin and looked at me. That was all. He just . . . looked at me, searching my face like he was trying to memorize it, like something must have changed while I'd been in Ohio. Finally, he took a deep breath.

"You didn't call," he said.

"I did," I objected.

"You didn't call *enough*."

"I'm sorry." I worried the hem of my sweatshirt between my thumb and forefinger, resisting the urge to look away. Eye contact doesn't make telepathy easier the way skin contact does. It just makes me faintly uncomfortable. "I was . . . for a long time, I wasn't myself. And then I was scared I *still* wasn't myself, but that I'd lost so much I couldn't actually tell anymore. I'm sorry, I really am. I didn't mean to worry you."

"Didn't mean to—Sarah, I thought you were never coming back." Frustration and fear rolled off him in a wave: wordless, formless, and oppressively strong. "I thought I'd lost you forever. You're my best friend. Do you know how scary that was?"

"I thought I'd lost me, too." My voice came out in a whisper. "I know about scary, Artie, because I've been scared since the day I got hurt. I thought I was never going to be okay again. I thought I'd broken my own brain so badly that I'd never be able to control myself around people who weren't wearing anti-telepathy charms. It's still . . . I'm still not like I was. I pick up more things from people I'm not attuned to. The world is *loud*, and when I sleep, I wind up walking in dreams that aren't mine if I don't set up barriers in the room to keep my thoughts from getting out. I thought I was never going to see any of you again because Mom wouldn't let you into the house in Ohio unless I told her it was okay, and I wasn't going to say it was okay until the thought of you feeling sorry for me wasn't so terrifying that it put me back in my bed for a week. So yes, I know how scary it was. I know how scary all of this was. I'm sorry I didn't call. Getting myself to Portland without freaking out or hurting myself was the last big test of whether or not I was recovered."

Slowly, Artie blinked. "You mean you came here on your own?"

I nodded.

"How?"

"I flew." Bit by bit, I explained the day I'd had, starting with saying goodbye to Mom outside of security. I mentioned my suspicion that a cuckoo had been hunting in the Cleveland Airport, but I didn't mention the cuckoo I'd actually seen here in Portland. That needed to wait until I saw Evie. She'd know what to do, and her resistance to Johrlac influence was almost as good as a born Price's, thanks to growing up in a house with Mom. Long exposure leads to increased resistance to the negative aspects of cuckoo influence, along with the easier telepathy. I guess it's a balance thing. Otherwise, cuckoos would just keep their favorite humans with them always, malleable and obedient and open books.

By the time I finished, Annie and Elsie had given up on giving us space and drifted over to join us, forming a rough little circle between the bleachers and the doors. Annie looked at Artie, looked pointedly at the open space between us, and rolled her eyes.

"All right, since it looks like the big reunion is over, we should probably go tell the rest of the family that it's time to throw a welcome home party for Sarah," she said. "Elsie, you have room in your car for one more?"

"I can give Sarah a ride," said Artie.

"Did you offer?" asked Annie. "Because dude, if I were you and this were Sam, I would already have been in the car and driving away as fast as I could."

"You don't know how to drive," said Elsie.

"My point stands," said Annie.

"Sarah and I aren't . . . like that," objected Artie, cheeks flushing. His thoughts turned into a tangled mess before shutting off entirely once again, blocked by the defensive action of his own empathic abilities. Full incubi can not only sense the emotions of the people around them, they can influence them, making direct changes to other people's moods and hence minds.

I can't change minds. I can't even directly change thoughts. I can manipulate memory and insert myself into someone's emotional landscape, but it's a lot less of a precision job than Uncle Ted or even Artie can manage. Artie's empathy had always been mostly receptive and defensive, allowing him to pick up on feelings or block out other psychics, including me. It might even have improved since I'd seen him last. The walls between us certainly felt sturdier.

"No, of course you're not," said Annie, with withering sarcasm. "Sarah, you're coming back to the compound tonight?"

"Yeah," I said, not looking at Artie. "I'm still not stable enough to sleep just anywhere. The room Mom and I set up is going to be best for me." It had triple-strength anti-telepathy charms worked into the walls, creating a psychic null space that never moved, never varied, and would last as long as the house was standing. I could sleep peacefully there, without worrying about picking up on any dreams I shouldn't be part of.

"If she's going home with you, I want to drive her." Artie squared his shoulders. His thoughts were still too sealed off to let me understand his expression; it could have meant virtually anything. "I need to come over anyway. Sam borrowed a bunch of my comic books, and I want them back."

"Sarah?" asked Elsie. "That okay with you?"

"Sure," I said, not looking at Artie. "I'll see you both at the house." I turned and walked to the bleachers to retrieve my backpack, waiting for some crack in the shell around Artie to open up and let me know what he was thinking.

It didn't happen.

Evie and Uncle Kevin understood the importance and necessity of privacy. In their line of work, having neighbors could mean way too many visits from the police, and they'd always known they wanted to be a safe space for the kind of people they were likely to associate with. Not just family members: other crypto-zoologists and researchers, cryptids like me or Artie, and bounty hunters like Grandma Alice. All kinds of folks could be found in the living room on any given day, and that meant having the space and the distance to host them.

Artie kept his hands on the wheel and his eyes fixed on the road as he drove past the Portland city limits, heading into the deep, dark woods outside. The trees pushed down on us from all sides, swallowing the ambient light, leaving us dependent on the headlights' glare.

According to my Aunt Rose, a lot of people die on that road. She ought to know. She died on a similar road more than sixty years ago, and when we're talking about death, we know to treat her as the expert that she is.

"This is going to be a long drive if you don't talk to me," I said.

Artie didn't reply. The shell around his thoughts was like a wall, built solely to keep me out.

Vexed, I shot a quick arrow of thought at his ramparts. *You say you missed me, but this doesn't feel like missing me.*

"Oh, come on, Sarah," he snapped. "You know that's not fair."

"So you *can* hear me."

"I can't help hearing you." He kept his eyes on the road. I guess it seemed easier than looking at me. "I hear you even when you're not around. I hear you having opinions on things I'm reading, and I hear you complaining when people talk during movies, since it's not like you can read the actors' minds and know what they were trying to say, and I hear you making nasty gagging noises every time I choose chocolate over strawberry. I hear you *all the time.* But you weren't hearing me, or you would have called."

"I called as much as I could," I said in a small voice.

"Then you didn't hear me, because I needed you to call a lot more than you did."

I closed my eyes, sagging in the seat. "Phones are hard. I can hear what you're saying, but I can't hear what you mean, and it makes my brain itch. I like text more. Text is always flat. It doesn't have tone or nuance; it just has what the person on the other side of the keyboard said. I texted you all the time."

"I'm sorry the phone made you so uncomfortable, but I needed to hear your voice a lot more often than I did." Artie abruptly smacked the steering wheel, the sound echoing through the cab. "I thought you were *dead*, and then I thought you were gone forever, and then I thought . . . I thought you didn't care about us anymore, because you were never coming back. I thought a lot of things. And you wouldn't let me see you, and so the thoughts didn't go away. They didn't get any better."

"Artie." I opened my eyes and reached for him. If I

was touching him, he wouldn't be able to keep me out. I could finally make him understand why I'd stayed away, and why I'd come back; I could show him, and he'd *see*, and this would all get better. We'd get better. We'd—

The truck came out of nowhere, roaring down a side road that was barely more than a logging trail. It slammed into the passenger side of my cousin's ancient Camaro, sending us spinning out of control. Artie shouted. I screamed. There was a roaring crash as we hit a tree, the front end of the car buckling. Glass filled the air, and for a moment it seemed to stop, shining and spinning in front of us, unable to touch us. Then my head hit the dashboard, and everything was darkness.

Five

$$\pi_2(n) \sim 2C_2\frac{n}{(\ln n)^2} \sim 2C_2\int_2^n \frac{dt}{(\ln t)^2}$$

"Disaster's not like a rattlesnake: it doesn't give you any warning before it strikes. It just happens, and you'd better hope to heaven and hell at the same time that you're not in the path of its glory."
—Frances Brown

Somewhere in the woods outside of Portland, regaining consciousness after a bad accident

SOMETHING STICKY COVERED MY cheeks and forehead, and there was a sweet, almost floral taste in the air, like someone had been spraying perfume inside the car. I sat up with a groan, feeling the seatbelt dig at my waist. I was going to have bruises in the morning, ghostly webs of broken capillaries that wouldn't show very clearly from the outside but would sure as hell hurt.

Everything was dark. I couldn't even see my own hand when I waved it in front of my face. It was possible I'd hit my head hard enough to leave me with a temporary form of traumatic blindness, but it seemed more likely—a lot more likely—that it was just a natural consequence of being in an accident in the middle of the woods at night.

An accident. I'd forgotten. That seemed impossible as soon as the memory came back, but trauma can do strange and terrible things to the way the brain processes information, and for a moment, I'd forgotten about the truck, the way it had roared out of the darkness, and—

"Artie!" I reached out frantically, with both my hands and my mind, and sagged in relief as my fingers found his shoulder and my mind found the distant, blurry shadow of his thoughts. Unconsciousness isn't the same as sleep. A person who's been knocked cold can sometimes seem to disappear entirely, as good as dead, unless I know exactly where to look—or I'm touching them. To test that theory, I took my hand away from Artie's shoulder, and winced as his thoughts seemed to wink out in the same instant.

Okay. He was alive. He was hurt, and he was unconscious, and he was probably bleeding; the floral taste in the air was from his pheromones working overtime to protect him from the presumption of a threat. I needed to get us out of here.

My backpack was on the floor by my feet. I tried to reach it. The seatbelt pulled me up short, tightened to its absolute limits by the crash. I fumbled for the belt. If I could just get to my bag, if I could get to my phone, I could call Annie. She and Elsie hadn't been too far ahead of us. They'd be able to double back and help, preferably before some Good Samaritan happened across the crash and decided to call the police.

Artie was leaking liquid love, and he wasn't awake enough to control the negative aspects of his influence. I was bleeding something that looked more like antifreeze or spinal fluid than human blood. Any cop who responded to this accident report would get a lot more than they were bargaining for, and they probably wouldn't enjoy it. We needed to keep this in the family, both literally and figuratively.

The seatbelt was jammed, presumably also by the accident. I took a deep breath, trying to keep the panic from rising up and overwhelming me. I knew that cars didn't explode nearly as often in real life as they did in the movies, but something was ticking, and something was dripping, and I wanted to get *out* of here. I wanted to go home. I wanted—

I could feel my thoughts getting wild around the edges, slipping through my mental fingers like snakes and slithering toward the endless equations that had kept me company through my convalescence. I stopped and took another deep breath. *This is nothing like what happened before,* I told myself sternly. *Your body is hurt, not your mind.* My head ached from its impact with the dashboard, and there was a chance I'd suffered a concussion, but those were injuries to my surface self, not to the strange, obscure structure inside my brain that controlled the parts of me that weren't a mirror to humanity. I wasn't going to lose control of my telepathy over this. I wasn't going to lose myself again.

The seatbelt came loose with a click. I shook it off like I was fighting all my fears at once, grabbing my backpack and fumbling for my phone. My hands were shaking. They weren't cut, though; the glass that filled the car around me seemed to have missed me somehow. I remembered the way it had seemed to freeze in midair, not quite touching our skins. Something about that moment . . .

It was probably the trauma speaking. Glass doesn't just stop in midair. I forced my hands to steady enough to let me unlock my screen and scrolled through my contacts until I found Annie's number. I'd never been happier that she didn't drive.

She picked up on the third ring. "Tell Artie to stop being a butt or we *will* double back and get you," she said. There was laughter in her voice. I could hear Elsie in the background, singing loudly along with some piece of bubblegum pop that I hadn't been subjected to yet. They sounded so *happy.* I hated to ruin that for them.

I hated to die alone in the forest even more.

"Please," I croaked. My voice was weaker than I expected it to be. I swallowed, tasting the sweet, almost syrupy tang of my own blood at the back of my throat, and tried again. "Please come back. There's been an accident. Artie won't wake up. There's a lot of blood." Unspoken was the fact that it didn't matter which of us was bleeding; it would be bad for a human rescuer either way.

From Annie's sharply indrawn breath, she didn't need any more details than that. "Do you know how far back you are? We're almost to the house."

It was an hour from Portland to the house. We'd been in the woods for less than five minutes when the impact occurred. We must have been unconscious in the car for at least half an hour. Artie was still unconscious. "Way back," I said. "We were barely in the woods when it happened. Artie won't wake up. Please. Come get us."

"We'll be there as fast as we can," said Annie. The line went dead. I pushed back the sudden urge to cry. Artie was hurt and everything was dark, and I was alone.

At least my phone battery was in pretty good shape. I turned the screen toward Artie, swallowing hard as I braced myself for what I was about to see.

He was draped over the steering wheel, eyes closed, glasses askew. Blood oozed from a long gash down the side of his cheek, vivid red and sluggish. After a moment's hesitation, I wiped the blood from my own forehead and held my hand over his wound, letting it drip gently down. Yes, as disgusting as it sounds, but not quite as ridiculous; cuckoo blood is a natural antibiotic agent. It's harmless to humans and other mammals, and it substantially reduces the chances of infection. He'd have a better shot at recovery without needing heavy drugs or having a scar. And it was something I could *do*, something that wasn't just sitting there and waiting for Annie and Elsie to come save us.

I wiped my sticky hand on my leg before reaching over and gently shaking his shoulder. "Artie? I don't think we should stay in the car. I think . . . I know the car probably won't *explode*, but it's making weird noises and I don't like it. So if you could wake up now, that would be great. Okay? Wake up."

I brushed my pinkie finger against the blood-tacky skin of his neck, and added, *I really need you to wake up now. It's important. Please, Artie, please.*

There was no response, either verbally or mentally, only the tangled, murky thoughts of the unconscious mind. At least I knew he was alive, even if I couldn't tell how badly he was hurt, or whether he was going to need medical attention beyond what Evie could provide in her living room. We don't currently have a cryptid-specific hospital on the West Coast. I'd never considered what a failing that was until just now.

The car continued to click and groan around me, and I remembered abruptly that we hadn't been the only vehicle involved in the accident: the truck that slammed into us out of nowhere must have had a driver, even if I'd been too distracted to pick up on their presence until it was too late. I reluctantly pulled my hand away from Artie and reached for the handle of my door. I needed to check on the other driver. And while I was at it, I could get the first aid kit out of the trunk and mop up some of the blood. The less there was in the cabin, the better.

The door refused to open. I winced. It had taken the brunt of the impact—it was honestly a miracle I hadn't been killed, and *that* was something I wasn't going to think about more than I absolutely had to—and something had bent inside the frame, jamming it in place.

"This is going to suck," I said aloud, and twisted in my seat, grabbing the headrest. Glass bit into my hands and knees as I crawled into the back, careful not to

kick Artie in the head. He didn't move or make a
sound, still sunk so deeply into unconsciousness that
he was unaware of my borderline gymnastics. That was
probably a good thing. I wasn't exactly what I'd call
"dignified," especially not when I overbalanced and
toppled onto the seat, landing in a heap of fast food
wrappers, empty cans, and junk mail. I wrinkled my
nose. Something back here had gone bad enough to
smell sort of like death.

"Dammit, Artie," I mumbled, feeling around in the
junk until I found my phone. I held it tight in one hand
as I unlocked the rear driver's-side door with the
other. This side of the frame wasn't bent. The door
opened easily, and the cold forest air rushed into the
car, striking me across the face, washing everything
else away.

Gingerly, I got out, focusing on my body with every
movement, waiting for some sign of additional damage
to make itself known. The small cuts in my hands and
knees from climbing over the seat stung, and the cut on
my forehead throbbed, but that seemed to be it. Artie's
old Camaro had somehow managed to absorb most of
the shock, rather than passing it along to its passengers.

Good old car. This was probably the end of the road
for it, at least based on what I'd been able to feel and
see by the dim light of my phone. But it had done its
best, and Artie had loved it since his sixteenth birthday, when the keys had fallen out of his cereal box.
Maybe Aunt Rose would come and carry it onto the
ghostroads, where it could keep on driving forever, a
shadow among the dead. Artie would like that.

Thinking about Aunt Rose and Artie at the same
time made something ache deep in my gut, a sharp,
anatomically unfocused pain, like my whole body was
rebelling from the natural continuation of my thoughts.
I tried to focus myself, closing my eyes as I stood and
allowed my mind to spread out around me, questing

for signs that I wasn't alone. If the other driver was still alive—

I found nothing sentient. The forest was alight with minds, but all of them were small, simple, the sort of thing that blended into so much background noise when I wasn't actively looking for it. I found deer, owls, raccoons, tailypo, even a few cautious wolpertingers, but no humans, and no other sapient cryptids. I might as well have been alone in the woods.

That didn't mean the other driver was necessarily dead. I couldn't pick up on Artie's mind, either, when I wasn't actively in contact with his skin. I held up my phone, turning in a slow circle as I looked for the truck that had slammed into us.

It wasn't there.

A trail of destruction led from the back of the Camaro and up a slight incline, leading back to the road. There would have been more damage if the truck had followed us into the woods. Whoever had hit us, they'd slammed into the side of the Camaro hard enough to send us spinning off into the brush, but they hadn't suffered enough damage to stop them. That seemed wrong. If they'd been okay after impact, why hadn't they come to see if *we* were okay? Why hadn't they called the authorities?

I glanced back at Artie's motionless form, suddenly uneasy. If he woke up and found me gone, he'd probably panic. My blood was everywhere inside the cabin, and even though it looked more like mucus to the human eye, he understood cuckoo biology well enough to recognize it for what it was.

But if he woke up, his thoughts would spike enough that I could pick up on them, and I could tell him where I was. Staying here because he *might* wake up and be upset was silly. Finding out what had happened to the other driver was smart.

I'm not going far, Artie, I thought at him, and started walking.

None of my bones were broken, but the bruises from the impact were starting to make themselves known. I groaned as I pulled myself up the incline, using the broken branches of the trees we had crashed through for leverage. I paused when I reached the top, still holding onto a snapped-off limb for balance as I held up my phone and moved it in a slow arc, scanning the road. There was no truck. Only a little broken glass glittered on the pavement as a sign that anything had happened here at all. Whoever had hit us had kept on driving, out of shock or fear or concern about their insurance premiums. It didn't matter. Whatever their reasons had been, we were alone. They had run us off the road and left us alone and injured in the woods to die.

The fact that having them gone was better for keeping our secrets didn't matter. In that moment, my hate was like a bonfire, burning hot and fierce and borderline out of control. How dare they. How dare they just leave us here like this, when we needed help, when Artie wouldn't wake up. How *dare* they.

Anger forced my thoughts out even farther, the small, non-intelligent minds of the woods lighting up like candles in the black field of my awareness. I found possums and snakes and coyotes. I found bears, three of them, larger and more ponderous than anything else around them. I found a chupacabra, too far away for me to ask for help—we had never met, much less touched, and my telepathy wouldn't stretch that far. I found everything except a single human mind. Even Elsie and Annie were out of my range.

I took a shuddering breath, anger collapsing and taking my scan with it. I needed to calm down. I was going to strain myself again, and then we'd be in even deeper trouble. With Artie unconscious, I needed to stay on my feet so I could flag down help when it came, whatever form it took.

Something brushed against the edge of my consciousness.

It was a delicate touch, like the fluttering of a moth's wing, soft and quick and almost imperceptible. If I hadn't been so attuned to the minds around me, I wouldn't even have noticed it. I snapped to attention, turning my thoughts in the direction of the contact, reaching out as broadly as I could.

Cuckoos aren't the only telepaths in the world. True mind-readers are rare, but "rare" isn't the same thing as "unique." Succubi have limited telepathic abilities. Apraxis wasps are technically telepathic, although their abilities are mostly focused on devouring thoughts, not sharing them. Some human sorcerers figure out a way to project their thoughts. There are probably other psychics I haven't had the opportunity to meet. It didn't *have* to be another cuckoo in the woods with us. It didn't *have* to be proof that this was my fault.

But it probably was. It seemed improbable to the point of impossibility that the thought should have been coming from anything but another cuckoo. Elsie's telepathy was too weak to reach me from as far away as I knew she currently was, and she didn't like to use it unless she absolutely had to; she'd be calling my phone, not my cerebral cortex. Nothing else in these woods had the capability to communicate like that.

A cuckoo would.

Cuckoos are rare, one in a million, thanks to the way we feed and fight and protect our territory. Cuckoos are rare, and I'd already encountered two of them—one directly, one through inference—since leaving home. Logically, I shouldn't have been worried about seeing another one. Logically, we wouldn't have been the victims of a hit and run in the middle of nowhere. Someone was hunting us.

I shoved my phone into my pocket and balled my hands into fists, reaching out in all directions as hard as I could. My eyes burned as the chemical changes in my vitreous humor caused them to glow a lambent

white, and I felt a spreading dampness on my upper lip.
I was bleeding again. This was too much; I couldn't
keep it up for very long, or I was going to hurt myself.
A sudden wind whipped around me, stirring my hair
off my shoulders, making the cut on my forehead sting
even worse than it had before.

Don't, I thought, slinging the word like a stone into
the darkness. *You won't like what happens if you do.*

Maybe I was being paranoid. Maybe the brush of
another mind against my own had been fear or hope or
some toxic combination of the two: I didn't want to be
alone, but I didn't want to be found and so no matter
what happened, I was going to lose. Maybe. But I
didn't think so. My injury, and the anti-telepathy
charms my family had taken to wearing in its
aftermath—the charms Alex and Shelby still wore, to
keep me from slipping accidentally into their minds,
even though I'd been mostly able to control myself for
over a year now—had left me more sensitive to the
presence of other telepaths than I'd ever realized I
could be. They were gunshots in a silent field, so loud
that they couldn't possibly be overlooked. Not even
when I wanted to.

The wind continued to whip around me. Something
moved on the other side of the road, barely visible in
the dimness. I snapped around to look at it. A deer was
standing at the tree line, body outlined in the faint
glow of the moonlight. I blinked.

The wind wasn't blowing on the other side of the
road. The leaves didn't rustle; the dust didn't stir. The
deer was standing perfectly still, and so was the world
around it. I blinked again and the wind around me
died, my eyes burning as the light bled out of them.
There was a warm gush as my nosebleed increased in
both strength and severity, and then the ground was
rushing up to meet me, and the darkness drew me
down again, into a place where there was neither light
nor motion, but only peaceful stillness.

"This would be a lot easier if she had a *pulse*," Annie complained, her hand clamped around my wrist like she thought she could somehow force my anatomy to rearrange itself and provide her with a heart to monitor. "Who designs a biped that doesn't have a *pulse*? That's just inefficient. I call shenanigans."

She sounded nervous. The thoughts rolling off her proved it. As usual, she was masking genuine fear under a veil of sarcasm and annoyance, like she could somehow bluff the universe into believing she was the badass she always pretended to be.

"Evolution works in mysterious ways." Elsie's voice was accompanied by the sound of branches breaking. "Artie's still out cold, but he's breathing, and he, at least, has a good, steady pulse. I think he'll be fine, once we get him home and patch up that cut on his cheek. It looks like Sarah bled on him before she got out of the car."

"Good." Annie let go of my wrist. "Let's move Artie first, make sure we have anything he'll miss, and torch the car."

"Are you sure—"

"His blood is *everywhere*. A human finds the thing, they're going to be in love with him for the rest of their life. And the frame is bent to shit. I don't think there's a mechanic in the world who can save it. I know Artie loves that car, but all good things come to an end." Her thoughts roiled, turning oddly warm against my mind. "Besides, I'm freaked out and angry. I need to burn off a little flame."

Something clicked. I opened my eyes, staring up at the dark canopy of the trees above me. "You're a *sorcerer*," I said.

"And you're awake." Annie bent down to offer her hand. "I'm surprised no one told you."

"I'm not. People don't tell me much these days."
Alex and Shelby were always worried they were going
to upset me. Mom and Dad probably didn't know.
They were almost as out of the loop as I was, where
family news was concerned, although in their case it
was because they didn't want to risk getting involved.
"When did this happen?"

"A couple of years ago now." Annie pulled me to
my feet, let go, and stepped back, holding one hand out
in front of her, palm toward the sky. She flexed her
fingers and a small ball of lambent flame appeared
above them, glittering orange and blue against the
darkness. She closed her hand, and the fire disappeared. "I mostly just do elemental tricks so far—we
haven't exactly been able to find me a reliable teacher—
but I've stopped setting my sheets on fire, so we're calling it a win."

"Huh." A wave of weary sorrow washed over me. It
was probably partially exhaustion and partially the result of the adrenaline crash I'd suffered after I collapsed, but that wasn't all of it.

Five years. I'd lost five years with my family, and no
matter how much they'd tried to keep me updated, I'd
always known there would be things they couldn't, or
wouldn't, explain to me until I was feeling well enough
to come home. Things like Annie discovering she
could pull fire out of the air. Big things. Things that
changed everything around them, like any new variable introduced to a formerly stable equation.

"Yeah," said Annie. "It's been weird for me, too. I'll
shout if I need any help getting Artie out of the car."
Then she was gone, sliding down the incline on the
sides of her feet, off to set Artie's Camaro on fire.

Elsie moved to steady me as I watched Annie go. In
a carefully light tone, she asked, "Why were you up by
the road, Sarah? I don't think you should have moved
if you were already feeling dizzy."

"I wasn't. I . . ." I pulled away from her, grabbing my

phone out of my pocket, and ran across the road to where I'd seen the deer. Elsie shouted behind me. I ignored her. There were no cars coming; I was perfectly safe.

The ground on the other side of the road was the usual welter of debris, fragments of leaf, bark, dirt, even bits of shattered glass from other accidents. I stopped, squinting at it. I couldn't tell if the wind had been blowing recently. Maybe I'd been seeing things. There was a crust of dried blood on my upper lip; it broke and flaked away when I touched it with the tips of my fingers, falling into the darkness. It wasn't a stretch to think that if I was still unwell enough to get nosebleeds at the slightest provocation, I was unwell enough to be seeing things.

But there were hoofprints in the dirt at the edge of the road, perfect and pristine. I knelt, placing a finger at the very edge of the nearest print. The gesture made an instant indentation in the soft, dry earth. Portland is a damp city in a damp state, but it can dry out sometimes, and when it does, the ground moves. If the wind had been blowing on *this* side of the road, the prints would have collapsed inward on themselves. They would have blown away. They hadn't blown away.

"Sarah, what the *hell*?"

I looked over my shoulder. Elsie was beside me, radiating confusion and wary distress. She didn't understand what I was doing, or why I was doing it, and she was worried. I wasn't "Cousin Sarah, who does weird stuff sometimes" anymore. I was "Cousin Sarah, who got hurt, and might not be making good choices." I was someone to worry about, not someone to accept.

The change stung. Elsie and I had never been particularly close—not like Artie and me, or Annie and me; the nerds of our generation, closing ranks against the people who didn't understand—but she'd never looked at me like I was someone she needed to protect before.

It didn't matter how much better I felt, or how much I had recovered from my actual injuries. The process of getting everyone else to see me as better was going to take so much longer than I wanted it to.

"The wind," I said, standing and turning so that I was facing her properly. "It was blowing on the other side of the road, but it wasn't blowing here. Do you know of any cryptid that can control the wind?"

"Sorcerers can," said Elsie uncertainly. "Not Annie, not yet—she's mostly all about the fire—but I know it's a thing they can learn to do."

Two sorcerers in one city when they weren't working together was even less likely than two cuckoos in one city. It was still an explanation, and that made it better than nothing. "I'll ask Evie about it. Maybe she can help."

"Maybe," agreed Elsie. She was still radiating wariness. I found myself suddenly glad I couldn't read her expression as well as I could read her mind. At least her mind was honest. "For right now, how about we don't run across dark roads at night with nothing but a cellphone, okay? I really don't want to have to explain to Aunt Evelyn why you're a smear on the pavement."

"Right," I said. "You want to go back?"

"Please," said Elsie.

Whatever else she might have said was lost as Annie shouted, "A little help down here? This jerk's heavy and bleeding, and I'm worried about getting an overdose of incubus juice."

"I get to tell him she called it 'incubus juice,'" I said. "Just me. No one else. I get to tell him, and then you get to tell me how ridiculous his face looks."

"I will grant you this great boon because it means he'll be awake for you to tell," said Elsie, speeding up. Her concern for her brother was getting larger, sending jagged spikes through her thoughts. She was focusing on it hard enough for me to pick up the reason she'd allowed Annie to risk incubus overdose in the first place: she'd been afraid his injuries might be even worse than they were, and she couldn't handle the idea of pulling her brother's body out of the car. I followed her and didn't say anything. She wasn't the only one who was worried, but she was maybe the one who had the most right to her concerns.

Annie had managed to wrestle Artie out of his seatbelt and halfway out of the car, and was now just standing there, blood on her hands and forearms, hands hooked under Artie's arms. He still wasn't moving, and although he was breathing, he wasn't conscious enough to be projecting thoughts outside his little bubble of personal space. My blood had clotted over the cuts on his face, stopping the bleeding. That was a small improvement.

"I wish Sam were here," said Annie, adjusting her stance to avoid dumping Artie on the ground. "He's stronger than I am."

"Sam's the boyfriend," explained Elsie, moving to help Annie by sliding her arms under Artie's middle. "He's a former carnie."

"There's no such thing as a *former* carnie," said Annie primly. "He's just temporarily a carnie without a carnival. And forever, unless he decides he wants to go home and take over from his grandmother."

"Uh-huh," said Elsie. Working together, the two of them were able to slide Artie out of the driver's seat and get him into a comfortable carrying position. "Sarah, can you get whatever the two of you are going to want from the car, please? Artie will never let me hear the end of it if we set the thing on fire with his comic books in the backseat or something."

"Sure," I said, with an uneasy glance at the unconscious Artie. My fingers twitched with the desire to touch him, just long enough to find the distant shadows of his thoughts and reassure myself that he hadn't gotten worse. I couldn't. I'd be in the way, and if he *had* gotten worse . . .

We needed to get him home. We needed to get him to where he could get help. There was nothing we could do here, except grab our things and go, and all I'd do was slow us down. I climbed into the car through the still-open driver's-side backdoor, feeling around on the seat for anything Artie might be planning to keep. I found a plastic bag of comics, as predicted; a first aid kit, which could be useful, and more, had probably been tailored to his specific physiology; a jacket of his, which I shrugged on despite not feeling cold the way true mammals do; and my own backpack, still tucked into the front footwell. I went around the car and leaned in through Artie's door for that, not feeling like participating in the seat-climbing Olympics twice in one night.

Artie's phone was in the cupholder. I took that as well, tucking it, his keys, and the phone charger into the pocket of his jacket. There was glass everywhere in the front seat, pooled around the spaces where his body had been. My seat was oddly clear, like the glass had been somehow shunted around me, rather than slicing into me when it went flying. That was odd. I brushed it carefully aside to make it easier for me to get out of the car without cutting myself.

Annie was waiting outside; Artie was nowhere to be seen. I must have looked alarmed, because she held up her hands and said, "Relax. Elsie is hauling him up to her car; you're going to have to ride with him in the backseat. Hope you're okay with close quarters." She wiggled her eyebrows, a broad motion that needed no nuance to be understood.

"Don't be weird," I said.

"Being weird is, like, ninety percent of my day," said Annie. She raised both hands, palms once again turned upward. "Move away from the car, okay? This is pretty cool, but you're not fireproof."

"Are you?"

Annie nodded distractedly, most of her focus on the air above her hands. "As long as the fire remembers how to be mine, I am. Once it grows into something else, it can hurt me, but when it starts, it starts in my bones, and it loves me too much to do me any damage."

The world seemed to tense for a moment, and I got a flash of what I could only describe as calculus, like someone was revising the equations that made up the universe. My eyes itched the way they usually did when I was actively using my powers. And two small balls of fire appeared above Annie's hands, burning white-hot despite their apparent lack of fuel.

"All sorcerers are elementalists," she said, as casually as if she weren't holding two impossible fireballs with her bare hands. "Not the classic 'earth, air, fire, water' gig, but sort of physical forces. Heat, cold, gravity, that sort of thing. I got heat. So did Grandpa Thomas. His journals are full of useful tips about how to make your own burn cream from things you probably have in the herb garden, and how to convince the chaperones you need new sheets because of 'nocturnal emissions,' not because you set them on fire in the middle of the night." She sounded amused and disgusted at the same time. "Guess growing up a Covenant boy makes suddenly becoming one of the things you were raised to hunt a little hard on the psyche. He was an amazingly good liar."

I took a step back. She might not have been bothered by the heat boiling off her palms, but I could feel my hair starting to frizz, and had no desire to be caught in what she was about to do.

"Almost ready," said Annie. The fire above her hands grew in both size and heat, edges becoming blue-white, crackling growing louder. She rolled her hands over, the fire dancing along the backs of her fingers, before flicking the balls into the car. They balanced for a moment on the seats, like they were going to go for a drive. Then they burst, spreading flames everywhere, transforming the interior into an inferno.

"Wow," I whispered.

"I'm getting better at it," said Annie. "It used to be pretty random whether I got fire when I asked for it or not. Go help Elsie, okay? I'll be up in a minute."

There was something in her voice that told me not to argue. "Okay," I said, and turned and fled, leaving my cousin and her pet conflagration behind.

Elsie had her headlights on, as well as the light inside the car itself, creating a safe oasis of civilization in the middle of the deep dark woods. She was leaning against the hood, texting furiously, when I came scrambling up the incline. She raised her head, nodded to me, and turned her attention back to her phone.

"Aunt Evelyn and Uncle Kevin are standing by for our arrival," she said. "Mom and Dad are on their way here, to make sure the scene is sterilized before they join us at the compound. Did Annie set the car on fire?"

"She did," I said. "She's still down there. Why—"

"Once she's sure the car is burnt enough not to be a problem anymore, she'll call the fire back into her body," said Elsie. "She couldn't contain like, a forest fire or anything, but something as small as burning out a car, the fire won't have time to forget who it belongs to. That way, we don't have to worry about accidentally burning down Portland or anything. Global climate change means we have to be responsible about our pyrokinesis." She laughed, sudden and bright and absolutely mirthless.

I winced. "He's going to be okay, Elsie. I promise."

"Did you turn into a Caladrius while I wasn't looking?" She lowered her phone. "Because unless you have special healing powers that you've never mentioned before, you can't promise anything. My baby brother has head trauma. People can die from head trauma."

"He's a Lilu," I said desperately. "Lilu heal faster than humans."

"Sure, but we're not superheroes, and healing at roughly three times the human rate doesn't mean we can't be broken." Elsie glanced over her shoulder at the brightly lit car. "So you know, if he dies before the two of you get to talk this out, I am never going to forgive you."

"Talk what out?"

A wave of irritation washed off Elsie as she focused back on me. "You're not this stupid. Stop trying to be."

"Whoo!" We both turned. Annie was trudging back up the incline, her hands dark with soot, radiating contentment. "Car's done. Fire's contained. Let's get the hell home before something else goes wrong."

"This isn't over," said Elsie, attention on me.

"I know," I said, and walked toward the car. I was tired, I was injured, and I already wanted to go home.

Sometimes recovery's not everything it's cracked up to be.

Six

$$\pi_2(n) \sim 2C_2 \frac{n}{(\ln n)^2} \sim 2C_2 \int_2^n \frac{dt}{(\ln t)^2}$$

"Every relationship, good or bad, is different. Some of them are just more different than others."

—Enid Healy

On the way to a safe, secure, intentionally isolated family compound in the woods outside of Portland, Oregon

SHARING THE BACKSEAT WITH Artie meant riding with his head resting in my lap, since the seatbelt could keep him safely restrained, but it couldn't keep him upright. I stroked his forehead with one hand, savoring the foggy glimpses of his thoughts that came with the contact. It wasn't enough to tell me what he was thinking—or whether he was aware enough to be thinking anything at all, rather than displaying flashes of random brain activity—but it meant he was alive. That was what really mattered. Artie was alive.

I let my hand rest against his skin, reaching deeper, looking for signs that the faintness of his thoughts was somehow related to the damage he'd suffered in the accident. Elsie's words from before were haunting me, making it difficult to focus on anything but worrying.

People die from head trauma. People *die*. Artie was people, and Artie had hit his head, and no matter how silly and overdramatic the thought might seem, Artie could die. I could wake up tomorrow to a world that didn't have an Artie in it, and I would never have told him—

And that didn't matter, because I was pretty sure he didn't feel the same way about me. He loved me because I was his cousin, not because I was a girl who liked him more than girls are supposed to like their cousins, even the ones who belong to a completely different species. All I could do by saying something was make it weird.

Still, I pushed deeper into his blurry, half-formed thoughts, looking for some sign that they were anything out of the ordinary. What would thoughts born of a concussion even look like? Would they be tattered around the edges, or too scrambled to hold themselves together, or something else, something worse and more confusing?

"—are you listening?"

Annie's voice. I raised my head, pulling myself out of Artie's thoughts, and said, "Huh?"

"You weren't listening." She twisted in her seat so she could look at me. "I said, we're almost to the house. How's Artie doing?"

"Still knocked cold, but I'm not finding anything scary in his head. Just a lot of jumble. Pretty normal for someone who's hit their head. I'm not too worried. I'm pretty sure I'd be able to tell if something was really wrong in there."

"And if you couldn't?" asked Elsie.

I took a deep breath. She was worried about her brother. Of course she was worried about her brother. Drew was enough older than me that we'd barely ever lived in the same house, and I'd still be worried about him if he'd been in a car accident. "If I couldn't, if I can't, then Evie will be able to figure it out. He's going to be okay."

Elsie didn't say anything.

The woods unrolled around us, dark and tangled

and so crowded that they became featureless, a solid
wall of black wood pressing in from all sides. I tensed
every time we passed another road, waiting for the
truck to make a second appearance. It never came. We
were driving on a virtually deserted road, deep into
the middle of nowhere, and while we might not be safe,
we weren't in active danger.

Artie stirred in his sleep, mumbling something that
was almost, if not quite, a word. I stroked his forehead
again, stealing glimpses of his tangled half-thoughts.
Were they getting stronger, or was that just wishful
thinking on my part? I wanted him to wake up so badly
that I could be imagining signs of improvement.

We were moving too fast for me to have any good
sense of the minds in the woods around us. I would
have known if there'd been a large gathering of
humans—campers are surprisingly psychically noisy—
or anything like that, but the smaller, individual
thoughts of the night were slipping through my mental
fingers before I could really clamp down on them.

Then we turned a corner onto a half-concealed private road, and a new set of thoughts washed over me,
strong and bright and terribly familiar, now that we
were past the charms buried at the borderline.

My family.

Evie was there, as fierce and quick and eager to help
as always. She was the best big sister I could have asked
for, unjudgmental and constantly willing to take the
time to make sure I understood what was going on. Her
husband, Kevin, was with her, and while he had more
of a core of worry than she did, he was still ready for us.
There were two more minds in the house, both male,
both unfamiliar enough that I couldn't pick up anything more than the most superficial of impressions—I
needed to meet them before I'd be able to get more
than that without pushing. And I didn't want to push.
After the day I'd had so far, pushing seemed like a terrible idea.

"Almost there," said Elsie, and she sped up, taking us around the curves of the long road to the front gate like she thought she was being timed. It would have felt unsafe if I hadn't known that she'd done this hundreds of times over the years, speeding up a little more with every trip, sometimes while *actually* being timed.

The Oregon compound started out as Kevin's idea. His mother, my Grandma Alice, hadn't really been there when he'd been growing up; he and his sister, Aunt Jane, had both been raised by the Campbell Family Carnival, which was sort of like growing up with family, and sort of not at the same time. He'd been dreaming of real roots, a home he could design and defend, since he was a little boy. After he met Evie and realized it was time to settle down, he'd set about making his dreams a reality. A house, isolated from the nearest human communities, big enough to host not only his immediate family, but every other living relative and maybe a dozen extras. Outbuildings and barns and fences and floodlights. Everything your average small militia needs to feel like they're not going to be crushed under the heel of "the Man," only in this case the militia was more like a wildlife conservation convention, and "the Man" was the Covenant of St. George.

Elsie screeched to a stop at the front gate, which was towering, solid, and very locked. Annie hopped out of the car to enter the code. Elsie looked over her shoulder at me.

"Everything all right back there?" she asked. *Is my brother alive?* her thoughts asked.

When I was a kid, I couldn't always tell the difference between the questions people asked out loud and wanted you to answer and the questions they thought so loudly that I couldn't avoid overhearing them. There *is* a difference. Thoughts can be soft or loud, but they always sound exactly like the person they belong to.

There's no distortion, no getting drowned out by the sounds around them, no getting lost.

"He's still asleep, but I can hear him," I said, trying to sound encouraging. "I don't know enough about head injuries to be absolutely sure what's going on, but I've been with Verity when she had a concussion, and he sounds clearer than she did then."

Of course, Verity had been awake with a concussion, not knocked cold. I didn't think saying that to Elsie would be a very good idea.

Elsie's thoughts were a roil of half-formed notions and questions she couldn't quite put into words. She opened her mouth, a question starting to crystalize, and stopped as Annie threw herself back into the passenger seat. The gates began creaking open.

"They're ready for us," said Annie. "Drive."

Elsie drove.

The compound "yard" was really more the compound meadow: a long stretch of reasonably flat ground that had been divested of trees and major obstacles, but otherwise left alone. Sometimes the carnival pitched tents there, when they were in town and wanted to visit their extended family. I had spent hundreds of hours there as a kid, racing around with my cousins, shrieking, having the normal childhood that most cuckoos are denied by their territorial, homicidal natures.

My species isn't inherently evil—my existence, and Mom's, proves that—but wow can we do a lot of damage when we're not raised right. And almost none of us are raised right.

All the lights in the main house were on, turning it into a beacon against the grasping hands of night. As we got closer, I felt Evie's mind snap into focus against mine, the sweet, generous thoughts of my beloved big sister instantly soothing me. If anyone could help Artie, it would be Evie. Kevin's mind came into focus a few seconds later. We hadn't spent quite as much time together, since he wasn't my sibling *or* someone my own age. Still, he was a stable presence, calm, steady, ready to do whatever needed to be done. I relaxed a little, my hand still resting against Artie's forehead. They would know what to do. They would fix this.

The other two minds I'd detected in the house were nearby, both bright and unfamiliar and subtly . . . off . . . from the human norm. I didn't have enough of a grasp of what they *were* to understand the deviations I was picking up on, but neither of them felt hostile. That would have to be enough.

Elsie whipped down the driveway fast enough to make my shoulders tense, screeching to a stop in front of the porch. Evie and Kevin immediately descended the brick steps, moving toward the car. Evie opened the door next to me, warm welcome radiating from her.

"Hi, Sarah," she said, leaning quickly in to brush a kiss against my forehead. The brief skin contact let me pick up more of her thoughts. She was frightened but keeping it under rigid control, not wanting to worry Elsie more than she already was. Injuries are common in our family. Injuries bad enough to leave a half-incubus unconscious for an extended period of time are not. "Mom told me you were coming. Can you keep your hands where they are while I check Artie's pulse? I want you to say something if his thoughts change at all."

"Sure," I said. "Mom wasn't supposed to tell anyone, though. In case I didn't make it to Oregon."

"I know, and she told me as much, but I'm out of practice at controlling my thoughts around a cuckoo, so I figured it was best to get things out in the open." She leaned into the car, checking Artie's pulse with practiced hands. "She wanted to make sure your room would be ready when you got here. We haven't had a telepath in residence for years."

Not since I'd gone and hurt myself. Cuckoos don't normally make good house guests. "Thank you."

"You're family, silly. You don't thank us for welcoming you home. You thank us for letting you settle in before we put you on the chore rotation." Evie felt her way along the sides of Artie's neck and skull before looking at the gash along his cheek. "You bled on him?"

I nodded.

"Good girl. That should slow down any infection enough that we can deal with it. No hospitals needed."

Taking Artie or Elsie to a hospital was always a fraught thing, since their blood had a tendency to scramble human emotional responses in negative ways. I paused, realizing that the three of us were alone in the car. Elsie was talking to Kevin, and Annie was . . .

"Evie, why is there a monkey?" I asked, in a small, tight voice.

"That's Sam," said Evie. She stepped back. "He's Annie's boyfriend. He's a fūri—a kind of yōkai therianthrope. We try not to call him a monkey; he doesn't like it."

"I can hear you, you know," said the monkey—sorry, fūri—without taking his hands off Annie's waist. He was easily six feet tall, with a tail almost as long as the rest of his body. He was also wearing jeans and a denim jacket, which made him unique among the monkeys I had known.

Humans are a kind of monkey. This was no stranger than Aunt Jane and Uncle Ted, or than Mom and Dad, honestly. Love finds a way.

"Sorry," I called back. "Didn't mean to be rude."

"Hey, Sarah," said Kevin, stepping up next to Evie. His thoughts radiated joy and concern in almost equal measure. He was as relieved by my return as my sister, which was nice. "Can you get out of the car? We want to move Artie inside."

"Sure." I undid my belt, sliding carefully out from under Artie. Kevin answered the question of what I was supposed to do next by ducking in and placing his own hands under Artie's head, keeping it supported in basically the same position.

I stood, and Evie and Kevin crowded me out, attention focused on getting Artie out of the vehicle without jostling him more than he already had been. I took a step backward, and then another, wrapping my arms tightly around myself. I was still wearing Artie's jacket. It was too big on me, and I didn't need the warmth, but I didn't take it off. Anything that made me feel like I was still anchored would be better than feeling like I was about to float away.

How had everything gone so wrong? And why had the wind only been blowing on one side of the street? Something about that seemed wrong. It seemed like a threat. I just couldn't figure out what it *was*.

"So you're the mysterious Sarah."

The voice was new. I turned. There was a human man behind me, dark-haired, pale-skinned, and dressed in what I thought of as "mathematician casual"— button-down shirt, dark jeans, a light windbreaker. I got the feeling he didn't stand out in crowds even when he was dealing with people who could see faces the way humans saw them. His thoughts were curious, wary, concerned, a swirling maelstrom of vaguely negative emotions that made him feel as prickly as a nettle under the questing fingers of my mind.

"I'm James," he said, apparently reading the blank confusion in my expression. "Annie adopted me after she decided my father didn't deserve me anymore."

"He never deserved you in the first place," called Annie. "You're a Price now. Deal with it."

"It's James Smith, actually," said James, and extended his hand toward me.

I looked at it warily. "I'm not sure you want to do that," I said. "Did Annie tell you anything about me, other than 'that's Cousin Sarah'?"

He shook his head, hand still outstretched. "She said you'd been injured and were convalescing, and that she hoped I'd have the chance to meet you someday, but that was all."

James wouldn't be living at the family compound—or, apparently, be an honorary member of the family—if he hadn't had a high tolerance for weirdness. From the spiky, almost crystalline edges of his thoughts, I was willing to bet there was something out of the ordinary about him, some little tweak or twist to his DNA that made him safer here than he'd be in the world outside. But he was still *human*. I could tell that as easily as I could tell that he was breathing. And unlike Evie, who'd grown up in a cuckoo's house, or the biological members of the family, who'd inherited Fran's inexplicable resistance to cuckoo influence, he didn't have any protection from me.

Crap.

"I can't shake your hand." I took a big step backward. "I shouldn't touch you at all, ever. And as soon as we're done taking care of Artie, you need to ask my sister for an anti-telepathy charm. It's dangerous to let me into your head."

His thoughts turned quizzical—and oddly excited. "You're a telepath?"

"Um. Yes." Behind me, Evie and Kevin had managed to pull Artie out of the car and were carrying him toward the porch steps. Annie and her boyfriend moved to help. The four of them moved quickly, heading toward the light and warmth of the living room.

I itched to follow. I wanted to know that Artie was okay, and more, I wanted to talk to Evie about what had happened in the woods. If anyone would be able to reassure me, it was going to be her.

"Are you a sorcerer?"

I paused, blinking at James. "What?"

"A sorcerer." His excitement was growing. "My mother's journals mentioned that some sorcerers can learn how to project their thoughts, and that it's a knack, like any of the elemental affinities. Annie and I have been trying to find instructions, but—"

"You want to *learn* to be telepaths?" This was just getting more confusing.

"Yes, exactly."

"Um, no." I shook my head. "I mean, sorry, but no. I can't teach you. I'm not a sorcerer. I'm sort of . . . not human?"

"Ah." James laughed, wryly. "Seems like that's half the people around this place. It's been a bit of an adjustment."

"Humans have been the dominant species for so long that they don't know what it's like to be outnumbered anymore." Evie and the others had made it inside. I realized with a start that Elsie was gone, too, following her brother into the house. Sudden suspicion arrowed through me. I narrowed my eyes. "Did Annie ask you to keep me distracted out here?"

James shrugged. "Maybe."

"Did she tell you *why*?"

"She said you and Artie have been dancing around each other for years, and she didn't want to upset you if there was something really wrong with him." He didn't even have the good grace to sound sheepish.

I stared at him for a moment, open-mouthed. Then I whirled and ran for the house, shouting, "Get that charm!" over my shoulder. I didn't slow down to see whether he was following me or staying where he was. I just ran.

Houses designed by eccentric cryptozoologists who grew up with a traveling carnival are rare, and they all have one trait in common: they're idiosyncratic at best, and seriously weird at worst. The family compound fell into the "seriously weird" category. The front door opened, not on a foyer or stairway or other reasonable architectural choice, but on the mudroom connected to the kitchen, on the theory that the kitchen had a lot of flat, relatively sterile surfaces, and most people would either need hot water or food when they got to the house, depending on how injured they were. And as a theory it wasn't *wrong*. It was just strange.

I ran into the empty kitchen and looked wildly around, reaching out to try to figure out where my family had gone. There wasn't any trace of them, which meant they'd continued on to one of the shielded parts of the house. Only the cuckoo-friendly guest room was *completely* shielded from psychic influence, but there were charms and protections built into various areas, largely because someone who's injured can make a lot of psychic noise when they wake up, and sometimes that attracts unwanted attention.

"Think, Sarah," I mumbled. They wouldn't have wanted to take him up any unnecessary stairs, and Evie would never have allowed a still-bleeding incubus on her couch, not even when it was her nephew. Which meant . . .

I turned toward the pantry door. It was standing very slightly ajar. I walked over and gave it a push, revealing the packed shelves that lined the small, square room, stopping at the door on the back wall. It was almost hidden behind its burden of spice racks, but the knob was visible enough. I turned it, pulling the door open.

The thoughts of my missing family members washed over me like a wave: Elsie scared, Annie angry, Evie and Kevin trying to smother their fear under a veil of calm practicality. Even Sam was there, although his thoughts were still too unfamiliar to betray much beyond his presence. I stepped through the doorway, walking down the short hall on the other side until I reached the recovery rooms. There were three of them, each kept perfectly sterile, each warded against all possible negative influences. Even the dead couldn't enter the recovery rooms, a fact our collection of friendly family ghosts found annoying, if understandable. There are a lot more hostile spirits than helpful ones.

That's true of cuckoos, too. That's why I've never taken the anti-telepathy charms personally. At the moment, however, it stung.

Evie looked up when I stepped into the room. Artie was stretched on the bed in the middle of the space—hospital issue, of course. We like to be prepared for any eventuality in this family. He still wasn't moving, and there was no crackle of his thoughts in the air, no psychic sign that he was there at all.

"Sorry to run off on you like that," she said, and her thoughts turned her words into a lie, because she wasn't sorry; she wasn't sorry at all. She was doing her best not to think about how worried she was, but she was out of practice, and all she was doing was throwing her fear at me, over and over again, like a series of stones. "I wanted to get Artie someplace secure."

Annie and Sam were on the other side of the room, sitting on the industrial-green couch. Sam had his tail wrapped around Annie's waist. Elsie was standing next to Evie, one of Artie's hands clutched in hers. Kevin was at the head of the bed, fussing with the machines hooked to the frame.

Those machines would be hooked to Artie if he didn't wake up soon. Machines to make sure he kept breathing; machines to make sure he had all the fluid and nutrition he needed. All because I'd come home—and he'd come to the warehouse to meet me. All because I was *here*.

"Did he crack his skull?" I moved to the head of the bed, shoving myself in next to Kevin. They had already sutured Artie's cheek, stitching it up with a series of quick, tidy lines. Between that and my blood, he might not even scar. That would be good. People don't like it when they scar.

"There's nothing physically wrong enough to be keeping him unconscious," said Evie. "He's taken worse hits running around the yard. I'm not sure what's going on. It could just be shock. He'll probably wake up soon."

She didn't sound like she believed it because she *didn't* believe it. Her thoughts were a tangle of fears and concerns, none of them fully formed, all of them centered on the idea that if Artie had just been knocked unconscious, as I had been, he would have woken up already. Something was genuinely wrong.

"I don't think he's going to wake up on his own," I said slowly. "And I don't think . . . I don't think it was an accident."

The room grew tight with tension as everyone turned to look at me. I felt a flicker of unfamiliar thought behind me; James had arrived. That was probably good. It meant I'd only need to explain this once.

"There was another cuckoo at the airport," I said, eyes on Evie. "A woman. She tried to attack me for trespassing on her territory."

"I take it she didn't succeed?" asked Evie.

"I mean, she *did* attack me," I said. "She just didn't win." Technically, I'd attacked her, turning her ambush around on itself. That was just semantics. She had come into that bathroom intending to do me harm, and that made everything I'd done a matter of self-defense.

"What's a cuckoo?" asked James.

"I'll explain later," said Annie.

A feeling of growing horror slithered through the air, as venomous as any snake. I turned. Sam was looking at me. The horror was coming from him. I sighed, shoulders slumping slightly. This was a complication I hadn't been expecting in my sister's house, and one I certainly didn't need right now.

"Sam knows," I said.

"I've never heard them called 'cuckoos' before," he said, eyes still on me. "But she's pale and dark-haired and that cut on her forehead isn't bleeding when it should be. She's a Johrlac. I thought they were a myth. Something people made up to scare little carnie kids into staying away from weirdoes on the midway. She's real. *They're* real, and one of them is in your house, and I think maybe we should all be running away now."

"Evie?" I said plaintively.

"Sam, Sarah has always been a Johrlac—a cuckoo— and so is my mother, and she's a part of this family. No one's running anywhere." Evie's voice was calm, level, and left no room for argument. "We can explain more later, once Artie's awake. Sarah, why don't you think Artie will wake up on his own?"

"Because it doesn't make sense for a cuckoo to attack me in the airport, and then for us to have an accident like that," I said. "The truck came out of nowhere—I didn't hear the driver's thoughts before they hit us. How does that make sense? Our headlights were on. If they'd been drunk, they would have been louder than usual, not quieter. I think the cuckoo I beat up decided she wanted to get back at me, and she set an ambush."

We'd stayed at the warehouse playing reunion for too long. I should have been more careful, should have treated my family the way I'd treated the strangers who'd carried me from the airport to the city—like potential casualties. But no. I'd been too tired and too happy to see them and too certain that they could handle any threats that came their way. I'd left plenty of time for the cuckoo to find me, figure out who I was with, and make plans to get back at me.

"This is my fault," I said softly, brushing my fingertips against Artie's cheek and getting rewarded with another burst of blurry, half-formed thought. "He's not going to wake up on his own because there's nothing physically wrong with him."

"Sarah—" said Evie warningly.

"I'll be fine," I said, and closed my eyes, and drove myself into Artie's thoughts like a knife through ice. The world cracked around me, crystalline and perfect, and I had time for exactly one second thought—*I shouldn't be here*—before everything shattered and was still.

Seven

$$\pi_2(n) \sim 2C_2 \frac{n}{(\ln n)^2} \sim 2C_2 \int_2^n \frac{dt}{(\ln t)^2}$$

"Trust the numbers. The numbers don't lie. Even if everything else in the world is trying to deceive you, the numbers will always, always tell the truth."
—Angela Baker

Still technically at the family compound, but also inside the mind of Arthur Harrington-Price, without an invitation

THE SHARDS OF THOUGHT and mind and math and memory fell down around me in a glittering veil, dusting the ground-not-ground at my feet, lighting up the darkness. I was standing in the middle of a vast plain of stormy nothingness. The nothing itself was the blooming purple black of a bruise, lit up here and there with blooming halos of vivid pink and red. Flashes of what looked like lightning lit up the horizon in a thousand shades of rose.

"Artie?" My voice sounded strange, like a recording of myself. There was no bone conduction here, because my bones weren't really with me; they were outside this space, standing or sagging next to a motionless man in a hospital bed. Right. Hopefully, Evie or Kevin would have the good sense to grab me and hold me up. I wasn't sure what would happen if the contact between us was broken while I was still flung almost wholly into Artie's mind.

That would be a hell of a way to make him understand that I was interested in his body: taking it over seemed a little bit extreme, but it seemed like a reasonably likely outcome of this particular act of raging stupidity. I'd been in Artie's head before, both with and without an invitation. I'd never been so far inside his head that I wound up in his mindscape.

"That is such a stupid word," I muttered, and took a step forward . . . or tried to. My legs worked, but I got the distinct feeling that I wasn't actually *moving*. The lights on the horizon certainly didn't move. They stayed exactly where they were, bright and shimmering and impossible, and I stayed exactly where I was, pale and lost and stranded in an infinity of bruised blackness.

"Artie?" My voice echoed as if bouncing off unseen canyon walls. I cupped my hands around my mouth and tried again, shouting louder this time. "*Artie!*"

The ground began to crack and crumble underfoot. I glared at it. "You stop that."

It stopped that.

Great: so I had some control over my environment, which was also Artie's mind, which meant I should probably be careful about how many orders I wanted to give. Since I also didn't want to plummet into the next layer of the—ugh—mindscape, a few orders were going to be necessary. I cupped my hands around my mouth again, forming a primitive megaphone.

"Artie! It's Sarah! I know you can hear me, I'm inside your head!"

No reply.

"If you don't come talk to me *right now*, I'm going to make you wish you had!"

No reply.

"Okay. You did this to yourself." I took a deep,

unnecessary breath, and began to sing at the top of my lungs, "I am a happy banana! A happy happy happy ba-na-na! Happy happy happy—"

"I hate that song."

I stopped singing and turned, beaming when I saw Artie behind me in the darkness. He scowled and the expression made perfect sense. I was inside his head; I didn't need to read his mind to know why his face was doing the things it was doing. That was a nice change.

In here, I could also see that he was handsome, and that was a nice change, too. Oh, I would have thought he was handsome no matter what he looked like, because I really was in love with his mind—his weird, sweet, comforting mind—but Artie's brain knew how to process human faces and I was inside his head and that meant that for right now, I could do the same thing. And he had a *nice* face, sweet and open and expressive. I spared a moment's resentment for the fact that I belonged to a species that didn't get to enjoy faces like his, because we simply didn't see them. It wasn't fair.

"I know you hate that song," I said. "That's why I was singing it."

"Couldn't you come up with a better way to get on my nerves?" Artie rubbed the back of his neck with one hand. "You could do your multiplication homework or something."

"I haven't done math inside your head since we were kids."

"Yeah, but it was always really annoying when you did it." Artie lowered his hand. "Where are we, Sarah?"

The vague hope that this was normal for him—that his mind always looked like this from the inside, and so he'd be able to tell me how to get us out of here— faded to wistful nothingness. "We're inside your head. Don't you know the inside of your own head?"

Worry strong enough to verge on panic spiked in his eyes and rolled through the mindscape around us, fuzzy and static on the idea of my skin. "Wait, we're inside my head? *You're* inside my head? You're not . . . looking . . . at things, are you?"

"I promised a long time ago that I wouldn't rifle through your memories uninvited," I said, feeling suddenly tired. "Don't you trust me anymore, Artie?"

"I trusted you not to hurt yourself and shut me out for five years, and look how well that went." His eyes widened and he clapped a hand over his mouth, like he thought he could somehow manage to take the words back. "Oh, jeez, Sarah, I'm sorry. I didn't mean to . . . I'm sorry."

"Like I said, we're in your head. It's harder for you to lie to me in here, unless you're also lying to yourself." A dozen questions sprang to mind, each of them more inappropriate than the last. I pushed them all down. It wouldn't just be an invasion of his privacy to ask those questions when I knew he'd have to answer them truthfully. It would be a violation of our friendship, of the careful, questionable peace we'd constructed between ourselves, one promise and compromise at a time.

Being a telepath in a non-telepathic world is *hard*. Sometimes I think my ancestors made a big mistake, leaving whatever dimension they originated in. Then I usually think that no dimension is awful enough to deserve us, and I'm glad to at least be in a world where the Internet exists. Telepaths would never have invented the Internet.

It's easier on the Internet. Everyone is the words they use and nothing else. It's fair.

Artie was still staring at me, guilt written broadly across his face. Maybe being able to read expressions wasn't such a good thing after all.

"I didn't get hurt on purpose," I said.

"I know."

"I wouldn't have done that to you. I wouldn't have done that to *myself*."

"I know."

"So why are you mad at me?"

Artie looked at me for a long moment. When he spoke, his voice was soft, almost distant, like he was remarking on the weather and not talking about one of the most important relationships in my life.

"Because you shut me out," he said. "You let Aunt Angela and Uncle Martin take care of you, and that was fine. You let Alex live in the same house as you, while all the rest of us were being told you were too dangerous to be anywhere near us, and that was fine. You let Alex move his human girlfriend into the house, you let her sleep right down the hall, and that was fine. But every time I asked if I could come to Ohio to see you, you said you weren't ready yet. Every time I asked if I could help, you told me 'no.' You said you were fine when you weren't fine, and I don't think you ever lied to me before, and I didn't like it. Five *years*, Sarah. You left me scared that I'd lost you for five *years*. That's such a long time. I'm mad at you because I'd almost finished grieving for you, and now you're standing inside my head, and I can't get away from you. Why couldn't you come back sooner? Why couldn't you stay gone?"

His voice broke on the last word. He looked away, off at the distant, prismatic horizon.

"Oh," I said.

He didn't say anything.

"I didn't . . . Artie. Please. Look at me?"

Slowly, Artie turned his face back toward me, expression unreadable not because of the way my brain was wired, but because he didn't know how to feel. Everything was jumbled up and tangled, and I'd done this to him. This was my fault. Whether I'd intended to do it or not, this was all still my fault.

"I didn't let you come to Ohio because I was scared

you'd never look at me the same way again," I said. "I wasn't . . . I wasn't *good* most of the time. I wasn't myself. Even when I could pull it together enough to chat online, I was still falling apart. Mom was putting me back together every day at first, and then every week, and then . . . they had to wear name tags."

"Name tags?" he asked blankly.

"So I could tell everyone apart because it wasn't safe to be around me without an anti-telepathy charm. There was too much of a chance I'd reach out, stumble, and grab something I shouldn't. I could have erased pieces of people's personalities and never even realized I was doing it. They had me on house arrest until last year, and I didn't notice for the longest time, because I was too deep in my own head to know what I was missing. I couldn't even do *math* on my own for almost two years." Endless hours of PBS had helped with that. I could still hear the *Square One* theme when I closed my eyes.

Artie blanched. "I didn't know. They didn't tell me."

"I asked them not to. Mom and Dad promised not to tell anyone they didn't have to about how bad it was. They were afraid Verity would show up on our doorstep looking for forgiveness, and I didn't know what that was, so I couldn't exactly go giving it to people. I was *broken*. I made them keep you away because I was *broken*, and I was trying to put myself back together without any sort of map or instruction manual, and I knew if you saw me—if you, specifically, saw me—and turned away because I was too broken to care about anymore, I'd give up. I'd stop trying to repair myself. There wouldn't be any point to it. So yeah, Artie, I kept you away. Until I was better. And maybe that wasn't right and maybe it wasn't fair, but I can't change it now, okay? I can't undo what I did."

"I'm sorry," whispered Artie.

"Don't be sorry. And be mad at me, if that's what

you need to do. Just don't tell me I was wrong to shut you out, and then shut me out because you're angry. Revenge isn't going to get us out of here."

"Here being inside my head."

"Yes."

"Sarah?"

"Yes?"

"Why are we inside my head?"

I relaxed a little. If he was asking questions, he wasn't so determined to stay angry that he'd let us get trapped here rather than work with me. Which, well, yay. "Do you remember the accident?"

"Sort of." He frowned, forehead wrinkling. "I remember . . . I was asking you why you didn't call more while you were in recovery. I don't want to be mad about that—honestly, I don't—but I am, and it seemed like you didn't understand why I'd be pissed. And then there was this *truck* . . ." Artie's eyes widened. "Holy shit, we got hit by a truck."

I laughed. I couldn't help myself. "Yeah, we got hit by a truck. It ploughed right into us. It never even slowed down."

"And the glass in the car was all floating."

He could see that, too? I blinked at him. "Um, what?"

"When the truck hit us. I looked over at you before my head hit the wheel. Your eyes were white, and the glass was floating. None of it hit you at all. None of it hit me, either. We should have been cut to ribbons, but the glass from the windows went *around* us. I remember it was so weird, and I thought I might be seeing things, and then your head hit the dashboard and it all fell out of the air, and my head hit the wheel and everything got real fuzzy for a while."

I stared. I couldn't think of anything to say to that.

Artie paused, expression growing grave. "And then I woke up, and you were standing outside the car. But you were inside the car, too, all slumped over against your seatbelt, not moving, and I realized there were two of you. I thought I had a concussion or something? Only seeing double usually isn't that literal."

"Artie . . ." I whispered.

"I know." He sounded utterly resigned. "I mean, I know *now*. At the time, though, I couldn't understand what was happening. Not until she touched me. When you're inside my head, it usually feels like . . . like a sunbeam in October. It's warm and it's welcome and I want it around as long as it wants to be there. This lady, though. Her mind felt like sticking my hand into clear water and hitting a layer of slime I didn't know about. I couldn't move, and I couldn't fight, and she was inside me. It was awful. And then I was asleep, and it didn't matter anymore."

The other cuckoo. She'd followed me somehow, and she'd arranged the accident, and it was her fault that Artie wouldn't wake up. I should have been relieved to know that he wasn't injured beyond our capability to fix. Instead, I was livid. She had no right to chase me. She had no right to endanger the people I cared about, and she absolutely had no right—no right at all—to do things to Artie's head without his consent.

"I hate cuckoos," I muttered. Louder, I said, "I'm in your head because you won't wake up. There's nothing so physically wrong with you that you should be in a coma, but I'm afraid you're going to wind up in one if we don't do something. Do you trust me?"

Artie stared at me. "What kind of a question is that?"

"You're mad at me. You're mad at me for going away, and I'm not going to say that isn't fair, but it means maybe you don't trust me right now."

"You're literally *inside my head*. Can't you see that I trust you?" Artie shook his head. Or the idea of his head. Mindscapes are weird. "Of course I trust you. You're my best friend. I've always trusted you, even when you were a jerk and shut me out."

"Right now, I'm in your head, and this is deeper than I usually go, but it's still surface level," I said. "That's why you're 'talking' to me. This is all your brain trying to make sense of someone being where people really don't belong. You're already inside your body, so why do you have a body? Why do *I* have a body?"

"Because it's more comfortable to talk to people when they have bodies?" ventured Artie.

I nodded. "Exactly. This is sort of a hallucination, but the good kind, like seeing your hand when you're in a totally dark cave. Your brain is protecting itself by giving you a reasonable framework for an unreasonable experience."

Artie frowned. It was sort of neat, seeing the muscles move and actually understanding what the expression was supposed to mean. "Meaning you want to do something my brain is going to think of as even *more* unreasonable, huh?"

"Yeah. I do." I took a step closer to him. "The woman who looked like me—she was a cuckoo. The bad kind, not like me or Mom."

"I picked up on that," he said, sounding resigned. "She whammied my head, didn't she?"

"Yeah," I repeated. "She must have followed me from the airport. Whatever she did, it's not here, at the surface level. That would be too easy for me to find and untangle. It's somewhere deeper inside your mind, where I don't usually go. I need your permission to go down and find it, even though I may see some things you don't want me to see. If you're okay with that, I think I can wake you up."

"What if I'm not okay with it?" There was a brittle bravado to Artie's words that took me a second to recognize.

He was scared. Of me.

Sometimes I'm glad I don't have a heart. It means it can't be broken. "If you're not okay with it, I can step out of your mind, tell everyone that I can't get consent for treatment, and call Mom. Maybe you'd be okay with her seeing your secrets."

To my surprise, he shook his head and stepped closer to me. I could have reached out and touched him. "I don't really want *anybody* digging around that deep in my head," he said. "But if it's going to be someone, I'd rather it was you. Is that silly?"

"It's sweet," I said, and reached for his hands. They were slightly too cold, like his mental image of himself didn't quite know how to keep things circulating properly. I offered him a small, hopefully encouraging smile. "I won't look at anything I don't have to, I promise."

"Cool," he said. He exhaled, slowly. "Is this going to hurt?"

"I don't know," I said, and tightened my grasp on his hands. There was a glint as his eyes reflected the light growing in mine, and then the thunder rolled on the lightning-lashed horizon of his mind, and I was falling, Alice toppling into Wonderland, dropping down, down, down into the dark.

Artie didn't fall with me, which made sense, since I was technically falling *into* Artie. He was everywhere, all around me, and I had left the conscious levels of his mind behind: there was no reason for his brain to project an avatar of the man when I was dropping into memory and autonomous systems.

The darkness around me twisted into an almost funnel-like shape, apparently influenced by my thoughts of Wonderland. Doors started appearing in the walls as I dropped past them, some labeled with words, others with images. These were the vaults of Artie's memories. I knew that, just like I knew that if I'd wanted to, I could have reached out and opened any one of those doors, stopping my descent. They weren't real doors, and I wasn't really falling; much as Artie's mind had attempted to protect itself by creating a landscape he could deal with, my mind was now protecting its core by giving me a framework to hang this whole unreasonable experience on.

"School" said one door, and "Girls" said another door, and "Comic Books" said a third. Then there were the more abstract labels—a leaf, a bat in flight, a bird. I slowed to a stop, frowning at the bird. It had a dark back and a pale belly, wings spread as if it was getting ready to flee.

A cuckoo.

This was the door to Artie's memories of me.

Opening it would be an invasion of his privacy. Yes, he'd given me permission to be here, but he was expecting me to use that permission to find the snare the other cuckoo had set in his mind, not to peek at whatever secrets he'd kept from me, *about* me. I still hesitated for what felt like a shamefully long time before shifting slightly backward and allowing myself to resume my descent.

The labels on the doors got more and more abstract and more and more broad as I dropped—fruit becoming food becoming bowls of what looked like porridge and mashed vegetables. Several doors appeared for immediate family members, almost as if he sorted the memories of them differently depending on their age as well as his own. When I started seeing doors labeled with things like "Numbers" and "Language" and "Sleep," I knew I was getting close.

There, almost at the bottom of the tunnel, was a door labeled "Dreams." Unlike the doors around it, this one was covered in a thick, cottony layer of what looked almost like spiderweb. I stopped in front of it, barely managing not to recoil. Standing in front of that door was like standing in front of an open freezer. Each individual strand in the web was putting out waves of cold, strong enough to almost knock me backward in the air.

This was the door. This had to be the door. None of the others had been protected this way, not even the ones I was sure Artie didn't want me opening. It's one thing to agree to let your weird telepathic cousin poke around in your head. It's another to know that she's planning to look at the door labeled "Masturbation." If he'd been able to seal doors against me, he would have done it with at least a dozen of the ones I'd passed getting to this point.

"It can't hurt you," I muttered. "It's a booby trap planted by someone who isn't here, and you *are* here, and you're stronger than it is. It can't hurt you."

But it could hurt Artie. I had no idea how to go about placing a psychic landmine, which meant I didn't know how to disarm one, either. Mom wouldn't be any help with this. Even if I pulled all the way out of Artie's head and called home, her powers were too limited compared to the cuckoo norm. She couldn't tell me what to do. I had to feel my way through the situation and hope I didn't make things worse.

No pressure.

Annie had fire in her fingers. That was her phrase, stolen from the surface of her mind while she was focused on burning the car: fire in her fingers. I thought about what that felt like, how the heat moved through the skin, how warm it was, how safe. How much the fire loved her. It didn't have a mind, not in the sense that I could reach out and touch it, but it loved her all the same; some things are more important than thought or logic.

In the real world, there was no fire in my fingers. But here, deep in the tangle of Artie's mind, I was as close to a superhero as I would ever get, and if I understood what it was to have fire in my fingers, why couldn't I choose it for myself? I focused on my hands and smiled as they burst into lambent blue-white flame, hot enough to turn back the cold from the webbing. I stepped forward, hands held in front of me, and watched as the web shriveled away, shying back from the possibility of my touch.

"Not yours," I said aloud, in case it would help my fire catch hold. "Not your door to bar; not your mind to steal. Not yours."

The web charred and blackened and finally fell away, revealing the label on the door. "Consciousness," it said. It was a little on the nose, but it could have been worse. She could have blocked the door that said "Breathing," or the one that said "Heartbeat." I was deep enough in Artie's mind that I was sure those doors existed somewhere nearby, functions of the self that were almost as old as Artie himself.

I stepped forward. The door wasn't latched. It was closed, but barely; a stiff wind could have blown it open. Shaking the memory of flame from my fingers, I reached out and pushed it gently. The door swung inward, revealing a small domed room, filled with pale light.

The cuckoo from the airport was standing in the very middle of the room.

She looked at me and smiled, her red, red lips curving upward in a gesture that was far more predatory than pleasant. "Hello, little girl," she purred. "Tracked me to my lair, did you? I bet you feel very clever. I bet you feel very *competent*. Look at you, personal disaster wreaking havoc through the world. Most of us find and break our targets inside of a year. You've been twisting this boy around for decades. You sure do play a long game."

"You're not really here." I started prowling around the edges of the room, shoulders loose, head high. She wasn't a threat. I wasn't going to give her the satisfaction.

No matter where I stood, the woman remained exactly the same, like one of those flat paintings that somehow becomes three-dimensional when viewed from the right angle. She was an illusion, not an actuality, and she had no business here. No business here at all.

"A knife is really inside a body, even when the person who did the stabbing is gone," she countered. "They truly seemed to care about you. I could hear it in every stray thought they had. How long have you been lying to them, little girl? How long have you been working to convince them you can be tamed, redeemed, brought to heel? I'd be impressed, if I weren't so disgusted."

I kept circling. The threads of her trap were coming clearer, suspended in the air above her. Seen from this angle, they were less like spiderwebs and more like strands of cotton candy, fine and fair and almost invisible unless they were looked at precisely so.

"Nothing to say for yourself, little girl? I'm sorry. Did I break your toy? You can find another one. Maybe even turn this to your advantage. The others will be so *very* sorry for you, when they realize he's not going to wake up."

She was just a phantom, a fragment, a psychic trap laid by the other cuckoo to take Artie out of commission—but why? I'd been unconscious. She could have attacked me directly, rather than trying to hurt someone I cared about. What was the point of targeting Artie instead of me? Did she think that would hurt me more, somehow? I knew there wasn't a code of honor that kept her from attacking a fellow cuckoo. Cuckoos don't do anything as petty and potentially limiting as "honor."

"Talk to me." She was starting to sound uncomfortable, eyes tracking me around the edges of the room. Even an echo can be afraid, given the proper motivation. "You're supposed to be angry. I touched your things. You're supposed to challenge me."

"I don't need to," I said, and stopped moving,

bracing my feet as I looked at her. She had no mind for me to grab hold of. She was a cluster of Artie's own neurons, overwritten with a set of hostile instructions by someone who had no reason to care about whether or not she hurt him in the process of baiting me. I reached out silently, hands still by my sides, and mentally grabbed hold of the threads in the air around her, snapping them cleanly off, forcing them back into the idea of her skin.

She screamed, and it sounded so real that I almost lost my nerve. But Artie was asleep in a bed back in the physical world, surrounded by our worried family, and his parents would be showing up soon; I needed him to be awake before my Aunt Jane started demanding to know what had happened. She can be terrifying when she wants to be. Uncle Ted wouldn't yell. He'd just look at me, radiating silent disappointment, and that would be enough. No. Artie needed to wake up, and for Artie to wake up, this unwanted figment needed to be chased out of his mind. She didn't belong here. She wasn't a part of our family. She wasn't a part of *him*.

The threads whipped through the air around her. I grabbed for them again, still not moving, and fed them back into the flesh of her. One of them whipped out too quickly for me to catch, wrapping around my wrist and burning like it was coated in some sort of acid. I lifted my arms then, clawing the thread away. It left no mark on my skin, which wasn't really here anyway, only the idea of it, drifting through Artie's mind like an intrusive thought, unwanted and unavoidable.

The figment screamed again. I lowered my hands and snatched the threads again with my mind, wrapping them tighter and tighter around her.

"You're not *wanted* here," I spat. "You're not *welcome* here. Get out."

She wailed and collapsed in on herself, becoming a gray, cobwebby mass that was more form than figure.

Then she burst into pale flame, burning away to nothing.

But in the instant before she disappeared—the instant before I released my hold on Artie's mind and allowed myself to rise back to what passed as the surface—she smiled, and I felt a sickening certainty take root below my breastbone.

This wasn't over yet.

Eight

$$\pi_2(n) \sim 2C_2 \frac{n}{(\ln n)^2} \sim 2C_2 \int_2^n \frac{dt}{(\ln t)^2}$$

"Some people are good at music. Some people are good at sports. Some people are good at both. People are people, and every person has their own strengths and weaknesses. Biology is just one aspect of the greater whole."

—Jane Harrington-Price

Back in the recovery room, surrounded by family, with a lot of explaining to do

I OPENED MY EYES with a gasp, staggering backward, losing contact with Artie in the process. Elsie caught me before I could hit the wall. I sagged against her, struggling to make my breathing smooth out. I didn't have a pulse that could race, but I could feel the muscular contractions that propelled the blood through my body happening faster than they were supposed to, until my limbs ached from the effort.

And Artie opened his eyes.

Evie laughed in relief. Kevin clapped a hand on Artie's shoulder.

"There you are, sport," he said.

Artie turned his head to look at him, lost and perplexed, radiating confusion. "Where's Sarah?" he asked. "She was here. She was just here. Was she really here?" He tried to sit up.

Kevin pushed him gently back down. "Sarah's here," he said. "Sarah came home. Sarah? Honey? Can you come over here?"

Meaning could I come over there before Artie hurt himself trying to move. Right. It was a good idea. The trouble was, I wasn't sure whether or not I could. Try as I might, I couldn't seem to get my feet under myself. Everything was rippling around the edges, the same way it had—

Oh, no. The same way it had rippled when I'd hurt myself. Pushing my telepathy too far had consequences, and while I wasn't going to pretend to be sorry I'd made it possible for Artie to wake up, I'd only just come back from five years lost in my own head. I didn't want to go back there.

I closed my eyes. *One,* I thought desperately. *Two, three, five, seven, eleven, thirteen . . .*

Prime numbers are some of the most soothing things in the universe. They're always the same, perfect, calming constants that don't change, don't vary, no matter how much everything else gets twisted in on itself. I could feel Elsie's hands on my shoulders, keeping me from falling over. She had them positioned so that she wasn't touching my skin. That showed good sense on her part, even if it stung a little. I wasn't rude enough to surge in and take over her mind just because she touched me.

Then again, there had been times when I wouldn't have been able to help it. Maybe she was being even more sensible than I'd thought.

Hands grasped my upper arms. "Sarah, you need to hang on," said Artie, distressingly close and even more distressingly urgent. Uncle Kevin said something in the background. I couldn't understand him. I hoped whatever it was wasn't important enough to be a problem.

Artie tightened his grip. "Whatever you're doing, keep doing it," he said. "You just came back. You can't go away again. I won't let you."

Nice how you think your opinion matters, I thought.

He barked sudden, unsteady laughter. "Yeah, well, your stalker trashed my car, so I think I get to give a couple of orders. Hang on. Just, whatever you have to do, hang on."

I wanted to laugh. There wasn't enough air in the room. *I don't think I can.*

"I know you can," said Artie, and took his hands off my arms, and pressed them to either side of my face.

Thoughts and feelings flooded my mind, all flavored with that unmistakable emotional stamp that shouted "Artie." I laughed unsteadily, and the thoughts melted into memories. Artie, looking at a computer screen, waiting for the alert to pop up that would tell him I was online. Artie at the comic book store, picking up the contents of my subscription box to make sure I wouldn't miss anything. Artie, phone in his hand, wondering whether he had the nerve to call me again when he knew I probably wouldn't pick up, because I never picked up anymore.

I gasped a little, almost taking a step backward, out of his grasp. He tightened his hold, keeping me exactly where I was.

"No," he said. "You don't get to leave again."

This wasn't—the last time I'd been hurt, Mom had done her best to keep *anyone* from touching me, so I could have the space I needed to heal. She'd isolated me, and maybe she'd been doing the right thing at the time and maybe she hadn't, because it wasn't like there was a manual for this stuff. Even the cryptid doctors I'd met didn't necessarily know how to treat injuries in cuckoos. They normally didn't get the opportunity. This wasn't what we'd done last time. Maybe that wasn't a bad thing.

I wasn't sure my family could handle losing me for another five years.

"Your name is Sarah Zellaby," said Artie firmly. "You're a part of this family. You're my best friend.

You're a cuckoo, and I know you don't like that about yourself, I know you'd be human if you could, but I'm so glad you're not, Sarah, I'm *so glad*, because you wouldn't be the same person if you were something else, and I lo—I like the person you are."

"Even now, he can't say it?" Elsie sounded more like a little annoyed. "Congrats, Artie. You've found the most unquestionably stupid telepath in the entire world. There should be some sort of an award. Oh, wait, maybe there is. She puts up with you."

"Stop it," he snapped.

"No, you stop. I've been listening to you whine for *five years*. I'm tired of it."

The memories I was pulling through Artie's hands were getting more fragmentary, moving backward through time to when we'd been much younger, still innocently convinced that by the time we were adults, the world would somehow mysteriously have changed for the better. We'd believed we would be the first generation of cryptids to walk in the open, moving among the humans like we belonged there. Like this was our planet, too.

The memories flickered faster and faster, like I was watching one of those flipbooks that had so enchanted us all as children. Put enough still images together and you can see them move! Wow! In a world of monsters and magic, somehow that had been the most incredible thing of all.

Half of them passed so quickly that I couldn't really see them, and that was all right; these weren't my memories to enjoy. I wasn't even sure Artie knew he was showing them to me, for all that he was the one holding onto my head, keeping me from tumbling down into the pit of my own splintered self. The other half lingered.

Me in the dress I'd worn to Antimony's junior prom, both of us giggling behind our hands. She'd worn a suit, tie striped in her school colors and left hanging suggestively open, makeup Adam Ant extreme, the cheerleader playing with New Romantic ideals and absolutely killing it. I'd worn a dress in cornflower blue, dusky and soft and supported by a dozen layers of taffeta, so that the whole thing seemed to float with every step I took.

I remembered Artie pinning the flowers in my hair, strangely quiet, meticulously careful not to let his fingers touch my skin. At the time, I'd thought it was because he wanted to avoid the glitter highlighter Annie had smeared liberally over every exposed inch of me. Watching it though his eyes, I half-wondered whether there might have been another reason.

Me on the first day of fifth grade, coloring at the kitchen table when Kevin brought Artie and Annie home from school. Annie had been icing her knuckles, jaw set in the stubborn thrust that meant she had looked at the world, considered her options, and decided everyone else was in the wrong. Her left eye had already been starting to swell. Artie had clearly been crying and was just as clearly trying to hide it. He and I had spent the rest of the afternoon playing video games and pretending not to hear Annie arguing with her parents over the times when it was acceptable to fight at school.

Me the day I'd come to Oregon for the first time, pale and scared of these new family members, excited to see the cousins I'd met on the day of my adoption and not since. My hair had been pulled over my shoulders in thick pigtail braids, and I'd looked substantially younger than my ten years. Artie had been in the living room when Evie led me into the compound. He'd looked up, and seen me, and smiled, and I'd known instantly that we were going to be best friends forever. He'd had the most soothing mind I'd ever touched.

He still did. I breathed in through my nose and out through my mouth and opened my eyes, looking at his face, only inches from my own. Relief radiated from

him, so loud that it felt like even the non-telepaths in
the room should have been able to pick up on it. Relief and—

"Really?" I blurted.

Artie went pale, thoughts turning alarmed. He
pulled his hands away from my face, taking a stumbling step backward.

"I'm sorry," he said, and fled from the room.

I tried to twist and run after him. Elsie kept hold of
my shoulders.

"Believe me, we've been waiting for this for a long,
long time, and no one wants it to happen more than I
do, but there's a gigantic gash in your forehead, and
you need to tell the rest of us what just happened," she
said. "He'll be lurking around for you to have uncomfortable conversations with when we're done."

"Sorry, honey, but she's right," said Evie. "I've never
seen anything like that. I *have* to call Mom and tell her
about it, and that means I need to understand it."

I stared at her. She shook her head, walking around
the bed to take my hands and tug me toward a seat.
The connection brought her thoughts into sharper focus, which didn't help, not really; she was worried
about me, she was concerned about Artie, she was already making plans for mobilization of the family if
there was further cuckoo activity in the area. Evie had
been practicing her whole life for moments like this
one. She wasn't going to lose her focus now.

I temporarily put all thoughts of Artie from my
mind and grudgingly allowed her to push me into the
room's one open chair. Annie and Sam were still on
the couch. They had been joined by James, forming a
line with Annie in one corner and James in the other,
with Sam in the middle between them. I frowned. Sam
and James were too new. I couldn't pick up their
thoughts clearly yet, apart from the subtle sense of
presence that kept me from being surprised by the
people around me. They couldn't be here.

"They have to leave," I said, eyes still on James and Sam.

Annie bristled. "They're family, too," she said.

"It's not that. They don't have . . . they need telepathy blockers. They're family, but they're not *family*." James had a mind that felt like frostbite and Sam had a mind that felt like the moment when a roller coaster began its descent down the first big hill on the track, and neither of them had any defenses against me. If I was hurt again, if I was dangerous again—

Annie's thoughts turned suddenly static and sharp. "Oh," she said.

"Yeah," I agreed. "Oh."

"Come on, guys," she said, standing. "Crash course on cuckoo biology and anti-telepathy charms in the kitchen. I think there's leftover pie."

"Well, why didn't you say so?" asked Sam, and followed her. James trailed after the two of them, his thoughts hopping back and forth between sensible wariness and the growing desire to stay in my presence. Meaning he needed that charm sooner than later, if we didn't want him declaring me to be his long-lost sister and trying to protect me from my own family.

Sometimes the way cuckoo powers work is really, really annoying.

Evie waited until they were gone before she focused on me and said, "I've seen your eyes go white before. This was more than that. They lit up."

"Like you had fireflies inside your skull," said Elsie.

I bit my lip. Bioluminescence is a fact of nature, and more common than most people realize. Even humans glow a little bit, under the right conditions, although human eyes aren't engineered to see it. The fact that my eyes glow sometimes is a quirk of biology, unremarkable on the greater scale of things. That didn't mean I liked hearing that they'd gotten brighter.

Being one of the only reasonable people out of an

entire species really makes it hard to understand my own biology. It's frustrating.

"I went into Artie's thoughts," I said. "I had to if I wanted to defuse the trap the other cuckoo set. It was a nasty one. She set it all the way down at the bottom of his brain, so that he couldn't wake up. He could still think, it was just . . . buried. Covered over by everything else. I found it, and I ripped it apart, and he woke up. That's all. But we should probably find that cuckoo. She knows who Artie is now."

"That's not going to be a problem."

The voice belonged to my Aunt Jane, which was odd, since I hadn't felt any trace of her entering the building. I turned to look over my shoulder. She was standing in the doorway with Uncle Ted behind her, a silver anti-telepathy charm dangling from a chain around her neck. She raised one hand in a small wave when she saw me looking, bending her fingers into the American Sign Language for "I love you."

That helped. Since I can't read faces, anti-telepathy charms turn people into inscrutable monoliths, making their moods and expressions virtually impossible for me to understand. Simple hand signals can make all the difference between me being totally lost in a conversation and me knowing what's going on.

"Jane?" Evie straightened. "Hi, Ted."

"Hi," said Uncle Ted, with a distracted wave. He sniffed the air. "Artie was bleeding here. I'm going to go find him, make sure he's okay. Jane will fill you in on what we found in the woods."

That sounded ominous, a feeling that only intensified as a wave of dismayed concern rolled off of Evie. She put her hand on my shoulder, pinky finger against the skin of my throat, and the feeling intensified. I knew she was doing it to make up for the functional black hole that was Jane, but in the moment, her feelings were so big, and mixed with so many other things, that I almost pulled away.

Uncle Ted turned and walked back toward the kitchen. Aunt Jane stepped into the room.

"Annie did a good job burning the car," she said. "I checked the whole thing for signs of contamination, and I didn't find any. No one's going to come hunting Artie down because they've decided he's destined to be their one true love."

"That's good," I said uneasily.

"The indents on the side were definitely made by a truck—it's not that I don't believe you, Sarah, it's just that it's important to verify that sort of thing directly, to be sure we haven't missed anything."

I nodded. "Of course."

"There was no sign of the vehicle or the driver. They really must have hit you and then kept on going. Elsie said you didn't get any warning before the accident?"

"No, none." I shook my head. "They came out of nowhere. I should have heard the driver's thoughts, even if they were drunk or drugged—I should have had *something* to tell me what was about to happen. The fact that I didn't hear anything before the impact means they must have been being masked somehow. An anti-telepathy charm, maybe—although that wouldn't be very safe, since wearing one of those is like shutting myself in a lead box—or the other cuckoo was the one driving, and she was pulling herself way, way back."

"The other cuckoo wasn't driving," said Jane. "She wasn't even in the car."

I blinked. "How do you know?"

"Because we found her body."

Aunt Jane drove the sort of solid, sensible, mid-sized minivan beloved by soccer moms and field biologists the world over. She could pack literally hundreds of pounds of specimens into that thing, concealing them all in brightly colored plastic tubs labeled things like "PTA supplies" and "recycling." I've seen her get pulled over, produce a plate of fresh peppermint brownies seemingly out of thin air, and charm the police into waving her on her way. She calls it her "weaponized white woman" routine, and it's a calculated ruse she's taken everywhere from cryptid extraction runs to political protests, where she spends a lot of time putting herself between the authorities and anyone she deems to be more vulnerable. Which is everyone.

Mom once said that everybody on the Price side of the family has a savior complex bred into their bones. Aunt Jane got it, too. She just does a better job than some of making it look accidental.

We stood around the open back hatch of the minivan, staring in silence at the body of the cuckoo from the airport. It had been concealed behind the first row of totes, tucked safely away from prying eyes. Now . . .

In life, she'd been a threat. As a shadow in Artie's mind, she'd been an enemy. Now, here and real and dead and gone, she just looked . . . small.

"I guess we know what you'd look like as a corpse," said Elsie, in a strangled voice. "I don't like it."

"I don't like it either," I said. The sutures Evie had put into the wound on my forehead were close and tight and mostly covered by my bangs, but they still ached. It didn't matter that they weren't going to leave a scar. That didn't take the pain away.

"I'm going to go check on Artie," Elsie said, and fled.

The cuckoo didn't have any visible injuries. Her limbs were straight, and her face was undamaged. I could see why Jane was so sure that she hadn't been in the other vehicle. With as badly as Artie's car had been smashed in, there was no way the passengers in the truck had gotten away without at least a few bumps and bruises. Cuckoos may not have the pretty colors humans do, but there should have been scratches, scrapes—*something*. Not just this pristine nothingness.

A trickle of what looked like snot was dried on her upper lip and crusted around both nostrils. I leaned closer. There was a faint blue undertone to the film. Not mucus, then: blood.

As if she were the telepath, not me, Evie leaned forward and pried one of the cuckoo's eyes open. "Look at this," she said.

We looked.

Cuckoos have blue eyes. It's one of the few places where we have any variation in our appearances, because when I say "blue" I mean any one of a dozen shades. This one's eyes had been a few shades lighter than mine, more ice than morning sky. They still were . . . but her pupils had contracted to pinpricks of black against the blue, and the edges of her irises were foggy, like they'd frosted over, or been burned.

"What the hell happened here?" asked Kevin.

"I think she had the cuckoo equivalent of an aneurysm, is what happened," said Jane. She looked straight at me as she asked, "Is there anything you want to tell us?"

My Aunt Jane loves me. I sometimes think she doesn't want to, but there's no questioning her affection. I'm part of her family. More importantly, I'm her reclusive son's best friend. And none of that matters, because she grew up surrounded by people who not only knew what cuckoos were, they knew precisely why we shouldn't be—couldn't be—trusted. We're natural predators who prefer the simplicity of a hunt where everyone involved is sapient. We destroy things for fun. *She* wasn't the Price sibling who'd married a cuckoo's daughter and been forced to admit that maybe there was more to us than a knife in the dark and a mind twisting inward on itself. She could love and fear and hate me all at the same time.

It was sort of a relief, though. At least now I knew

why she was wearing an anti-telepathy charm, and why Uncle Ted was doing the same thing. She must have insisted, choosing the possibility of offending me over the chance that I'd come back from my convalescence somehow wrong.

"I already told Evie everything," I said. "The cuckoo attacked me at the airport. I fought back. I thought I got away. She must have followed me to the warehouse, where Artie picked me up, and decided that she deserved a little revenge. We were on our way here when a truck hit us from the side." I hesitated before going on. She was going to find out eventually. Better that she hear it from me. "She could tell that Artie was important to me, so she put a psychic snare in his head to keep him from waking up. When I realized what she'd done, I went into his mindscape and defused it. He woke up."

There: factual, straightforward, and unlikely to make me seem even less trustworthy to my justifiably paranoid aunt.

Jane turned toward the cuckoo again, studying her. Finally, she said, "If this were a human body, I could tell how long she'd been dead by checking her blood coagulation and degree of rigor. But she's not stiffening the way I expect her to, and it's impossible to tell how the blood is pooling. When do you think she died?"

"I don't know," I said honestly. "I didn't feel anything connecting her to Artie when I went into his head. Defusing her trap shouldn't have done anything to her."

"What if it wasn't *defusing* the trap that killed her?"

Jane turned toward Evie when she spoke. I didn't move. Evie wasn't wearing an anti-telepathy charm; I could pick up her meaning just as well while I was looking at the cuckoo.

She looked so small. She had been a terrifying threat, and now she was so small, and she was never going to threaten anyone again. What in the world could have possessed her to follow me so far from the airport? Cuckoos are territorial, but that doesn't normally make them *stupid*.

"Explain," said Jane.

"Sarah got hurt when she modified the memories of the Covenant operatives who were threatening Verity and Dominic," said Evie.

"Thanks for that, by the way," said Kevin.

"No worries," I said, leaning closer to the cuckoo. The distant, faintly acidic scent of cuckoo blood tickled my nose and made me want to sneeze. There was a film of blue-tinged blood crusted around her ears as well as above her mouth. She'd bled out fast and catastrophically. Given the damage to her eyes, I was willing to bet that if we'd taken swabs, we would have found more blood in the soft tissues around them. Her death had probably been relatively painless, because it hadn't given her time for anything else.

"According to our mother, the physical signs of injury included bleeding from the eyes and nose, hypoxia, and temporary clouding of the irises," Evie continued.

I snapped around, staring at my sister. "What?" Mom had never told me about the damage to my irises. My eyes had always looked perfectly normal to me.

But that wasn't entirely true, was it? During the first few months, when I'd walked in a cloud of hazy disorientation, the whole world had been cloudy around the edges. I'd attributed it to my bruised brain. What if some of it had been due to other physical causes?

How many things about my own health had my parents concealed for my own good?

"Mom thought they might be cataracts at first, until she realized they were receding as you got better," said Evie, apologetic discomfort rolling off her in waves. "The damage to the eyes seems to be tied to excessive telepathic 'pushing.'"

"You're saying this cuckoo hurt herself the same way Sarah did, by pushing things into Artie's brain?" demanded Jane.

"No," I said numbly. "No, she's saying this cuckoo *killed* herself that way. I just don't understand . . . I don't understand why hurting us would have been worth dying."

"I don't think it was about hurting Artie at all," said Evie. "We've dealt with ordinary cuckoos before. They don't consider humans or Lilu worth their time. She killed herself to hurt *you*."

"But all I did was hit her with my backpack," I objected. "That's not worth dying over."

Evie shrugged. "Doesn't change the fact that she did."

No. It didn't.

Something was going on—something bigger than one dead cuckoo. I just wished I knew what it was.

While I was still trying to put my feelings into words, Kevin said, almost apologetically, "We don't get access to many dead cuckoos."

"I'll get the dissection kit," said Jane.

"I'm going to go find Artie," I said, and turned and fled before the autopsy could begin.

My family is my family. I wouldn't have them any other way. But sometimes they can be a little much to deal with. Especially when the knives come out.

Nine

$$\pi_2(n) \sim 2C_2 \frac{n}{(\ln n)^2} \sim 2C_2 \int_2^n \frac{dt}{(\ln t)^2}$$

"Nobody gets to pick where they're born
or who they're born to, but everybody gets
to pick their family. Make good choices
with yours."

—Alice Healy

*Roving through the family compound, trying not to
think about what's about to happen in the barn*

DISSECTION IS A FACT of life—and death—when your
whole family is involved with the biological sci-
ences. Evie needs to understand cryptids if she's going
to help heal them. Kevin needs to understand them so
he can document them as accurately as possible, an
activity that matters both now and in the future. We
wouldn't even know that there used to be two types of
wadjet if not for some of the old family notebooks,
which meticulously documented the differences between the Egyptian and Indian branches of the species
before the Egyptian wadjet disappeared, probably
forever.

But that doesn't mean I have to like it, and it didn't
mean I had to be happy knowing they were about to
take a member of my species apart, piece by piece, like
she was some sort of puzzle to be solved. People aren't
puzzles. At least, they shouldn't be.

I found Annie and the others in the kitchen. Both

James and Sam had become the sort of blank spot that I associated with anti-telepathy charms, although Annie was as bright and visible as ever. Elsie was sitting on the couch, sullenly drinking a glass of orange juice. It was amazing how much resentment she could direct toward citrus.

"Hi," I said, offering a small wave to James and Sam. "Now that you have your telepathy blockers, I won't be able to read your minds. That's for the best, for all of us, but you should be aware that my brain doesn't process facial input very well."

"Meaning?" asked Sam.

"Meaning that if you didn't have a tail, the two of you would be essentially identical to me."

Sam and James exchanged a look. "I can't decide whether that's racist or just insulting," said Sam.

"Technically, I think it's speciesist," I said. "All humans look basically the same when I can't read their minds."

"Okay, definitely insulting," said Sam. "Not human. Hence the tail."

"Yes human, hence the no tail, but there are humans with this condition," said James. "Face blindness is usually a result of something being wired slightly differently in the visual processing center of the brain."

"Well, I don't know whether that's my problem, since we don't have an MRI, or a reasonable assortment of cuckoos to put *in* the MRI, but it doesn't matter, since we're living with the reality of my situation, not the theory," I said. "I can recognize voices. I can't read your expressions, and if you want me to know what you're thinking—emotionally—you may need to say it out loud, just to be sure."

"Do we have to wear these things forever?" James plucked at the chain dangling around his neck. "I've never been overly fond of jewelry. It gets caught on things, and the chain gets cold."

"That's because you're secretly a snow cone machine who walks like a man," said Annie fondly. Her mood when she looked at him was a fascinatingly complicated mixture of regret, fellowship, and a fierce fondness that felt very similar to the way she thought about Alex.

"He's your *brother*," I blurted, and paused, feeling the embarrassing tingle in my cheeks that would have been a blush, if I'd had the capillary response to fuel it.

Annie simply nodded. "He is. I found him in a cardboard box labeled 'free to good home,' and decided I was going to keep him. He has his own room now and everything."

"I wish that were less accurate," muttered James.

Their trio was starting to make more sense now. I offered Annie a wan smile and waved a hand toward the stairs. "I'm going to go find Artie."

"Good luck with that," said Elsie. "I've looked everywhere. The jerk is hiding."

"Yeah, but I know he didn't leave the house—I would have heard him go—and I can't hear him now, which means there's only one place he can be." I started across the room. "I'll be back down as soon as we've hammered this out."

"Good luck," called Annie.

I waved vaguely over my shoulder rather than looking back and kept walking.

My family is remarkably effective in the field. We have to be. Hesitate when there's a Covenant operative or a hungry lindworm in front of you and there's a good chance you're going to wind up dead. Not cool. But this means that we're also incredibly relaxed and disorganized when we don't have to keep it together. When we relax, we *relax*, becoming as difficult to herd as a clowder of cats. If I'd stayed to finish saying goodbye, I would have found myself caught in an endless loop of just one more thing, until something important enough to break the cycle happened. Bedtime is an eternal trial.

At least James and Sam had their anti-telepathy charms now. Annie must have explained why they were necessary. Neither of them had seemed afraid of me, but with their minds sealed off, how could I tell?

Sometimes coming from a predatory species really sucks.

A constellation of smaller minds came into focus as I climbed the stairs. They were too small to project very far, although each of them was fully sapient, as complex as any human. Some of them were blurry: we'd never met before. Others were bright, crisp and clear, elders of the colony who knew exactly who I was and would be thrilled to see me home. I took a deep breath, steeling myself. Then I kept climbing.

"HAIL! HAIL THE RETURN OF THE HEART-LESS ONE!"

Aeslin mice are small, but when that many of them shout in tandem, they're capable of making a hell of a lot of noise. There were at least a hundred mice spread out across the second-floor landing, perched on the bookshelves and clinging to the banister. I stopped, blinking at them. About a third of the gathering wore the colors of Verity's clergy, bedecked with more feathers than any mouse had any business wearing. The rest were a mixture of the active family liturgies, including a few I didn't recognize. That made a certain amount of sense. Dominic, Shelby, now Sam and James . . . we'd had a few new additions to the family since the last time I'd been home in Oregon.

"Hello," I said.

The mice cheered.

Aeslin mice are evolutionary mimics. They look like ordinary field mice, save for slightly larger heads and slightly more developed hands—two attributes most people would never be in a position to notice. They nest like mice, breed like mice, and happily infest the walls of human habitations, again, like mice. It's just that they do all this while practicing a complicated, functionally inborn religion. Aeslin need to believe in something. Anything. Our family colony believes in, well, the family. We are, and have always been, their objects of worship.

No pressure. I mean, "these adorable, cartoony creatures love and trust you, and believe that you have the power to keep them safe when their species is otherwise functionally extinct" is a perfectly normal situation, right?

"Long have we Awaited your Return," intoned one of the older mice, stepping to the front of the group. He used a long kitten-bone staff to hold himself upright. From the twinges of pain that laced through his thoughts, I could tell that bipedal locomotion was no longer as easy for him as it had been when he'd been younger. "Hail to the Heartless One! Hail to the Savior of the Arboreal Priestess!"

"Of course I saved her," I said. "Verity's my family. I had to."

"We understand," said the priest gravely. I frowned. He wasn't wearing nearly enough feathers. "We also understand that we have been Unfair to you."

That didn't make any sense, but he meant it. All the thoughts rising from him were sincere ones. "What do you mean?" I asked. "You helped me locate Verity when she needed me. Well. Not you, exactly, but the splinter colony she had with her in New York. You were totally fair to me."

"Please." The priest bowed until his whiskers brushed the floor, easing some of the crackles of pain from his spine. "Please. We seek Forgiveness and Absolution. Allow us to petition you for these things, for only then may we be Properly Made Clean."

Sometimes the Aeslin ability to make any letter into a capital one was enough to make my head spin. "All right," I said. "What do you need from me?"

The priest straightened and turned, looking at another, younger mouse. This one was wearing glasses, twists of wire around magnifying lenses that made its tiny oildrop eyes look absolutely enormous. The rest of its livery was nothing I recognized, beads and bits of bone counting out complicated patterns across its back. They almost looked like a Fibonacci sequence. I smiled at the thought.

The younger mouse cleared its—her—throat, forced her whiskers forward, and said, "I am come to petition you, O Heartless One, called Sarah Zellaby, called Cousin Sarah, to Forgive us our trespasses against you, to Forget our refusal to clearly see what was before us, and to Formally Allow us to sanctify the clergy which has been assembled in your Name."

I blinked. "Um, what?"

"We understand now that we were unwilling to set aside our prejudices and our fears for your species of Birth, and to acknowledge that what matters is not Blood, but Belonging," said the younger mouse. "You are a daughter of this line, as truly as any who have been Born to it. You carry in your motions the Grace of Beth, the Forgiveness of Caroline, the Canniness of Enid, the Viciousness of Frances, the Determination of Alice, and the Persistence of Evelyn. You are a Priestess, and have always been, and we are sorry not to have seen it before now."

I gaped at her, unable to figure out how I was supposed to respond to that, or whether there *was* a good response.

The mouse sat back on her haunches, whiskers still pushed forward as she focused her full attention on me. "We have assembled as much as we can of your catechisms, for you have never been a stranger here. Will you allow me to lead your temple, to learn your mysteries, and to reveal them to the acolytes who come before us with time, ready to pledge themselves unto your divinity?"

I stood there in silence for a long moment—long enough that the mice began to mutter nervously amongst themselves, their thoughts radiating concern and fear of rejection. Me? They wanted *me*?

If I didn't say something soon, this was going to get ugly. I swallowed my fear and confusion and asked, "Are you sure? I'm not—I mean, all the other priestesses are—"

"The Polychromatic Priestess is not human, nor ever aspires to be," said the younger mouse, sounding relieved. "Her veins carry the blood of the Lilu, and still she stands beside her family, and still she cares for them as well as any other of her kin or kind. Nor was the Violent Priestess fully human, for all that none has ever Learned precisely what else she drew from, and that inhumanity has kept her bloodline safe from the crueler of the Heartless, for their claws find little purchase on family minds. You will not be the First. You will not be the Last. Will you permit us to worship you as well as you deserve, and to be held in the regard we have always owed to you?"

The mice looked at me, whiskers vibrating, radiating hope, and I gave them the only answer I could:

"Yes."

Their cheers could have woken the dead.

I'm not sure how long I spent on the stairs with the rejoicing mice. Eventually, Annie poked her head around the corner, called, "Celebratory cheese and cake in the kitchen!" and withdrew, leaving me to stand fast against the sudden rodent tide. I wasn't sure she knew *what* the mice were celebrating, just that they were, and I couldn't get past them.

A priestess. Me. A Priestess, as the mice would put it, slapping on that all-important capital letter. They didn't have priestesses among their clergy, only priests, regardless of sex, showing how confusing they found human gender roles. Everything they did, they did because it was tradition, and this colony's traditions had started with Beth Evans, a British farmwife and member of the Covenant of St. George who had been willing to bend her own traditions far enough to offer safety and succor to a small group of talking mice. According to Covenant law, she should have killed them on sight, condemning them for the crime of being unusual and unnatural and all the other things the Covenant didn't approve of. She had refused to be recognized as a god, saying that it was improper for a woman to set herself above her husband, and so generations of labels had been indelibly set.

Watching Annie argue with the mice had always been a fun way to kill an afternoon when we were kids. She'd wanted to be a goddess—of course she had—and she'd wanted me to be a priestess, and Artie had been willing to give up his titles altogether if it meant the mice would stop shouting every time he came into a room. But the mice had always been firm on the idea that I could never be a priestess, because I wasn't human and wasn't a Price and was a member of a predatory species. And now I was a priestess.

I walked slowly along the silent hall, trying to wrap my head around the idea. Apparently, saving Verity's life had been enough to make the mice change their tune. It was weird. I didn't know if I liked it. But I knew that it would make Verity happy, and Annie, and probably Evie. That was what mattered. More than anything else, that was what mattered.

The door to my room was at the very end of the hall, near the stairway to the attic. It was closed. I hesitated for a moment, looking at it, before I took a deep breath and turned the knob, pushing the door open.

The room on the other side was good-sized, with pale green walls and a dark green carpet. Like most of the house, it was furnished in mismatched oak. Kevin liked to go to thrift stores and yard sales, find the sturdiest, most battered pieces he could, and then restore and refinish them out in the workshop. It meant nothing quite went together, but everything could be used to barricade doors or smashed for makeshift weapons if a situation suddenly went south. My family doesn't believe in single-use décor when there's another option available.

I didn't mind the fact that the bedframe, desk, and dresser all looked like they'd come from different decades and schools of interior design. It made the room feel homey, like I lived here even when I wasn't living here.

Artie was sitting on the bed.

I stopped in the doorway, looking at him, letting the soothing background radiation of his thoughts wash over me. Maybe it was weird to use him to calm myself down enough to *deal* with him, but weird is sort of what we do. Weird is normal, for us.

His attention was focused on his laptop, but he knew I was there, and was doing his best not to think about me. Naturally, this meant that the longer I waited, the more he couldn't stop thinking about me. It was a vicious cycle. Finally, he looked up from his screen, radiating a combination of angry wanting and desperate unhappiness. It stung a little. It didn't sting as much as his absence had.

"Can't I get, like, five minutes of peace around here?" he asked. "Five minutes. That's all I'm asking for. Is that too much?"

"It is when you look for peace by literally hiding in my room, yeah," I said. "You do remember that this is *my* room, right?"

"We carved our initials into the bedframe when we were eleven," he said, lowering the lid so that he could see me better. "When we decided we were going to be best friends forever."

"Annie was *so* mad about that," I said. "She told her mom, and Evie made us sand and varnish the whole frame, because it's not safe to leave proof that something used to belong to you."

"Move like ghosts, disappear when you leave," said Artie, half-agreement and half-repetition of one of the many warnings that had haunted our childhoods. With a sigh, he closed the laptop and set it aside. "I know this is your room, but I can't leave until my folks do, since my car's all smashed-up and not here. I'm going to be dealing with mechanics for the rest of the year."

I winced. "Um. About that."

Artie's thoughts turned wary. "It's not smashed-up?"

"It was."

"Now it's. . . ?"

"Annie set it on fire." His mouth dropped open, shock rolling off him in a wave. I put my hands up, like that would be enough to ward it off. "She had to! You'd bled all over the inside of the cab, and there was no other way to make sure some hiker or police officer wouldn't come along, get a whiff of you, fall in love, and track you down to kidnap you. Remember what happened when you came to the mathletes competition with me?"

"Like I could ever forget," he mumbled uncomfortably. His shock tempered itself into a more customary level of discomfort and discontent. "Why couldn't I have inherited a nice, normal genetic condition? Annie sets things on fire with her mind. Sam turns into a big terrifying monkey-dude. Something nice and simple, like that, instead of 'congrats, if someone's into dudes, they're into you, whether they want to be or not.'"

"It's not fair," I said. This was an old song. I knew which lyrics were mine.

"It's not!" Artie shoved his laptop aside, turning so that he was facing the wall. I couldn't read his expressions, but a lifetime of trying to keep them under control meant that sometimes he didn't want me to see them anyway. "It's not fair. It's not fair that I can't have friends without worrying about making them fall in love with me by mistake, and it's not fair that Dad didn't think about whether his kids would be able to control their pheromones before he went and married Mom, and it's not fair that I never get to know whether—"

He caught himself, but the thought was already fully formed. It escaped despite his best intentions. *Whether anyone really likes me, or whether it's just these stupid pheromones.*

I winced and walked over to the bed, sitting carefully on the very edge and facing the wall. Humans get weird when people focus on them during moments of emotional distress, and Artie, despite his biology, is very much culturally human. We all are, these days. We never had a choice in the matter.

"I really like you," I said softly.

Artie didn't say anything.

"I don't know how many times we have to go over this. Your pheromones don't work on me. I'm too biologically different."

"You're a mammal," he said. "You have hair, you have three bones inside your inner ear, you can—" He caught himself, suddenly radiating embarrassment.

"Lactate, yes; so I've been told. Not that it's ever going to happen. Can you imagine me hanging around with a cuckoo man long enough to get pregnant, even if I wanted children?" I shuddered. "If I want to subject myself to toxic people, I'll just read the comments on literally any article about female-led comic book properties. It'll be a fun reminder of why I should never, ever read the comments."

"Your life is reading the comments."

"Yes, and the things people think when they don't know anyone can hear them are even worse than the things they're willing to write down. Thanks but no thanks." I took a deep breath, still staring at the dresser. "We're getting away from the point, Artie. I'm a mammal, maybe, but I'm not a mammal from anywhere around here. You're a mammal from around here."

"That's not what Dad thinks," Artie said. "He thinks Johrlac aren't the only ones who figured out a way to move between dimensions."

"Okay, not from around here, but maybe from the next town over," I said. "It's close enough. Lilu are cross-fertile with humans. That means you can't have traveled far."

"It's the cross-fertility that's the problem," said Artie.

"I don't know. I think I like a world with you in it better than I'd like a world without you."

Silence answered me, broken by the slow, roiling boil of his thoughts, which were too jumbled and fragmentary to let me pull anything specific out of them. Most people are like that, most of the time. Humans don't walk around narrating their actions to themselves unless they're trying not to forget a step in some unfamiliar chore; I've seen Annie load the dishwasher, wipe down the counters, and make herself a sandwich, all while thinking about nothing but the plot of some anime she's been watching. Conscious thought and habitual action aren't always friends.

Finally, Artie said, "I don't want to have never existed. I just wish parts of this weren't so hard."

"They're hard for everyone."

"Try having everybody you meet fall in love with you even when they don't want to."

I twisted around, finally looking at him. "You mean the reason they really kept me in the house for five years? That's what cuckoos *do*. You want to talk about violation? You make people fall in love with you. Fine. Only really, they're falling in lust with you, and that's gross, it's icky and inappropriate and unfair, but all you have to do is walk away from them. You've been you for your entire life. How many people have you taken advantage of?"

Artie shook his head. "None."

"I took advantage of at least four people *today*. That's how I got here. And yeah, I tried to make sure they were people who deserved to be taken advantage of, but you know how I did that? I rooted around inside their heads, in their private thoughts, where they thought they were safe, and I found the things that would convince me it was okay to do whatever I wanted to them. I'm *so* much worse than you are. All I need to do is let my guard down and *everyone* falls in love with me. The whole world falls in love with me. I just have to want it and it's mine. You really want to tell me you're worse? Really?"

"At least you can go outside," he said, refusing to meet my eyes.

"So could you, if you wanted to learn how to deal with what you are," I snapped. "Elsie goes outside. Elsie spends all her time with *roller derby girls*. She has the same pheromones you do. She has the same problems dealing with humans as you do. She still dates. She still talks to people. You're making choices, Artie. Here's a fun one for you: if you'd been willing to *choose* to fly to Ohio, and *choose* to take a cab to the house, Mom would never have left you standing on the porch. You could have come to me a long time ago. So why didn't you?"

He stared at me, trembling, eyes so wide that even I could pick up on his distress. Finally, in a small voice, he said, "You didn't want me there."

I considered closing my eyes. It wouldn't do me any good. He'd still be in the room if I did that, thoughts still audible, turmoil still echoing through my head like a small, captive storm. I clenched my hands in the covers, balling them between my fingers until my wrists began to ache.

"I wanted you there," I said. "Every day, I wanted

you there. Except on the days when I was afraid that I'd never be myself again, because I was too broken, and I knew that if you came, you'd turn around and walk away and never want to talk to me again. And I couldn't do that. I couldn't *survive* that. That's why I didn't ask you. It's why I didn't beg. I wanted to beg. I knew I couldn't beg. If I begged, you might actually come, and if you came, you'd never want to see me again, and if I lost you on top of everything else, that would be it. I'd be done. I'd be *over*. I couldn't lose my best friend. I couldn't, I couldn't, I couldn't—"

Artie suddenly leaned over and grabbed my hands, pressing them deeper into the mattress. I stopped talking and stared at him. He stared back.

This close, I could see every detail of his irises, every line and tiny gradation of color. They were beautiful. I didn't need to be able to read his expression to know that they were beautiful, or that I wanted to keep staring at them for the rest of my life.

With his skin touching mine, his mind was barely shy of an open book. He was thinking of how much he'd missed me, how much he hated that I was right, and how wrong I was at the same time, because he would never have run away from me, no matter how broken I'd been; he would never have rejected me, because he . . .

He.

And here it was again, the thing I'd felt from him downstairs, the thing I hadn't been ready to deal with then. The thing I wasn't ready to deal with now. The thing I might never be ready to deal with.

"No, you don't," I said miserably. "You think you do, because I'm a cuckoo. You can't help it."

"My pheromones don't work on you," he said. "That's what you keep telling me over and over, like it matters. I can't force you to do anything you don't want to do."

Silent, I nodded.

"Do you remember my side of the family tree?"

"Um," I said slowly. "Your father is Theodore Harrington. Your mother is Jane Price."

"And her mother was?"

"Alice Price."

"And *her* mother was?"

"Frances Price."

"Frances Price," repeated Artie. "Not even the mice know where she came from. She was found as a baby and raised by the carnival and she married Jonathan Price and they were happy. They were really, really happy."

Slowly, I started to understand what he was saying. "And when they met a cuckoo, Jonathan got caught, and Fran didn't."

Artie nodded. "Fran didn't. Fran was resistant. We still don't know why, because we don't know anything about her side of the family tree, but Fran was resistant. And her daughter is resistant. And *her* kids are resistant. Which means I . . ."

"You're resistant." I bit my lip, staring fixedly at him. "You don't get caught."

"No. I don't get caught." He looked down at his hands, still clasped over mine. "Even when it would be easier, I don't get caught, because whatever it is you do to peoples' heads, I'm resistant to it. Because of who my great-grandmother was."

"I don't like you because of your pheromones," I whispered.

"I don't like you because you changed my mind so I wouldn't have a choice," he said.

"I like you, though," I said. "I like you . . . I really like you, really a lot." The words didn't feel big enough for the way I felt about him. They felt too big to be comfortable. I was teetering on the edge of the sort of thing that couldn't be taken back once it was said, the sort of thing that could change everything, because sometimes people didn't want to hear it. Sometimes people just wanted to go on pretending they couldn't see the things that were right in front of their faces.

"I like you, too," said Artie.

I bit my lip. "So now what?" I asked. "Do we . . . I don't want you to hide from me. I wouldn't have come back if I wanted you to hide from me. I don't want you to do anything that makes you uncomfortable, but I can't be here if you're going to—"

He kissed me. Hands still locked over mine, pressing them down against the mattress, he leaned over and he kissed me. My eyes widened, very briefly, before they closed, before I melted into him like this was the thaw I'd been waiting for all my life, because I stopped trying to keep him out of my mind and myself out of his and let us come crashing together, him into me and me into him and he was kissing me, he was *kissing* me, his lips were on mine and my lips were on his and he was *kissing* me.

Then he pulled away with a soft hiss, letting go of my hands at the same time. The sudden loss of connection was dizzying. I blinked at him, half dazed and utterly confused.

"Sorry," he said, rubbing his cheek and wincing. "I sort of forgot I had seventeen stitches in my face. Um. Ow?"

"Oh," I said, and started laughing. Artie blinked at me, his bemusement hanging almost audible in the air. I shook my head. "I forgot, too. I forgot you got hurt, I forgot I got hurt, I forgot the whole—I *forgot*."

"That's a lot of forgetting," said Artie. He started laughing, too, and leaned forward until our foreheads were touching. Some of the feeling of connection came springing back, but not all of it; not enough to be anything more than pleasant. I could feel his thoughts, a distant swirl of confusion, delight, and disbelief.

"I had other things on my mind," I said. He laughed again. I leaned in, intending to go for a second kiss before this mysterious interlude into everything I'd ever wanted came crashing to an end.

Someone cleared their throat behind me. I pulled back and whipped around. James was standing in the doorway, one hand still raised to knock.

"What," said Artie flatly. He didn't sound happy.

"I lost the coin toss," said James. "I was tasked to, and I am quoting here, 'sneak up there while they can't hear you coming and see whether they've figured their shit out.' Was your shit making out like teenagers? Because if so, you appear to have figured it out, and I will hopefully never be asked to do anything like this ever again."

"So you're leaving," said Artie.

"Sadly, no," said James. "I would pay almost anything to not be standing here right now. Unfortunately for me, your Aunt Evelyn wants to see you. Downstairs. Now."

"Why?" I asked. I was having a hard time imagining anything more urgent than what we'd been doing.

"They've finished their initial autopsy." His voice turned grim. "There's apparently some information she feels you need to have."

Well. Anything but that.

Ten

$$\pi_2(n) \sim 2C_2 \frac{n}{(\ln n)^2} \sim 2C_2 \int_2^n \frac{dt}{(\ln t)^2}$$

"Life happens. So does death. The trick is putting as much time as possible between the two."

—Mary Dunlavy

Heading for the living room, because that's way better than making out with the boy you've loved since you were just a kid

THE REST OF MY family snapped back into clear psychic focus as soon as I stepped outside the room that had been warded for my use. Their minds were ... loud, even for them. We're a boisterous, argumentative lot, and we're fully capable of violating most noise ordinances in the process of figuring out what we want to do for dinner. This, though—this was something else. All of them were screaming, but only inside their own minds. No sound was coming up the stairs.

That was enough to make me walk faster. James and Artie paced me, Artie radiating a degree of anxiety that nicely mirrored my own. His empathy had to be picking up the disconnect between the waves of anxiety rolling up the stairs and the dead silence that accompanied them.

We were almost to the stairs when Artie reached over and took my hand. His anxiety immediately calmed, and mine dropped in response. We could handle this. Whatever it was, whatever it meant, we could handle it. We didn't have a choice.

Annie and Sam had joined Elsie on the couch. Evie and Kevin were standing nearby, their heads close together, murmuring to each other. Their thoughts were opaque, veiled in trivial inconsequentialities, which made my anxiety spike again. Everyone in our family knew how to mask their thoughts, if not always their emotions, because Mom and I weren't the only cuckoos they were likely to encounter on a regular basis. If I could read them, so could the enemy. Better to use me as a means of testing their defenses.

Aunt Jane and Uncle Ted were nowhere to be seen. I reached out automatically, finding the flickering traces of their minds in the barn. They were disposing of the cuckoo's body, burning the parts that looked too human to be safe to keep around, preserving the rest in specimen jars. I got a flash of the cuckoo's eyes, floating in a jar of clear fluid that was probably the cuckoo's own blood, and pulled myself away from them, physically shuddering. Some things are better off unseen. This was one of them.

"I found them," announced James, heading for the couch, where he took up a position leaning against the arm, next to Annie. "I'm choosing to view this whole experience as a form of familial hazing, to make up for the fact that I spent my foolish teenage years in another time zone. Please, can you be done torturing me soon?"

"Nope," said Annie, and punched him amiably in the arm.

"About damn time," said Elsie, radiating smug satisfaction as she looked at my hand, still firmly clasped in Artie's.

My cheeks warmed with an invisible blush. I squared my shoulders and looked toward Evie and Kevin. "What's going on?" I asked. "What did you find?"

"Honey, do you want to sit down?" Evie took a step forward, spreading her hands like she was trying to soothe a panicky animal. If I hadn't already been a little bit freaked out, that gesture would have been enough to do it. "We need to talk to you about what happened. Both of you."

"I'm not going to be all weird about Sarah because a cuckoo decided to mess with my head," said Artie. He let go of my hand with a sudden bolt of self-consciousness, like he'd just realized he was still holding it. Which, to be fair, he had.

I couldn't blame him. The thoughts rolling off Annie and Elsie were curious, amused, and even relieved, all covered by a thin veneer of worry. Evie and Kevin mostly just felt worried. I didn't want our relationship, whatever it was actually going to be, to become their next topic of dissection.

"I know, dear," said Evie. "Nothing's ever going to make you weirder about Sarah."

"That's the truth," said Annie.

Elsie snorted laughter, covering her mouth with her hand. I shot her an imperious glare. She laughed harder, abandoning any pretense of swallowing it. Sometimes having cousins can be really annoying.

"We dissected the cuckoo who attacked you in the woods," said Kevin, apparently realizing that the only way forward was to barrel straight through without hesitation. "The blood we found in her nose and ears was the result of a massive aneurism, leading to an even more massive brain bleed."

"Is that what killed her?" I asked.

"Not quite." He removed his glasses, wiping them on his shirt as he spoke, so he wouldn't have to see my reaction. I almost wished I could do the same. He was thinking too loudly for that; every word was accompanied by an image, whether I wanted to see it or not. And I didn't want to see it.

"Most intelligent creatures have highly crenulated

brains. It's a matter of biological necessity. Smooth brains have less surface area, which means less space for the neurons to do what they need to do. Crenulated brains have more surface area, allowing for greater intelligence, memory retention, all the requisites of intelligence as we currently understand it. A domestic dog may have a larger brain than an Aeslin mouse, but due to the crenulations, the Aeslin mouse actually has greater surface area and hence more potential for intelligence."

This was biology 101; we'd all learned this stuff when we were kids. Well, maybe not James and Sam. I still couldn't catch sight of their minds through their telepathy blockers, and so I had to assume they looked interested enough to be considered an appropriate target audience for this little anatomy lesson.

Kevin didn't notice that I was confused, or maybe he just didn't care. He put his glasses on as he continued, "We've seen Johrlac brains before, although not many of them, and only one that was undamaged. Our current model for their morphology says that we should have found a brain of the same approximate weight and size as a comparable human brain, but with deeper crenulations, creating a greater surface area and allowing for the development of psychic powers such as telepathy."

"I know you're trying to tell us something, but this is all making me feel uncomfortably like I'm going to be the next one on the dissection table, so it would be really swell if you could get to the point before I have to leave the room," I said.

"I'm sorry, Sarah. I know this isn't easy."

I laughed unsteadily. "A member of my own species—which is predatory and sort of evil, and that sucks for me—attacked me. Twice. And then she attacked Artie, and now she's dead, and you're tiptoeing around actually telling me why that is. So no, this isn't easy. It's confusing and it's scary and I just want to know what's going on. Please, can you tell me what's going on?"

Kevin sighed. "We opened her skull to confirm she'd suffered from a brain bleed, and to add her brain to our specimen collection. We get better equipment every year. We may eventually be able to design better anti-telepathy charms by looking at the structure of the Johrlac brain."

"We *did* find evidence of the brain bleed," said Evie. "It was catastrophic in scope. She must have died almost instantly. I don't believe she would have had any real time to suffer."

It was difficult to worry too much about whether or not the cuckoo had suffered. She was dead and that was sad, but mostly because her being dead meant I couldn't track her down and hurt her for what she'd done to Artie. Being near me shouldn't have been considered enough to make him a target. It wasn't right, and it wasn't fair, and I wasn't okay with it.

"We also found some alarming morphological changes to the brain itself," said Kevin, sounding suddenly grim. "Most of the crenulations were either shallower than we expected them to be based on earlier specimens, or entirely gone. The tissue was both dehydrated and less stable than it should have been."

"He means the brain fell apart as soon as we touched it," said Evie. "It was like brain pudding. No structural integrity. No elasticity. The trauma she suffered was incredible."

And unnerving. "Do you think it was pathogenic?"

"We've never discovered a single disease in this dimension that can infect cuckoos," said Evie. "But I thought of that, and I started some cultures. We should know more soon."

Meaning she didn't think it was a virus. That was good, since I'd been close to the dead cuckoo both before and after she collapsed. It was also bad. It meant we didn't know anything. "What else could have done this?"

Evie and Kevin exchanged a look, discomfort rolling off them in waves. Artie twitched, picking up on it as clearly as I was.

"I need to know," I said.

Evie sighed. "When you had your . . . accident . . . you were lucky enough to be near an actual cryptid hospital," she said.

I nodded slowly. St. Giles' Hospital was cryptid-owned and cryptid-operated and maintained solely for the care and keeping of people who couldn't walk into a human emergency room and expect to have any chance of walking out again. It had been the nearest available source of medical care when I'd been hurt. I didn't remember anything of my time there—not even the names of the doctors who'd helped me—but Mom had sent them an edible arrangement every year since I'd come home.

"St. Giles has an MRI machine," she continued slowly. "They were able to take some pictures of your brain, both immediately after your injury and when they were getting ready to let Mom take you home. The initial pictures showed . . ." She stopped, glancing at Kevin.

Wearily, I rubbed my left temple and said, "You're thinking about how you don't want to tell me this so loudly that you might as well be shouting it. Please just say whatever it is out loud, so everyone will know it, and we can move on to whatever comes next, okay? I'm a big girl. I can handle it."

"The initial pictures showed reduced crenulation," said Evie. "The later pictures showed *increased* crenulation. It was like your injury had caused the surface of your brain to contract in preparation for expansion."

I blinked. "Wait, what?"

"The crenulations of your brain grew deeper," said Evie. "According to the doctor who worked on your case, it looks like the changes are permanent. We don't know what could have caused that sort of morphological change. It's possible that your disorientation after the incident was partially because your brain had literally reconstructed itself, and it didn't know how to think yet. It was still relearning what it meant to be a brain."

I lowered my hand from my temple, staring at her. I couldn't think of what to say.

On the couch, Sam put up his hand and said, "Wait, do cuckoos not get doctor-patient privilege? Because none of this sounds like stuff you should be telling us."

"None of this sounds like stuff you should *know*," I said. "I didn't know any of this. Why do you get to know things about me that I don't know?" The injustice of it burned brighter than I would have thought possible.

"Mom was scared," said Evie. "I don't think you understand how terrifying it was when you first went down. We didn't have another telepath we could ask to look at your actual thoughts, but your vital signs were all over the map. Sometimes you'd have so much brain activity that it overloaded the machines. Other times, you'd have no brain activity at all. If you were human, you would have been declared brain dead several times, because you *were*. It was like your brain was shutting down by stages. So yes, she talked to me, and maybe she told me some things you'd rather she hadn't mentioned, but I'm not going to feel bad about that. I refuse to feel bad about that. My *sister* was *dying*."

"Why didn't she tell *me*, then? I was the one who was hurt!"

"Because she didn't want to worry you."

I turned.

Artie looked at me, fear and concern and quiet resignation coloring his every thought. *Guess we only got to do that once,* he thought, clearly enough for me to hear it, and said, "I wouldn't have told you, if I'd known. I was scared, too. I thought . . . I didn't know any of this, and I wouldn't have told you, because what if it had been the last straw? What if you'd decided not to try getting better because you heard that from me? I would have kept it a secret until I was dead to make sure it didn't hurt you."

"Artie . . ." I reached for him, and hesitated, not sure what I was supposed to do next.

His fear dimmed, replaced by wariness. "It's okay. I know you don't want us to treat you like you're broken. You're not broken. You're just Sarah."

"Always have been," I said, and finished reaching for him, wrapping my fingers solidly around his before looking back to Evie. "I wish you'd told me."

"I'm sorry," she said.

"I know," I said.

"Given the pictures we have of what happened to your brain after your injury, and what happened to this cuckoo's brain around her time of death, we think she may have killed herself in the process of planting that trap in Artie's subconscious," said Kevin. "Her brain started to do what yours did, and then it, well, failed. It couldn't expand again after it contracted."

I stared at him. "Did my biology have to get weirder?"

"We're pretty sure you evolved from insects," said Annie. "There are lots of insects that metamorphize during their lives. Maybe the brain thing is like that. It's a physiological change triggered by some outside factor, and it's perfectly normal, and she just couldn't cut it."

"Not helping," I said.

"Why does she have a rack like that if she used to be a bug?" asked Sam.

Annie hit him in the arm, her amusement coloring the air around the pair of them like sunlight.

"This is all really interesting, but what does it have to do with me?" I asked.

"Sarah . . ." Evie sighed. "Do you have any idea why this cuckoo would have been willing to risk her life for the sake of hurting you?"

I didn't. Not only did I not know, but I wasn't sure I wanted to. "She's dead," I said. "Does it matter?"

Kevin and Evie exchanged a look.

"I hope not," Evie finally said. "I really, really do."

"Come on, nerd," shouted Elsie, gesturing for Artie to follow her down the driveway. "You can text her like the sad geek you've always been."

"I hate you," Artie called back, conversationally. "I hate you like I have hated nothing else in my life. My hatred is the sun, and you are the fields which it will burn."

"Love you, see you in a second," chirped Elsie. She waved to me. "Later, Sarah. See you in the morning."

"Bye, Elsie," I called, before turning my attention back to Artie. "Um. So."

"Yeah," he said. "So."

"Are we—?"

"I don't know." He glanced at me, thoughts tinged with hope. *Are we?*

"We could be. I mean, if you wanted to. I mean . . ." I took a deep breath and stopped talking. *I mean, I want to. I've wanted to for a long time.*

He blinked. *Why aren't you talking out loud?*

Because Evie's right inside, and she's listening to everything we say. She and Kevin were waiting by the front door for me to come back. They'd been willing to give me a little bit of privacy while I said goodbye to Artie and Elsie, but that was about all.

Ted and Jane were still in the barn, and probably would be for the rest of the night. There's nothing like a cryptozoologist when there's something to be taken apart. It's basically Christmas morning for them, and when they have the opportunity to wallow in it, they *really* wallow. Evie and Kevin would be joining them once they were sure I was safely in for the night. I could hear Kevin thinking distantly of all the tests he wanted to run on the dead cuckoo's tissues, now that they were reasonably sure she'd died of something I couldn't catch.

Oh, thought Artie. Then: *Kissing was nice. I liked kissing. Did you . . . I mean, can we do more of that? If you liked it?*

I liked it a lot. I'd like to do more of it. Maybe not with our family watching, though. That's a little bit much.

Yeah, thought Artie, with chagrin.

Elsie had reached her car. She leaned on the horn, sending it blasting through the night. I laughed before I could catch myself.

"Okay, you win," I said. "Text me when you get home, Artie?"

"I'll text you from the road," he said, and leaned over to plant a glancing kiss on the corner of my mouth. The contact was brief, but long enough for me to feel his thoughts brush against mine, warm and familiar and suffused with a lemony brightness that I was coming to accept, finally, as love.

He loved me. Artie loved me. Artie loved me, and Artie *had* loved me for a long time, maybe as long as I'd loved him. We'd just been too stubborn and too stupid and too scared to tell each other.

Artie walked down the driveway and got into the car with Elsie. She pulled out, waving through the window to me, and then they were gone, heading for the gate, their headlights a bright spot against the darkness.

How was it still so dark? It felt like so much time had passed since my arrival in Oregon that it should be near morning, but the moon was still high and not even the glimmer of false dawn could be seen on the horizon. I watched until their lights faded out of view, and then I turned and went inside.

Evie pounced immediately. "Well?" she asked, thoughts going so bubbly with excitement that they were like sipping champagne. "Did the two of you finally decide to sit down for a real, adult conversation?"

"You mean after everyone in this family spent forever not so subtly trying to get us to hook up?" I demanded. "You're all so inappropriate. We're younger than you. I'm telling Mom."

"Yes, *please* tell our mother," said Evie. "She won't believe it from me, and she's been in despair thinking the two of you would never figure things out and you'd be pining in your room forever."

"Evie!" I squawked.

"Okay, fine. Your room, various coffee shops, and the local college math department. Romance isn't the end-all, be-all of existence, and you don't need it to be happy, but when you're talking about someone as bound and determined to see herself as a monster as you are, it's just nice to see you putting yourself out there." Evie pointed to her mouth. "I know you can't see this, but I'm smiling. I'm happy for you, sweetheart, I really am."

I folded my arms. "I never said we had 'an adult conversation,' as you so horrifyingly put it."

"You didn't have to," she said. "You're glowing." She reached out and grasped my arms, long enough for me to feel the joy and relief flowing through her, before letting me go and stepping back. "Kevin and I need to head out to the barn to help Ted and Jane with the dissection and preserving the samples. I don't think you want to come out there, but if you need anything . . ."

"I'll call." I tapped my temple with one finger.

She nodded, relief palpable in the air. "Okay, sweetheart. I'll see you soon."

I stayed by the door, watching as she walked away,

before turning and heading through the kitchen to the living room.

Annie and Sam were gone. James was still seated on the couch. I offered him a nod as I went to pick up my backpack from where it had been dropped by the entertainment center.

"It's James," he said.

"I know."

"I thought you didn't see faces." He sat up a little straighter, turning toward me. "Was that not . . . ?"

"I don't see faces the way humans see faces," I said. "That doesn't mean I can't tell people apart once I get to know them a little. You're tall and pale and you have floppy hair and you don't have a tail. Sam has a tail. Which means you have to be James." I sat down at the dining room table, unzipping my backpack. "Also you have a very distinctive accent. Where are you from?"

"Maine," he said. "You?"

"Ohio, mostly." My laptop was still shrouded by the layer of clothing I'd packed it in. I pulled it out gingerly, relieved when nothing rattled or fell to the floor. Maybe it was okay despite the beating I had given it. "My parents live there, and I sort of bounced back and forth between their place and here in Oregon when I was a kid. Depending on what was going on and how much work Mom had on her plate."

"What does she do?"

"She's an accountant. Cuckoos are good at math." The screen wasn't cracked, and all the keys on my keyboard were still firmly in place. I relaxed a little. "So when tax time rolled around, she'd bundle me onto a plane or a train or the local carnival convoy and ship me off to stay with my cousins. We all grew up together."

"I see."

I glanced over my shoulder at James as I pressed the power button. "I know we can be a lot, and I'm a weird new variable. It's nice to meet you."

"I think 'a lot' may be the most charitable description of this family," said James, with a dour chuckle. "When Annie informed me that I was being adopted, I thought she was being fanciful. And then she got me back here, and I found myself with a bedroom, a space on the chore chart, and an offer of a new identity if I wanted to actually *become* a Price, rather than carrying my father's name around with me all the time. I'm still mulling that last one over. It's tempting."

"Family is always tempting," I agreed. My laptop screen bloomed to beautiful electric life, finishing its bootup cycle flawlessly. I relaxed further. "So you're a sorcerer, too, huh? That's fun. Do you and Annie set stuff on fire together?"

"I'm better at freezing things."

I cocked my head. "Freezing them as in making them stop moving, or freezing them as in making them cold?"

"To be fair, I've discovered that when I make things cold enough, they usually stop moving." James wiggled his fingers at me. "I can make things very cold, very quickly. Annie says I'm a menace. Annie set her own hair on fire last week, entirely by accident."

"Annie was setting pit-traps for her siblings when she was six; Annie doesn't get to talk," I said.

James laughed, apparently surprised. "I'll be honest: you're nothing like I expected you to be."

"You had expectations?" It was weird to think he already knew about me, when I'd never heard a word about him. I wanted to ask him to take his anti-telepathy charm off, to make this conversation slightly more normal for me. I needed to know what he was feeling, and to hear the wisps of thought that would reach me even without physical contact. Instead, I tucked my hands into my lap, where I wouldn't be so much as tempted to reach for his protection.

James was too new and too unaccustomed to cuckoos and most of all, too not a Price. He didn't have

Fran's immunity. I would rewire his brain without meaning to, and he'd be the brother I'd never wanted inside of the evening. That wouldn't be fair to him, or to Annie, who had actually gone to the trouble of adopting him and bringing him home.

"They told me you were this amazing mathematician, and a little shy, and totally in love with your cousin Artie—which, to be fair, seems to have been true, so I assume the rest is also pretty accurate," said James. "Annie said you weren't human, but she didn't go into a lot of detail, not the way she did tonight. I'm assuming she didn't want to prejudice me against you."

"We've had problems with that before," I said. "Mom says that when Kevin and Evie got married, Grandma Alice actually tried to break up the wedding. I don't mean 'disrupt'—although she did that, too—I mean *break*. She didn't like cuckoos, which is understandable. We're hard to like." She still didn't like most cuckoos or trust them as far as she could throw them. As a species, we're dangerous.

The last few hours had been a perfect demonstration of that. I shivered at the thought of how close Artie had come to slipping into an actual coma. We weren't medically set up for that, and there weren't any cryptid-friendly hospitals within a day's drive. He could have died because of what that cuckoo had done to his brain.

And what about what *this* cuckoo had done to his brain? No matter how much he liked to lean on Fran's vaunted resistance to our influence, I'd been inside his mindscape and making changes while he was unconscious and unable to fight me. Our cousins and his sister had been saying we were being stupid about each other for years, sure. He'd never been willing to make a move before. He'd never even implied that he might want to. Had I changed his mind in the process of freeing him from the other cuckoo's influence?

Was I just as bad as she was?

"Is something wrong?" asked James.

I blinked, shaking my head a little as I tried to focus on him. "What?"

"You zoned out for a moment there."

"Oh." I gave my head another small shake. "I'm sorry. It's been a really long day, and I'm not used to being around this many people anymore. I've been pretty isolated while I was recovering from my injuries."

"Which you got saving Antimony's older sister from the Covenant of St. George," said James.

I nodded.

"That was fairly brave of you, to hear the story. I'll admit, I always thought you were another magic-user, and that your spell had gone somehow wrong. 'Actual, literal superhero' never occurred to me."

"Oh, no," I said. "Annie and Verity are way better superheroes than I am. They actually work for what they can do. When we were kids, Verity was never around, because she was always going to another dance lesson. And Annie spent half her time on the balance beam or the trapeze rig. I'm a freak of nature. They're amazing."

"Telepathy is fairly amazing, too," said James.

"Not when the rest of the world isn't telepathic." I looked at my computer screen. It wasn't connected to the house Wi-Fi, which was sort of a relief. If Artie had allowed them to stick with the same password for five years, I would have been forced to yell at him. A lot. "No one thinks about what they're thinking. The number of people who've spent hours being friendly and helpful and kind to my face, all while wondering what I'd look like naked, is sort of genuinely horrifying. Do you have the new Wi-Fi password?"

"It's on the fridge," said James.

He seemed to take my request as a cue that the conversation was over; by the time I'd walked to the fridge, found the paper he was talking about, returned to my computer, and figured out the necessary transcription key to find the actual password, he was once again deep in his book. Honestly, it was a bit of a relief. He seemed nice enough, and Annie usually had good taste in people, but I needed some peace before I went up to bed and cut myself off from the world again.

With no one more specific to focus on, my mind relaxed and reached out, locating and identifying my family members one by one. Annie was upstairs, her thoughts preoccupied with a fiercely immediate physicality that told me where Sam was. Evie, Kevin, Ted, and Jane were all out in the barn, focused on their work. The mice were like glitter in the walls, bright and constant and ever-moving, too small and quick for me to really focus on them.

I could. They had minds like anything else, and if it has a mind, I can read it. But minds that small take work, and I wasn't in the mood for work. I was in the mood for letting myself go, sinking deeper and deeper into the comforting lull of answering email and looking at pictures of kittens and basking in the quiet glow of the thoughts around me, letting them wrap around me like a blanket.

At some point, James got up and left the room. It didn't change the noise around me. Anti-telepathy charms are dangerous that way. When you evolve to depend on a sense, whether it's as basic as touch or as esoteric as telepathy, removing it from the equation can unbalance and upset things.

I pulled up a math game, one where I had to merge squares to form larger and larger numbers, chasing a distant, golden goal. The tension slipped out of my shoulders as I focused on the screen. I'd done it. I'd made it to Oregon without getting hurt; I'd defeated the cuckoo who wanted to chase me out of her territory; I'd saved Artie. It was sad that the cuckoo had died, but not sad enough for me to grieve for her. She'd made her choices. She didn't deserve and probably wouldn't want my pity.

The numbers on my screen shifted and increased, one flowing into the next. It was a dance of simple addition, and it was so soothing. I relaxed further, watching the numbers dance. It was going to be okay. The cuckoo in the woods had been a threat and she wasn't anymore. I had my family around me. I was safe.

My computer beeped, telling me I had an email. I switched tabs. Maybe it was Artie. Maybe he'd realized that he didn't want to kiss me again; now that he was far enough away, any influence I'd been exerting over him would be fading into nothingness, leaving him free to make his own decisions. If he decided he didn't really want to be with me, it would sting. But if it was the truth, that would also be a good thing. I didn't want to make him love me with a lie. I wanted him to love me because I was worth loving.

The email wasn't from Artie. I didn't recognize the sender's name, and the subject header—"Can you give me a second? I just want to talk"—didn't exactly look like spam. There were no attachments. As long as I didn't click any links, I'd be safe. I still frowned as I opened the message.

If you want your family to be left to their own devices, you'll come outside now. I'll know if you try to tell anyone, through any means you have available to you—and that includes telepathy.

Do us both a favor, Sarah. Don't try to find a way out of this. You know it's only what you deserve.

P.S.: Her name was Amelia.

I stared at the screen in silent horror for a long moment before I turned and looked toward the door.

Someone was out there waiting for me. Someone had been able to come close enough to home to threaten my family.

The danger wasn't over yet.

Eleven

$$\pi_2(n) \sim 2C_2 \frac{n}{(\ln n)^2} \sim 2C_2 \int_2^n \frac{dt}{(\ln t)^2}$$

"Never go anywhere unprepared, unarmed,
or unaccompanied. The difference between success and suicide is often a matter
of prior planning."

—Evelyn Baker

*Getting ready to leave the living room, wondering if
stupid things are any less stupid when you know
that they're a really bad idea*

MY MIND WHIRLED AS I tried to think through the
implications of the email. It was a threat, absolutely:
someone who just wanted to sell me Girl Scout cookies
wouldn't have told me not to ask for help. I didn't know
how a stranger could have made it past the gate, but there
are always ways, for someone determined enough.

They'd told me not to call for help, not even telepathically. I'd been careful, though; there was no way
my system had picked up a virus from the email, not
with all the firewalls and barriers I had in place. I could
send Annie an email, and—

A chat window appeared at the bottom of my email
client. Don't even think about it.

My gut twisted. Who are you?

The person you're about to come outside to see.
Don't try to send an email, Sarah. I'll know. Get up
and walk away. Don't make a fuss. Do it now. Or else.

Or else what?

Or else there will be consequences.

If I'd had a heart, that last word would have been enough to make it seize in my chest. "Consequences." That wasn't the word of someone who was playing around or making idle threats. That was the word of someone who was willing to do serious damage to get what they wanted.

My parents raised me to know my own worth and value myself as an individual. But nothing—*nothing*—would make me more important than the rest of my family. I couldn't let it. Part of what separates me from the other cuckoos is knowing, really knowing, that other people matter. An ordinary cuckoo couldn't be lured outside by a word like "consequences." I . . .

I had to go.

Carefully, I stood, leaving my computer where it was. Annie would know something was wrong when she came down and saw it sitting there unattended. I don't like other people using my things. I never leave them out in the open if I have any other choice. She'd notice. She had to notice. Someone would notice.

Someone would notice I was gone.

I walked slowly toward the kitchen, and through it to the front door. The temperature outside had dropped even further, becoming just shy of freezing. I could feel it, but it didn't affect me the way it did the true mammals. Wherever we came from, it was a much colder place.

I paused when I reached the edge of the porch, mentally reaching out into the yard, looking for any mind that didn't belong there. I found him near the fence, a silent, unremarkable presence that had somehow managed to go unnoticed until I started looking. This was bad. This was very, very bad. Awareness of his presence came with awareness of the static that had been growing in the back of my mind, lighter and more subtle than I expected it to be, a fizzing, bubbling proof of presence.

I resumed walking. Every step took me closer to that unknown mind. It came further and further into clarity, resolving from a presence to a person to a cuckoo. There's a certain sharpness to a cuckoo's thoughts, like biting into a strawberry and suddenly discovering that it's actually a lime. They tingle and fizz and even burn.

These thoughts didn't quite burn. They were sharp, yes, curling in on themselves like the fronds of a fern, protecting themselves from being read. I could see their superficial lines. Nothing more. They were too deeply rooted in the man they belonged to, and they didn't want to let their secrets out.

I walked silently toward him, wishing my inhuman capabilities had come with some good, old-fashioned night vision. Part of the question was answered when I reached the fence: the man who'd emailed me wasn't inside the boundaries. He hadn't managed to get past the gate. Instead, he was standing at the very edge of the trees, a pale blur in the darkness, lit by the glow from his cellphone screen. He glanced up, raised one finger to signal me to silence, and returned his attention to the phone, finishing whatever message he'd been preparing to send.

"You know, it's rude to demand someone come outside and then ignore them," I said.

Don't speak. His words were clumsy, distorted, like he was pushing them through a wall of water. *They might hear you if you speak.*

Who are *you?* I demanded.

His head snapped up, eyes glowing white. I resisted the urge to take a step back. I'd known he was a cuckoo, known he had to be a cuckoo, but knowing and seeing are different things.

Like the female of our species, male cuckoos all look essentially alike, pale-skinned, dark-haired, blue-eyed. We were designed by the same evolutionary forces, intended to survive the same environment. To someone whose brain was designed to process the information, his face would look enough like mine that he could have been my brother, and dissimilar enough that if we'd held hands and walked down the center of a mall together, no one would have looked twice. Oh, the ones who looked once might think we were a little narcissistic for dating someone so similar, but they wouldn't jump straight to a bad conclusion.

Two cuckoos in the same place *is* a bad conclusion, almost always.

He was wearing jeans and a dark sweater, helping him blend into the trees. Amusement colored his distorted tone as he replied, *You can call me Mark. You want to come over here and hold my hand? This would be easier if you were touching me.*

I'm not touching you. The thought was revolting. *How are you here?*

You really don't know anything, do you? It's amazing. It's like finding a diamond in the middle of a chum bucket. You have to wipe off all the gore before it can shine.

I narrowed my eyes. A faint wind rose around me, fluttering my hair. *I know enough to know I want you gone.*

Mark made a small scoffing sound. It was the first audible noise he'd made since my arrival. *It's cliché, I know, but make me.*

I couldn't. He knew it, and I knew it, and so we were at an impasse. Or maybe not. "I don't have to make you," I said aloud, enjoying the way he tensed at the sound of my voice. "All I have to do is call my family."

"Funny," he said, his own voice pitched low and tight to keep it from carrying across the grounds. "I was under the impression that you cared about them."

That gave me pause. Narrowing my eyes further, I shot a sharp thought at him. *You touch them and you die.*

"Oh, now you'll talk to me like a civilized person?

You've been living among the humans for too long, Sarah. What went wrong inside that pretty little head of yours? You should have entered your second instar when you reached puberty, and you didn't. You held it off for *years*, and look at you now. Frightened. Pathetic. *Moral*." He sounded genuinely disgusted by the last word, practically spitting it at my feet. "How did you delay your metamorphosis?"

"What's an instar?"

His eyes widened. "This is worse than I thought. Why in the—it doesn't matter. It isn't my problem, I'm just the retrieval guy. Here's what you're going to do. You're going to walk to the gate, and you're going to let yourself out. You're going to come with me. No alarms, no attracting attention to yourself, no funny business. And then we're going to leave."

"Why the hell would I do that?"

"Because if you don't, then you'd better be prepared for a siege." He leaned forward. "The blood of Kairos isn't enough to protect these people from us. We'll hem them in, pin them down, and have them, one by one—and that's just the ones within these walls. We know where the Lilu live. Their defenses aren't as good as they ought to be. They'll be dead by morning, all of them, and it will be your fault, Sarah. You'll finally have done what a good little second-instar cuckoo ought to do and killed the family that raised you. Is that what you want?"

He wasn't making any effort to shield his thoughts or emotions from me. Calm conviction radiated around him, colored with the absolute serenity of truth. He wasn't lying. He wasn't trying to deceive. He genuinely believed every word he was saying.

"You can't . . ." I began. Words failed me, so I continued in silence, *You can't. They're* Prices. *They've beaten cuckoos before. They've beaten everything.*

"Three of them are Prices," said Mark. "Two of them married in. The Lilu and the one who thinks of herself as your sister—and that's disgusting, by the way, do you always let your pets have that much power over you? It's vile. They're not Prices, not genetically. The boys aren't Prices either. The fūri might be a problem. He could probably hurt a few of us before we shut him down. The sorcerer is less than half-trained, and he *wants*. He wants so badly that we know everything we need to know. We can break him. We can break them all. It's your choice, Sarah. Come quietly, come now, and we leave them alone. Sound the alarm, fight us, and we take them down before we take you anyway. The end result is the same."

He was utterly sincere. I couldn't see his thoughts well enough to know how many cuckoos he had with him, but I got the impression of at least five—a larger swarm than anyone had ever documented. Cuckoos usually work together only at mating time, and then only for as long as it takes the child to be conceived, carried, delivered, and deposited with an unwitting host family. Six cuckoos in one place wasn't just dangerous: it was a natural disaster.

"Seven," he said.

I snapped my head up, staring at him. "You're starting a countdown now? Don't those usually begin with 'ten'?"

"Not a countdown," he said. "A clarification. There are seven of us. You're a cuckoo, too."

The cuckoo choice would be to go back inside and sound the alarm. I would be safe. I would be protected. I would be selfish. I'd be putting my entire family at risk. I looked at the other cuckoo, who looked politely back. He somehow managed to look like he was focusing on my face, the lines and angles of it, as if he could actually see it like a human would. It was a good trick.

I took a slow breath. My whole body ached with the stress of the moment, and with the knowledge of what I was about to do.

"If I come with you, you stay the hell away from

them," I said. "You don't come back and start making trouble as soon as my back is turned."

Amusement radiated through his thoughts, warm as morning sunlight. "How are you going to hold me to that?"

"I don't know. But I am. If you ever come anywhere near here again, I will kill you. Maybe only you. Maybe the rest of the cuckoos get away. Maybe you kill me in the process. Doesn't matter. It means there's one less cuckoo on your side, and that shifts the numbers in a way that I can live with."

"Two less," he said.

I frowned. "What?"

"You said there would be one less cuckoo on my side. There would be two less. I *would* kill you, princess. It might be the last thing I ever did, but I'd do it."

"I'm not on your side."

"You will be." He cocked his head, like he was listening. I didn't hear anything. He was the only cuckoo close enough for me to detect. He must have been playing relay with someone who was in his range but not in mine.

That didn't necessarily mean he was stronger than me. There are plenty of things a cuckoo can do—plenty of things I knew how to do—to increase their range where a specific person was concerned. Maybe he'd been willing to stay in contact with another cuckoo long enough to become attuned to them. It was strange. A whole pack of cuckoos coming for me was even stranger.

"Fine," he said finally, eyes flashing white. "We give you our word that no one will come back here to interfere with your family. We can't promise they'll be spared if they track us down. Take it or leave it, because we've already been out here too long."

They wouldn't thank me for this. Family is supposed to be the most important thing in our world, and by walking away, I was as good as saying that my family couldn't protect me. The thing was, they *couldn't* protect me. Not against this. Not against an enemy that could get inside their heads. Anti-telepathy charms are the solution against one cuckoo, acting alone or trying to defend their territory. They wouldn't hold the line against a group of them. They would just make the enemy harder to see coming.

My family had protected me after New York. It was my turn to protect them. I looked the cuckoo in the eye and nodded, once, before I turned and started for the door next to the gate.

Tucking the family compound away in the forest had been a good way to control traffic in and out. It hadn't eliminated the need for things like getting the hell away from your family, hence the occasional doors set into the fence. Without them, my cousins—Verity especially—would have been forever setting off the motion detectors along the top as they climbed their way to freedom. Sure, freedom looked like an evergreen forest in the middle of nowhere, but it was still freedom.

Or it had been. I keyed in the gate code, which I'd lifted from Kevin's mind without even thinking about it, and stepped out of the supposed safety of the yard into the dangerous darkness of the woods. It didn't feel like freedom anymore. It felt like walking into a trap.

The cuckoo nodded approvingly. "Come with me," he said, then turned and led me deeper into the trees.

Lacking any real choice, I followed.

We walked until the compound lights dwindled to nothing behind us. Only then did Mark produce a flashlight and click it on, directing its watery beam toward the ground.

"Sorry to make you come all this way, but, well, we both know things would have gotten really ugly back there if we'd parked any closer," he said. He sounded almost jovial, like we were old friends going for a walk, and not virtual strangers in the middle of an abduction. "We'll be at the RV soon."

"An RV?" I couldn't quite keep the disbelief out of my tone. "You brought an *RV*?"

"Had to," he said. "We don't squish well, not even when we have a good reason to be working together. It's a really nice one, too. Modern. There's even a bathroom it's not physically painful to use. Amelia and David took a few recreational trips back there while the bedroom was occupied. He's pretty mad at you, by the way."

"For what?" I asked. "All I did was hit her with my backpack."

"I didn't say it was logical, just that it was there," said Mark. "Amelia saw you first. That meant she got the duty and the honor of triggering your next metamorphosis. Unfortunately, she couldn't exactly survive something like that. She died like she lived. Pissed off at the entire world and willing to do whatever she could to destroy it. Honestly, I think David's mostly angry because he knows that if their positions had been reversed, Amelia would be perfectly happy to have him gone, if it meant you were progressing to your next instar."

I stopped walking. Mark continued for a few more feet before turning to look at me, projecting polite confusion.

"We're not there yet," he said. "Like I said, we have to keep walking."

"You keep using this word, 'instar,'" I said. "What the hell does it *mean*?"

"Can't you take the definition from me?" he asked. "You should be able to reach out and snatch it from my mind. If you can't, that's not my problem."

"That's not how I do things," I said.

"That's not how *humans* do things," he said. "You,

though, Sarah Zellaby? That's exactly how you do things. You act like you have some moral high ground because you only hunt people you've decided somehow deserve it, but you're just like the rest of us. You take. You take, and you take, and you take, and you don't give anything back. You can't help yourself. If you could, you'd be useless to us. You want to know what an instar is? *Take* it."

I stared at him, feeling my eyes burn as they went white. How dare he talk to me like that, like I was doing something wrong by trying to be careful. Even more, how *dare* he remind me of what I already knew and wanted to forget about. There were no questions left in my mind, only anger, and the brush of the wind against my cheeks as I focused on him, trying to punch my way through his mental barriers and claim what I needed to know.

His walls were strong. Not as strong as mine, maybe, and not as strong as an anti-telepathy charm, but strong enough that I couldn't smash through them the way I'd wanted to. I pictured my thoughts as hands, grabbing chunks out of his defenses and pulling them free. They came back as quickly as I could discard them. I made a frustrated noise.

"Okay, you can stop now." He sounded winded. "That really hurts, you know."

I stopped grabbing for his mind. "How can it hurt? I'm not touching you."

"You're not touching me where anyone can see it, but you're definitely touching me," he said, rubbing his temple and wincing. "Wow, you're strong. I'll give you this much, princess: you're almost as impressive as I hoped you'd be. Now come on."

"I still don't know what an instar is." My voice came out plaintive and tight, like a child who expected to be smacked. My gut was roiling. My whole life, I've tried not to hurt anyone. Now I couldn't even bring myself to hurt another cuckoo. Instead, I was following him through the forest, so close to willingly as to make no real difference.

I paused. I was following him through the forest. No other cuckoos had appeared. If I turned and ran back to the compound now—

"Please don't even think it," he said wearily. "I wasn't lying about my backup. They may not be right on top of your family's property, but they're close enough, and you'd never make it. This is the kindest way of doing things."

"It doesn't feel very kind to me," I said.

"That's because you're the prize," he said. "The prize is, well, prized. It's desired and valued and it doesn't get to have opinions of its own. Opinions are for soldiers and flunkies. You get to sit on a shelf and look shiny until it's time for you to go to work."

"What are you talking about?"

"You'll see," he said, and started walking again, taking our only light with him.

The woods were so dense and dark around us that I wasn't sure I could *find* the compound on my own. We'd gone far enough into the trees that even the minds of the family members I was attuned to had faded into true silence—not just the static of a present but inactive connection. Maybe I'd been complicit in my own kidnapping, but at this point, I was committed.

Something rustled in the bushes behind me, something without enough of a mind for me to latch onto. I shuddered and chased after Mark and the safety of his flashlight.

"Thought so," he said, once I drew up level with him. "Like I said, we're almost there."

"Why aren't you answering my questions?" I asked.

"Prizes don't get to ask questions," he said.

"I'm not a prize."

"Yeah, you are, princess. Come to terms with that sooner rather than later, if you can. This will be a lot easier for you if you do." He stepped over a fallen log and paused to offer me his hand. "Careful. The footing's treacherous here."

I stared at his hand for a split second before grasping it and using it for leverage as I both stepped over the log and drove myself deep into his mind, past the layers of mental defenses, past the walls whose construction I paused long enough to both admire and study. He knew some tricks I didn't. I wanted them. I wanted everything.

He wanted me to take? Well, he was going to get everything he wanted, and he was going to get it *now*.

The word "instar" was floating near the surface of his mind, almost like he'd been waiting for me to come and get it. That was silly—tell a person not to think about elephants and they won't be able to think about anything else—but I still shrieked silent triumph as I seized hold of it and drew it into my own vocabulary.

Instar: a developmental stage of insects. There was more wrapped up in the definition, science and analysis and images of butterflies bursting out of cocoons, ants breaking out of their exoskeletons, but the core of it didn't waver, didn't change. I dropped Mark's hand. He staggered back, eyes wide and glinting white as he stared at me with new, slightly frightened respect.

"Skin contact," I snarled. "Shouldn't have given it to me." His thoughts were clearer now. They almost formed words even without him trying to project them. "Think next time."

"There's not going to be a next time," he said. "There should have never even been a first time."

"You really want to tell me you've never touched anyone before in your life?"

"I've touched plenty of people," he said. "I've never touched anyone like you."

"Because I've reached my third instar," I said.

He turned his face away.

"Don't make me go into your thoughts again. Neither of us is going to enjoy it." I made a motion like I was going to grab his hand. He flinched. "You don't want that? Then talk."

"You have no idea what you're messing with, Sarah," Mark said. He took a step backward, away from me, out of easy reach. That didn't matter. Skin is easy. When all I need is skin, I can do anything. "This is so much bigger than either one of us. You need to stop."

"You're kidnapping me, taking through the woods to hand me over to a bunch of strangers, and taunting me with all the things I don't know, and *I'm* the one who needs to stop?" I narrowed my eyes. I could see them reflected in Mark's irises, little glints of light that meant my abilities were still on high-alert and informing everything about me. "I think you got your pronouns wrong."

"You'll understand soon," he said, a note of genuine pleading in his voice. "Please. We're almost there."

I glared at him for a moment before I pulled myself back, taking a deep breath. We were too deep in the woods for me to make it to the compound on my own, and I needed to know why this was all happening. Whatever the fourth instar was, it was enough to frighten Mark. Maybe it would be enough to frighten the rest of them. I could resolve this without endangering the rest of my family. I could handle it. Whatever this was, I could handle it.

"All right," I said, and let him lead me into the dark.

Twelve

$$\pi_2(n) \sim 2C_2 \frac{n}{(\ln n)^2} \sim 2C_2 \int_2^n \frac{dt}{(\ln t)^2}$$

"Didn't think I'd ever have a family. Didn't think I'd ever want one. It's funny, how much a person can change without even noticing what's happening."

—Frances Brown

A logging road deep in the Oregon woods, isolated from everyone but the enemy, about to make a terrible mistake

THE RV LOOKED PERFECTLY normal, if a little swankier than most people in this neck of the woods could afford. All the lights were on, even the headlights, turning the slice of road and grassy shoulder around it buttery-yellow against the darkness of the rest of the woods. Mark huffed a sigh, radiating relief, and started walking faster. I reached for him.

"Please don't," he said. "I don't want you in my head again."

"You're the one who kidnapped me," I said. "I'm not sure you get to make requests."

"I didn't kidnap you," he said. "I liberated you from your kidnappers." He looked over his shoulder at me, eyes glinting momentarily white. "I know there's a lot you don't understand yet, but you will. You're so close to understanding, and once you do . . . everything's going to change, for all of us. Come on."

He sped up again, pulling ahead of me, so that there was no possible way I could grab his hand. It was too late for me to change my mind. I followed.

The RV's side door opened as we approached, and two more cuckoos stepped out, their minds reaching for mine in a telepath's . . . not handshake, exactly, since that implied contact, something we were all dedicated to avoiding. It was more like a meeting between two wolves with no humans around to observe them. Our thoughts brushed by each other, taking stock, taking measure, and then moving quietly on. I caught nothing from them aside from caution and a sense of wary excitement, like they were waiting for me to do some uniquely exciting trick.

"David," said Mark. "Heloise."

"Out loud?" asked the one he'd called Heloise. "Like humans? Ugh. I knew the girl was provincial, but that's disgusting." She gave me a slow look up and down, pausing when she reached my hair. She sniffed. "Bangs. It has bangs. Mark, how dare you not tell me it had bangs. I might have chosen a different role."

"I hadn't seen her before she landed in Portland, any more than the rest of you had," said Mark, sounding unruffled. "You'll be thrilled to hear that she was hurt in the crash. There's a cut concealed under those bangs. A nice long one."

"How do you know that?" I asked.

"Your relatives should really wear telepathy blockers if they don't want people to wander in and take whatever it is they want to know," said Mark. "Honestly, if they're the best humanity has to offer, it's a wonder we didn't conquer this planet centuries ago."

"Too much work," said David. He looked at me, eyes glinting white as a wave of malice rolled off of him like approaching thunder. "You killed Amelia."

"I didn't kill anyone," I protested. I had never been around this many cuckoos in my life. The staticky hum of their presence was like white noise, making my head bubble and fizz. "I don't know any of you people, and I still don't know why I'm here."

Heloise approached us, walking a circle around me as she continued her inspection. "You're so innocent— and so domesticated. It makes me sick. We should never have allowed this to happen."

"I don't know you," I repeated. "I don't understand why you're so worried about me."

"You don't seem to know much," she said. "I'm not worried about *you*. I'm worried about the message it sends when we allow ourselves to be domesticated. We should have stolen you away years ago, before all this damage had been done. We could have hollowed you out ourselves. Kept you where no one would ever see. Where you wouldn't be able to do us any damage. David? I need your phone."

The other cuckoo pulled a phone out of his pocket and lobbed it toward Heloise. She caught it without looking and aimed it at my face, clicking several quick pictures. I blinked.

"What was that for?"

"Bangs," she said, and tossed the phone over her shoulder. David caught it and put it back in his pocket. "I can't cut my own hair, and I'll need to give the stylist something to work from. Mark? Get her inside."

"Why me?" he asked.

She looked at him, eyes glinting white as irritation sparked along the surface of her thoughts, bright and fierce and judgmental. "She's already touched you," she said. "The damage is done." Turning, she stalked back to the RV. David followed.

Mark looked at me. I could feel the regret rolling off him, although I couldn't tell whether he was sorry this had to happen, or sorry he was the one doing it to me. It didn't matter. He wasn't going to let me go, and he wasn't on my side.

"I'd really rather not get close enough to grab you," he said. "I don't suppose you could do me a favor and come quietly? You won't get anything else useful from me unless you rip my mind apart, and you're not ready for that yet. I don't want to be on your bad side once you are."

It was tempting to lie to him, or to refuse to go along with anything he wanted from me. I was too tired to push it that way. I needed this to be over. I needed to understand what they were trying to accomplish so I could break free and go home, back to my family, back to the people who would take care of me, who I could take care of in turn.

"Fine," I said, and flounced toward the RV.

The static white noise of the other cuckoos got stronger as I got closer. I faltered. Six cuckoos, not including myself; that was what I'd sensed from Mark back at the compound. Six cuckoos, and I was the only one who didn't belong to their hive.

Hive. The word came easily, naturally, like it had always been the right noun for this sort of situation. It was tied to "instar," somehow connected to the concept of insect metamorphosis, and so *right* that I couldn't even try to question it. A group of cuckoos was a swarm. A group of cuckoos who had put aside their natural distaste for sharing space and territory, who had decided they could work together for some reason, was a hive. I was walking into a hive.

The RV door was unlocked. I pushed it open and stepped through, into a space like nothing I had ever seen before.

David and Heloise were in the little kitchen area, David making some sort of hot mixed drink, Heloise leaning against the counter. A massively pregnant female cuckoo reclined on the window seat, rubbing her belly in small, concentric circles, her posture radiating discomfort and suspicion. Two more cuckoos were seated toward the back, both male, both watching me enter with glowing white eyes, their suspicion hanging heavy in the air.

Mark pushed through behind me, careful not to

touch me at all as he pulled the door closed behind himself. "I got her," he said.

"We can see that," said the pregnant cuckoo. She leveled a flat gaze on me, eyes sparking white as she reached out and brushed the fingers of her mind against my own. Her lip curled. I would have known it was disgust even if she hadn't been broadcasting the emotion loud and clear. "This is what we've been waiting for? Are you sure? Have you *looked* at her?"

"More closely than I wanted to," said Mark. "She took my hand for a second when I helped her over some debris—"

"Suck-up," said one of the men. The other snickered.

"—and she had half my brain on the table in front of her before I could let go," Mark continued, like he hadn't heard them. "She's a damn battering ram."

"That's what we need," said the woman. She focused on me again. Her next words were silent ones, less distorted than Mark's had been; while he'd sounded like he was talking underwater, she sounded like she was talking next to some piece of loud machinery, something that fought to steal every syllable away. *You're a fascinating experiment, Sarah Zellaby. I'd been hoping to have the chance to meet you.*

"How do you know my name?" I asked.

She rolled her eyes. *Have you adapted so completely to life among the humans that you've forgotten how to be a telepath?*

"No," I said. "Have you adapted so completely to life among the cuckoos that you've forgotten that it's rude to talk telepathically in public?"

"Who told you that?" she demanded. "Your petty so-called mother, denying you the pleasures she'll never experience? She's never even managed to enter her first instar, you know. Her kind are meant to be smothered in their cradles, not allowed to go around acting as if they're real people."

I felt a spike of discomfort from behind me. Mark didn't like the things she was saying, for some reason. That might be worth looking into later. I was going to need allies among the cuckoos if I was going to get out of here in one piece.

"You people keep using that word, 'instar,'" I said. "I know it means the space between metamorphosis, but I don't understand what you think it has to do with me. I've never spun a cocoon or cracked my exoskeleton. I've only ever been me."

"Those are activities for insects, and we're not insects; not anymore," said the woman. "I'll make it a trade. If you can say my name, I'll tell you what an instar is."

"I don't know your name."

"Telepath, remember?" She cocked her head, a gesture that was familiar enough to be upsetting. I did that same thing when I was annoyed. So did Mom. It was clearly a family trait; it was just that the family was bigger than I'd ever thought.

"Right." I narrowed my eyes and drove my thoughts forward, trying to break into her mind.

I bounced off her shields almost immediately. They were tightly woven, so interlocked and unstable that trying to slide past them was like trying to wrestle with the wind. Every time I grabbed for a weak spot, it reinforced itself, becoming twice as thick and three times as complicated. I breathed in, breathed out, and pulled back, "looking" at the shifting walls of thought and intention.

Math is the underpinning force of the universe. That's something people don't always understand when I try to explain it to them, and it's so basic—so primal and perfect—that I don't have the words to make it any clearer. How do you explain air to a bird, or water to a fish? There's no explaining things that simply *are*. That's how I feel about math. Math is everywhere. Math is everything. Even the seemingly effortless, uncomplicated things like walking and breathing and, yes, telepathy, they're all math.

The other cuckoo's mental shields were made of instinctive equations, so tightly knotted together that they seemed like a single continuous piece. They weren't, though. An equation that large would be clumsy, awkward . . . slow. Her shields were fast and adaptive because they were built like a living thing, with numbers in the place of single cells.

Where there's an equation, there's an answer. I cocked my head in imitation of her earlier gesture, picking at the wall until it all came into sudden, perfect focus. I wrapped the answer to her equations in a soft shell of my intentions and lobbed it at the shields.

They went down all at once, a cascade of falling defenses. The whole process had taken only a few seconds. Back in the real world, outside our minds, the other cuckoo gasped, hand clutching at her swollen belly. The last of the shields fell. I looked at her levelly.

"Your name is Ingrid," I said. "Now what the hell's an instar?"

"Get out of my head," she hissed.

I pulled back, enough that I was looking at her with my eyes more than with my mind, and said, "I met your conditions. I learned your name. It's your turn to answer my questions."

"She has you there," said Mark.

"He's on her side now," said Heloise, in a jeering tone. "They went for a long, romantic walk in the woods together, and now he's ready to switch to the winning team."

"He's already *on* the winning team," said one of the male cuckoos in the back. The other male cuckoo said nothing, only sat in sullen silence, his mental glare overflowing the RV until the air felt like it was too heavy to breathe.

I did my best to ignore the lot of them, focusing instead on Ingrid. "Tell me what I need to know," I insisted. "I know enough to know that I don't know enough. Unless you'd rather I went in and took it . . . ?"

"No," she said sharply, raising one hand in a warding gesture. The other hand remained clamped to her belly, cradling its precious contents. "You won't take anything. But I can show you, if you'll accept the knowledge. No forcing your way in. No digging for anything I haven't offered willingly. Do we have an arrangement?"

There was fear in her words, lending them a spicy brightness that hadn't been there before. I wanted to hear more of it, I realized; I wanted to hear her *beg*. That wasn't like me. That didn't change how much I wanted it.

Something was wrong. "Yes," I said, and swallowed, suddenly dry-mouthed. "But you have to promise me the same. No looking at things I'm not intentionally showing you. No digging around."

"The compact is sealed," she said, and her eyes flashed white, and I was falling.

The infant cuckoo was pulled, purple-gray and squalling, from its mother's womb. It kicked its tiny legs and thrashed its tiny arms until its father passed it into its mother's arms, allowing her to guide it to her breast, where it latched on and started sucking greedily. Unlike a human baby, it seemed to know immediately what to do and how to do it.

"We have no instincts left," said Ingrid. I turned my head, unsurprised to see her standing next to me. "We don't need them. Everything an infant cuckoo needs to know is passed down, parent to child, before birth. They're passive receivers in those days, unable to talk back, only able to learn." She caressed her own swollen belly with one hand. "They stay passive for a week,

maybe two, after birth. Long enough for us to be sure
they're whole and healthy before we pass them on. It's
not cruelty that makes us find better homes for our
children. It's mercy."

"My parents left me with human strangers," I said.
"They died."

"Yes, and that's very sad, but it had to happen," said
Ingrid. The little family in front of us jumped forward,
the man disappearing, the woman going from naked in
her bed to clothed and composed and walking calmly
up a driveway in a nice suburban neighborhood, a
swaddled baby in her arms. "Babies are larval, you see.
They're easily influenced, easily *changed*. We give
them everything we can before they're born, and then
we place them with hosts who won't be able to manipulate them. We protect them by allowing them to
incubate in peace. Larvae give off a sort of a . . . signal,
like those wireless fences people buy for their dogs. No
one can see that anything's wrong, but the dog won't
cross the invisible line. Well, adult cuckoos won't go
anywhere near an infant that's old enough to have
started radiating, not before they've reached their first
instar. Our children are safe from us. They claim and
keep territory just by existing."

"Are you going to abandon *your* baby?"

She looked at me like I was dim. I realized, numbly,
that I could read her expression perfectly. It was just
like being back in Artie's mindscape. Here, everything
was thought, and I could visualize it all without even
trying.

"Of course I am, you stupid girl," she said. "This
isn't my first, and it won't be my last, if I have anything
to say about it. I'm a wonderful mother, by the standards of our kind. I create them, I nurture them, I
birth them, and then I let them go. Can you swear to
me that you'd do half as well?"

"I never really thought about it," I admitted.

"Of course you didn't. You've been living with another species, living with another species' rules. We don't keep our children with us because we're *bad* for them. They'd never become their own people if we kept them. They'd grow into little mirrors of their parents, because we'd be inside their heads every hour of every day, keeping them from becoming anything else. We love them, so we leave them. We give them a *chance*."

I'd never considered the way cuckoos abandoned their offspring in quite that way. I twisted my fingers together, watching as the mother cuckoo rang the doorbell, smiled at the woman who answered, and stepped inside, out of view. Then I frowned.

"What about the families you leave the babies with? Do you give them a chance?"

"Why would we do that?" The scene shifted again, a discarded bicycle appearing on the lawn, a few bright stickers appearing in the window. The door banged open and a little girl ran out, pale-skinned and black-haired and identical to every other cuckoo child in the world. "There are so *many* of them. They're predators, and they've overbred their habitat to a degree that would be appalling in anything else. If every cuckoo in the world had a baby every year, we still wouldn't have a large enough population to threaten human superiority. Who died and gave them this entire planet? Oh, right. The dragons." Her laughter was high and bright and giddy, like she'd just made the best joke the world had ever known.

The little girl grabbed the bike and maneuvered it up onto its wheels. Ingrid sobered.

"She's larval," she said, indicating the girl. "She has perfect camouflage at this age. All her telepathy does, ever, is convince the people around her that she *belongs*. It doesn't revise them. It doesn't tell them 'this is your daughter.' It just makes it so that when she skins her knee, they see blood; when she goes to the pediatrician, the doctor finds a heartbeat. This is a normal part of our development. It's meant to last until the start of puberty. Trauma can trigger the first instar early. Do you remember when your first set of parents died?"

I swallowed, not looking at her. It was easier to focus on the child, who was bright and happy and fictional and uncomplicated. She was walking the bike toward the street, both hands on the handlebars.

"I don't remember them at all," I said quietly.

"No. I suppose you wouldn't, not after what that butcher did to your mind."

"Don't talk about my mother that way."

"You've had three mothers. The one who gave you away to save you, the one who died, and the one who stole you. I'll talk about the third any way I like. She had no right. She stole everything you had, and she made you thank her for it." Ingrid's anger was a stinging swarm of gnats, swirling through the thoughts that shaped the illusion around us. "Children are supposed to come to their first instar in their own time. They grow, they mature, and one day, the little egg inside them breaks, and they see the world for what it is."

The girl with the bike seemed to age five years in the blinking of an eye. She straightened, the suddenly too-small bicycle falling from her hands, and turned to look at the house with a thoughtful eye.

"That egg contains everything they need to know about being a cuckoo. It tells them what they are and where they came from. It tells them what's going to happen to them, how to survive it . . . how to adapt." The girl—the teen—walked back into the house, shutting the door behind her.

Someone screamed. A splash of blood hit the window. I flinched.

Ingrid was untroubled. "The entry into first instar can be a trifle violent, it's true, but it's a natural part of our development. The individual gets overwhelmed by the weight of the collective memory of a hundred generations, but not forever. They always resurface."

"It turns them evil," I said.

"It reminds them that they're predators, surrounded by predators who wouldn't thank them for pretending to belong," said Ingrid. "The average age for metamorphosis from larval to first instar is thirteen. Your morph was delayed. Severely. That *woman*—the one you call your mother—had no right to steal your future from you."

"She stole nothing," I said. "She made it so I could care about other people."

Ingrid turned to look at me, weary regret written clearly across her face. I was suddenly glad I couldn't normally read expressions the way humans did. It was exhausting, looking at people and knowing what they were thinking, even if I wasn't reaching out to read their minds. Telepathy was kinder.

"Who told you we don't care about other people?" she asked. "Yes, we care more about ourselves than we do about humans, but humans care more about humans than they do about anyone else. Why are the rules different for them? Because they have the numbers? Because that means they get to decide what's wrong and right? She took your past away. She reached into your head with bad tools, broken tools, and she sliced out everything that should have been yours."

Something about that seemed wrong. I fought the urge to take a nervous step backward, and said, "Mark said I was on my third instar. How is that possible, if I never had my first?"

"Oh, you had it. It just took years. It should have happened almost instantly and unlocked all the answers to your questions. Instead, it unspooled day by day, making its changes a little bit at a time. We get stronger after a morph. It changes the configuration of our minds. It makes them deeper, more complicated. We can *do* things after a morph that we couldn't do before."

I thought uneasily of the way my telepathy had strengthened as I got older, until what had been a trial when I was a child had become easy, even casual. Had I been going through an instar? If we'd been taking regular scans of my brain, what would we have found?

"Most of us go through metamorphosis into our first instar and then stop. First instar is necessary. It's what changes a larva into a worker. We're industrious. We keep ourselves busy. And we very rarely need second-instar soldiers to keep us safe. Second instar is a matter of necessity. Few of us survive the morph to reach it. Those who do find themselves substantially stronger and more versatile than a first-instar worker. You have no idea what you're capable of now, do you? That *woman*," and the venom in Ingrid's voice was startling, "stole your first instar from you, and she sliced your second up and spoon-fed it to you in little pieces, and now you're lost. You don't know how to be a proper cuckoo. You don't know how to be a proper soldier. But that's all right. You were never meant to be a soldier."

"What are you talking about?" I couldn't stop myself from replaying the conversation with Evie, where she'd explained what the doctors had seen on my MRI.

Ingrid saw it, too. She nodded solemnly, looking distantly pleased. "That was your second instar," she said. "The channels are deeper for you now than they were before. First instar is automatic. Second instar is triggered by the self. Third instar is triggered from the outside. Fourth instar is a myth and a destiny and a sacrifice, and you're going to do so amazingly well, my dear. You're going to make me so proud, and I'll name this little girl 'Sarah' in your honor. You're going to be magnificent."

"I don't want this." I took a step back, or tried to; we were inside Ingrid's mind, still, and she refused to let me move. "I just wanted you to explain things to me."

"I am," she said, and leaned forward, and kissed my

Thirteen

$$\pi_2(n) \sim 2C_2 \frac{n}{(\ln n)^2} \sim 2C_2 \int_2^n \frac{dt}{(\ln t)^2}$$

"No matter how much we learn, there's always something we don't know. A map labeled 'here be monsters' is better than one that reads 'we have no idea.'"

—Thomas Price

A private home in Portland, Oregon, down in the basement, waking up from a dead sleep, not quite screaming

I SAT UPRIGHT WITH a gasp, shoving my hand into my mouth to keep myself from screaming. Elsie would hear me—Elsie always heard me—and come stampeding down the stairs from her room to make sure I was okay. She took her duties as big sister and designated responsible person very seriously.

And of course, when she realized I'd just been having a nightmare, not anything more serious, she'd take her duties as mocker of little brothers and tormenter of the sleepy equally seriously. I didn't want her coming down. Not when my heart was hammering against my ribs like it wanted to break loose and run away, and not when my eyes were still heavy with exhaustion.

Sarah. I'd been dreaming about Sarah. That wasn't super weird—I was usually dreaming about Sarah, and sometimes they were good and sometimes they were nightmares, but since she'd been hurt, she'd had a starring role in almost every dream I had. I dreamt she'd never gone away and everything was fine, and I dreamt she'd come back and professed her love to me, and I dreamt she'd died in New York and that I'd never been able to even say goodbye to her, and I dreamt she hadn't died but hadn't woken up either, that she was going to sleep the rest of her life away on a machine in the basement of some cryptid hospital.

But Sarah was home now. Sarah had come back to us, come back to *me*, and she'd finally kissed me, she'd finally let me kiss her, and everything was going to be amazing. Like, really amazing, the kind of amazing I didn't deserve but had no intention of refusing. So why was I having nightmares *now*?

The dream was breaking apart in my memory. I remembered a little girl with a bicycle, and something called an "instar." It was weird. I didn't like it.

Shaking the fog away, I slipped out of bed and padded across the dark room to my computer. A wiggle of the mouse woke the screen. I pulled up my chat client first; no Sarah. Well, that made sense. It was almost two in the morning, and she'd just come from Ohio. She was probably asleep, safely behind the charms and wards worked into her bedroom walls, so the rest of us wouldn't wake her accidentally. That was sort of a relief. She didn't need to share my nightmares.

Being in love with—and admitting I was in love with—a telepath comes with its own list of unique complications. More so now that Sarah had recovered from her accident. She'd never been this sensitive before. When she'd kissed me, it had felt like I could see everything in her mind, and like she could see everything in mine, and that had been okay. That was the sort of worrying part. There were finally no barriers between us, and it didn't matter.

It was probably supposed to matter. I tried to picture having no boundaries between me and literally anyone else, and the idea was creepy and a little bit upsetting. I like people, but I also like privacy sometimes.

At least I knew it was just because I was totally into her, and not because she'd cuckoo-ed me the way she'd always been afraid she would. I couldn't whammy her into loving me—or lusting after me, I guess; my pheromones are way more oriented toward getting me laid than getting me cared for and respected—and she couldn't rewire me into accepting her. We really were perfect for each other.

"Elsie's never going to let me forget it, either," I muttered, and opened Wikipedia. When all else fails, ask the Internet.

Typing "instar" into the search box got me a page on insect metamorphosis, and a slow-growing sick feeling in my stomach. I'd sort of hoped it would be a made-up word, something from a comic book or an anime series or whatever. Instead, it meant the stages arthropods went through between molts. They would transform, enter an instar, and then stay there until they were finished growing and could molt again. Which was weird and kind of gross and it didn't make sense that I'd come up with it in a nightmare about Sarah.

(Not that bugs couldn't show up in dreams about Sarah. According to Mom, cuckoos are biologically more like really big wasps than they are like monkeys—hominids but not primates, in other words. So, yeah, there was probably an evolutionary stage way back in Sarah's family tree where she would have gone through molts. But I tried not to think about that too hard, because it was weird to dream about kissing a girl and think "the girl is secretly a giant wasp" in the same sentence.)

Still feeling a little awkward and out of sorts, I got up, grabbed a shirt from the floor that didn't have any visible stains on it, and pulled it over my head as I started up the stairs toward the kitchen. When all else fails, orange soda and toast. Even at two in the morning, orange soda and toast. They can cure many ills, and if they can't fix the problem, at least you won't be hungry and groggy anymore. Elsie likes caffeine, but I say sugar does basically the same thing, without the nasty crash at the other metabolic end.

Elsie was sitting in the kitchen when I got there, sharing a bowl of chicken noodle soup with several members of the family Aeslin colony. They offered me a somewhat dismissive cheer, their attention way more focused on mining her soup for chunks of chicken and celery—the former to eat, the latter to ritually place in the compost bin. Aeslin mice are weird.

"Hey," I said.

Elsie looked up, smiling wanly. "Hey, stupid brother," she said. "Couldn't sleep?"

"Bad dreams." I crossed to the fridge. "You?"

"Same. I don't remember what they were, just that they were bad." She gave her soup another stir, kicking more chunks to the surface. The mice cheered again, but softly. Mom has opinions about appropriate volume after midnight, and even the mice don't usually cross her. She's scary when she's angry. "Hey, Artie. You awake enough to play dictionary?"

A sudden wash of cold dread swept across my skin. I forced myself to open the fridge and take out a can of orange soda before I turned to face her, keeping my motions smooth and easy, like this was perfectly normal. Like I wasn't direly afraid I knew what she was about to ask me.

"Do you know what 'instar' means?"

Sometimes I hate being right. I walked over and sat down across from her at the table, deciding to skip my toast for now. Toast is for people who don't feel like they're about to throw up. "It's a biology thing. It means the growth stage insects go through between molts. It's metamorphic—they tend to change shapes and stuff—but I don't really understand it. Why?"

"Because it was in my dreams," she said, and gave me a worried look. "Artie, why was it in my dreams?"

"I don't know." I glanced at the clock above the stove. Less than five minutes had passed since I'd entered the kitchen. It was still too early to call anyone. Sarah was asleep. That was all. "It's a weird word."

"It's a weird word for you to know."

"I looked it up." I took a deep breath as I looked at her. "I wanted to know what it meant, since it was in my dreams, too."

Elsie's eyes widened slowly, until they were practically bulging in their sockets. She pushed back her seat, standing, and glanced to the mice. "The rest of the soup is yours," she said. "Please don't try to put the bowl in the sink. You know what happens."

The mice mumbled muted agreement. They could get the cutlery to the sink—could even get it into the dishwasher if they were feeling motivated—but when they tried to move plates or bowls, things inevitably wound up getting broken. Mom hates losing dishes.

"Where are you going?" I asked.

"To get my keys."

"Why?"

Elsie paused long enough to give me an absolutely withering look. "Our telepathic cousin comes home from Ohio for the first time in years. You finally figure out how to get over yourselves and hook up. And that same night, you and I *both* have a weird dream that ends with a new word being planted in our brains? Yeah, that's not normal. Even for us, that's not normal. So we're going back to the compound to make sure Sarah's okay."

"Couldn't we just call?"

"At two o'clock in the morning? If we call and she says nothing's wrong, we won't believe her, and we'll go over there anyway. If we call and she says something's very wrong, we'll be too far away to help. No, getting in the car is the right decision. We can stop and pick up donuts or something in case someone has a problem with us rolling in before the sun comes up."

There was an urgency in her tone that made me stop, blink, and look at her more closely. "You're really freaked out."

"We come from a family of biologists. One way or another, we've been exposed to more science lessons than those poor kids on the Magic School Bus. But you know what I've never studied voluntarily? Bugs." Elsie shook her head. "I don't like bugs. They're weird and they're creepy and they have too many legs. They skitter. I am not a skittery person."

"Okay . . ." I said, not sure where she was going with this.

"I know, without a doubt, that I've never heard the word 'instar' before. It's a whole new word. And somehow, it's in my head, which tells me someone *put* it there. Hopefully, it was Sarah. I'm not sure why she'd be putting words in our heads, and we're going to have a talk about privacy and boundaries if she did, but that's the good option. That's the option where no one's violating what should absolutely be a safe space. If it wasn't Sarah, she's in trouble. So we go. You, and me, and right now."

"Mom and Dad—"

"Are still at the compound."

That explained some of her urgency. We were alone in the house. If someone was playing with our heads, that wasn't good.

"I'll get my shoes," I said.

She nodded tightly. "Meet me at the car."

I turned and walked back toward my room, speeding up as I went, until I was practically running down the stairs.

Being a Price means spending your life preparing for an emergency you hope won't ever come. Elsie and I aren't as physical as our cousins—we can't be, not when our blood tends to make people fall in love with us—but that doesn't mean we got out of the basic training. I grabbed clothes and yanked them on before picking up the bug-out bag that leaned against my desk and slinging it over my shoulder. Inside I had medical supplies, rope, a flashlight, batteries, water, a compass— all the low-tech answers to low-tech problems. Well, most of the low-tech answers.

The handgun I took out of my desk and clipped to my belt would provide the rest of them.

I'm a pretty good shot, and my parents have always been careful to make sure Elsie and I are comfortable with firearms. Verity prefers knives and Antimony prefers anything that keeps the fight at a comfortable distance, but Alex and I bonded over shooting when we were in elementary school, and I'm good enough at it that even Grandma Alice says I have potential. From her, that's the next best thing to being given an actual medal.

The last thing I grabbed was my phone, fully charged and ready to work. I don't know how anyone had the nerve for cryptozoology before we had a decent cellular network. I mean, Sarah's a pretty good substitute, but telepaths are rare, and most of them can't be counted on to play mission control. Assuming Sarah was okay.

Sarah was okay. She had to be. We just got her back. There was no way she could be hurt again, not so soon after she'd come home.

I tried to hold onto that thought as I made my way up the stairs and out the garage door to where Elsie was leaning against the side of her car, impatiently waiting for me.

"I would have left without you if we hadn't just set your car on fire," she said, getting into the driver's side. She turned the key in the ignition. The radio immediately began blasting K-pop, bright and peppy and infectiously enthusiastic, even though I couldn't understand a word.

I got in and buckled my belt. "Let's go."

"How's your cheek?" Elsie pulled out, eyes on the road. "I don't like going into whatever this is with you already wounded."

"Almost better." Lilu—both incubi and succubi—heal faster than humans. Dad can snap a broken bone back into place and be fully recovered an hour later. Elsie and I don't have quite that kind of regeneration, but we don't stay down for long. Mom thinks it's because our blood is so potent that our bodies have evolved to keep as much of it inside us as possible. I think that sounds like revisionist bullshit, even though I'd never say that out loud. Evolution isn't that careful. Evolution just *happens*, and the consequences fall on the evolved.

"Good. Let me know if we need to pull the stitches out."

I touched the side of my face, self-consciously. I knew Sarah didn't register faces the way a human girl would, but it still felt weird to be seeing her with a big gash in my cheek. "I think they're okay. They're already starting to break down."

"Good." She hit the gas harder, accelerating along our sleepy suburban road like she believed speed limits were things that happened to other people. The night blurred around us, and we were on our way, racing against a catastrophe that might not even have happened.

Please, let it not have happened, I thought, and listened to the music, and tried not to be afraid.

My name is Arthur Harrington-Price. My friends call me "Artie," which really means my cousins call me Artie, since I haven't had any flesh-and-blood friends since I hit puberty and got hit with the wrong end of the incubus stick. I'm not devastatingly handsome or suave or capable of talking people into anything I want—which Antimony says is a good thing, since people who can get anything they want just by asking for it tend to turn into supervillains, and she'd hate to have to put me down. She means it, too. My cousin loves me, but she's ruthless. That's part of why I trust her. She'd never let me go evil.

Elsie and I come from a mixed marriage, human mother—well, mostly human; everyone seems to think Great-Grandma Fran brought a little something extra to the table, even if whatever it was is so diluted now that we can't identify it with anything short of full genetic sequencing, and we don't have the resources for that—and incubus father. Elsie got more of the control and less of the chemistry. I got the reverse. She can usually talk people into things, and she has some skill at dream-walking, wandering through sleeping minds and seeing what they have to offer her. Me, I got biological love potion number nine. When people who might be into me get a whiff, it's love at first whatever. And that's not cool. The only people who are immune are the ones who are actually related to me, which I guess proves that nature abhors inbreeding.

So I spend most of my time indoors, in my bedroom, or doused in cheap cologne when I absolutely have to go out somewhere. I read comics and I code and I work at making things easier for my family. I've been producing most of our false IDs since I was still in high school, that sort of stuff. It's something I can do when field work isn't on the table. And field work is almost never on the table. Lilu have what Uncle Kevin calls a flexible genetic structure, meaning we can reproduce with virtually anything and get children that are more Lilu than whatever their other parent was. It's a way of guaranteeing the species continues even when we have a tendency to piss off our neighbors and get ourselves burned at the stake. Which is honestly not as much of an overreaction as it seems. We're sort of bad for people.

Elsie didn't drive like she cared about other people. Elsie didn't drive like she cared about *us*. She hadn't strayed *too* far from the speed limit until we were outside city limits, but as soon as she'd been sure we were in the clear, she'd slammed her foot down on the gas and she hadn't let up once. The K-pop was gone, replaced by a playlist of Broadway songs, none of which had a BPM of less than oh-god-we're-gonna-die, and she seemed to be trying to match her driving to the music. I held tight to the grip above my door and wondered whether this was some sort of cosmic karma coming to get me for all the times I'd pictured Sarah— not biologically related to me, still technically my cousin—in that bikini she'd worn when we went to the lake house the year before she'd been hurt.

"Can you slow down?" I asked.

"Are you picking up any static?" she shot back, swerving around a corner like she thought she was auditioning for a *Fast & Furious* reboot.

That stopped me.

Telepaths are normally undetectable, which makes sense, since a telepath you can detect isn't going to sneak up on you very well, and every kind of telepath we know about is an ambush predator. They hunt by making sure their prey doesn't know they're coming until it's too late. Only it turns out that once a telepath has spent too much time around specific non-telepaths, they start creating a sort of psychic white noise that even non-psychics can pick up when they're around. They become detectible.

Maybe that's why cuckoos are usually such jerks: they don't want anyone to be able to track them. I could follow Sarah across the world, as long as I never let her get quite out of range. Even when I don't know exactly where she is, if she's in range, I know she's there. I know she's all right. That matters. It matters a lot.

We were too far away for the static to have kicked

in, but when it did, I'd be able to relax. Except if she was up in her room, there wouldn't be any static; the charms that keep the rest of us from projecting inward also keep her from projecting out. I'd need to wake her up if I wanted to be completely sure.

Dammit.

The drive from our house to the compound normally took about an hour. Elsie managed to get it down to forty minutes, mostly by ignoring any traffic law that inconvenienced her. She screeched up to the front gates shortly before three o'clock in the morning.

"Get out," she instructed. "Punch the code and let's go."

"I'll follow you up," I said. Something was wrong. I could feel it. "I want to count lights. See how many people are still up in the house."

She nodded, lips pressed into a thin line as I got out of the car and moved to the keypad.

The fact that entering the compound meant someone getting out of their vehicle or coming out of the house has always been a problem. It's more secure than putting the security system on wireless controls, which could be compromised, but it means someone's exposed every time the door opens. We were never allowed to order pizza when we were kids. Someone always had to be willing to go into town.

The air was cold—not strange for three in the morning—and weirdly silent. Even the owls and tailypo in the woods weren't making any noise. I moved toward the keypad, punching in the security code, and moved toward the door next to the gate as Elsie prepared to drive through.

It was already unlocked.

I twisted the knob back and forth several times, checking that it was actually unlocked, and not unlatched or something else mechanical. Even being unlatched would have been a little alarming—one of the only times I've ever seen Uncle Kevin really lose his temper, it was because Verity had run out too quickly and forgotten to make sure everything was secure, and she'd been thirteen at the time—but unlocked? Unlocked was barely this side of impossible.

None of that changed the door's condition. I stepped through, locking it properly behind myself, only glancing over my shoulder twice as I followed Elsie up the driveway. If someone was locked out now, they could call the house, assuming they had their phone. Or they could use the intercom. The door needed to be locked. The door shouldn't have been unlocked in the first place.

Something was really wrong. The feeling of wrongness only intensified as I moved toward the house without the white noise that would signify Sarah's presence kicking in. She was probably upstairs in her room. She was probably fine. That didn't make this comfortable.

Elsie was waiting for me on the porch. "See anything unusual?"

"The gate was unlocked."

Her face smoothed into quick, unreadable neutrality. "You're sure?"

"I checked it three times. It was unlocked."

"The lights in the barn are still on. Our folks were there when we left."

I caught her meaning quickly. "You want to go tell them something's up while I check inside for Sarah?"

"If you wouldn't mind?" She grimaced. "This whole situation has me twitchy. I just don't know what's going on, and I want some backup."

Annie was my preferred backup for situations like this one. Anything my cousin couldn't beat to death with a hammer wasn't worth being scared of. But she'd been sharing her room with Sam since her return from the road, and Sam didn't wake up friendly, or without throwing things. I didn't want to prod the giant monkey in the middle of the night if I didn't have to.

"It's fine," I said. "I'll see you in a few minutes."

"Scream if you need help," she said, and hopped down from the porch, heading around the side of the house.

I opened the front door.

It was unlocked, like the gate. Unlike the gate, that was normal. The front door was only locked when no one was inside; otherwise, anyone who'd made it past the fence could just stroll on in. Aunt Evie liked to explain it as a way to disorient people who expected military-grade security at all times, but honestly, I thought she just liked being able to run around without carrying her keys. Aunt Evie could be that sort of mixture of canny and careless, probably because she'd grown up in a household where her human privilege had been so completely world-changing.

It also helps that the house has a really weird layout. The front door—so called because it's big and has a porch and a doorbell and some decorative trellises with honeysuckle growing on them—leads, not to the foyer or the living room, but to a mudroom. The kitchen is on the other side, and the so-called "front room" is on the other side of *that*. It's a mirror of what people generally expect to find in a house like ours.

(Coming in through the back door gives a more normal experience, except for the part where getting there requires climbing the carefully rickety deck stairs and crossing an expanse of weather-treated wood decorated with a portable barbeque and a bunch of lawn chairs. It all works. It's all livable. But big chunks of it are intended to throw people who don't understand us off-balance, because someone who doesn't know whether they're coming or going is way less likely to unload a pistol into your head.)

The mudroom was empty. The kitchen was empty except for a small cluster of Aeslin mice bravely delving for crumbs in the toaster, which was still plugged in. Aeslin teens, then. The younger members of the colony were big on pushing boundaries and testing their faith, at least until they settled down and became respectable members of the clergy. A few of them tossed a muted cheer in my direction, but mostly they ignored me. It was late. Even the mice were tired.

I crossed the kitchen, intending to head for the stairs, and stopped dead at the threshold to the front room. There was Sarah, curled up on the big couch with one of the decorative throw pillows clutched against her chest, her knees drawn almost to her chest, so that her entire body formed a perfect letter "C."

She was still wearing the clothes she'd had on for the flight from Ohio, black leggings and a heavy sweater and sensible shoes. Her hair was an inky sweep across the pillows, her bangs almost hiding the cut on her forehead, and she had never looked so beautiful, or so breakable. What the hell was I thinking, getting involved with her? She was *family.* I mean, sure, we weren't related, and we'd only semi-grown up together—no one would be able to call this full creepy—but she was supposed to be off-limits. I was supposed to take care of her and protect her and make sure she was happy and not afraid. I wasn't supposed to make things worse.

But the way she'd kissed me, the way she'd talked about the idea of kissing me . . . maybe it was holding back that had been making things worse? Or maybe I was just trying to convince myself that something I really, really wanted to be true *was* true, and this was all a bad idea.

I drifted toward her, frowning a little. Something was still wrong. I couldn't quite put my finger on it yet; whatever it was, it was subtle. She was breathing slow and steady, clearly asleep.

I'd been on the verge of a coma earlier, according to her. I sped up, pausing when I reached the couch. Sarah didn't move, didn't react to my presence.

Sarah? I thought, as loudly as I could. She still didn't move.

I took a deep breath before leaning over to brush the hair away from her face. My fingertips barely brushed the curve of her cheek. She made a small, sleepy noise, lifting one hand and wiping the memory of my touch away, all without opening her eyes. I pulled my hand away and stepped carefully backward, first one step, then another, and another, until I was in the kitchen doorway.

The mice clustered around the toaster raised their heads and paid me exactly the amount of attention required to avoid being rude to one of their personal gods. It was a calculated snub, impressive for how well-practiced it was. I held a finger to my lips, gesturing for silence as I approached them, and crouched down by the counter so that my eyes were on a level with theirs. They looked at me with interest. A few of them vibrated with barely suppressed excitement, waiting to hear what I was going to say next. Hyper-religious mice can only pretend to be too cool for the clergy for so long.

"Hi," I whispered, voice pitched so low that it was barely a breath. Human ears would have strained to hear me. I hoped the mice would be a different story. "I need you to be quiet and do something for me. Touch your ears if you agree."

One by one, the mice touched their ears. I relaxed a little. Aeslin mice mean well, and they're utterly devoted to the family, but the further something is from human, shape-wise, the less human its reactions are likely to be. Sometimes Aeslin will do things because they're incapable of understanding that those things are a terrible idea. Sometimes that includes cheering when asked to be quiet, because the joy of receiving a direct request from one of their gods is so great that they simply can't contain it. It's not their fault. It's frequently our problem.

(When I was little, I used to have nightmares about the family colony falling in love with me because of my pheromones. Dad told me, over and over again, that it was never going to happen, that Lilu are only irresistibly attractive to species we're biologically compatible with whose sexual orientations are compatible with being attracted to us—and that's a fun conversation for a seven-year-old to have with their father—but nightmares aren't logical, and sometimes their blind, burning devotion could look an awful lot like love to a kid who was afraid of changing the world without intending to.)

"Were any of you down here when she went to sleep on the couch?" I pointed behind myself toward the couch.

The mice shook their heads.

Damn. I guess that would have been too easy, since it would have let me ask way more specific questions about what she'd been doing before that and how she'd looked before she curled up and put her head down. Oh, well.

"Watch her," I instructed, still in that nearly silent whisper. "If she moves, one of you follows her, and the rest go looking for someone who can help you. Do you understand?"

Again, the mice touched their ears.

"I'll bring you a pizza tomorrow," I promised. The mice, mindful of their promise to be quiet, mimed cheering. I gave them a thumbs-up, and rose.

Buying pizza for the mice is always a fun way to horrify the local Italian restaurants. They don't like any of the cheap take-out options—mice can have good taste, too—and they want everything on their pies. Everything. Pineapple and anchovies and when the seasonal specials line up, pears and walnuts and gorgonzola and balsamic vinegar. For them, it's like having an entire buffet delivered straight to their door. For the pizzamakers who have to put their horrifying concoctions together, it's like being punked by some asshole reality show.

As quietly as I could, I climbed the stairs to the second floor. All the doors there were closed, which is something we're supposed to respect. An open bedroom door means company is welcome, a closed one means go the hell away. I ignored them and kept walking, until I reached the door at the end of the hall.

KEEP OUT said the sign on the front, and YES, VERITY, THIS MEANS YOU said the amendment underneath it, and I CAN SET FIRES WITH MY MIND NOW, LET ME SLEEP IN said the third piece of paper, all of them written in Antimony's careful, tightly controlled hand. She had always been a big fan of block letters, which were unambiguous and easily read from a distance. Which was also a pretty good description of Annie herself, really.

I opened the door.

Everyone's bedroom is unique. Even hotel rooms, which start out sterile and identical, will take on the character of their occupants after a day or two. Annie had been sleeping in the same bedroom since she was two years old. She'd had a lot of time to settle in.

The walls were dominated by books and weapon racks. The closet—which had no doors, since closets with doors are practically an invitation for things to sneak in and jump out at innocent cryptozoologists who just want to sleep—contained her dresser, as well as all her clothes, and several polearms. The swaths of wall that weren't blocked off by other furnishings were covered in a patchwork quilt of posters and photographs. Some of them were new, and I assumed they'd come with the man who was curled up next to her on the bed, his tail wrapped loosely around her ankle.

Thankfully they were both clothed enough to qualify as "decent," and hence unlikely to throw things at me for the crime of seeing them in the altogether. I looked around the floor, settled on a pair of jeans that seemed unlikely to be booby-trapped, and flung it at the bed.

Sam reached up and snatched them out of the air before they could land. Then he tossed them aside and pressed his face into the pillow, all without apparently waking up.

"I think you two are a whole new category of 'light sleeper,'" I said, trying to pitch my voice into the room and keep it from being heard by anyone downstairs. My shoulders were starting to lock up from the tension. "I can keep throwing things, but we'd all be happier if I didn't have to."

Antimony sat up. Sam made an unhappy grumbling noise and slid an arm around her waist as she blinked blearily at me through the tangled curtain of her hair.

"Is it morning?" she asked. "It better be morning. There better be coffee. I don't smell coffee."

I stepped into the room, shutting the door behind me before turning on the light. Sam made a second grumbling noise, louder and unhappier than the first, and attempted to bury his head under the pillow. His tail uncurled from around Antimony's ankle and snaked around her waist instead. Antimony, for her part, shoved her hair out of her face and glared.

"Artie," she said, voice already much more clear than it had been only seconds before, "what the *fuck*?"

"There's a cuckoo sleeping on the couch downstairs," I said.

"Um, yeah. Happy fucking birthday. You've been praying for this for five years. Calm down, get out of my room, and enjoy it. Before I kill you and you don't get to enjoy anything anymore. Your parents have an heir and a spare. They'll be fine without you."

"It's not Sarah."

Silence so loud it was like a siren filled the room, drowning out everything else. Then Antimony swore and leapt out of bed, stepping with calm assurance over the piles of clothes, knives, and books littering the floor. She yanked open the top drawer of her dresser and started rooting through it, sending underpants flying in all directions before she finally pulled out a fist-ful of anti-telepathy charms. Each thin silver chain ended at a tiny vial containing a disk of copper and a sprinkling of herbs, preserved in water and sealed with wax. I blinked.

"Those are expensive," I said.

"Not when they're homemade," she replied, and tossed one at me. "Me and James, we're like Etsy for cryptozoologists. I mean, our first batch had a ten-dency to explode—"

"You promised we were never going to talk about that again," said Sam, voice muffled by the pillow.

"—but we've worked the kinks out. Put that on." Antimony slung a charm around her own neck before moving back to the bed and prodding her prone boyfriend. "Up. You need to shield your mind. Get moving."

"I hate you," said Sam, even as he reached up and took a charm from her outstretched hand. "I hate your whole family. You're garbage people. You're what fūri parents warn their children about."

"I love you too, asshole," said Antimony.

I gaped at her. "What—why—how—?"

"Which, where, and when," Antimony finished quickly. "Now you've taken a journalism class. What, you thought we weren't going to prepare for Sarah coming back wrong? I've read all the comic books you have. When a telepath breaks, sometimes they get bet-ter, and sometimes they go Dark Phoenix. I love Sarah as much as you do, but that doesn't mean I was going to sit back and wait for her to set my world on fire. Fire's my job."

"Why didn't you tell me?" I asked, wounded.

Antimony looked at me with sympathy and steel in her eyes. "I really do love Sarah as much as you do, but you love Sarah way differently than I do. She's my cousin, not my conclusion. If I'd told you I was afraid she'd come back wrong, we would have had an epic fight, you would probably have said some things you'd be regretting right about now, Sarah might not have come home in the first place, and you still wouldn't have an anti-telepathy charm, because why would you need one?"

I took a breath, intending to argue. Then I deflated. "Fine," I said sullenly as I put the charm around my neck. "You're right. I wouldn't have listened. But now you're not listening. The cuckoo downstairs *isn't Sarah*."

"If she's not Sarah, how did she get into the house?"

"The door in the fence was unlocked when Elsie and I got back."

That was enough to make Sam sit up. Unlike Annie, who was wearing an oversized roller derby shirt and a pair of jogging shorts, he was wearing nothing but a pair of sweatpants. When the blankets fell away, I was treated to more answers about how furry her simian boyfriend was than I had ever actually wanted.

"That door's never unlocked," he said. "I got found in the woods by a bunch of campers once and had to walk back here in human form, and Mr. Price made me stand at the gate for twenty minutes while he took his time finding his shoes and coming down to get me."

"Dad took pictures," said Antimony, reaching into the drawer again, this time to produce a Taser and several throwing knives, which she promptly dropped on the bed. "Artie, turn around. If I have to go downstairs and kick an imposter's ass, I want to put a bra on first."

"Superheroes never stop to put on their underwear before they fight the forces of evil," I said, dutifully turning to face the door.

"Most of them are telekinetic and have gravity-defying boobs," said Antimony as she rattled around behind me. "My boobs aren't gravity-defying. My boobs are very, very aware of gravity, and they don't like it. They want to be protected from it whenever possible, especially if I'm about to go up against a cuckoo. Why was the door unlocked?"

"I don't know." I stared at the posters on the inside of Annie's door, twitching slightly. "Maybe Sarah went outside for some reason. Maybe someone lured her outside. And she didn't lock the door."

"She knows to lock the door."

"Maybe . . . maybe she didn't lock it on purpose." The idea was appealing, which probably meant it was wrong. The most appealing ideas always are. Still, I pressed on, saying, "Maybe she knew she had to warn us somehow, and figured leaving the door unlocked would at least be a clue that something was wrong."

"Hang on," said Sam. "Why are you both focusing on 'how did an imposter get in,' and not on 'how can you be so sure it's an imposter'? I mean, is it just some weirdo wearing a Sarah mask, or what?"

"You can turn around now, Artie," said Annie. She continued, "Cuckoos are a low-individual dimorphism species. They all look alike. They have about the same degree of sexual dimorphism as humans or fūri, but their faces, their bodies . . . they tend to be identical, or very close to it. It wouldn't be hard for another cuckoo to take Sarah's place." She sucked in a sharp breath. When I turned around, she was staring at me.

"The hum," she said. "Even before I put the charm on, the hum was gone. I didn't notice because I was asleep. That's how you knew, isn't it? There was no hum."

Sam put his hand up. "Footnote, please?"

"We're all telepathically attuned to Sarah. Makes it easier for her to project thoughts *into* our heads, makes it harder for us to keep her *out* of our heads. When she's in range—so within, say, a half mile—we get a sort of static effect behind our thoughts. Like white noise. The hum came back when she stepped into the warehouse, for me. And now it's gone again. Sarah's out of range."

"My range is more than a half a mile," I said. "I can tell she's there when she's within three miles of me. She's not here. She's not in the woods outside the compound, either. She's gone." Panic was clawing at the back of my throat.

Antimony must have heard it in my voice. She stepped quickly across the floor, dodging several suspicious-looking piles that clearly contained more than just clothes, and gripped my shoulders. "Breathe," she said. "You need to breathe. We're going to find her."

"Um, maybe this is a bad time and everything, but if Sarah's gone and there's a cuckoo in the living room, we should probably worry about that before we worry about where Sarah is?" Sam finally got out of the bed, grabbing a sweatshirt off the floor and tugging it on. "I don't know as much about cuckoos as I want to. I know they're bad news. Not something we want to mess around with."

"Elsie's getting our parents from the barn, and I have some of the mice watching the cuckoo who isn't Sarah," I said.

"Can she telepathically control the mice?"

Thankfully, I knew the answer to that. I shook my head. "They're acclimated to Sarah and Aunt Angela, which means they're resistant to telepathic control. She could hit them with a shoe or something, but she can't take over their minds unless she really works for it."

"Fun times." Antimony clipped the last of the knives to the waistband of her shorts. "Let's go say hello to our uninvited guest, shall we?" Her grin was too broad to be anything other than a threat.

For a moment, I felt sorry for the cuckoo who was waiting downstairs. But only for a moment. If she was here, that meant Sarah was in trouble, and if Sarah was in trouble, I was going to help her.

This time, finally, I was going to help.

Fourteen

$$\pi_2(n) \sim 2C_2 \frac{n}{(\ln n)^2} \sim 2C_2 \int_2^n \frac{dt}{(\ln n)}$$

"Family is the only thing you can't re-place."

—Kevin Price

The front room of an isolated compound about an hour outside of Portland, Oregon

THE CUCKOO WOKE WITH a gasp, eyes widening and then going narrow as she realized she was looking at the barrel of a gun.

"Um, what?" she said, in a tremulous voice. "What's going on?"

I have never been so glad not to be the one taking point on an interrogation. She sounded like Sarah. She sounded *just* like Sarah, enough that it would have made me second-guess myself if not for the ringing silence in my head where the steady, comforting presence of the cuckoo I knew and loved best belonged.

Take off the charm and you'll be able to hear her, whispered the small voice of my doubt. I shoved it aside. Doubt is one thing, but I've been training my whole life not to doubt what I know to be true, and even when I'd touched her, I hadn't been able to hear anything. Whoever this was, it wasn't Sarah. Sarah was gone.

Sarah needed me.

"Who are you?" I asked.

Her eyes widened again, glinting briefly white before returning to a cool, glacial blue. Something in my chest unclenched, because her eyes . . .

Her eyes were wrong. Oh, they were the right color, even the right shade, but they were still wrong. I'd spent way too many hours trying not to look into them to not recognize the pattern of her irises, the subtle gradations of light and dark and in-between. This wasn't Sarah.

"I'm Sarah," she said, in a small, injured voice. "I'm your cousin. I live in Ohio with my parents. I just came home. Why are you doing this? You're scaring me."

"What's my name?"

The cuckoo went still. "What?"

"If you're my cousin Sarah, and you belong here, what's my name?"

Her eyes narrowed again as her expression turned sullen. "You're wearing an anti-telepathy charm. You know I can't see faces the way you humans do. I can't tell who you are."

"You can't see faces, but you can hear voices," said Annie. "You should be able to tell who we are by the sound of our voices. Why can't you?"

"Jet lag," said the cuckoo. "I only just got back here from Ohio. I'm still tired. I'm not used to being around you yet."

"You've been in love with Artie since you were ten years old," said Annie, voice mild, almost pleasant. That was a warning sign, even if this cuckoo didn't recognize it as such. She really didn't know my cousin, or what Annie was capable of. "You two spent more hours on the phone together than I did with my entire cheerleading squad. There's no way you don't recognize Artie's voice. Jet-lagged or not, you know him."

The cuckoo looked frantically at the three of us, an expression of profound misery and confusion on her face. She looked so much like Sarah that it was difficult to see her so unhappy without wanting to do something about it.

But she *wasn't* Sarah. That was the problem. "Where is she?" I demanded, and my voice sounded gruff and strange, like it belonged to someone else, someone bigger and tougher and meaner than me. Someone who could get things done.

The cuckoo turned wide, guileless eyes toward me. "I'm right here," she said. "Take off the charm, and you'll see. I'm *right here.*"

"Don't," said Annie tightly.

And that was the problem, because I wanted to. I really, really wanted to. It wasn't telepathic influence. It was panic, pure and simple. Sarah had been gone for so long, and now we finally had her back, only to lose her again. I'd been able to tell this cuckoo wasn't her because she'd been asleep. She was awake now. She was awake and she was scared and she was willing to push as hard as she had to in order to make us see things her way. If I took the charm off, she would *be* Sarah. She would shove her way past the protection I'd inherited from my great-grandmother and make sure I never had to miss her again. I wanted that so badly.

But it would all be a lie, and Sarah would still be lost. I shook my head. "I don't think so," I said. "You're going to need to find another patsy."

Those not-quite-right eyes widened further, into an expression of almost comical surprise. Then they narrowed, her expression becoming one of composed calculation. "If you say so," she said.

"Hey," snapped Antimony. "Focus on me. Where the hell is my cousin?"

"Ew," said the cuckoo, disgust dripping from that single syllable. "Do you actually consider her your cousin? That's gross. She's so much more evolutionarily advanced than you are. That's like me saying a honeybee is my new fiancé. It's inappropriate. You're perverts, every single one of you."

Antimony raised an eyebrow. "So you admit you're not Sarah."

"I just wish I hadn't cut my hair for this gig," said the cuckoo, with a one-shouldered shrug. "Bangs are so passé. Anyway, it doesn't matter."

"Why's that?" asked Sam warily.

"Because that one," she nodded toward me, "told me how to get out of this. You might not thank him for that."

"What are you—" began Antimony.

That was as far as she got before something hit her in the back of the head. She stopped for a moment, expression comically dazed, before she toppled forward, losing her grasp on the gun in the process. Sam yelped. He had a choice in that moment—catch his falling girlfriend or catch the gun—and sadly, he chose wrong, grabbing Antimony before she could hit the floor. The ball of ice that had knocked her down fell, unheeded, to the carpet.

And the cuckoo caught the gun.

"James, what the *hell*," snarled Sam, looking over his shoulder toward the stairs, where our second resident sorcerer was presumably standing. James specialized in cold things. James specialized in cold things, and James wasn't a biological member of the family; he didn't have the protections against cuckoo influence that the rest of us had inherited.

I didn't turn. Turning would have meant taking my eyes off the cuckoo, who was now holding Annie's pistol aimed squarely at my forehead.

"If you move, I shoot," she said. "If you say anything I don't like, I shoot. Honestly, I'd shoot anyway, if I didn't think we might need you later. What she sees in you, I have no idea."

"Of course you don't, I'm wearing an anti-telepathy charm." I winced inwardly. Maybe backtalking the murderous cuckoo who had replaced Sarah was a bad idea.

"This would all be so much easier if you'd take that nasty thing off."

"I'd rather not, if it's all the same to you." The temperature in the room was dropping steadily. I still didn't dare look behind me, but every hair on Sam's shoulders was standing on end, and he looked like he was fighting a silent war between staying where he was and serving as possible backup and getting Antimony the hell out of there.

She wasn't moving. James must have hit her just right to knock her out, or at least daze her for a while. I refused to consider anything worse. Antimony was the best of us or, at least, the most bloody-minded and tenacious. She'd figure this out. I just needed to buy her the time.

And just like that, I knew what I had to do. I took a step backward, away from the cuckoo. She bared her teeth in a snarl.

"Stop where you are, incubus," she spat. "You're mine now."

"Are you all right, Heloise?" James sounded half-drunk, or maybe drugged, like he didn't fully understand what was going on.

The cuckoo winced. "I'm fine, Jimmy," she said. "I'm just explaining to Artie here why he needs to come with me."

"He'll come with us because we're on the right side of the fight," said James. "He's smart enough to know that. Not like *them*." There was pure venom in his voice, and I knew that if I turned, he'd be looking at Annie and Sam, hands full of ice, ready to attack.

I took another step back. "Sam," I said quietly. "Run."

Under other circumstances—if Annie hadn't been taken by surprise, if we'd been able to fight ice with fire, if the cuckoo hadn't managed to get her hands on a gun—I knew Sam would have argued with me. He's not family by blood, but he's still family, thanks to Annie's fiat, and he knows better than to leave a man behind if there's any other choice. Right now, there

wasn't a choice. Out of the corner of my eye I saw him
tense, nod, and gather Annie even closer to his chest.
Then he leapt into the air.

There's almost nothing as fast as a fūri who has
somewhere to be. I've watched Verity—who has re-
flexes that border on preternaturally sharp—throwing
knives at Sam while he was in motion, and she's never
come anywhere near hitting him. When Sam wants to
get away, he gets away.

His first leap carried him to the banister, one long
arm clutching Annie's unconscious form. He landed
easy, grabbing the rail with both feet and his free hand
before he leapt again, this time heading up the stairs to
the first landing. The cuckoo swore loudly. James
hurled a ball of ice after the fleeing fūri. It missed
widely enough to become comic, smashing into the
wall between two framed family portraits. One of
them fell to the ground and shattered.

I didn't move. The cuckoo still aiming her stolen
gun at me made that an easy decision. If she'd been
more mammalian . . . for the first time, I found myself
wishing that my pheromones could affect a cuckoo. If
she'd shot me, I could have swayed her completely over
to my side.

Telepathy versus chemically-induced attraction,
round one, fight. The cuckoo stood, eyes narrow, gun
still aimed at me.

"Jimmy, grab his gun," she said. "He's a Price. They
always have guns."

"You know you hate being called 'Jimmy,' James,"
I said. "If she was whatever she wants you to think she
is—your sister or your girlfriend or your confessor or
whatever—she wouldn't keep calling you that."

"I don't like *you* calling me Jimmy," said James, stepping up to me and grabbing the handgun off my belt.
The temperature dropped again as he got closer. The
cuckoo didn't seem to notice. Having antifreeze for
blood comes with an annoying degree of cold resistance.

James sneered at me as he tossed my gun on the couch and stepped back toward the cuckoo, slipping an arm around her waist and pulling her closer to him. Her aim never wavered. "I don't like *you* calling me anything," he continued. "Hel, are you sure we need to take him with us? You could shoot him right now for what he did to you."

I wanted to ask what I'd supposedly done to her. For once in my life, I kept my big mouth shut. Whatever lies she was shaping in his mind would only get stronger if I gave her an excuse to make him repeat them out loud. Lies are like that. The more they're told, the more realistic they tend to become.

Heloise looked briefly disappointed when she realized what I was—or wasn't—doing. Then she jerked her chin toward the door. "All right, incubus," she said. "Move."

"Do I have a choice?" I asked.

"Yeah. I shoot you."

I moved.

This is fine, I thought as Heloise marched me across the lawn, the barrel of her stolen gun digging into the skin between my shoulders. *Mom will know what to do.* It was a little weird that Elsie hadn't come charging back with the various parents yet, but that was probably because they were busy coming up with some sort of plan for getting the unfamiliar cuckoo out of here. They had to have a coherent failsafe for this sort of thing.

A gun went off in the distance, from the direction of the barn. I stumbled, nearly losing my balance. Heloise laughed, sounding utterly, horrifyingly delighted.

"I know what you were thinking," she said. "You were thinking what people like you are always thinking. That you had a way out of this. Guess what? You don't. You're coming with me, and you're never going to see your precious family again. You lose. Got that? You lose."

"You're so good at this, Hel," said James admiringly.

I could hear the cuckoo preen behind me. "I know," she said. "I should have been in charge of this extraction from the beginning. Ingrid's too soft on the little freak."

"Don't call Sarah a freak," I said. It was a wild guess, but it was better than focusing on the real bombshell:

There was at least one more cuckoo, maybe two. No one else would be giving this woman orders. I mean, they could try, but she wouldn't *listen*. Cuckoos aren't big on following other people's plans.

"Why not?" asked Heloise. "I thought you were into cryptid rights, 'live life out loud,' all that hipster Etsy bullshit. She's a freak. She's in her third instar now, and we only need her to molt one more time and she'll be able to crack this world open like an egg. That's not normal. That's the sort of thing only a freak can do."

Instar. The word was starting to take on an ominous cast, like it was the key to a secret I had never been meant to hear. "She's not a freak," I said. "I don't know what an instar is or why you're so afraid of it, but she's not a freak."

Heloise dug the barrel of the gun harder into my back, forcing me forward. "I'm not afraid of some sheltered little princess who doesn't know what it means to be a Johrlac," she spat. "Don't even say that."

"Whatever." The grass was slippery. It would be easy to fake a fall . . . but then what? I had lost my handgun. I still had a knife with me, and a weighted sap in my left pocket. Neither of them was going to be enough to stop a cuckoo with a gun *and* the sorcerer she had in her thrall. Maybe more importantly, neither of them was going to make her give me Sarah back.

There had been four people in the barn before Elsie went to talk to them. Of the four, three were resistant to cuckoo influence, Mom and Uncle Kevin because of biology, Aunt Evie because of long exposure. Dad was the only one really at risk, and while he could dial his pheromones up to try to affect Aunt Evie, she was smart and knew how to protect herself from an incubus. No one in their right mind gets turned on by the smell of formalin and rot, both of which she had available to her in convenient pre-jarred form out in the barn.

One gunshot meant one person had gone down. Dad wouldn't have thought to start out by grabbing a gun—it wasn't the way he preferred to fight, when he had to fight at all—and that meant he was probably the one who'd been shot. I was remarkably okay with that. Lilu heal quickly, and none of the people in the barn would have been shooting to kill.

It probably says something weird about my family that "I bet my mother shot my father in the leg" was a comforting thought, but I'm a Price. Weird is sort of what we do.

"I'm not afraid of her," insisted Heloise, voice getting higher and shriller. "Jimmy, make him stop."

"With pleasure." James flicked me in the side of the head. The flash of cold was immediate and intense enough to leave me with a ringing headache.

I winced. "Dude, what the hell?"

"I froze your eardrum," he said. "Don't make me do something worse."

I rubbed the side of my head, slanting a sidelong glare in his direction. "When this is over and you're yourself again, I'm going to tell the mice you want them to sing you to sleep every night for a month."

"I *am* myself," he said, scowling at me. "Hel understands me. She appreciates me for the scholar that I am, and not because she feels sorry for me. She's going to help me find Sally and bring her home."

"Sure she is," I said, still rubbing the side of my head. "How did you meet her again?" I half-expected Heloise to break in and make us stop talking. Only half. Cuckoos are notoriously arrogant and convinced that their weird mind games are unwinnable by anyone but the cuckoos themselves. As long as we were talking *about* Heloise, she probably wasn't going to interrupt.

"We went to elementary school together," said James. "Me, her, and Sally."

"Sally. Your best friend. The one the crossroads took."

"Yes."

"If Heloise was there, why did Sally go to the crossroads alone to get taken? Shouldn't Heloise have stepped in and made her do something else?"

"That's enough of that." Heloise withdrew the gun from my back long enough to rap me lightly on the crown of the head with its grip. "Don't try to confuse my Jimmy. I don't like it when people do that."

"She's so good to me," said Jimmy, in a dreamy, puzzled tone. "She takes such good care of me."

"Yes, I do, don't I, Jimmy?" There was a soft smacking sound, and I knew without looking that she had just blown him a kiss. Gross. Evil people shouldn't blow kisses at my honorary cousins.

We had almost reached the fence. James jogged ahead to unlock and open the door, holding it for us.

"Thank you, James," said Heloise, and started to push me through. The woods loomed dark and tangled and all-consuming, and I knew, all the way down to the bottom of my heart, that if I went into them with her, I would never come back out. My body could molder among the roots for years before anyone stumbled over it.

I couldn't help Sarah by getting myself killed. I couldn't help *anyone* that way. So when Heloise urged me forward again, I did the only thing I could do, and grabbed hold of the fence with both hands, swinging myself around in the process, so that I was blocking the exit.

Heloise blinked at me, clearly nonplussed. "What do you think you're doing?"

"Stopping."

She lifted both eyebrows. "If you say so. Jimmy?"

"Right away." James moved toward me, hands outstretched, air around them crackling with cold.

I blinked. "She has you, but she doesn't *have*-you have-you, does she? Huh."

"What are you talking about?" demanded Heloise.

I kept my eyes on James. "I know you and Annie have been digging in the library, going through all Grandpa Thomas' old books, looking for ways to be better sorcerers. It's like, all the two of you do most days. I've seen you do all sorts of stuff, and now all you're doing is trying to turn people into ice cubes. She has you, because she's in your head and everything, but she doesn't *have* you, not really. You're pushing back. Is that a sorcerer thing, or a stupidly stubborn thing? Either way, keep it up."

James made a sharp growling noise and grabbed my hand.

The cold flowing out of him was intense enough to violate half a dozen laws of physics in the process of giving me virtually instant frostbite. I hissed through my teeth, fingers tightening on the metal, which did me the immense favor of freezing solid and adhering to my skin. That was going to hurt when it came time to pry me loose.

"Make him let *go*," snarled Heloise.

James pulled my hand off the fence. My skin, frozen to the metal and taxed beyond all reasonable limits, did the only thing it could do, and tore. I staggered backward, staring at my red, raw fingers, which were slowly leaking blood. James lunged for me. I stuck my hand out automatically, catching him across the face, leaving a red smear behind.

James froze, eyes becoming slightly glazed as he stared at me.

My eyes widened. In the battle between cuckoo compulsion and incubus attraction, which would win? It wasn't a question I'd ever really wanted to ask myself before, especially since it meant being close enough to a non-family cuckoo for it to matter. Suddenly, it seemed like a very big deal.

"Jimmy! What the hell are you doing? Get him!" Heloise waved the gun in her hand like it was some sort of badge of authority.

Hell, maybe it was. But if she was going to kill me, she was going to do it here, where at least my family would have a chance of finding my body. "No, James," I said, voice calm and level. "Don't get me. I want you to stay right where you are, buddy, okay? We're friends, right?"

"Friends," he said, sounding dazed.

I winced. I'd never actually *bled* on anyone who wasn't related to me before. Even in elementary school, when I'd been young enough that people just wanted to be my friend and maybe give me their pudding cups, I'd been careful enough to avoid skin contact with people who could be enthralled. How long was this going to last? And was James ever going to forgive me?

Not that it mattered if I was dead. *Sorry, buddy,* I thought, and nodded vigorously. "Friends," I echoed. "We're friends, and Heloise here, she's not your friend. No matter what you think you remember, you only met her tonight, and she's not acting like a friend, is she? Friends don't hold their friends at gunpoint."

"What the fuck is this, an episode of Mr. Rogers? Grab him!" Heloise adjusted her stance, once again taking careful aim at my chest. Headshots are tricky. Even the best marksman can miss. Chest shots, at close range, are much more likely to do the kind of damage jerks like Heloise prefer. "Grab him, or I'm going to shoot you both."

Slowly, James turned to face her. His motions were jerky, like he was fighting some force I couldn't see. I wanted to cheer for him. I kept quiet. The last thing I wanted to do right now was attract more potentially deadly attention to myself.

"You're my friend, Hel," he said.

"I know, Jimmy. I know." Her voice was treacly sweet, a parody of a friend's concerned tone. It made my skin crawl. The way she batted her eyelashes at him made it worse. "He's a bad person. You need to stop him."

James nodded in that same jerky manner. Then he reached up, swiped his thumb through the blood on his cheek, and stuck it in his mouth. His eyes cleared. He lunged for Heloise, who shrieked and stumbled backward on the lawn, aiming her stolen gun directly at his face and pulling the trigger.

Nothing happened. There was a dull click and that was all, and I had to swallow the urge to laugh even as I pulled the cosh out of my pocket with my uninjured hand. In all the chaos and the triumph of getting her hands on the gun, she had forgotten one essential step.

She had forgotten to take the safety off.

If this had been a movie, I would have said something pithy about safe shooting, some stupid little quip that would probably have alerted her to the problem. Thankfully, while we all come from the Spider-Man school of combat—the bad guys can't hit you if they're too busy trying to figure out what the hell you're talking about—my parents had always been very clear that there was a time and a place for helping your enemies improve. The middle of combat was neither of those things.

I rushed for Heloise, swinging my arm around so that the cosh hit her in the shoulder. She yelped with pain. She dropped the gun. James lunged for her again, barely missing as she staggered backward.

And that's when Sam dropped down on her from

above like the two hundred pounds of furious pseudo-simian he was. He landed feet-first on her shoulders, toes gripping hard. For one glorious moment they stood there like cheerleaders getting ready to do a really impressive trick. Then physics kicked in, and Heloise went down hard, Sam on top of her, lips pulled back from his teeth in a genuinely impressive snarl. She screamed. The sound was almost enough to drown out the click of a hammer being pulled back. I looked behind me.

There was Antimony, a scowl on her face and a gun in her hands. This one was bigger than the one on the ground, and the safety was most definitely *not* on. She looked like she was ready to start shooting people. It was a mood I could absolutely support.

"Hey, cuz," I said. "You okay?"

"You mean after James hit me in the head with an ice cube the size of a golf ball? Oh, I'm *dandy*."

"You don't sound dandy. You sound like you're about to kill somebody."

Annie's smile was more like a snarl. In that moment, it was easy to see why she was Sam's perfect girl, even if I would have sooner gotten involved with a live wolverine even if we hadn't been related. She was way too scary for me. "That's probably because I'm about to kill somebody. Sam! Get off the fucking cuckoo so I can shoot it!"

"You can't shoot her," said Sam, and slammed Heloise's head into the lawn with a sharp shove of one foot. "No. Stay down. This is the part where you stop fighting so my girlfriend doesn't kill the living shit out of you."

James clutched the sides of his head with both hands, bending almost double. "Can you please, *please* knock her unconscious?" he moaned. "Half of me still wants to save her from you because she's been my best friend since grade school, and I know that's not true."

"Listen to your sister, meaning me," said Antimony.

"She's not your friend, she's not your long-lost bestie, and she's not the secret to bringing Sally home. She's just a complication we didn't ask for. Sam?"

"On it," said Sam, and gripped Heloise by the hair, pulling her head far enough off the ground to snake his tail around her throat and squeeze.

The effect was immediate. Her eyes bulged as she reached up and clawed at the offending appendage with her one free hand, trying to break what looked like a fairly unbreakable grip. She began to thrash and wheeze.

"Cuckoos breathe, right?" asked Sam, as casual as if he weren't choking a woman right in front of us. "Like, I'm going to knock her out if I squeeze long enough?"

"Or you're going to kill her," said Antimony. "It's not like we strangle Sarah for fun. James, why the hell weren't you wearing your anti-telepathy charm?"

"I was in bed," he said, still holding the sides of his head, like he was afraid his skull might fly apart at any moment. "You said Sarah's room was warded to keep her from wandering into our dreams at night."

"More to keep our dreams from wandering into hers, but yes, it is," said Antimony. "That doesn't mean taking off that charm was a good idea. There's no bathroom in her bedroom."

"Go easy on him," said Sam. "Not everyone's as paranoid as you are."

"It's not paranoia when you find an actual cuckoo in your living room."

"Fair," allowed Sam. Heloise wasn't thrashing anymore. "Hey, James, you still have a weird lady in your brain telling you to kill us all?"

"No," said James, shoulders sagging in relief. He dared a glance over at Annie. "I'm sorry about the hailstone. I don't know what came over me."

"Don't worry about it. The cuckoo came over you. Sam, can you get her out to the barn?"

"Not back inside?" asked Sam, as he uncoiled his tail from around Heloise's neck and stooped to pick her up. I finally realized that he'd stopped to put on a long-sleeved sweatshirt at some point; except for the very brief moment where he was grasping her arms and hoisting her over his shoulder, he was never touching her skin directly. The fur on his tail was thick enough to insulate him.

"Did you take so long coming to my rescue because you felt the need to stop and change clothes?" I asked.

Annie rolled her eyes at me. "You're a Price, nerd. You can take care of yourself."

"Against a sorcerer and a cuckoo?"

"You're still standing, aren't you?" She gave James a measuring look. "But that's not his blood. Artie, what did you do?"

"He gave me frostbite on purpose and took off the top layer of my skin."

"I didn't do it out of malice," protested James. His cheeks and the tips of his ears were red, like he was embarrassed or running a fever. "The cuckoo was in my head. Everything she said sounded perfectly reasonable."

"Sure, it was just the kind of reasonable that ends with me in a shallow grave somewhere." I glanced to Antimony. "That's my blood. He probably needs some aconite, and maybe a cold shower."

"That would be . . . welcome, yes," said James stiffly. He didn't look at me. Whoops. "I'm not currently fit for polite company."

"Sorry about that," I said.

He dared a glance in my direction, the tips of his ears flaring an even deeper red, until he looked like he was on the verge of a stroke. "Please, don't apologize," he mumbled. "You did what was necessary to break that woman's control over me. Honestly, I prefer this. At least I know you won't take advantage. Now if you'll excuse me, I need that shower now."

"Meet us at the barn!" Antimony called as he fled for the house. She turned and looked at me, nodding approvingly. "Nonstandard approach, but you're alive and only bleeding a little, so we're going to call it a win. Now let's go. Your sister should be done patching up the hole in your dad by now. Oh, and did you know my dad's bi?"

"I did not know that and I did not want to know that and why do you know that?"

She shrugged. "He made a pass at *your* dad when he started bleeding. Now come on. We need to figure out what we're going to do next."

Sam started across the lawn, heading for the barn. After a moment's hesitation, Antimony and I followed. We were definitely not going to get any more sleep tonight.

Fifteen

$$\pi_2(n) \sim 2C_2 \frac{n}{(\ln n)^2} \sim 2C_2 \int_2^n \frac{dt}{(\ln n)}$$

"I thought I'd seen the worst of what this world had to offer when I saw the Covenant. Then I saw my first cuckoo, and I knew I'd been wrong."

—Alexander Healy

In the barn, preparing for war

WHEN I WAS A kid, I'd thought everyone had a barn filled with taxidermy and weird, wonderful tools, like a mad scientist's lab crossed with a veterinarian's office. I'd giggled at Vincent Price movies, both because he looked like he should be a distant relative—he wasn't—and because he'd been moving through a world that looked so much like the one I had at home. He'd been familiar in a way so few things were.

As I got older, I learned that not everyone knows their way around a scalpel before their tenth birthday, and that maybe taking jars of organs preserved in formaldehyde for show and tell wasn't a good way to make friends. I'd learned, in short, to be ashamed. But none of that changed the way the smell of the barn swept over me, chemicals mixed with wood rot and hay and clean, freshly-sharpened steel, all of it blending together to say "home" and "you are safe" and "boy, I hope you've had your tetanus booster recently."

The smell of bleach hung heavy in the air, drowning

everything else out. I took a breath, then sneezed. "Dude, what the hell? Why does it reek of aconite in here?"

"There's Benadryl in my purse," said Elsie. She was standing next to one of the surgical tables, taping a piece of gauze down on Dad's shoulder. He was shirtless and sheepish, hands braced to either side of his knees while she worked. "After Mom shot Dad, all the grownups got squirrely and horny. Mom's out walking the perimeter to make sure there's nothing else coming."

I paused, looking around. Mom was accounted for, but Aunt Evie and Uncle Kevin were missing.

Antimony must have done the same math I had. Her whole face screwed up in an expression of radiant disgust. "Ew," she said. "I didn't need to know that. Why did you make me know that?"

"Because I was here when my father got shot—meaning I was here when my mother shot my father—and everything tried to turn into the world's most embarrassing orgy," said Elsie.

"I'm sorry, sweetheart," said Dad. "I don't have any control of what happens when I'm bleeding."

She sighed. "I know, Dad. You can put your shirt back on now."

"Please," said Annie.

"You're never that anxious for *me* to put my shirt back on," said Sam, and dumped the unconscious Heloise onto another of the surgical tables.

"Yes, because you're not twice my age, related to me, and capable of making me stupid with lust just by flexing a bicep." Annie holstered her gun and moved to help Sam strap Heloise down. "Okay, maybe that last one applies, but it's not creepy because you're not my uncle."

They made an efficient team, and if I focused on that, I didn't have to pay attention to my father squirming back into his shirt, or—somehow even worse—the fact that the woman they were securing to the table was a dead ringer for Sarah. With her hair askew after Sam landed on her, it was apparent that she had even mimicked Sarah's injuries. This had been very carefully planned, and they hadn't expected us to catch on.

I paused, frowning. "Hey, so, you know how there's that mental hum when you've been around a telepath for too long?"

"We went over this earlier," said Annie.

"Sure, but Dad and Elsie weren't there," I said. "This cuckoo doesn't have the hum, because she's not Sarah, so we're not attuned to her the same way we're all attuned to Sarah."

"Not all, but sure," said Sam.

"Why didn't she know?"

That was enough to make everyone pause and turn to look at me.

Dad spoke first. "What do you mean, Artie?"

"I mean she's wearing clothes that look like Sarah's, or maybe are Sarah's, and I don't want to think about that, so I'm not going to think about it anymore than I have to, and she made some snarky comments about wishing everything had gone wrong before she'd cut her hair, since she doesn't like having bangs, and she even has a cut on her forehead that looks just like the one Sarah got in the accident. She planned for an *insertion*. She thought it was going to take us time to figure out that she wasn't who she was pretending to be. But she also knew that being a Price makes you resistant to cuckoo powers."

"Meaning what?" asked Elsie.

"Meaning she didn't think she could fool most of us telepathically," said Annie, taking up the thread. She stared at me with dawning comprehension. "She thought she could pretend to be Sarah so well that we'd all believe her, which means she *didn't* know we could pick up on the hum."

"I don't think ordinary cuckoos spend enough time

around people to even know about the hum," I said. "I think they just . . . come and go, and leave things broken behind them."

"That's pretty much the long and the short of it, yes," said an unfamiliar voice from behind me.

We all turned, except for Heloise, who was both unconscious and tied down. The man standing just inside the barn door raised his hands.

"I surrender," he said. "Or I come in peace, or whatever you need to hear in order to not shoot me immediately. Because we need to talk, and we don't have a lot of time."

His skin was pale and his hair was black and his eyes were blue and I didn't have to be a genius to know that if I hadn't been wearing an anti-telepathy charm, he would have been nudging the edges of my mind, looking for a way past my natural resistance. He was wearing blue jeans and a University of Portland sweatshirt and he looked like Sarah's brother and I saw red, I literally saw red. I was moving before I had a chance to think about it, striding across the barn to knot my hand in his sweatshirt and yank him toward me even as I raised my fist and cocked it back.

He looked at me impassively, resigned, not flinching. "If it's going to make you feel better, go for it," he said. "Like I said, we don't have a lot of time. Get it out of your system."

I hesitated, hand still raised, unable to decide what to do next.

Antimony saved me from myself. She appeared next to me, pushing down on my fist until my arm was back by my side. She didn't touch the hand clenching the man's sweatshirt. "Hi," she said, in the brightly pleasant tone that meant she was about five minutes away from setting everything in sight on fire. "Who are you, why are you here, and why should we let you leave?"

"My name is Mark," he said. "I'm here because I

need your help if we're going to save the world, and you shouldn't let me leave. I'm a cuckoo. I know you know what that is. You have one of us tied up on the table over there."

"They're cuffs, not rope, but continue," said Antimony. I looked at her. She shrugged. "Precision is important, even when you're talking to people you're probably about to kill. Maybe especially when you're talking to people you're probably about to kill. That way they get to the afterlife with an accurate idea of what took them out."

"I don't think cuckoos go to this dimension's afterlife," said Mark, in a resigned tone. "If they do, I've never heard about it, anyway. We're not from around here. Presumably, after we're dead, we go wherever the hell it is we actually belong."

"I'll have to ask Mary about that," said Antimony. Her hand moved in a complicated pattern, and she was suddenly holding an actual fireball. It flickered orange and red and blue, looking strangely like a pom-pom from her cheerleading days, if the pom-poms had been actively terrifying. "Later. Maybe when it's time to hide your body."

"I would really, really prefer it if you didn't kill me," said Mark. "I didn't have to come here."

"Yet you came," Antimony purred. Sam loomed up behind her, apparently done with his adventures in bondage. "Your mistake."

The cuckoo's eyes flashed white. "Living things want to stay alive," he said quietly. "Please don't remind me how much I want to survive this. You won't like what happens if you do."

"We have you pretty solidly outnumbered," said Elsie, joining our little cluster. I glanced over my shoulder and saw Dad heading for the back of the barn. Whether it was to get a chainsaw or find Aunt Evie and Uncle Kevin was anybody's guess.

Aunt Evie and Uncle Kevin. Fuck. I turned back to

Mark, raising my fist back into the perfect punching position. "Where's my mother?" I asked.

"She's not wearing one of those pesky telepathy blockers," said Mark. "I could 'hear' her coming as I was on my way in. She wasn't hard to evade. I didn't hurt her, if that's what you're worried about. I came here to ask for your help. Hurting people would be contrary to my own interests. And I'm a cuckoo. Everything I do is about my own interests. Now please. What can I do to convince you that I come in peace?"

"Let us cut your hands off?" suggested Elsie.

"What *else* can I do to convince you that I come in peace?" Mark eyed Elsie, clearly alarmed. "You're awfully vicious for one of the self-proclaimed good guys. Are you always like this?"

"Only with the people who deserve it," said Elsie. "You deserve it."

"Because I'm a cuckoo?" Mark scowled. "I expected resistance. I expected some honest caution. I didn't expect *bigotry*. Not after everything Sarah had to say about you people."

I didn't think. I just moved. My fist slammed into his face hard enough to knock him free of my grip. He fell, sprawling in the doorway, and stared up at me with narrow, white-tinted eyes as he raised one hand to rub his chin.

"Don't say her name," I spat, taking a stiff-legged step toward him. "Don't say it, don't think it, don't do *anything* unless you want me to hit you again."

"That's going to make this difficult, since I'm here because I need you to help me save her." He touched the trickle of clear liquid now connecting his nose to his upper lip and grimaced. "You hit hard."

"You can thank us for that," said Dad, now fully clothed, as he walked over to join us. He looked around our little group before shaking his head. "Five on one isn't fair, even when the one's a cuckoo. Give the boy some space. He didn't have to come here, and if he's really trying to help Sarah—"

"I am," said Mark hurriedly. "Look. Tie me to a chair or something, okay? You'll trust me more if you know I can't touch you, and you need to trust me. We don't have a lot of time."

"Before what?" I demanded.

"Before Sarah finishes the morph into her fourth instar and the rest of my hive uses her to destroy the world."

I suddenly felt like I wanted to vomit and pass out at the same time. It wasn't the most pleasant of sensations.

"Oh," I said faintly. "Is that all?"

Mom, Aunt Evie, and Uncle Kevin had all come back to the barn while we were in the process of tying Mark to the chair. He'd held perfectly still during the process, not complaining at all, not even when we got a little overenthusiastic with the knots.

"I don't think anyone has ever successfully captured a cuckoo alive before, and now we have two in one night," commented Mom, looking approvingly at the cuffs holding Heloise to the table. "Does this mean we can take one apart?"

"Again, really bloodthirsty for the good guys," said Mark. "Do you ever chill?"

"Sarah's missing," said Antimony. "Your friend over there tried to use my *brother* to murder my cousin. Oh, and you just told us your hive was planning to destroy the world. Why would we chill, exactly?"

"Because you're the good guys," said Mark.

"Anyone who thinks good means chill needs to spend more time with my family," said Elsie. She had produced a nail file from her purse and was meticulously filing her nails, checking them carefully for snags and imperfections. She managed to look completely unconcerned with everything that was going on around her. That was when she was at her most dangerous.

"We've never been chill," she continued, still filing. "Chill doesn't save anybody. We like saving people. The ones who can be saved, anyway. Some of them were always beyond salvation." She blew on her nails. "Those ones, we bury in the woods."

"Where is Sarah?" I demanded.

Mark turned to look at me, eyes glinting white again. "Who makes those charms for you people? They deserve a raise. I can't even get past the first layer."

"I make them," said Annie. "Me and James. Who your friend over there aimed like a gun and fired. I'm not happy with her."

"She's not my friend," said Mark. He leaned back as far as the ropes would allow, looking at us all one by one. "Do you not understand how cuckoos work? We don't have friends. We don't have families. We're every man for himself, all the time, from the day we're born until the day we die. A hive only comes together when absolutely necessary, and it's never for a good reason."

"So why did yours come together?" I asked.

"For Sarah." He looked momentarily almost ashamed. It was a strange expression to see on a cuckoo. "How much do you know?"

"What?"

"You heard me." His eyes flashed white again. "Everyone knows about you. The Prices. The Healys. You were the first people to figure out that we existed, and *keep* knowing that we existed, even when we tried to make you forget. It's because of you that this world has turned dangerous for us." He paused to chuckle, darkly. "Well. Because of you, and because of video surveillance. We can change a mind, but we can't change a camera. Another few years and this whole world is going to be like London. Too filmed to risk. Still, we might have held out a few more decades if it weren't for you people screwing everything up for us. So I'm asking you, how much do you know? I need to know where to start."

"We know nothing," said Mom, stepping forward. "Start there. Start with the assumption that we know nothing, and we need you to tell us everything. And if you're wrong, we'll just have a few things confirmed. It's not like most of the enemy cuckoos we've dealt with have been inclined to give us good intel."

"Fine," said Mark. He took a deep breath. "This is what you need to know in order to understand what's about to happen . . ."

Sixteen

$$\pi_2(n) \sim 2C_2 \frac{n}{(\ln n)^2} \sim 2C_2 \int_2^n \frac{dt}{(\ln t)^2}$$

"People feel smart when they tell you 'Frankenstein' was the doctor, not the monster. They're wrong. Frankenstein—Dr. Frankenstein—was always the monster. That's the whole point. Sometimes evil is so damn beautiful it hurts."

—Martin Baker

In the barn, getting a history lesson from a monster

WE COME FROM A dimension called 'Johrlar.' I don't know where the root word came from. No one does anymore. We're the children of exiles, people who'd been thrown out of Johrlar for breaking the rules. I don't know what rules we broke, either. Johrlac—cuckoos—don't write anything down. Our history is given to us while we're in the womb, passed down from mother to child as we gestate. Every cuckoo is born with the whole of our living memory already waiting for us. But we're still larval. We haven't even reached our first instar yet. If we had access to everything we knew, it would overwhelm us, and we would never be able to mature into individuals. So the knowledge is hidden from us until our minds are developed enough to absorb it without being overwhelmed. Our first metamorphosis looks like human puberty. Our bodies change, our brains expand, and the whole history of our people unlocks. It can be . . . a shock, to the developing psyche."

"You mean they snap and murder everyone around them," said Antimony.

"Something like that," said Mark. He didn't sound sorry about it, exactly; more resigned, like this was some nasty mess that he had somehow ended up responsible for. "A cuckoo in morph is incapable of understanding that anyone else actually exists, even other cuckoos. We assume they must have had some way of leavening the shock on Johrlar, but if they did, it's part of the missing history. We know there are big swaths of knowledge that have been cut out of our inherited memories."

"Cut out how?" asked Mom.

"As I said, we're the descendants of exiles, even if we don't know what their crimes were," said Mark. "The memory transference is not exact, or we'd all be clones of our parents, little buds carrying their precise personalities into the future. We get more of a general sense of history, things that were big enough or catastrophic enough to carry forward. We get the rules of behavior. We get something that looks a lot like instinct, which is good, because we don't *have* instincts anymore."

"You don't need them," said Aunt Evie. "Not if you're getting a handbook to proper behavior straight from your mother's mind. Instincts would only get in the way."

Mark nodded, looking relieved that at least one of us understood what he was talking about. "Exactly. And the memories, they play an essential role in our maturation, because their release triggers a chemical response that properly finishes our metamorphosis."

"If you don't start explaining what this has to do with Sarah, I'm going to cut your toes off one by one and make you eat them," I said.

Everyone went quiet as they turned to look at me. Sam let out a long, low whistle.

"Damn, Harrington," he said. "You're cold."

"I'm *terrified*," I corrected.

"You're right to be," said Mark. "Look. When Sarah was a child, her adoptive parents were killed. It was a tragedy, absolutely. When a cuckoo child is in sufficient distress, they can sometimes unlock a level of telepathic strength they shouldn't have been able to access for literally years. She called for help. Your family replied. Specifically, Angela Baker replied."

"Be careful what you say about her," said Aunt Evie pleasantly. "She's my mother."

"She's not a receptive telepath," said Mark.

Aunt Evie blinked. "You didn't call her broken. Usually, cuckoos call her broken, or a freak, or something even nastier."

"She's not broken. She's perfectly normal. There are one or two like her born every generation, and most of the time we're not preparing to force a Queen, so they're killed. But they keep cropping up in the populace, and sometimes they're allowed to live, because sometimes we know we're going to need them." Mark managed to sound apologetic as he said, "Once she acquired Sarah, and it was clear that she was going to keep and properly prepare her, everyone else pulled out of the region. Angela was to be left alone to cultivate our Queen."

"Talk faster," said Antimony, in a voice that was suddenly devoid of emotion. I glanced at her. She had gone pale and was looking at Mark like she couldn't decide whether to slit his throat or run for the hills.

Mark looked placidly back. "You're finally catching on," he said. "A non-receptive cuckoo never receives the histories. They don't go through the first traumatic morph, and they don't understand why the rest of us are the way we are. They call us cruel, call us evil . . . and when one of them somehow acquires custody of a normal cuckoo child, their first instinct will always be to crack the child's mind open and scoop the offending pieces out. They still get instincts, those non-receivers. They have room for them. They don't understand that normal cuckoos don't have that. They take out every scrap of the history, of the law, and they leave a void behind. A void that heals so slowly. But it does heal. It comes together the tiniest bit at a time. Puberty happens, but the metamorphosis doesn't. The larval stage stretches on and on, years past when it should have ended.

"Sometimes that's the end of it. Those stunted cuckoos live their whole lives in a suspended larval state, never quite becoming full adults, no longer children, and they try to be good, and they hate themselves, and they never learn what they're capable of, and eventually they die." Mark shook his head. "It's a terrible, self-loathing way to live, but it's part of our life cycle, and it can't always be avoided. Sometimes, though—sometimes they don't stay stuck that way. Sometimes they either trigger their own metamorphosis or have it triggered for them, and when that happens, something wonderful can follow. The metamorphosis continues past its normal limits. They become adults and, when their brains can't find the missing information, they enter their second instar and metamorphosize again almost immediately, entering a *third* instar."

"Sarah never metamorphosized at all," I said. "I'd notice if she grew wings or an ovipositor or something."

"Our metamorphosis is internal," said Mark. "Cuckoo children don't turn into giant wasps when they hit puberty. They simply . . . well, change their minds."

Slow-growing horror filled the pit of my stomach. "When she hurt herself in New York," I said. "That's what made it happen, isn't it?"

Mark nodded. "She pushed so hard that her mind, which had healed up completely around the missing pieces, finally understood that it was supposed to transform. It contracted, losing most of its ability to form coherent thought, and then it expanded, growing in potential, growing in strength. She entered her first instar years later than most of her kin and entered her second instar inside of the week. She was well on her way to becoming the strongest of us. Becoming something we only know exists because of the information in our heads, the information passed down from our ancestors. She was becoming a Queen."

A life lived around Aeslin mice can make capital letters pretty easy to hear. "What's a Queen? Are you saying that Sarah's going to become your leader or something?"

"No. We don't have 'leaders,' as such. We're too solitary. We can't stand each other long enough to give or receive orders. I think maybe we *did* have leaders, back on Johrlar. That feels right, somehow. It feels like an evolutionary inevitability. But here, in exile, we prefer to stick to ourselves. Queens don't lead. Queens are powerful. They have the kind of strength someone like me can only dream of. They—"

Mark stopped mid-sentence, eyes going gray, like they had frosted over. He began to shake.

I knew, immediately, what had to be happening. I whirled, and there was Heloise, still cuffed to the table where we'd left her, eyes now open and solid, blazing white, staring at us with the kind of hatred that starts wars.

There wasn't time to think about what I was going to do next. I ran across the barn to the cabinet where we kept the actual gardening and yard supplies, jerking it open and grabbing the big can of Raid. Then I ran to Heloise's side, shaking the can with every step. I aimed it right between her eyes.

She shrank back, the glow in her eyes dying, replaced by blue irises and utter terror. Behind me, I heard Mark gasp for air.

"You're a big bug," I said flatly. "I don't judge—I'm

in love with a big bug—but you're a big bug, and this is bug spray. What happens if I squirt this in your eyes? Nothing good, I bet. Nothing you'd be too excited about experiencing. Want to find out?"

"You wouldn't dare," she whispered.

"What's that? Oh, sorry, it may be hard to talk for a while, since my cousin's boyfriend crushed your trachea and all. Which you totally deserved, and I hope it hurts like hell."

"Here, bud." Dad took the can of Raid from my hand. "I'll keep her busy while you hear the rest of what our other prisoner has to say. And then we'll figure out whether or not we're taking one of them apart."

Heloise sneered at him.

"I vote this one," I said, before walking back over to Mark. "Talk faster."

"Everything is math," he blurted.

I blinked. So did everyone else.

"That's what my mother always says," said Aunt Evie. "She says the universe is numerical in nature, so the better a mathematician someone is, the closer they draw to the divine. It's why she became an accountant. For her, that was like joining the priesthood."

"Only without the celibacy," said Uncle Kevin, and snickered as Evie elbowed him in the side.

Mark nodded, ignoring my uncle entirely, and said, "Exactly. Everything is math, and everything is *made* of math, and if you can manipulate the numbers, you can change the world. Literally change the world. You need to know the right equations, or you need the raw power to punch your way to the correct answer without taking the steps in the middle. But if you can accomplish one of those two things, there's nothing you can't do."

A cold ball of dread was growing in the center of my chest, filling the space where my heart was supposed to be. Wherever my heart had gone, it would stop beating at any moment, I just knew it, forced out by that killing cold. "Cuckoos aren't from around here," I said quietly.

Mark met my eyes, not flinching away. "No."

"But we've never seen any evidence they could travel between dimensions. They don't use magic the way most sapient species use it," I said. "They don't make charms or cast spells or bend the laws of physics. They just influence minds and do math."

"Yes," said Mark.

"Is cuckoo magic math-based?"

"Yes," said Mark again. "But the equations are . . . they're huge. They're resource-intensive in a way that almost always results in the death of the person who completes them, and those are the ones we still have. There are pieces of the math missing. Whole sections that were wiped clean when our ancestors were put into exile."

The urge to sit down was suddenly overwhelming. "You're saying that when the people back on Johrlar decided to throw your ancestors out, they stole the math that would have allowed them to go home."

"Shut *up*," snarled Heloise.

There was the distinct sound of an aerosol can being shaken, and she stopped talking.

"Yes," said Mark. "We don't know what our ancestors did, we don't know whether they were political dissidents or cultural outcasts or criminals—"

"Can I vote 'criminals'?" asked Antimony. "I'm going to vote criminals."

Mark ignored her. All his focus was on me, which was a little unnerving, even knowing that the charm around my neck was preventing him from doing anything to psychically influence my reactions. "—but when they were expelled from their home dimension, the knowledge of how to get *back* was wiped from their minds. They were supposed to remain where they were, forever. They hadn't been killed, but they had been cast out, and their exile was intended to be eternal."

"I don't think I like where this is going," said Sam.

"We know the original equations were beautiful and subtle and kind," said Mark. "We know that when our ancestors were exiled, Johrlar survived. We know the equations could be performed over and over and over again."

"Yeah, because they were being performed by a whole bunch of people," said Elsie. Everyone turned to look at her. She glanced up from her nails and shrugged. "What? You know I'm right. Look, you're talking about math that's so big that it kills people. Well, that's what research teams are for. That's what *think tanks* are for. If you have a spell that's so resource-intensive it uses a sorcerer up, you get a whole bunch of sorcerers to come and cast it. If you have an equation that's so resource-intensive it melts brains, you get a whole bunch of smart people to think about different pieces of it at the same time, so nobody's brain gets melted. The equations aren't meant to be a solo voyage. No big. Why are you telling us all this?"

"We don't know the equations, but this isn't the dimension where we were first exiled," said Mark. "We found another way. A cruder way. It's like a sledgehammer instead of a scalpel. The equations we have, the ones we've developed, require a Queen to resolve them. Once she finishes her final morph and enters her fourth instar, she can do the math. She can find the right answers. And she can rip a hole in the fabric between dimensions, allowing us to move on."

Antimony's eyes widened. "That's how you got here," she said. "You ripped a hole in the fabric of our dimension, and you came through it."

"Not me, personally, but yes," said Mark. "It was centuries ago. The world where we'd been was no longer . . . welcoming. Once the beings native to a dimension figure out that we exist, things tend to grow unpleasant fairly quickly, and we have to move on to better, safer hunting grounds. It's a matter of survival. We don't really have a choice."

"Other things followed you through the hole you made, you prick," snapped Antimony. She took a step backward, flexing her hands. Tiny balls of flame danced around her fingertips, burning lambent white.

Sam gave her a concerned look. "Uh, if it's cool with the rest of you, I'm going to take my sort of overly-excited girlfriend inside to check on James before she sets the barn on fire."

"Not interested in dying in a fiery conflagration today, so that sounds great, thanks," said Aunt Evelyn. She glanced at Antimony. "Remember your calming words, sweetie. Ask the mice if you need help with guided meditation."

"Sure, Mom," Annie mumbled, and let Sam pull her out of the barn, reducing our numbers by two and lowering the temperature by several degrees. I hadn't even realized how warm it was getting with her standing there, setting herself on fire.

"Eyes forward, missy," said Dad, giving another shake of the Raid can. "You want to stay focused on me, unless you want a blast of pesticide to the face."

"Can I just say how much I'm enjoying this?" asked Mark. "I mean, there's still a chance you're going to murder me rather than letting me go, and that'll suck pretty badly as far as I'm concerned, but I'd probably die anyway when the world ends, and at least this way I get to watch you all torment Heloise first."

"Wait." I held up one hand. "Why do you keep saying the world is going to end?"

"Because it is, if you don't stop it." Mark looked at me levelly. "Sarah Zellaby is the daughter of an ordinary cuckoo woman. There was nothing special about her until her parents were killed and she was adopted by a crèche-keeper—Angela Baker. Angela instinctively rewired Sarah's brain in the process of removing what she registered as negative conditioning, creating space sufficient for the brain to undergo substantial physical transformation when Sarah pushed herself too far and strained her psychic capabilities. That was her morph from first instar to second. The second instar lasted less than a week before she entered her second morph, which lasted *years*. Second morph is dangerous. It's rare, and cuckoos who enter it are usually ripped apart by their own kin, rather than allowed to finish the process. They have too much power when it ends."

"So Sarah's a super-cuckoo," I said.

"So Sarah was in her second instar when she arrived here," he said. "She triggered and completed her *third* instar in the process of removing the trap Amelia had placed inside your mind. The morph into third instar is brief. It's painless, compared to the variant form of second. It's a preparational step, if that makes sense."

"None of this makes sense," I muttered.

"Biology rarely does," said Uncle Kevin, eyes gleaming. I realized he was excited. Thanks to the anti-telepathy charm, I couldn't sense his emotions the way I normally could, which was how I'd been able to miss it for this long.

I glanced at Mom. She had the same half-hungry look on her face, barely concealed behind the veil of her concern for Sarah. I managed, barely, not to wince.

We're all Prices, even me and Elsie; there's never really been any question that if and when we marry, it'll be the "Harrington" part of our names we shed, because we're Prices. We were born to this fight and to the endless scholarship started by our ancestors when they left the Covenant and realized how little work had been done to preserve the secrets and stories of the various sapient beings who shared this world with humanity. People talk a lot about what it means to be a Price. We're terrifying to the ones who oppose us, we're weird to the ones who stand with us, we're heroes to the ones who depend on us. But there's one thing that tends to get left out of the conversation, treated as less important than the need to keep fighting and keep winning until the war is over:

We're *scientists*. Mom and Uncle Kevin even more than Elsie and me. They're the direct descendants of Thomas and Alice Price. They were raised to believe that the world can make sense, if they just try hard enough and refuse to stop poking at its soft bits. The cuckoos have been one of the greatest mysteries our family has ever encountered. We'd tried for years to learn more about their biology, without taking apart one of the two cuckoos we considered part of the family. To have one walk into our home and just start talking was, well . . .

It was no wonder this was going so slowly. The people who would normally have hurried things along—the people we instinctively still listened to, thanks to their age and our familial relationship—were too enthralled by the potential to learn something to focus on what actually mattered.

I was focused on what actually mattered. I was focused on Sarah. I took a step toward Mark.

"Third instar is a preparational step, fine," I said. "Preparing for *what*?"

"When there are multiple potential Queens ready for their fourth instar, we test them," said Mark. "I don't mean 'we' as in 'me,' I mean 'we' as in 'whoever has them.' They're tested, and they're tried, and when one of them proves stronger than all the others, she's given the numbers she needs to unlock her fourth metamorphosis. First morph is a necessity, second morph is a gift, third morph is a challenge, and fourth is an ascension."

"So Sarah's a god now?" asked Elsie. I doubted Mark could hear, or understand, the warning in her tone. "That's going to make Thanksgiving dinner awkward."

"If she survives the process, she's not going to be a

god, she's going to be a Queen," said Mark. "She'll have the strength to do the math and put enough power behind it to blow this dimension to pieces. She's going to smash this world like an eggshell. She's going to open the way for the cuckoos to go somewhere else. If you don't stop her, she's going to destroy everything she's ever cared about, and she's going to destroy you in the process."

"That sounds like something you'd want," said Mom.

"It does, doesn't it? I know it's something *she* wants." Mark jerked his chin toward the silent, furious Heloise. "But no. I'm here to help you stop this. I'm here because this needs to not happen. There's one thing you need to do first, though, and it's going to be hard."

"What's that?" asked Uncle Kevin.

Mark took a deep breath. "You're going to need to trust me."

Seventeen

$$\pi_2(n) \sim 2C_2 \frac{n}{(\ln n)^2} \sim 2C_2 \int_2^n \frac{dt}{(\ln t)^2}$$

"There are losses we don't move past, no matter how hard we try. Some wounds, once inflicted, bleed forever underneath the skin. All we can do is learn to live with them."

—Jonathan Healy

Back in the house, with two monsters in the barn, no big deal (very big deal)

T HIS IS A BAD idea!" Mom was right up in Uncle Kevin's face, shoulders locked, one finger jabbing at his chest like she thought she could poke him into seeing things her way. "We can't let them go just because one of them is a good liar. Lying is what cuckoos *do*. You'd see that, if not for the part where you—"

She seemed to realize she was treading on dangerous ground and stopped herself mid-sentence. Not quickly enough; the damage was done.

"Which part, Janie? The part where I married a cuckoo's daughter? The part where I welcomed my wife's sister into my home? How much of this is about Sarah, and how much of it is about the part where you don't want Artie to be in love with Sarah? You can marry an incubus, but God forbid the boy wants to date outside his species?"

Mom's eyes went wide for a moment before narrowing

into a menacing expression I knew all too well. "Kevin Alexander Price," she said, grinding each word between her teeth before spitting it out, so his name became a condemnation, "I can't believe you would say something like that to me. I can't believe you would *think* that."

"I can," said Aunt Evie.

Antimony was suddenly at my elbow, grasping it and steering me away from the unsettling sight of our parents ripping into each other. I started to open my mouth. She shook her head, pulling me along to the kitchen, where James and Sam were waiting.

"You know the plan?" she asked, eyes on James.

He nodded, his still-damp hair sticking to his forehead and ears. "I'm good with intransigent parents," he said. "Go save your cousin."

Antimony nodded and started walking again, not letting go of me until we had reached the front door and slipped outside to the porch. Sam followed, easing the door shut again once we were all safely through. Annie let go of my elbow.

"Come on," she said. "Let's go get our cousin back."

"What are you—we can't go without them." I gestured toward the house. "We don't have the numbers to go up against a whole *hive* of cuckoos. It'll be a bloodbath!"

"That's why we're picking up some reinforcements before we leave," she said, and started across the lawn toward the barn, not looking back.

"Come on." Sam clapped me on the shoulder with one massive hand. "She's not going to wait for us, and I know you'll be pissed if she goes running off to the rescue without you."

"I can't believe we're doing this," I said, and followed Annie.

She didn't look back once as we walked to the barn and inside, to where Elsie and Dad were still standing watch over our two captive cuckoos. Elsie studied her nails, tucked the file into her purse, and stood.

"Took you long enough," she said. "Dad owes me five bucks."

"To be fair, I couldn't estimate how long it would take Annie here to get tired of waiting for Artie to move," said Dad, voice mild. He gave the can of Raid another shake, still aiming it directly at Heloise's face. "You can't have this one, kids. I'm sorry if your plan was depending on her, but I don't trust her enough to let her up."

"We only need one asshole for this extraction," said Annie, producing a knife from inside her shirt . . .

. . . and using it to cut through the ropes holding Mark to the chair. I attempted to protest. All that came out was a garbled squeaking sound.

Mark stretched his arms over his head, grimacing. "You people don't care much about chiropractic health when you're tying someone down, do you?" he asked.

"What the hell, Annie?" I managed not to shout. I was pretty proud of myself for that.

"He's going to lead us to Sarah," said Annie. She made the knife disappear back into her clothing. "Relax, Artie. He can't reach our minds through the charms we're wearing, which means he can't do anything to hurt us. Unless he knows how a gun works. And managed to get his hands on one, which, not going to happen."

Mark laughed wryly. "My parents never allowed firearms in the house. Too much of a chance Cici would pick one up and manage to hurt somebody with it."

"Your parents?" I asked. "I thought cuckoos always left their babies with host families."

"Shut *up*," hissed Heloise.

"I thought we had finally come to an agreement," said Dad, and shook the can again before giving a small, warning squirt of pesticide in the air above her head. Heloise whimpered. She didn't say anything else.

"You know, I gotta say, I'm really impressed with how terrible you people are," said Mark. "I've been listening to Ingrid talk about her daughter the princess, and how she was going to make her a Queen and use her to destroy the world, for *years*. She never mentioned that the people raising her were genuinely awful. You hate us because we're the competition, right?"

"We hate you because you're dangerous predators who murder innocent people and make things worse for absolutely everyone, but thanks for playing." Elsie stood, slinging her purse strap over her shoulder. "Dad, you're cool with staying here, right?"

"Of course, pumpkin." Dad gave his can another shake. "Your mother's going to be furious when she realizes what's happening. I'm hoping this little gift bag will keep her from getting too angry. It's not every day you get a cuckoo to play with."

"I'm not a *toy*," snarled Heloise.

"Sort of are," said Elsie. "Sort of turned yourself into one when you decided that a bad haircut and a pair of yoga pants meant you could pretend to be our cousin without getting in trouble for it. Because your friend is right: we're not good people. We can't afford to be. We're one side of a three-sided war, and you're the enemy."

"Hey!" I hadn't realized I was going to shout until I was actually doing it. Everyone except for Heloise turned to look at me. I glared at them, trying to encompass the whole room at once. "If somebody doesn't tell me what's going on *right now*, I'm going to march back inside and tell Mom that this is happening."

"We're going to rescue Sarah," said Annie bluntly. "Mark here is going to lead us straight to her, and we're going to get her back."

I looked at Mark. He turned his face slightly away, not meeting my eyes, and I knew. I knew what he wasn't ready to tell us yet; what I wasn't ready to hear, because there was still a chance he might be wrong. He'd said there hadn't been a Queen in centuries, not since the cuckoos had ripped a hole in whatever innocent dimension they'd parasitized before this one. He could still be wrong.

Sarah could still be saved.

"Fine," I said. "Elsie, you're driving."

"I am," she said. "It'll be a tight fit, but I've crammed five people into my car before."

"So let's go." I shook my head. "I can't imagine Sarah wants us to keep her waiting any longer than we have to."

"She's never been that kind of patient," Annie agreed. The five of us started for the door, forming a tight little clump with Mark in the middle, where he couldn't run away.

"Have fun, kids!" Dad called, and then we were outside, and everything was happening.

Mark got the front passenger seat. I didn't like putting him up there with my sister and easy access to the steering wheel, but it was that or cram him into the backseat, which would increase the odds of accidentally touching him without a layer of clothing in the way. Our anti-telepathy charms were good. They weren't good enough to stand up to extended skin contact. We might have decided to trust him for the moment, but that didn't mean we wanted him inside our minds.

That was where a cuckoo could do the most damage. Once they were past your defenses, they could basically do whatever they wanted, and there was no way to catch or stop them.

No one came out of the house as we drove down to the gate, and through it to the road. Elsie still waited until we were clear to turn on her headlights, and slumped slightly as she did, the worst of the tension leaving her shoulders.

"Okay, that's one hurdle down," she said.

"My parents are going to kill me," said Antimony. "Actual murder. Let's really enjoy this little rescue mission, because it's the last one I'm ever going to go on." She was sitting in the middle, one leg slung over Sam's to make the footwell less crowded.

Sam snorted. "Your parents are going to be arguing about how they're supposed to handle this until the sun comes up. We'll be home and making waffles by then."

"I like waffles," said Elsie.

"I know this is only confusing because I can't read your mind, but your parents aren't *actually* going to kill you, are they?" asked Mark. "If they are, I say again, absolutely terrible people. How you got a reputation for being the good guys, I may never know."

"We have a good propaganda arm," I said. "You mentioned *your* parents before. I thought all cuckoos killed their parents when they hit puberty."

"And a sister," added Antimony. "Cici. What gives?"

"Right." Mark sighed. "You know how I don't want to destroy the world and head off to terrorize a fresh dimension with the rest of my merry band of predators? Well, Cici is why. She's my little sister. Cecilia. She's a holy terror. Smart and funny and awful. Really, really awful. She might be as terrible as you. It's hard for me to measure."

"Another cuckoo?" asked Elsie.

"Human," said Mark. "You're not the only ones who come from a mixed family, you know."

"I thought you . . ." I stopped, unsure how to finish my thought without sounding like an ass. Then I remembered that Mark was still technically our prisoner and had been working with the people who kidnapped Sarah and forced her into a dangerous, involuntary physical transformation. "I thought cuckoo kids prevented their human parents from having more children."

"Normally, we do; cuckoos are selfish even as children, and the majority of us are happy as only children," said Mark. "We don't like to share. But my parents left me with my grandmother for six months when Dad got a job with a German robotics firm. They must have gotten pregnant their first night in Europe. Mom was *huge* when they came back." He sounded frustrated and fond at the same time, like any big brother thinking about the moment when his life turned upside-down. "She waddled when she walked, it was hilarious. And then there was this baby. This screaming, red-faced, wailing baby that everyone said was my little sister. And I remember . . ."

He paused for a long moment. When he spoke again, his voice was softer. "I remember thinking 'I could wish for this to go away.' I hadn't reached my first instar yet, I didn't have conscious access to the history, but I knew I wasn't like my parents. I knew sometimes I scraped my knee and I bled clear and everyone acted like that was normal. I knew I could hear other people's dreams. And that baby . . . I knew, just by looking at her, that *she* would bleed red like our parents. She wouldn't feel like she was somehow outside the family, like she came from another planet. It would have been easy to hate her."

"Why didn't you?" I asked.

"I know it sounds cliché and stupid and all that bullshit, but I poked her. And she grabbed my finger, and her hand was so tiny, and her grip was so strong, and I thought, who cares what color her blood is? Who cares if she looks more like Dad than I do? She's my sister. She's *mine*. I guess I was still selfish—I'm a cuckoo, after all—but selfish doesn't have to mean bad. You people, you're selfish. You think you'd be riding to some random cuckoo's rescue? Fuck, no. You want Sarah back because she's yours. She belongs to you, and you didn't agree to lose her, and now you're going to go get her. Selfishness can be a strength."

"What about that first instar you were talking about?" asked Annie. "Shouldn't you have killed your whole family then, like a good little cuckoo? All the ones we've been able to talk to have told us that they loved their adoptive parents right up until the moment when they didn't. Usually that conversation happens right before they try to kill us, so they're probably biased, but still."

"Oh, I hit it," said Mark. "I woke up in the middle of the night with the knowledge and laws of my entire species filling my head, crowding out everything else, making it almost impossible for me to breathe. I was fifteen. Cici was four. I thought she'd probably scream and wake our parents, so I knew I had to kill her first if I wanted it to be easy. It mattered that it be easy. I didn't want to upset her. That's probably when I should have realized something was wrong, when I was thinking 'I don't want to upset my sister' and 'I'm going to murder her' at the same time, but I was fifteen and I was being eaten alive by memories that weren't mine, so I think I did okay, all things considered. I got a knife. I went to her room."

He paused, long enough to turn his face toward the window and watch the dark trees rolling by outside. "She had this doll. This stupid doll. If you squeezed it, it was supposed to say 'Mama.' Cici was hard on her toys—she still is—and she'd bashed it against the wall until the voice box broke, and all it did when you squeezed it was make this awful moaning sound. I stepped on it on my way into her room. She woke up. She looked at me with those big brown eyes, and she asked if we were playing a game called 'horror movie.' And I said yes, we were, and the first person to scream would lose." Mark chuckled darkly. "I figured it would keep her quiet long enough for me to take care of her, you know? Only instead, she jumped out of bed and ran off giggling, and I had to chase after her so she wouldn't wake our parents, and every time I almost caught her, she'd get away again. It was almost morning before I realized I was *letting* her get away. She'd managed to keep me running until the murderous period passed and it didn't matter that I knew what I was. It didn't matter because I loved her, and I loved my parents, and I wasn't going to hurt them."

"And so you kept them," I said.

"I kept them," Mark agreed. "Cici's twelve now. She's a living nightmare pretending to be a little girl, and I'm grateful every single day that she woke up before I could do something I couldn't take back. It's why I knew the plan—the big, amazing, this-is-gonna-work plan—was going to fail."

"How's that?" asked Sam.

"A couple of years ago, I lost her at the mall. Turned around and she was gone. I pretty much hate most humans. Being able to read their minds will do that to a guy. The things people think when they don't know someone's looking . . ." He shuddered. "Anyway, she was just gone. So I freaked out and went looking for her, thinking the worst, thinking I'd forced myself not to be a monster for her sake and then failed to protect her from the other monsters, when she came running out of this store, grabbed my arm, and said a man who looked just like me but wasn't had tried to take her. I knew she had to mean another cuckoo—we'd clearly wandered into someone's hunting grounds, and he'd assumed I was poaching, so he'd taken her to teach me a lesson—but I also know that we all look alike to humans. I asked how she knew it wasn't me. She said he didn't hum. Humans who spend enough time around us after our first instar acclimate to our presence. They learn how to tell us apart, and we can't change their minds the same way we can before they get attuned to us. It's a double-edged sword. The more time we spend with someone the more we can influence them, at first, but eventually they get desensitized, and it gets so much harder."

"You know about the hum," I said.

"Once Cici told me, yeah. I started watching for it. I always know when she's around, or our folks. They change the texture of the air." Mark shook his head. "I won't lose them. They're mine."

"What happened to the cuckoo who took your sister?" asked Elsie.

"I went back to the mall the next day, alone, waited for him to approach me, stabbed him in the stomach fifteen times, dumped him out back, and set his corpse on fire," said Mark, as matter-of-fact as if he'd been placing an order at McDonalds. "Nobody touches my family."

"But you helped Heloise touch ours," I said.

"I helped Ingrid, who, please remember, is Sarah's biological mother, lure her away from you. I'm not saying I didn't. She knows where I live. She knows where my *family* lives. I have no real desire to be at war with you—you are all terrible, terrifying people—but I wasn't going to risk Cici's life because your cousin was somehow more important than she is. She's not. I did what I was told, I escaped as soon as I could, and now I'm helping you. Be grateful for that part. I could have told Ingrid about the hum. I could have sided with my hive against humanity. I'm not, because I love my sister. Take the fucking win."

Elsie took the next curve more sharply than she needed to. Mark's forehead thumped against the glass of the passenger side window. He swore, rubbing his head as he turned to glare at her.

It was really a pity cuckoos couldn't understand the nuances of human expressions. The sweetness of Elsie's smile was a thing of pure and genuine beauty.

"Oops," she said.

Mark kept rubbing his head but didn't say anything.

"How many cuckoos are in your hive?" asked Antimony.

"With Heloise out of the picture, and not counting

myself, three," he said. "If Sarah's already finished with her instar, four, and the fourth is a big fat 'game over' for the rest of us. She'll be suggestible. Ingrid is right there to make suggestions."

"Sarah won't hurt us." My voice wavered, making my statement sound almost more like a question.

Mark twisted in his seat to face me directly. He looked almost sorry. Somehow, that was the most terrifying thing to happen in this entire terrifying night.

"Sarah won't have a choice," he said. "No one really knows for sure what a Queen is like, because we get one per dimension. She enters her fourth instar, she blows a hole in reality, and if she's lucky, it kills her, because if she's not lucky, she melts her own brain in the process of getting the math to work just the way she wants it to, and we're not a species of caretakers."

"You mean you'd just leave her to die?" asked Sam.

"Sure," said Mark. "Let's go with that."

"Maybe she hasn't entered her fourth instar yet," said Antimony.

"Then maybe we have a chance," said Mark. He turned back to Elsie. "I'd drive faster if I were you."

Elsie slammed her foot down on the gas.

I closed my eyes. The anti-telepathy charm around my neck suddenly seemed impossibly heavy. If Sarah was in range, I didn't know it. I couldn't know it. And that meant she couldn't know we were coming for her. She was cut off. She was alone.

She had to be so scared.

We're on our way, Sarah, I thought, and wished there was any way I could lie to myself and believe she would hear me. *Hold on, because we're coming. We're coming just as fast as we can.*

Hold on.

Eighteen

$$\pi_2(n) \sim 2C_2 \frac{n}{(\ln n)^2} \sim 2C_2 \int_2^n \frac{dt}{(\ln t)^2}$$

"Breathe, baby, breathe. You breathe and
you keep on breathing. That's the only
thing I'm going to ask of you today. You
just keep on breathing."

—Enid Healy

In the shining whiteness of the infinite void, which sort of sucks, to be honest

"HELLO?"

My voice didn't echo. An echo implied a wall,
however distant, for it to bounce off of. Instead, it
dropped away like a stone falling into a well, dense and
dull and disregarded.

There was no ground under my feet, but I was standing anyway, toes pointed outward instead of dangling
down. I raised one foot and stomped experimentally.
There was no feeling of resistance; my foot simply
stopped when it hit what my brain insisted on thinking
of as the floor.

Maybe the thought was the problem. I closed my
eyes. *There is no floor,* I told myself sternly. *There is
nothing for me to stand on.*

The sensation of falling was immediate and
stomach-churning, as the not-a-floor beneath me took
my thoughts to heart and dissolved, leaving me to
plummet through the nothingness. I screamed before

I could think better of it, and my terror sounded as wrung-out and empty as everything else.

"There's a floor!" I shouted. "There's a floor there's a floor *there's a floor*—"

The impact when my feet hit the reconstituted floor was enough to send me sprawling, my entire body aching from the sudden stop. I lay where I was, suspended on a flat, seemingly solid surface that looked exactly like everything else surrounding me. No walls, no ceiling, but there was a floor now, called into existence by my demands.

I rolled onto my back and stared up into the nothingness. My throat hurt from the screaming and my ankles hurt from the landing and everything was awful. Everything was absolutely, utterly, no questions about it, awful.

Laboriously, I sat up and looked around again. Any hopes that the void would have changed during my fall were for naught: the world around me was as blank and white and empty as it had been before. The only thing to indicate that I had moved at all was the ache in my butt and ankles, and even as I thought about it, the ache faded away, like my body couldn't hold onto even the idea of pain.

That was actually a good thing. It meant I wasn't really here; this was another mindscape, like the one I'd entered when Artie was caught in the cuckoo's trap. Only this time, the mindscape was *mine*, and I was the one in the trap. There was no one coming to get me out of this.

I needed to get out on my own.

"This sucks," I announced, on the off chance that one of the cuckoos who'd stolen me happened to be listening. "If you were hoping to convince me to help you do some horrible cuckoo thing, this is not a good way of going about it. This is frightening and inconvenient and . . . and *mean*, and I don't work with people who are mean to me."

There was no answer. To be fair, I hadn't been expecting one.

I looked around the void again, searching for anything that would break the endless whiteness. Then I paused. This was my mindscape. It, and everything it contained, belonged to me. Which meant that anything I could think of should be right at my fingertips.

"I want a chair," I said to the air in front of me. "Not too comfortable. A chair where I can sit and think."

I turned.

There was a chair behind me.

It was simple, plain black leather with polished brass casters, the sort of thing that belonged behind a desk in a home office. It could have been placed in the window of any office supply store in the world, glistening in the light, inviting weary souls to set their burdens down for the low, low price of a few hundred dollars with an available installment plan. I took a step toward it, reaching out to run my fingertips along one faux-mahogany arm.

It felt solid and real, as real as I was. Which made sense. In here, we were both thoughts, and my thoughts were sufficient to change the world.

I sank down into the leather, tucking my legs up under myself in a cat-curl position that had been my preference when working since I was a kid. I stared at the nothingness in front of me.

"I need a chalkboard," I said, and blinked, deliberately slow.

When I opened my eyes again, the chalkboard was there, old-fashioned and tall, green slate pristine as it awaited my genius. Two fresh erasers sat in the tray beneath it, alongside sticks of chalk in multiple colors. It was a chalkboard out of a children's movie, pushed into place by the set designer of my thoughts, ready for me to begin.

I didn't move.

The chalkboard was tempting—more tempting than

any chalkboard I'd ever seen—and there were numbers
nibbling at the edges of my mind, glorious numbers,
numbers that whispered promised solutions to every
problem I'd ever had and every dilemma I'd ever faced.
I could use those numbers to get myself out of here, I
just knew it. Something was holding me back.

I'd seen numbers like this before. Not often. They
shifted and twisted when I tried to focus on them directly, flickering like candles in a soft wind, never quite
going out, never quite holding still. I'd seen these same
numbers when I injured myself in New York, blossom-
ing around the edges of my consciousness before I hit
the ground and everything went away. They meant
something. They resolved to something.

I closed my eyes again. "I need a desk, a laptop, and
an Internet connection."

They were there when I opened my eyes. The desk
was old and scarred, and I recognized it from my father's office. He'd built it himself out of reclaimed
wood, blending oak and mahogany, pine and cedar. It
was a patchwork thing, like he was, and when I reached
out to caress the wood with one trembling hand, it was
almost like he was there with me, watching over me.
Tears burned at the corners of my eyes. I blinked them
away. If I didn't find a way out of here, I was never going to see him again. I couldn't let that happen.

The laptop was much newer, sleek and futuristic
and generic. I tugged it toward me and opened a chat
client.

My entire family was offline. That was a disappointment, but not a surprise. There was no way of knowing
whether the Internet connection I'd imagined would
correlate in any way to the world outside my mindscape. But I hoped it would.

In an earlier era, I might have imagined pigeons
with notes tied to their legs, or hunting horns, or some
other clumsy mechanism of communicating across
great distances. Here and now, the Internet was the

answer. I kept scrolling through the listed names, each with the little grayed-out dot that meant they weren't available to talk to me. I scrolled faster and faster, past every person I'd ever touched, every person I'd ever made a connection with, every person who might have been able to hear me. There were so many of them. There weren't nearly enough.

The last name on the list, *Ingrid*, was the only one with a green dot.

I hesitated, staring at that name, staring at that dot, before finally clicking on it and pulling up a chat window.

What did you do to me? I typed.

The cursor blinked for several seconds before the reply popped up: *Sarah?*

Yes. This is Sarah. What did you do to me?

How are you talking to me right now? You're in the middle of your metamorphosis. You can't be talking to me.

I narrowed my eyes, glaring at the computer screen like I thought she could somehow see it. *No one bothered to tell me the rules, so I guess I don't have to follow them,* I typed. *Where am I? Why is this happening to me?*

Again, the cursor blinked, longer this time. Finally, the response came: *You're going to change the world, Sarah. I'm very proud of you. More proud than you can possibly know. You need to do the math now. You need to solve the problem, so we can move forward.*

At least this was easy. *No.*

You don't have a choice.

I think I do, I typed. *I think I can just sit here and not touch the numbers. I have a computer now. I can look at pictures of cute cats on Tumblr.*

Forever?

That gave me pause.

This was my mind, yes, but it was functionally an exercise in solitary confinement at the same time. Yes,

I had a computer, with a telepath's makeshift connection to the illusion of the Internet, and yes, I could call things into being by wanting them strongly enough, and no, that didn't change the fact that I was alone in here. My family was out of range; the only person I could talk to was Ingrid, and she could just decide to stop talking whenever she wanted to. She could cut me off. She could leave me by myself in this blazing whiteness, until I started doing the math out of the desperate need to get out, to get away.

Maybe. Or maybe this was like a holodeck in *Star Trek*, and I could start calling people out of my memories of them, using them for company, for stability, for a way to keep myself from doing what the cuckoos wanted from me. Because if there was one thing I knew for sure, it was that doing what the cuckoos wanted wasn't going to end well. Not for anyone.

"Took you this long to come to that conclusion, huh? Maybe you're not as smart as you've always said you were."

"Verity!" I looked up and there she was in all her glory—literally. She was dressed like she was heading for a dance competition, wearing heels so high that it seemed impossible she could walk in them and a short, fringed garment that barely qualified for the name "dress." "Moderately long shirt" might have been a better description. The individual crystals stitched to the fabric gleamed and sparkled in the light, and her short blonde hair had been crimped into perfect finger waves, making her look like the very image of a Gibson Girl.

But her dress was gray, and her lipstick was gray, and neither of those things made sense. I wouldn't imagine her that way.

"What's wrong with your lips?" I blurted.

Verity smiled a little. "I can say this because I'm not really me and you know it, which means you know this, and you just never wanted to tell yourself. You can't see the color red."

"Of course I can. My favorite sweater is red."

"And you know that because you've seen it through your father's eyes. You know what red is because you borrow it from the people around you, so naturally that you don't even notice that everything red is gray for half a second before the color turns on. That's how it's always worked for you."

I looked at her blankly. "What does that have to do with anything? Why isn't the color turning on in here?"

"Normal cuckoos don't see the color red. They've never cared enough about how humans work to learn how to see it. Biologically, structurally, you can't see it. It isn't there for you. Socially, emotionally, you can see it. You had to learn how in order to be happy." Verity took a step backward, leaning her hip against the chalkboard. "I'm not here."

"I know."

"You could make me think I was here, if you wanted to, but you'd know I wasn't."

"I would." I glanced around at the nothingness. "Right now, anyway. If we stayed here long enough, I wouldn't know it anymore. I could let this be the world. I could imagine more than just you."

A smile tugged at the corner of Verity's grayed-out lips. "No red."

"No red," I agreed. "But I'd be able to understand faces. That would be a nice change. You have a beautiful smile."

"You're remembering other people thinking that I had a beautiful smile," Verity corrected gently. "You don't *know*. Not really."

I glanced at my computer. Ingrid had apparently noticed that I wasn't responding to her anymore; she had typed my name so many times that it scrolled the chat client. Gently, I closed the screen and returned my attention to Verity.

"Does it matter what I know?" I asked. "If it's in here, and it seems real, it *is* real. Everything here is whatever I want it to be. I think . . . I think I could be happy."

"Hiding inside your own mind? Really?"

"Do you have a better idea?" I exclaimed, pushing myself out of the chair. I spread my hands, indicating the white nothingness around us. "All this is happening because the cuckoos *want* me to do the math! They *want* me to reach my next instar! I don't know if you were paying attention when Mom tried to teach us about cuckoos, but doing what they *want* is never the right answer!"

"Neither is running away and hiding, and that's what you're trying to do. We're Prices. We don't hide."

"I'm not a Price!"

"You took your last name from a science fiction novel about creepy telepathic children who want to destroy the world," said Verity. "That may be one of the most Price-like things you could have done. You're family. We raised you right. You're a Price, and Prices don't run, or hide, or refuse to do something because it might be dangerous."

"But the cuckoos—"

"Want you to do some math. You love math. Math loves you. Do their damn math so you can get the hell out of here and stomp their blue-eyed asses into the floor." Verity shook her head. "I believe in you. Artie believes in you. It's time you started to believe in you, too. You can't fight if you're in the hole. Get out of the hole, and then come see me for real. I miss you, you big jerk."

"What if I can't?" I whispered. The numbers nibbling at the edges of the world felt . . . big. They felt massive in a way I'd never encountered before, like they were the numbers that underpinned the entire universe. Tackling them wouldn't just be like adding two and two together to see whether I got four. It would be like reinventing calculus, written in starlight and graded by the moon.

"You're Sarah Zellaby," she said. "Of course you can."

I closed my eyes..When I opened them again, Verity was gone.

Slowly, I sank back down into the seat I'd conjured and opened my laptop. Ingrid was still filling the screen with my name, over and over again, an unending stream of letters that seemed to lose all meaning as they went on. Words were like that. They were fragile, mutable. Their meanings changed depending on the context. "Sarah" could be me, or someone else, or a pet, or a doll, or a piece of heavy machinery owned by an overly sentimental construction engineer. It wasn't fixed.

Math, though . . . math never changed. Math always meant exactly what it said, no more and no less, and refused to be written for anyone. Math was always math. If I turned myself into numbers, I would be a wholly unique equation, something so much bigger and wilder and harder to define than "Sarah." I looked at the screen again. I put my fingers on the keys.

Give me one good reason, I typed. *Give me one good reason I should help you after you hurt Artie, and threatened my family, and brought me here against my will. Give me one good reason I should do this math for you, and not for myself.*

Because if you do, she replied, *we'll go away forever.*

I stopped. Then, haltingly, I typed, *What do you mean, you'll go away forever?*

I mean the cuckoos. All of us. We'll take the answer you give us, and we'll open a door, and we won't look back. They're gathering, Sarah. The cuckoos are sending out the call, and they're gathering, ready for you to open the way. You can save this world from us. You can create a future without fear of what's lurking where you can't see. Isn't that enough for you?

There had to be a catch. There was always a catch.

But the numbers were nibbling at the edges of the world, and whatever it was, I couldn't see it.

I solve, you go, I typed. *Promise.*

Promise.

Something about this felt wrong. I took a deep breath and answered anyway.

Fine, I wrote. *Now go away and let me work.*

I closed my eyes. Only for a moment, but when I opened them the laptop was gone, taking the desk with it. It was just me and the chalkboard, pristine, inviting, waiting for me to get started.

I rose and walked over to the board, picking up the first piece of chalk. It fit perfectly against my fingers. The numbers whispered, urging me to begin. I pressed the chalk to the board.

I began.

Nineteen

$$\pi_2(n) \sim 2C_2 \frac{n}{(\ln n)^2} \sim 2C_2 \int_2^n \frac{dt}{(\ln t)^2}$$

"Well, bugger."

—Thomas Price

A sleepy residential neighborhood in Beaverton, Oregon, about to have a real problem

MARK'S DIRECTIONS HAD BROUGHT us out of the woods, past Portland to Beaverton, a suburb where the lights always seemed to turn off before the sun had fully committed to going to bed. The streets were asleep, lined in darkened houses, sidewalks empty.

Until.

We turned one last corner, and the sidewalks abruptly acquired a thriving, if silent, population of pale-skinned, black-haired people whose clothing came from all walks of life. One woman who looked like she'd just stepped off the pages of *Vogue* turned her head to watch us roll by, her eyes flashing briefly white. Two men dressed like bikers did the same, followed by a man in the pastel scrubs of a pediatric nurse and a woman in a bathing suit. She wasn't shivering, despite the chill of the early morning air. None of them seemed to be bothered even a little by the cold.

We passed what looked like an entire preschool class, all of them wearing pajamas. Some were clutching stuffed toys. All of them looked absent, somehow, like they didn't really understand where they were or what was going on.

"What's up with the kids?" I asked.

Mark glanced in their direction. "They're still larval. They haven't reached their first instar. They don't have the history yet. Someone had to go and get them from their host families. Most of them probably think they're having a really strange dream."

Voice carefully measured to contain her horror and growing rage, Elsie asked, "And the host families . . . ?"

"They weren't the target. A few of them are probably dead, if that's what you're asking, but most would have been asleep when the children were taken." Mark sounded utterly unconcerned, like this was nothing of any real importance. "Either you'll stop your cousin and they'll get their kids back, or you won't, and they'll be vaporized before they can wake up. So I guess they're fine."

"You *guess*?" snapped Elsie. "What happened to you being the kinder, gentler cuckoo?"

Mark turned to look at her. "I never said I was. I said I loved my sister and my parents. Three humans, out of however many billion there are currently running around this shithole of a planet. And before you judge me for that, how many cuckoos do you care about, again? Because I'm counting two. Two cuckoos, full stop. Seems like I'm doing a little better with the cross-species empathy project."

Elsie narrowed her eyes and kept on driving.

The house we wanted was at the end of the street, a small, standard, 1970s tract home that didn't stand out in any way from its neighbors, save for the seven RVs parked out front, and the dozen or so cuckoos standing patiently on the lawn. Their eyes were glowing a steady white, like Christmas lights strung through the air. Elsie stopped the car in the middle of the street, just staring at them.

"That's it," she said. "We can't get any closer."

"You don't need to," said Mark. "All of you are wearing anti-telepathy charms. You're basically invisible to me right now, unless I'm looking directly at you. All the cuckoos in the house have already sunk into the corona of Sarah's metamorphosis. They're watching her do the math, waiting for the moment when it all comes together and she wakes up with the knowledge like an egg waiting to hatch inside her mind."

"Meaning if we stay quiet, they won't realize we're here," I said slowly.

"Bingo."

"What's to stop you from telling them? We're outnumbered."

"There aren't enough bullets in the world," Antimony muttered.

"Nothing," said Mark. "If I want to betray you, I'll betray you, and you won't be able to stop me. So I guess this is the part where you either trust me or don't. If you trust me, we go get your cousin. If you don't . . ." He let his voice trail off.

His meaning was still perfectly clear. "If we don't, we lose her," I said. I unbuckled my seatbelt. "Fuck this."

The sound of the car door opening was incredibly loud in the eerily silent neighborhood. A few cuckoos looked our way, only to look away again immediately afterward. We weren't people to them. We didn't matter.

Mark waited until we were all out of the car before starting toward the house. We fell into step behind him, forming a short, terrified line. My palms were sweating. I wiped them on my jeans. I'd never wished my pheromones were *more* effective before, but in that moment, I did. If I'd been able to affect cuckoos, I wouldn't have needed to worry about a thing. I could have just wiped off my cologne and waltzed right into the middle of things, demanding they all love me, knowing that I would be obeyed.

Normally, I would have flinched away from that thought. If consent matters where the body is involved, how much more important is it when it comes to the mind? Normally, I wasn't walking into a cuckoo hive to retrieve my cousin, who I—who I was coming to hate calling "cousin" more and more, because it implied a blood relationship that wasn't there, and I had finally allowed myself to admit, to myself and everybody else, that I was completely in love with her.

The cuckoos didn't move as we approached, or as Mark began leading us through the invisible maze formed by the placement of their bodies. We couldn't walk in a straight line without bumping into them, but he seemed to know where to put his feet, or at least how to avoid overly attracting their attention. He walked and we followed, swallowing the sound of our own breathing, doing whatever we had to in order to go unnoticed.

Sam was so tense that he'd shifted back into human form, walking barefoot through the grass. Flames flickered around Annie's fingers, brief and bright and fading out as quickly as they appeared. Only Elsie looked perfectly relaxed, as calm as if she'd been waiting for a sale down at the Sephora. She was also the closest to Mark. I looked a little closer. There was a knife in her hand. If he betrayed us, she was planning to take him down before he could enjoy the fruits of his betrayal. It wouldn't be enough to save us, but it would be better than nothing.

I appreciate my sister. She can seem like a massive flake, but she's pragmatic as all hell when she needs to be. People get hung up on the sparkly nails and the neon hair and forget that she's still a Price. We all are.

I stood up a little straighter as I walked. Yes, we were marching into a cuckoo hive, and yes, there was every chance that one or more of us would die tonight, but we were Prices. This was what we were born to do.

Mark reached the door without incident. He turned to look at the rest of us, pressing one finger to his lips in an exaggerated sign for silence. Then he pushed it open and stepped inside. We followed, still in our straight line, until I pulled the door gently shut behind me. It wouldn't stop the cuckoos on the lawn from pouring into the house if they got the signal—it would barely even slow them down—but every little bit helps when you're going up against telepathic killers from another dimension.

Sometimes my life is more like an X-Men comic than I want it to be.

The house had been built along a much more predictable floor plan than the Price compound: the front door deposited us in a little atrium attached to the front hallway, with pegs for our coats and a rack for any muddy shoes. There was a pair of blue boots, sized for a small child, lying on their sides next to the rack. I gestured toward it, eyebrows raised in silent question. Mark followed my gesture, and grimaced. He shook his head before pointing to his chest and mouthing, exaggeratedly, "Not me."

Right. Whoever had owned this house before the cuckoos came to claim it was already dead, and there was nothing we could do to save them. It was sort of nice knowing that Mark hadn't been part of whatever group had decided that this was their new base of operations. I didn't really want to kill the only cuckoo who was actually helping us. He deserved to go home to his sister. He deserved a chance.

There were lights at the end of the hall, and voices, although no one was talking. Someone laughed; someone else made a dismayed grunting sound, like they'd stepped on something unpleasant. I couldn't get a sense of how many of them there were, but the house felt full, oppressive, like it was almost at capacity. Telepaths didn't really need to speak to give themselves away.

I pulled my phone out of my pocket, opened the notepad function, and typed a quick message before holding it out to Mark.

Where's Sarah?

He looked up from the screen and shook his head, spreading his hands in an indication of ignorance. Then he produced his own phone, and repeated my actions, finally flipping it around so we could all see his screen.

She isn't broadcasting, so she must still be in morph, he wrote. She could be anywhere in the house.

Great. We split up and look for her, I replied. Me and Elsie upstairs, you, Sam, and Annie down here. If you find her, Annie will text me. Same if we find her. Okay?

I looked around our little band of unlikely saviors— Earth deserved something way more organized, and even more heavily armed—until each of them nodded in turn. Then I put my phone back in my pocket and started toward the stairs, with Elsie on my heels.

Hold on, Sarah, I thought. *All you need to do now is hold on.*

The blue boots had belonged to a little girl, pigtailed and gap-toothed and displayed proudly along the length of the hall, sometimes by herself, sometimes in concert with her baby sibling, who had been too small to have teeth of their own in what looked like the most recent pictures. I wasn't studying them more than I had to. They were part of a story I didn't want to know, whose ending was signaled in tiny, terrible clues all around me. The smear on the edge of the bathroom door that looked like dried strawberry jam but probably wasn't; the open door of a small, silent room where a crib waited for an occupant whose naptime had ended forever.

"I hate them," whispered Elsie, voice low and tight and risky. Cuckoos have human-normal hearing—the ones downstairs wouldn't be able to hear us unless we spoke at a normal volume. But until we'd checked all these rooms, we had no way of knowing whether they contained a cuckoo, someone who'd slipped away from the rest of the hive for a nap and might find themselves in the enviable position of being able to catch a pair of intruders.

I nodded my understanding. Elsie spared me a brief, anguished look before starting toward the nearest door, knife in hand, ready to begin our search in earnest.

The room was empty. All the rooms along the front of the hall were empty, until we had one more door to check, and a lot of failure to carry on our shoulders. Elsie looked at me. I nodded again, then put my hand on the doorknob.

I wanted to remove the anti-telepathy charm that was keeping me safe. I wanted to know whether the comforting psychic hum of Sarah's presence would resume, as familiar as the sound of my own heartbeat, and somehow as essential to my mental health. I hadn't realized how quiet the world was until that silent song had gone away and returned again.

I wanted it back. I wanted *her* back.

I opened the door.

The room on the other side was dominated by its bed, king-sized, easily, with too many pillows mounded at the head and the sort of thick, ornately-carved frame that spoke of either family heirloom or more money than sense. A cuckoo was stretched out in the dead center, hands folded over her breast like she was being prepared for her own funeral, black hair fanned across the pillows around her, eyes closed. She was wearing a simple white dress, almost childlike in its cut and style.

Elsie crowded into the room behind me, knocking me out of the doorway. When I still didn't move, she pried my fingers off the doorknob and closed the door, creating a small bubble of privacy.

"Well?" she demanded, in a low, dangerous voice. "Is it her?"

"I don't . . . I don't know." My ears reddened with the shame of my admission. If this was Sarah, I should have known, the same way I'd known that Heloise *wasn't* Sarah. Even with the anti-telepathy charm, I should have known. She'd been a part of my life for as long as I could remember. She was my *Sarah*.

But all cuckoos look essentially alike, and this one was no different. Everything about her was right, and everything about her was wrong, because I never saw Sarah in this kind of silence. Even when she was asleep, I could hear her in the back of my head. I'd been listening to her my whole life.

"We need to hurry," said Elsie. "I don't know how long we can creep around in here."

"I know. Just . . . just hold on." Cautiously, I approached the bed. The cuckoo didn't move. She was profoundly asleep—if sleep was even the right word. She was so still that she might as well have been dead. Only the very slight rise and fall of her chest kept me from panicking. She was alive. She *was*. She was just . . . gone.

When I reached the head of the bed, I leaned over and gingerly brushed the cuckoo's bangs away from her forehead. There was a long, shallow cut there, held closed with butterfly bandages. It was clearly Aunt Evie's handiwork. I exhaled through my nose, trying to keep myself as quiet as possible, even as my hand started to shake.

"It's her," I said. "It's Sarah."

"Are you sure? Heloise had a cut on her forehead, too."

"This is the real one. Heloise had a cut on her forehead because someone put it there. The edges were too regular, and the cut itself was too deep. This is from Sarah slamming into the dashboard of my car. It's her."

I put my hand on her shoulder, pushing as hard as I dared. "Wake up. We're here to rescue you."

She didn't react.

I pushed again, even harder this time. "Sarah, come on. You need to wake up."

She still didn't react.

I sighed heavily. "Okay. I guess this is the way it's got to be." I bent forward and slid my arms underneath her, gathering as much of her weight as I could before I straightened.

She felt like a dried leaf, all shape and no substance. Her skin was burning hot where it touched mine. She was running a fever so intense that it seemed like it would have to be fatal, the sort of thing no one really walked away from. I pulled her close to my chest, one arm supporting her torso while the other held up her knees, and looked to Elsie.

"We need to get her out of here," I said.

"You think the cuckoos are going to let us walk out of here with their precious princess?" she asked. "We have telepathy blockers. She doesn't."

"I think we have to try," I said. "Get the door?"

Elsie looked at me grimly. Then she nodded and moved to clear the way for me to carry Sarah into the hall.

Every step felt like a mile, weighted down by both Sarah's body and my own growing fear. She wasn't waking up. Whatever they'd done to her, she wasn't waking up, and that meant she was defenseless; no matter what happened between here and home, we'd be the ones who had to keep her safe and get her away from the danger presented by her own kind. Would she understand why we'd done what we'd done? Would she forgive us?

The hall was dark, and I stepped on something that squeaked loudly, the sort of squeezebox that gets put into kids' toys to drive their parents up the wall. Elsie and I both froze, counting the seconds. No one came to investigate. We started walking again.

Elsie led the way down the stairs, ready to catch me and Sarah both if my balance failed me. We were almost to the bottom when a familiar shriek of rage and indignation shattered the silence: Antimony. Which meant the cuckoos were onto us.

Which meant we had to run.

I didn't look back as I raced for the door, and neither did Elsie, leaping several feet ahead of me to wrench the door open and start across the cuckoo-burdened lawn. Our approach had been quiet, careful, and masked by Mark's presence. None of those things were on our side now. As we ran, the cuckoos turned to track us, snapping out of whatever fugue they'd been wrapped in and beginning to move forward.

"It's Sarah!" I yelled. "They're following Sarah!"

"Great observation! Keep running!"

The car was still parked in the middle of the street, exactly as we'd left it. Elsie pulled one of the back doors open and I thrust Sarah inside, not bothering with the seatbelt as I shoved her across the back seat and started to slide in beside her. That's when I froze.

The cuckoos from the lawn were bearing down on us, their faces twisted with fury, their eyes glowing white. Annie, Sam, and Mark were nowhere to be seen. If we drove away now, we'd lose them.

"Artie! Get in the fucking car!"

I twisted to look at my sister, who was gesturing wildly for me to get in so she could start the engine. We had Sarah. We were saving Sarah. If we tried to wait and save the others—if that was even possible at this point—we'd lose her, and if Mark could be trusted, losing her meant losing the world.

This was what we'd been training for since we were old enough to understand what it meant to fight. This was what we'd always known was coming.

"I'm sorry," I whispered, and slammed the car door. I was still buckling my belt when Elsie hammered

her foot down on the gas, sending us rocketing forward, into the front ranks of the charging cuckoos. I
realized what she was going to do almost too late, and
threw myself to the side, holding Sarah's body in place
with my own. I didn't see the impact, or how many of
the cuckoos she hit, but I felt it, a shuddering jolt that
traveled through my entire body even as the car was
spinning into a full turn and we were racing away down
the street.

"How big is she broadcasting?" demanded Elsie.
"Check her eyes!"

I peeled myself off of Sarah and forced her left eye
open. A pale blue iris greeted me, the pupil so small that
it was virtually a pinprick. "I don't think she is," I said.

"Good. Hold on."

Elsie has never had a lot of respect for the rules of
the road, but normally she at least drives like she
doesn't want to go back to traffic school. Apparently,
having a swarm of cuckoos chasing us meant all bets
were off. I yelped as the car spun and I was slammed
against the door. I yelped again as I dove across the
backseat to stop Sarah from hitting her head on the
window. I didn't know exactly what was going on inside her head, but I couldn't imagine that a concussion
would make things any better.

"Slow down!" I shouted.

"No!" she yelled back. If anything, she accelerated,
heading for the woods faster than I had realized her
tiny car could manage.

Something crashed into the roof of the car. Elsie
screamed, as much in rage as fear, and slammed on the
brakes.

Antimony flew through the air in front of us, propelled by the physics of our sudden stop. Sam was
there before she could hit the road, snatching her
under one arm and leaping straight up, into the trees.
I blinked, my heart pounding, and struggled to say
something more coherent than a wheezing moan.

Sam dropped back down to the road, Annie in his arms, and set her feet onto the pavement. He was back in what I always thought of as his "natural" form, although his tail was held low—a sure sign of tension in the normally genial fūri. The pair approached the car, Annie climbing into the front while Sam opened the door next to Sarah.

"Mind if I move her over?" he asked, before doing exactly that. I was still gaping at him, too startled to speak. He raised an eyebrow. "What, did you think you left us to die? Because that's pretty shitty, if it's the truth."

Elsie shook off her shock and punched Annie in the arm. "What the *fuck*," she demanded.

"They caught on," said Annie. "Could you drive, maybe? I want walls. Big, thick, secure walls. Also, the parents, probably pretty mad, and coming back with Sarah is the best way I can think of to calm them down."

"What happened?" Elsie started the car again, driving more slowly now, like having flying cousins slam into the roof had been all she needed to snap her out of her maddened flight.

I focused on getting Sarah belted into the middle seat. Her skin was still too hot; touching her was like touching someone with a potentially fatal sunburn, half-cooked and in need of medical care. She didn't react at all, just listed gently over until she was supported by my torso, her head hanging limp against my shoulder. I put an arm around her to hold her up, trying not to focus on the fact that I still couldn't hear the hum of her presence.

The hum . . .

"We don't have an extra anti-telepathy charm," I said. "We don't know whether she's broadcasting."

"True," agreed Annie, even as she pulled a gun out of her waistband and flicked the safety off, keeping it below the level of the windshield as she watched

the rearview mirror for signs that we were being followed.

"We need to cut her off."

Annie's eyes flicked to mine, our gaze connecting
through the mirror. Then she smiled, the smallest twist
of her mouth, there and gone in the beat of a heart.

"I made a deal with the crossroads to save Sam before I'd even admitted I was in love with him," she said.
"Grandma Alice must be so proud of her disgustingly
dominant genes."

"Shut up," I said, voice sharp. "I'd do the same thing
for you."

"Sure you would," she said. "Now expose yourself
to the possibility of psychic attack so you can be sure
she's safe."

Elsie laughed, high and sharp and bitter. I glared at
the back of her neck.

Then I reached into my shirt and pulled the anti-
telepathy charm over my head, dropping it to the seat
between my legs, where it wouldn't count as "in contact" and block me from Sarah's mind.

The change in the car's atmosphere was immediate
and intense. The hum of Sarah's psychic presence
crashed against me like a wave against the shore, louder
and more present than it had ever been before. I
gasped, almost forgetting how to breathe in the face of
its weight, which bore down on me, crushing me into
the seat. I could still see the rest of the car. Sam was
watching me with obvious concern; Annie and Elsie
were sneaking glances at me in the rearview mirror as
they tried not to get too distracted to stop their respec-
tive tasks. Both surveillance and driving take a certain
amount of attention, after all, especially when you're
driving like you have special permission to ignore any
rules of the road that you don't like. The trees rushed
by outside the car, dark and barely distinguished in the
glow of our headlights, and none of that mattered, because it was all so far away. It was all beyond us.

Sarah's skin was pressed against mine where I was holding her up. I had time to realize that might not be a good thing—to realize that even though it had been my intention to give her the anti-telepathy charm, to keep the other cuckoos from following the giant mental signal flare that was her mind right now, I wasn't moving. I was just sitting there, the charm between my legs, not moving.

Move, I thought, and didn't move.

Oh, crap, I thought, and the world went white.

Twenty

$$\pi_2(n) \sim 2C_2 \frac{n}{(\ln n)^2} \sim 2C_2 \int_2^n \frac{dt}{(\ln t)^2}$$

"No matter how much we study, train, and prepare, there will always be situations we weren't ready for. That's the nature of reality. It's sort of neat, when it isn't trying to chew your face off."

—Kevin Price

Someplace that probably isn't safe for incubi or other living things

EVERYTHING WAS WHITE.

I turned slowly, trying to get my bearings in the infinite brightness. There were no walls, no floor, no ceiling: only the featureless sterility of a blank page, waiting to be transformed into something comprehensible by the addition of basic physical forces.

I cupped my hands around my mouth. "Hello?" I shouted. There was no echo. My words barely seemed to travel past my lips, like even sound was being swallowed by this terrible new landscape.

Panic seemed like a good idea. Panic often seems like a good idea. Unfortunately, experience has shown that panic is virtually *never* a good idea, and if it is, it's because you're already about to die, so why waste time on staying calm? I forced myself to take a deep, slow breath, in through my nose and out through my mouth. The panic receded a bit. I did it again. Then I paused, panic forgotten in the face of a new oddity. I breathed into my cupped hand and sniffed.

Nothing.

Most of the time, Lilu pheromones are virtually undetectable, which makes sense: if people could smell us coming, they'd do a much better job of avoiding us, and hunters like the Covenant of St. George would probably have eradicated us centuries ago. They get stronger when we're nervous—and I was definitely nervous. That's part of why I wear so much crappy cologne, and why Elsie has an addiction to small artisanal perfume companies. The Black Phoenix Alchemy Lab has saved a lot of people from becoming embarrassingly enamored of my succubus sister.

When our pheromones *are* detectable, they smell vaguely sweet and woody, like crushed aconite flowers mixed with sugar. And when I breathed into my hand, I couldn't smell them at all. There was nothing, not even the chemical tang of the cologne I use to smother them. I might as well have been a baseline human. Which was something I'd dreamed about my entire life but wasn't something I'd really been hoping would happen during an attempted rescue.

Something was wrong.

"As if the big white room didn't tell you that part," I muttered, and started walking. It wasn't necessarily the right thing to do, but it was *something* to do, and that made it better than standing around waiting for the invisible floor to drop out from under my feet and send me plummeting into the void. I am not a big fan of plummeting. If I had to commit to a position, I'd probably have to say that I was anti-plummeting.

I kept walking, and a smudge appeared on the horizon. Appeared *with* the horizon; until there was something to break up the infinite whiteness of it all, there couldn't really be said to *be* a horizon. It needed something to define it. I started walking faster.

The smudge began to take geometric shape. It was

a half-circle of blackboards, pushed together like a soundstage from a movie about mathematicians trying to save the world. There was a figure there, standing in the middle of the broken ring. I was too far away to make out details, but I could see that they were wearing an ankle-length skirt and a virtually shapeless sweater, the sort of thing that was more warm than fashionable, that would protect the wearer from notice.

I broke into a run.

The closer I got, the more details I could see. The figure became a woman became a cuckoo became *Sarah*, chalk smudges on her nose and chin, lips drawn down in the so-familiar, so-beloved expression of pensive contemplation that she'd been wearing since we were kids sitting and coloring at the same table.

(Well, I'd been coloring. She'd been doing calculus in crayon, and when we'd finished, Aunt Evelyn had pronounced us both to be amazing artists and hung our projects side-by-side on the refrigerator.)

"Sarah!" I sped up. I wasn't winded at all, which was, like the lack of my pheromones, probably a bad sign. There was a decent chance I was dead, and this was the afterlife, although if that was the case, my Aunt Mary had way underplayed how much eternity sucked.

Sarah didn't turn. She kept writing figures on the chalkboard, moving at a steady, unhurried pace, like she had all the time in the world. Which was probably true—if we were dead.

Maybe this was the cuckoo afterlife, and I'd been pulled into it because I'd been touching Sarah when—what? When the other cuckoos caught up with us and forced Elsie to crash the car? But that didn't make sense. Not only had Elsie still been wearing her anti-telepathy charm, but if Mark had been telling the truth—about anything—the cuckoos were going to want Sarah *back*. She was their key to escaping this world and this dimension and moving on to someplace that wasn't prepared for them. Which meant Sarah wasn't dead. Which meant I wasn't dead.

It was a bit of a relief to realize that this probably wasn't the afterlife. I know several ghosts personally—I have two dead aunts who I love a lot—but that doesn't mean I want to bite the big one before I see the next season of *Doctor Who*. But if we weren't dead . . .

"Uh, Sarah? Are we inside your head right now? Because I don't think I'm supposed to be inside your head."

She kept writing figures on the blackboard, not looking at me.

"Are you ignoring me, or can you not hear me? I mean, we're in a funky infinite whiteness, which is really Grant Morrison-esque and a little bit upsetting, so I'm trying not to think about it too hard, and I guess that could mean your perceptions are filtering me out, but I'd really like it if you'd talk to me."

She kept writing.

"Sarah?" I touched her shoulder gingerly. "Sarah, it's me. It's Art—"

She turned her head, not all the way, but far enough for me to catch the sudden flash of white in her eyes. I was knocked back immediately, going sprawling on the floor that wasn't a floor, landing hard enough to take my breath away. Sarah returned her attention to the chalkboard.

"Okay, that's not good," I muttered, pushing myself to my feet. "Come on, Sarah, you need to cut this out. Telekinesis? Really? When did you figure out how to move things with your mind?"

Was it my imagination, or did the corner of her mouth twitch? Since we were probably inside Sarah's head right now, I wasn't sure whether I actually got to have an imagination. Telepaths are really confusing.

More carefully this time, I began walking back over to her. "Do you know what's going on? Because I'm not going to lie to you, this shit is weird, and it's getting weirder all the time. I think we need to get out of here."

Sarah kept writing.

"I'm afraid if I touch you again, I'll get knocked across the—this isn't exactly a room, you know. More a featureless void. Please don't knock me across the featureless void. It's not fun. I didn't enjoy it the first time. I'm sort of worried that I might just keep flying away from you forever, since there's nothing to stop me. How is gravity even working here?"

Again that twitch, before she went placidly back to writing on her blackboard. I turned to face it. The numbers—well, partially numbers; her idea of math involved more letters than a bowl of alphabet soup—were arrayed in straight lines, broken here and there by little squared-off chunks of text that had been written smaller, like they were supposed to be the algebraic equivalent of a footnote. None of it made any sense. That wasn't new.

What *was* new was the way some of the strings of numbers seemed to phase in and out of reality, like they were too tightly written to maintain their grasp on a single linear plane. I squinted. They kept moving.

"This is bad."

Sarah kept writing.

"Look, I get that you're in a smart-person fugue and all, and normally I wouldn't bother you while you were undermining the fabric of the universe with mathematics, but you do understand that this is bad, right? Numbers shouldn't be sufficient to change the laws of physics. They should sit quietly and think about what they've done until it's time for someone to figure out the tip."

Sarah kept writing.

"Dammit, Sarah, *you're going to kill us all if you don't stop.*"

Sarah stopped.

So did I, just staring at her for a long moment, until I saw her hand—still holding the chalk—begin to shake. It was a small, almost imperceptible tremor. I decided to take the risk and reached out to carefully pluck the chalk out of her fingers.

She didn't resist. She also didn't fling me telekinetically away. I was willing to take that as a win.

"Can you hear me?" I asked.

She stared at the chalkboard and didn't reply.

"Sarah, if you can hear me, it's really me. It's Artie. We're not dead, so I think . . . I think this is your mindscape, and you're in the middle of what the other cuckoos called your metamorphosis. You're entering your fourth instar, which means you're becoming a better cuckoo. Bigger and stronger and everything. I'm really here. I'm with you in the real world, where your body is, and I'm touching you, and I think that was enough to let you pull me in with you. If you can hear me, please. Look at me? Say something? Say *anything*. I want to help you. I need you to tell me what you need me to do. I need you to tell me you're still . . ." I trailed off. There were no good endings to that sentence.

Sarah lowered her chin, until she was looking at the very bottom of the chalkboard, and said in a low voice, "I know you're just me trying to talk myself out of this, but I have to do the work. If I don't do the work, I don't wake up, and I don't go home. There's no part of me that doesn't want to go home. There's just all the parts of me that are too scared to believe that I can finish things. I can. I swear I can."

"Sarah, please." I dropped the chalk and grabbed her hand, only wincing after I was already fully committed to the action.

The repulsion blast I was expecting didn't come. I relaxed a little. Then Sarah raised her head and looked at me, and I relaxed substantially more.

"You're not real," she said softly. "I wish you were real. It would be so nice if you were real. But you're not real, and it's not fair of me to act like you are."

"Hey, that's sort of mean," I said. "After everything

I've been through today, the least you could do is admit that I exist. I mean, you're the one who got kidnapped."

"I wasn't kidnapped," she said. "I went because . . . because I had to. It was the only way to keep the family safe."

"Oh, sure, you call it 'keeping us safe,' like there was ever a chance that we weren't going to go after you," I said. "Mark told us how he lured you out of the compound. He's sort of an asshole, by the way. In case you were thinking he might be your new best friend, since he's the same species as you and everything. I can't say that he's someone I want to invite to join us for D&D."

"Mark?" Sarah raised her eyes, enough to blink at me in clear bewilderment. "You met Mark?"

"Black hair, blue eyes, total asshole? Yeah, I met him. I know it's cool for you to have other friends, but could you try having other friends who don't want to kill us all? Maybe?" I shook my head. "No, that's not fair. He's helping us. He has a sister who's not a cuckoo, and apparently if your species can convince you to work for them, she'll die along with the rest of us."

"You met Mark," she repeated, sounding faintly baffled. "You're really you."

"I've been saying that."

"But you can't be here." Her eyes widened. She took a step backward. "Artie, what are you doing here?"

"I told you—I took off my anti-telepathy charm while I was holding you propped up in the backseat. Not my smartest move, since it means we were in skin contact before I realized what was happening, but I'm not sure I'm sorry." I chuckled bleakly. "I was afraid you might not be you anymore. And now here you are, holed up inside your own head, doing math. We need to get you another hobby."

"I have to do the math," said Sarah. "The math is how I get out of here."

I frowned. "What do you mean? Just open your eyes. Wake up. There's no reason you can't."

"It's a physical process, Artie."

"What is?"

"Metamorphosis." She looked back toward the chalkboard, and for a moment—just a moment—I could see the raw longing in her expression, like she had never seen anything so beautiful. "This is like taking a final exam. I have to pass the class before I can graduate and go on to the next one."

"What happens if you don't? Can't you just . . . wouldn't that mean you repeated the class you'd already taken? Wouldn't that give us more time?"

"That's where the metaphor falls apart. Haven't you ever seen a butterfly who couldn't finish breaking out of the cocoon? They die, Artie. They get stuck, and their wings can't straighten, and they die."

"Are you saying you're trying to grow wings?"

"I'm saying that if I don't finish breaking out of this cocoon, I'm pretty sure I won't survive." She looked back to me, resignation and grief in her expression. Then she smiled. "You know, I think the best thing about meeting on a mindscape is being able to *see* your face. I never do out in the real world, not unless it's in a photograph. You're really pretty. Did you know that? I'm glad I know that."

"Um." I reached back and rubbed the back of my neck, or at least the idea of the back of my neck. Again, telepathy is confusing. "I don't think it's 'pretty' for me. Pretty sure it's supposed to be 'handsome.' And either way, it's not technically correct."

"You have a skewed sense of your own appearance, which is common," said Sarah. "I think you're beautiful. Right now, I'm going to be selfish and say that's what matters."

"That's not selfish."

"Isn't it?" Her smile was even sadder than before. "You can't stay here, Artie. I need to be alone with the numbers. I need to focus on them right now. I need to show them that I can handle them."

"They're just numbers."

"No. These numbers are different. These numbers are awake. They can see me, and they're trying to decide whether I'm good enough to see them." She glanced at the chalkboard, fingers twitching. Then she raised her hand.

The chalk pulled itself up off the floor and flew to her, smacking into her palm. She closed her fingers around it.

"I'll be home soon, I promise," she said. "The cuckoos can't make me do anything I don't want to do. I just need to finish this equation and I can come home."

"Sarah—"

"Kiss me one more time before you have to go?" Her voice was soft, plaintive. There was no way I could have told her no. I stepped forward, pressing my lips to hers, and she melted against me, languid and slow. I could have kissed her forever. I wanted to kiss her forever, the rest of the world be damned.

Sarah was the one to eventually pull away.

"Don't worry about me, Artie." She looked at me, and her smile was heartbreakingly bright, and devastatingly beautiful. I couldn't look at it. I couldn't look away.

"Please," I whispered. "What you're trying to do will destroy the world."

"It won't. Ingrid said—"

"She's a cuckoo. Cuckoos lie."

For a moment, I saw doubt in her eyes. "I'm a cuckoo. Do you think I lie?"

"Not to me," I said.

"I'll be fine," she said, and her eyes flashed white, and everything went black.

I sat up with a gasp, feeling the heavy weight of gravity settle over me, along with a dozen sensations I hadn't realized were missing—the whisper of the night wind, the cool dampness of the air, the looming shadow of the sky, which was considering whether or not it was time to rain. In Portland, the sky is always considering whether it's time to rain.

"Good," said Elsie. She was bending over me, her hands on her knees, an uncharacteristically solemn expression on her face. I could see the lights of the compound behind her. It looked like the whole house was lit up, even the rooms that were usually left closed-off unless more of the family was in residence.

Elsie's finger jabbed at the center of my chest, jerking me back into the moment. "I thought you were dead, you asshole."

"I told you he was still breathing," said Sam.

I craned my neck back. He was standing behind me, arms crossed, still in his vaguely simian form. His tail was wrapped tightly around his left leg, like he was anchoring himself in place.

"What . . ." My throat was dry. I swallowed hard and tried again. "What happened?"

"You dropped your charm and went *down*, dude. It was like someone had flipped your switch or something." Sam shook his head. "We couldn't figure out how to peel you off the cuckoo without touching her, and with the way you'd gone down, we were sort of worried you'd jerk us into whatever hallucinatory Wonderland you'd gone and tumbled into. So we left you alone until we got to the house."

"So how . . . ?"

"I opened the car door and unbuckled your seatbelt, and you fell out of the car," said Elsie. "You didn't wake up, so I stuffed your anti-telepathy charm into your pocket. That did the trick. And before you ask, Annie took Sarah inside."

Then she hauled back and kicked me in the hip.

"Hey! Ow!" I put my arms up to block my face, just in case she had some wacky ideas about continuing her assault. "What the fuck, Els?"

"Never, ever, *ever* do that to me again, you asshole." She dropped to her knees and wrapped her arms around me before I had a chance to respond, yanking me against her and burying her face in the front of my shirt. Her shoulders moved in uneven little hitches. I realized, to my dismay, that she was crying.

My badass big sister who could handle anything the world wanted to throw at us was *crying*.

"You're not allowed to leave me," she said, voice muffled by the way her head was bent, the way her lips were pressed to my shirt. She sounded . . . small. It was terrifying. "I thought you were going to leave me."

"I'm right here," I said, and awkwardly patted her hair. "I haven't gone anywhere."

She pulled back, letting go so she could look at me, and offered me a wan smile. I'm sure mine was just as bad, because we both knew the terrible truth behind my answer: one day, one of us was going to leave. One day, one of us was going to wind up in a situation we couldn't bluff or bully our way through, and we were going to become one more entry in the litany of the dead that the Aeslin mice recited twice a year, on the summer and winter solstices. That's what it means to be a Price. We fight. We do our best to win. But eventually, inevitably, we lose.

Sam was still standing behind me, silent and awkward as he watched his girlfriend's cousins try to comfort one another, and it was hard to swallow the urge to turn around and tell him to run for the hills as fast as he possibly could. Annie loved him and he loved her and if there's one thing that every Price child learns before we graduate from high school, it's that love is never enough. Grandma Alice loves Grandpa Thomas, has for more than fifty years, and what did that get her? An endless search through parallel dimensions for a man she can't let herself admit is dead. And she's the lucky one. At least she can pretend to have hope. For the rest of us, hope is something that dies quick and messy on the battlefield.

Sarah was fighting her own battle right now, trapped in the white nothingness of her own mind, and there was nothing that any of us could do to help her, and there was nothing that I could do to save her. All we could do was wait . . . and hope that she found a way to win.

I remembered the bleakness in her eyes right before she'd thrust me from her mindscape. Assuming that had been real, and not just a weirdly specific hallucination, I wasn't as certain as I wanted to be that she was going to come out on top. The cuckoo equations were eating her alive.

Gingerly, I pushed Elsie away from me and climbed to my feet, relieved when my legs didn't take the opportunity to collapse out from under me. The world spun a little before settling down. Elsie watched me, wary, waiting for the moment when I'd fall.

"You were out for more than half the drive," she said.

"It didn't feel that long," I said. "Come on. Let's get inside. I'm sure we're about to be yelled at."

"I'm not." Her expression was grim as she stood and brushed the grass off her knees. "Normally, sure, but normally, we haven't come racing back with a cuckoo in a coma and word of a whole hive behind us. This is war. Lectures about our malfeasance can wait until later."

"This is a swell family that I've decided to attach myself to," said Sam. "Totally normal. Way better than the carnie life."

"You said it, not me," said Elsie, and started for the house, leaving the two of us with no real choice but to follow.

Mom, Aunt Evie, and Uncle Kevin were all in the living room. Dad, Annie, and James were nowhere to be seen. Neither was Sarah. They had probably taken her upstairs to her room, where she could hopefully sleep without fear of the cuckoos finding her. That didn't make her absence any less distressing.

Mom surged to her feet as soon as she saw us appear in the kitchen doorway, almost knocking Uncle Kevin over in her rush to reach us and wrap her arms around our shoulders, crushing Elsie and me both against her for one long, desperate moment. Then she released us and shoved us backward at the same time. I bumped into Sam. Elsie hit the counter.

"What the *hell* were you thinking?" Mom snarled. For a moment, I could see why so many cryptids considered her one of the more terrifying members of the family. She mostly doesn't do field work—that whole "not wanting to wind up dead" thing she has going on, which honestly, I agree with—but when she does, she has absolutely no chill. Aunt Evie will try to empathize. Uncle Kevin will try to negotiate. Mom will just stab first and ask questions never.

"That we needed to get Sarah back," I said, voice cracking in the middle of the sentence, like my mother's disapproval had somehow hurled me all the way back into puberty. "We didn't have a lot of time, and you were all arguing about the best way to do this. I couldn't wait any longer."

"Arthur James Harrington-Price, did your father and I raise you to be a fool?" Mom took a step forward, virtually looming over me. It was a nice trick, since I'm taller than she is. "Because rushing in with minimal backup is the *definition* of foolishness."

"No, it isn't," I snapped, and stepped forward, toward her. It was like our heights reversed in an instant. Now I was the one looming. "I took a sorcerer, a fūri, and a succubus who drives like she's auditioning for Mario Kart, all equipped with anti-telepathy charms, assisted by a cuckoo who was willing to betray his own kind for the sake of saving this world, and I got Sarah back. Honestly, I would have been happier if I could have taken fewer people, because it wasn't like we were ever going to have a pitched battle in the middle of Beaverton. We needed to get in, find her, and bring her home. We did that."

"Artie . . ." Her face softened. "You know she's not well."

"He's not stupid, Aunt Jane."

We all turned. Antimony was standing on the stairs, her hair sticking to the sweat on her cheeks and forehead, a terrifying calm in her expression. She looked like someone who had come to deliver the news of a death to a family. My heart clenched.

She looked at me as she said, "Sarah's in the middle of what the other cuckoos called a metamorphosis, and when she wakes up, there's every chance she wakes up being driven by an equation so large that it breaks the brains that try to hold it. She'll be a fourth instar cuckoo. She may not be *Sarah* anymore, at least not the way that we think of her. And we may need to make sure she doesn't crack this world open like an egg. Artie knows all of that. He knew it before we went to find her. But he also knows that we're family."

"She's right," said Aunt Evie. "I hope and pray that Sarah can fight this—that she's more Price than cuckoo. But if she can't, it's better that we be the ones to stop her. It's better that it be her family."

She was talking about killing Sarah. That was what this really came down to. She was talking about taking a knife and driving it into the base of Sarah's skull, where it would sever her brain stem and kill her as quickly and painlessly as possible. Cuckoos don't have the same arrangement of internal organs and weak spots as true mammals. The fastest, cleanest way of taking them out is by targeting the brain.

The thought was enough to make my stomach churn, especially since I couldn't say that they were doing anything wrong. If it came down to a choice between Sarah or the world, we would choose the world. We wouldn't have a choice.

"Where's Dad?" I asked.

"Out in the barn with James," said Uncle Kevin. "They're trying to get the cuckoo we captured earlier to talk. The one you didn't lose."

"We didn't lose Mark," I said. "We just . . . didn't bring him back." If he had any sense of self-preservation, he'd already be on his way home, returning to the sister he loved and the parents he liked well enough to keep alive.

I somehow didn't think the cuckoos would be very forgiving of his role in our recovering Sarah.

"That sounds like losing your hostage to me," said Mom.

"Yeah, well, we had to do something, or we wouldn't even be having this argument." I shook my head. "I'm going out to the barn. Maybe Heloise knows what we can do to save Sarah."

"Artie."

I stopped and looked at Elsie, raising my eyebrows in unspoken question. She looked back at me, earnest and clearly grieving.

"What happens if she says there's nothing we can do?"

Again, my stomach roiled. I somehow kept my voice calm as I replied, "Then you take the mice into Sarah's room and you make sure they see everything. She's a part of this family. She's going to be remembered."

This time, when I started walking, she didn't stop me. Nobody did. I made my way across the living room and down the hall to the back door, letting myself out into the cool night air. My feet left clear impressions in the dewy grass as I made my way to the barn.

Inside, Heloise was still strapped to the table, and Dad was sitting nearby, the can of Raid in his hand. James was standing over the captive cuckoo, fingers spread wide, like he was soaking up the heat from a campfire.

"What's he doing?" I asked.

Dad glanced over at me, and I saw the flicker of grief in his expression before he clamped it down and said, with merciful neutrality, "Testing to see how much cold a cuckoo can endure before it starts talking. They can apparently survive in sub-arctic temperatures, which is pretty impressive. There must be something strange about their musculature. We'll pay close attention when we analyze the tissue we got from that other one."

"This is boring," said Heloise. She turned her head and smiled brightly in my direction. "Well, well, well, if it isn't the little half-incubus. I didn't expect to see you so soon. Or ever, really. The hive should have torn you apart."

"Annie's back," I said. "I bet cuckoos like heat a lot less. Sarah hates the middle of the summer."

Heloise's smile flickered, turning wary. "You wouldn't."

"You know, my family thinks I'm the nice one, because I spend most of my time in my room and I don't bother people unless I have to, and because I think it's not fair of me to use my pheromones on standard humans. They didn't ask to share the planet with a bunch of people who look like them but aren't them. This isn't the X-Men." I made my way to one of the trays of tools that had been set out for the first cuckoo's necropsy. There were several scalpels of varying size and sharpness. I selected one of the larger ones before turning back to Heloise.

She was still watching me. She wasn't smiling anymore. Not even a little bit. I started walking toward her, the scalpel in my hand.

"They think I'm the nice one because I don't give them any reason not to, but you know who never thought I was the nice one? Sarah. That's part of why we get along so well. She's always known that I *could* be really dangerous if I wanted to. I never wanted to. I just wanted to read comic books and play with my computer and love her. Even if I never told her I loved her, being able to do it was enough."

"I didn't do anything," said Heloise hurriedly. James had closed his hands and stepped back, expression going politely neutral. He wasn't going to stop me from whatever I wanted to do next. That was good to know.

"I think we might disagree there," I said, stopping next to the table. I lowered the scalpel until it was pressed, lightly, against the skin above her collarbone. I wasn't pressing down—not yet—and she wasn't bleeding, but she would be soon enough. Skin, whether human or cuckoo, is easy to cut, and difficult to heal. "We got her back."

Heloise's eyes went even wider. "What?"

"We went to your hive, and we were careful, and we got her back. She's here now, in a room that's warded against your little telepathic tricks, so the other cuckoos can't hear her." I pressed down slightly on the scalpel, until the blade was indenting her flesh. "Here's a fun question for you: why would I tell you this, knowing that you'll just broadcast it all to any cuckoo who gets close enough to potentially help you? Got any ideas?"

Heloise couldn't pull away from the scalpel, so she held perfectly still, staring at me. "You wouldn't dare."

"Why not? You're not my family. She is. You're just the monster that helped them hurt her."

"Because I look exactly like her," Heloise said, and for a moment, the smugness worked its way back into her voice. "You humans are so stupid. You can threaten me all you want, but you'll never—ahh!"

Dad winced when she screamed. So did James. I

raised the scalpel, blade now dripping with the clear lymph that serves cuckoos in place of blood.

"Want to say that again?" I asked. "You'll look a lot less like her if I start slicing pieces off. It might be easier to look at you. So it's not a bad idea." I started to bend over her again.

"Wait!" Heloise looked at me with fear and misery in her eyes, and maybe it made me a monster, but I didn't feel bad about putting it there. "What do you actually want from me?"

"I know Sarah's in morph."

"Yes."

"Tell me how to stop it before she enters her fourth instar."

Heloise blinked. Then she seemed to sag against the table, misery wiping every other trace of expression away. "You're going to kill me," she said. "I always knew that was a possibility. When Ingrid asked me if I'd be willing to be the decoy, she wasn't really *asking*. She's the strongest of us. Well. Was. When the little princess wakes up, she'll be able to wipe her mother off the map. Too late for me. Sorry, Heloise. For a member of an inherently selfish species, you sure did die stupid." She laughed, high and sharp and utterly mirthless. It was the laughter of someone facing the walk to the gallows and determined to do it without tears.

"I never said I was going to kill you," I said.

"You didn't have to," she said. "You can't stop a morph, little incubus. Once it begins, once that process kicks off, it keeps going until it's over. Instars can last forever, depending on the external stimuli we encounter, but metamorphosis is a limited-time offer. She's going to finish her transformation and she's going to wake up in her fourth instar and she's going to blow this stupid planet to kingdom come. Sorry. Guess that's probably pretty inconvenient for you. Look at it from my perspective, though: I'm about to be dead."

"Destroying the planet will kill the rest of us," said Dad. I flinched a little. I'd been so focused on Heloise that I'd almost forgotten he was there.

"So what? I'm the one that matters." She tilted her head back as far as the table would allow, glaring at him. "I'm the superior species. You filthy primates took the long route to becoming mammals, and you're still disgusting. All that sweating and bleeding and listening to your own heartbeats like having a crappy diesel generator for a circulatory system is somehow a good thing. It's vile. I don't know how you live with yourselves."

"I'm not going to kill you," said Dad, voice mild. "You can stop trying to make me."

"Oh, believe me, if I really tried, I'd get my way." Heloise's eyes flared white. "I don't need to be able to read your mind to know what *really* scares you. That wife of yours. She's human, right? Human enough, anyway. Does she love you? Or have you just overdosed her on those nifty pheromones you have?"

"Shut up," said Dad.

"You're not from around here either, you know. The dimension you came from may be closer than ours, and you may have arrived before we did, but this isn't the world you evolved to exploit. You people and your high horses and your fancy morals, when you're colonists as much as we are. We weren't the first invaders. We won't be the last. Or oops, I guess we will be, because when our queen comes out of her egg, she's going to murder every last one of you fucking—"

"I said, *shut up*," snapped Dad, standing. Looming, really, the can of Raid in his hand and a dire expression on his face. Heloise stopped talking, but she didn't flinch. If anything, she looked absolutely, transcendentally triumphant, like she was finally getting what she wanted.

"You don't know, do you?" She smiled like she'd just won something. "You can't look into her head and see—and even if you could, maybe she doesn't know. Maybe she thinks she loves you until she gets a head cold and realizes she can't stand you when she can't smell you. Are Lilu behind the push for free flu shots? Widening your target pool?"

Dad began to shake the can.

I dropped the scalpel, hurrying to put my hand on his arm. "No. Dad, *no*. You're letting her control the situation. You can't listen to her. She's a cuckoo. Cuckoos lie."

"All cuckoos? Because I seem to remember you making an impassioned plea for the life of one cuckoo in specific. Is she a liar, too? Or do you think you're special? You're not special, Lilu. You're just one more pawn for her to push around the board. We can't fight our natures, even when we want to. Biology always wins. Biology's a bitch that way."

"Mark fought his nature," I said.

"Did he? Or did he convince you to save the fair maiden from her wicked, wicked captors and bring her right back into your nest, the way cuckoos always do? You're protecting her while she finishes her metamorphosis. You're sheltering your own doom, and you think it's your idea because she would never lie to you, because she *loves* you." The sneer Heloise put into the word "love" was enough to make my stomach turn over.

I swallowed bile. "It's not like that."

"It's always like that, over and over and over again. You people renamed us when you realized we were here, called us 'cuckoos' like that would make us less, like that would make us weak enough for you to fight. Did you know that we returned the favor? We call you 'cowbirds.' You're too stupid to see what's in your own nest. You're too stupid to see *anything*."

"Right," I said. "That's enough."

The anti-telepathy charm was still in my pocket. I dug it out, careful to keep it against the skin of my palm as I leaned over and slipped it under the neck of her sweater—Sarah's sweater—and anchored it under the strap of her bra.

Heloise froze, eyes going wide once again as she stared at me. I offered her a cool smile. It didn't matter whether she could see the expression or not. I knew it was there.

"I'm tired of you, but I'm not going to kill you," I said. "Enjoy the quiet."

"Please," she whispered, sounding truly frightened for the first time. "It's too much. The world. You turned off the world."

"Yeah, I did," I agreed, stepping back. "If Sarah doesn't wake up, you'll wish I'd done worse than that."

I turned and started for the barn door. I was almost there when Dad caught up to me.

"That wasn't kind," he said, voice low.

"No, it wasn't," I agreed. "But then, what about this day has been?"

He rested his hand briefly on my shoulder. "I won't tell you she's going to be all right. None of us can know that. But I can promise that we're going to do everything we can."

"I know, Dad," I said. "Come on. Mom's waiting for us."

Side-by-side, we stepped out of the barn and started across the lawn, toward the house where the rest of our family was waiting, where Sarah slept, where everything was falling apart.

Even me.

Twenty-one

$$\pi_2(n) \sim 2C_2 \frac{n}{(\ln n)^2} \sim 2C_2 \int_2^n \frac{dt}{(\ln t)^2}$$

"There's a moment where everything comes together, where the numbers add up and everything is perfect, and nothing hurts. That's the best moment of them all. A person could spend their whole life chasing after it, and never feel their time was wasted."

—Angela Baker

In the shining whiteness of the infinite void, where everything is about to change

THE EQUATION EXTENDED OFF the chalkboard and into the air, wrapping around me, filling the void with numbers and letters and the sweet, simple logic of a world working exactly as it had always been intended to work.

"Oh," I said. "*Oh.*"

I had been so foolish. I had been so *stupid*. This was . . . this was everything.

The equation sang to me, bright and beguiling, begging to be completed. Begging to be carried out into the world and allowed to come to sweet fruition. All I had to do was wake up. All I had to do was open my eyes, and the work—the great work, the work that I had been moving toward since the moment of my birth, the work that had always been destined to be mine—would finally begin.

All I had to do was wake up.

So I woke up.

Twenty-two

$$\pi_2(n) \sim 2C_2 \frac{n}{(\ln n)^2} \sim 2C_2 \int_2^n \frac{dt}{(\ln t)^2}$$

"When it's a choice between saving your family and saving the world, I can't tell you what to decide. I can only tell you that, no matter what you choose, part of you will always know that you were wrong."

—Alexander Healy

The front room of a private complex about an hour outside of Portland, Oregon, in the calm before the storm

YOU SURE LEAVING A cuckoo alone in the barn is the right idea?" Antimony leaned against the wall next to me, taking a swig from a bottle of virulently pink liquid. It looked like she was drinking cotton candy, which was almost enough to put me off the idea of cotton candy forever.

"No," I said. The mice cheered in the kitchen behind us. Elsie had broken out the panini press as a means of dealing with her own nerves, and was making ham and cheese sandwiches for the colony. It was a weird coping mechanism, but, frankly, I've seen weirder. "At the same time, I don't really care. She's not going to escape without seizing control of someone's mind, and with my anti-telepathy charm on her, she's not seizing anyone's mind."

"Mean," said Annie approvingly. She took another swig of pink. "I hope she suffers. I hope she screams and screams, and no one comes to save her."

I shot her a sidelong look. "Seriously?"

"Seriously." Annie lowered her bottle. "Do you think she was lying when she said there was nothing to be done to make Sarah wake up before she's done entering her next instar?"

I hesitated.

Mom and Dad were sitting on the couch, talking quietly. Mom had her hand on his cheek; he looked miserable. Heloise had really managed to get to him. Aunt Evie was in her office, gathering medical supplies in case things got ugly, and Uncle Kevin was in the library, researching everything we had on cuckoo biology and other insect-derived cryptids. He'd called Verity in New York before he locked himself away, asking her to go and talk to the local Madhura, who might be able to help. They also might not—or might not be willing to. Madhura are bee-derived, while cuckoos originated from a wasp-like ancestor. Nobody's exactly friends with the cuckoos, as a species, but there's a special degree of hatred between the cuckoos and the Madhura.

Still, Verity's contacts knew Sarah, and they knew she'd helped to stop a Covenant purge, so there was a chance. That was all we were chasing at this point. A chance. A chance that maybe somehow we could stop this before it got any worse. We needed something to go right. We needed something to *change*.

"New subject," I said. "Sam and James. Where are they, exactly?"

"Sam's outside, patrolling the fence line," she said. "He moves faster than the rest of us. Between that and his anti-telepathy charm, if the cuckoos show up here, he'll be best suited for both dealing with them and letting the rest of us know what's going on."

"And you're okay with that?"

"Nope!" She toasted me with her bottle of pink liquid. "I don't like sending my boyfriend out to deal with psychic serial killers without backup. It sucks and I hate it. But he put up with me traveling backward through time so I could punch the spirit of the crossroads in their nonexistent face, so I'm trying to be cool."

I thought about that for a moment. "You know, sometimes I wonder what our family looks like from the outside."

"Like the Munsters if that edgy modern reboot had ever managed to get off the ground."

"Fair." I looked around again. "You didn't say where James was."

And that was when James started screaming.

It was a high, panicked sound. I shoved away from the wall. So did Annie, dropping her drink as her hands burst into flames. Mom and Dad both leapt to their feet, Mom's hands suddenly bristling with knives, Dad producing a handgun from somewhere inside his jacket. I couldn't see what Elsie was doing, but I had no doubt that it was impressive, possibly involving the weaponization of a grilled cheese panini.

The screams cut off. James came tumbling down the stairs, spinning head over heels, until he crashed into the wall at the bottom and was still. Annie yelped and ran to check his pulse, only remembering at the last moment that she should probably extinguish her hands before she touched him.

"He's alive," she said, looking up and over her shoulder at the stairs. "It was a bad fall, but—"

She stopped mid-sentence, breathing in sharply. I followed her eyes and felt myself go pale as all the blood drained out of my head, leaving me unsteady and breathless.

Sarah was walking down the stairs.

Sarah, in the white dress she'd been wearing when we found her at the hive, her feet bare and her hair loose around her shoulders, like some sort of sacrifice intended for an unspeakable divinity. But her hair was floating, surrounding her in a loose corona, like she was moving underwater, and the hem of her dress was doing the same, and her eyes were glowing a bright, steady white, like searchlights. She wasn't hurrying. She wasn't slowing down, either. She was simply moving in a steady, implacable line, descending toward the fallen James and the crouching Annie.

"Sarah?" I whispered, remembering a heartbeat too late that I wasn't wearing my anti-telepathy charm anymore. She could reach me if she wanted to. The second realization followed hard on the heels of the first, slamming into me hard enough to physically knock me back a step.

There was no hum.

Sarah was less than twenty feet away, not wearing an anti-telepathy charm, and I couldn't sense her presence. There was no comforting hum of "friendly telepath in the house." There was only the ringing silence that had become too damned familiar over the course of the past five years.

"Sarah?" I said, more loudly. I thought it at the same time, and in my mind, I was screaming.

She stopped walking and turned, slowly, to face me. The light in her eyes didn't fade. The air between us grew static, like it had been laced with an electric charge.

"Sarah, I don't know what's happening, but you're sort of scaring us," I said. No one else was moving, and so I moved, taking a step toward her. "Can you hear me? Can you understand what I'm saying? You're safe now. We went and we found you and we brought you home."

Home, she said, directly into my mind. Her voice was louder than anything I'd ever heard before, like the ringing of a cloister bell. I clutched the sides of my head. Mom moaned, and I heard something hit the floor. I didn't turn to see who had dropped what. Taking my eyes off of Sarah suddenly seemed like a terrible idea.

Yes, she continued, still in that silent, impossible scream. *Home is part of the equation. This is the wrong number.*

"I don't like the look of this," said Elsie. I glanced back, long enough to see her standing right behind me.

"I don't like it either," I said grimly, and returned my attention to Sarah. She seemed like the biggest threat, in the moment. "Sarah, you *are* home. Try to remember where you are. Try to see us. I know it may be hard right now, but we're right here. Please."

Sarah tilted her head to the side. Her hair didn't move. It stayed floating in the air around her, unmoving, unchanged. Somehow that was the most terrifying thing she'd done yet.

Yes, she said, as calm as if she had been trying to order something from a recalcitrant drive-through window. *You're right here. That's part of the problem. The math doesn't work if you're right here. But I can fix it.*

The air grew even heavier, like a storm was rolling in.

Aunt Evie had grown up in a house with a cuckoo. Had spent her childhood with a cuckoo for a mother, learning how to be human from someone who had had to learn those lessons second-hand. Maybe that was why the next voice I heard was hers.

"Get *down!*" she shrieked as she hurled what looked like a water balloon into the center of the room. It burst on impact with the floor, filling the air with a white, powdery substance. I clapped a hand over my mouth and nose. Unless someone has been beating erasers in a classroom, nothing that fills the air with powder is a good thing.

Interesting, said Sarah's echoing mental voice, as

the light in her eyes somehow grew even brighter, until looking at her face was like trying to look directly into the sun. The air around her pulsed, her hair rising further away from her shoulders, and the powder began moving in fractal swirls toward a single spot in the air, pulling itself together until it had formed a perfect sphere. It was as if she had somehow reconstituted the water balloon without the actual "balloon part."

A shiver ran across my skin. We'd talked about telekinesis before, how she felt like it was somehow connected to telepathy in the real world—not just in comic books, where good was good and bad was bad and everyone looked good in spandex. More importantly, we'd talked about the sheer amount of *power* it would require.

No wonder her eyes were glowing like that. She was eating herself alive, kicking off chemical reactions in her brain that would allow her to influence the world around her.

"Sarah." I took a step toward her. "You need to stop."

Why did you try to hurt me? She was still looking at the ball of white material she'd siphoned from the air. *This would have hurt me. That was foolish of you.*

I realized two things at the same time, and both of them were terrible.

The first was that the white stuff Aunt Evie had thrown at Sarah—her sister—must have been powdered theobromine. Cuckoos are allergic to theobromine. They love tomatoes, and they hate chocolate. It makes them itchy. That much of the stuff would have been enough to cause a serious reaction in a human or Lilu. In a cuckoo . . .

It could have killed her. Aunt Evie, who loved her sister, who loved her mother, who talked about the importance of family as much as anyone, had just happened to have a water balloon filled with theobromine in her office, waiting to be flung. She'd prepared for this. She'd known that it was possible, and she'd *prepared*.

The second was that everyone else was still wearing their anti-telepathy charms. They weren't flinching from the volume of Sarah's mental voice because they couldn't *hear* it. They didn't know how angry she was.

"Guys, she's pissed," I said, stopping where I was. "Aunt Evie, you might want to run."

The ball of compressed theobromine suddenly shot across the room like it had been fired by an invisible slingshot. I heard it strike something. I heard Aunt Evie start choking. Dad and Elsie ran to help her. Elsie was shouting, her words rendered incomprehensible by Aunt Evie's increasing respiratory distress and the sound of footsteps thundering across the floor.

Mom was suddenly next to me, hands bristling with knives. Most Prices have trained, at least a little, in throwing knives. They're less deadly than guns, but they're quieter, and they get the job done. "I'm sorry," she said, glancing to me, and pulled her hand back to start throwing.

Sarah looked at her, eyes flaring whiter still. Mom shouted in dismay as her feet left the floor. Then she slammed into the ceiling and stuck there, her arms stretched out from her body, her hands still full of knives.

"Mom!" I cried, in dismay. I looked frantically at Sarah. "Let her *down*. Sarah, you have to let her *down*."

This isn't the right location, and you're all being irrational. I need to remove you. I need to remove myself. Fine. Sarah moved her hands for the first time, swiping them through the air in front of her like she was browsing through a touchscreen, pulling up the pieces she wanted and discarding the pieces she didn't. There was a terrible, somehow meaty ripping sound, and a jagged tear appeared in the air at the middle of the living room, bleeding white light into the room.

I felt something run up my leg. The mice. They'd been watching this whole thing, and some of them were scared enough to take refuge with the nearest available divinity. More were probably hiding themselves in Annie's hair and clothes. And none of that was going to save them if Sarah brought the house down on us.

"Sarah!" I howled, and started toward her again, or tried to. The air itself was pushing back against me. It was like wading through quicksand, thick and clinging and terrible. "Sarah, *you have to stop*!"

Annie was staggering to her feet, James by her side, one arm draped around her shoulder so she could support his weight. I wasn't actually sure he was awake. I *was* sure that holding him like that was keeping her from accessing her fire. If she let go, he would fall down. Sarah didn't seem to have noticed them. Her attention, such as it was, was divided between the impossible tear in our living room and me.

For the first time in my life, I didn't want Sarah's attention and I had it. It was getting hard to breathe. Mom was still pinned to the ceiling, and Dad and Elsie were still somewhere in the house trying to keep Aunt Evie from dying of theobromine poisoning. We were far enough away from the library that it was possible Uncle Kevin didn't even know things had gone so terribly, terribly wrong.

This was up to us. Just us. And I didn't know if I could do it.

"Sarah, please," I said, still forcing my way through the heavy air toward her. "Please. It's me. It's Artie. You're my best friend. Don't you remember that? I . . ."

Annie was approaching Sarah from behind, James still draped against her. I didn't know what she was going to do. I wasn't sure *she* knew what she was going to do. But if there was any way to end this without hurting Sarah, she was going to find it. And with the anti-telepathy charm in her pocket, Annie was functionally invisible right now. Sarah didn't know she was coming. As long as I didn't think about it too loudly, there was a chance.

"Sarah, I love you."

The white light in her eyes seemed to dim for a second. It could have been wishful thinking. It could have been the first sign that her body was running out of the energy necessary to sustain this sort of output. I had to hope that it was something else. I had to hope that I was actually getting through to her.

"I've never told you that before, but it's been true for years. I love you. I'm *in* love with you. I want to wake up next to you. I want to watch you do math—you're so cute when you're doing math. I want you to tell me how soothing my brain is. So please, you have to stop this. You have to let us help you. Please, Sarah. Please don't leave me again. I only just got you back. I can't lose you yet."

Artie . . .

For a moment—just a moment—her mental tone sounded less distant and clinical, and more like the Sarah I loved. Then her eyes flashed again.

We're part of a different equation. You can't lose me. You never had me. I can't do this here.

And she stepped through the rift in the air.

Things began to happen very quickly. Annie, who had been close enough to reach out for Sarah—I saw the glint of an anti-telepathy charm in her outstretched palm and realized what her plan had been—stumbled under the combined weight of James and the sudden absence of her target. The air was thick and thin at the same time, making both movement and breathing difficult. And Annie, who was off-balance and probably faintly hypoxic, fell into the rift, dragging James with her.

I didn't hesitate. Hesitation is one of my great skills. I overthink everything. But in that moment, I threw caution aside and dove through the thickening air, into the rift, following my cousin and her pet sorcerer and the cuckoo I loved into the glittering, light-lined darkness.

I hope this isn't how I die, I thought, and blacked out.

Twenty-three

$$\pi_2(n) \sim 2C_2 \frac{n}{(\ln n)^2} \sim 2C_2 \int_2^n \frac{dt}{\ln n}$$

"Human morality is only absolute because the humans won the war to see who would be the dominant species of this planet. We live by the moral and ethical standards of a species whose dominion is built on bones."

—Martin Baker

Sprawled in the middle of the street in an unfamiliar city, because that's fun

"RTIE? Artie, can you hear me?"

So I wasn't dead. That was nice to know. Not that dead people can't yell—Aunt Mary yells plenty when she thinks her living relatives are doing stupid shit that could land us in the afterlife before she's ready for us—but dead people aren't usually that interested in whether or not I can hear them. Sort of like telepaths, dead people get their meaning across regardless of how many senses are functional at any given time.

I wasn't dead, and I was lying on something that managed to be uncomfortably hard and uncomfortably jagged at the exact same time. What felt like a rock was digging into my hip, and I was pretty sure there was gravel under my back. It sort of hurt. I opened my eyes, staring up into a chalk-colored early morning sky. It was that bleached bone-white that sometimes accompanies the very beginning of dawn, streaked with bands of cirrus clouds. The moon was still visible, hanging low and pinkish-red on the horizon.

Then Annie leaned into my field of vision, eclipsing everything else.

"Ack," I said, with all the coherence I could muster.

"You hit your head when we came out of the rift," said Annie, reaching down to offer me a hand up. "I recommend against doing that again."

"Okay, um, what the *actual* fuck?" I took her hand, letting her pull me into a sitting position. Being able to see my surroundings raised more questions than it answered.

We were in the middle of a street in what looked like a shopping district, only small and quaint and bizarrely agrarian. Even the suburbs near farm country outside Portland didn't look like this. There was something old-timey about it all, but modern at the same time, like a paradox that somehow managed not to contradict itself. This was a place where people lived. This was real.

"I didn't hit my head," said Annie, letting go of my hand. "I landed on James. Not super fun for James, but since he was already barely conscious, he wasn't too pissed about it, and I got him clear before you came tumbling through. He's awake now. Sarah didn't hurt him. She just terrified him. The rift closed a while ago. We're stuck here."

"Where's 'here'?"

"Ames, Iowa."

I stared at her. "What? That's like, I don't know—"

"It's eighteen hundred miles away." She held up her cellphone. "The wonders of GPS."

"Holy shit."

"Mmm-hmm." Annie put the phone back in her pocket. I realized how tired she looked. "I also called home while you were out. Everyone's all right. Mom had a nasty reaction to the theobromine powder—she inhaled more than she should have before your dad and Elsie got her out of the cloud—but she's going to be fine. Your mom fell off the ceiling as soon as the rift closed. She has a broken wrist. She'll recover."

"How is this possible?"

"Well, the cuckoos did say they wanted Sarah to rip a hole in the fabric of the world. I guess this was just a test run. We have a bigger problem, though."

There was something about her tone that put my teeth on edge. I eyed her warily as I pushed myself to my feet and brushed the gravel off my knees. "What's that?"

"We fell into the rift a week ago."

Oh. "Um," I said. "Yeah, that does . . . that does sound like a bigger problem."

Annie looked at me solemnly. "You think? Our family thought we were dead, so that's fun. Apparently, they summoned Aunt Rose—Mary's busy keeping an eye on Shelby, since the baby's due soon—and had her searching the twilight for us. I think the fact that she couldn't find us may be the only reason nothing's currently on fire."

"Where's James?" I hesitated before asking the question I really wanted to have answered. "Where's Sarah?"

"James is taking a quick turn around the block while I try to wake you up," said Annie. "Sarah is . . . Sarah's with the rest of the hive."

My heart sank.

Sarah had attacked us; Sarah had ripped the rift in the air that had led to us losing a week and winding up stranded nearly two thousand miles away from the rest of the family, with no backup and only the weapons we happened to be carrying when we fell through. And yet, somehow, I'd still been hoping that we'd be able to talk her down.

"The Calculating Priestess conducts the Rites and Rituals of her Kind," squeaked a voice next to my ear. I glanced to the side. The Aeslin mouse standing on my shoulder was wearing a scrap of one of my old flannel shirts as a cloak, and a necklace made from a small USB drive. One of my clergy, then. It was nice to know that if I died out here, I'd have at least one of my own mice with me.

"What did you call her?" asked Annie.

"She has been Named and Acknowledged as a Priestess," said the mouse, wiping its forepaws across its whiskers to emphasize the statement. "We are sorry to have taken so long."

"Okay, that's . . . new." Annie looked down at the pocket of her coat, a thoughtful frown on her lips. "You could have said something."

"You didn't ask," squeaked her pocket.

"Fair enough." She turned her attention back to the mouse on my shoulder. "Do you know anything about cuckoo rites or rituals?"

"Only that they Must Be," said the mouse gravely. "What fragments we know pre-date the Faith."

Meaning that at some point before they came to our family, ancestors of the current colony had encountered a cuckoo. I exchanged a startled look with Antimony. It can be easy to forget that the mice had an existence before us. They're some of the last Aeslin mice left in the world. We have to protect them. That can limit the way we look at them, like we think of them as accessories and not individuals.

"Fragments?" asked Annie carefully.

Aeslin mice have utterly flawless recall. If a mouse hears or sees something once, they'll be able to repeat or describe it perfectly for the rest of their lives. Unlike the cuckoos, with their implanted histories, the history of the Aeslin mice is learned, handed down without alteration or editing, for as long as a faith endures.

The mouse scrubbed at its whiskers, looking embar-

rassed. "The faith came before the faith which pre-
dated our discovery by the Kindly Priestess," it said.
"We have failed you by remembering any piece of it. It
is Heresy, and should long have been Forgotten."

"It may save our asses now, so whatever it is, I de-
clare it part of my catechism," said Annie bluntly. "It's
a Lost Mystery. Now tell me what you know."

"When the Heartless Ones choose to do a great
ritual, they will gather together, one unto the next, until their numbers are terrible to behold," said the
mouse. "When this happens, the wisest thing is to Run
Very Far, and Not Look Back. Those who fail to Run
will not be seen again."

I looked around. "I don't see any cuckoos."

"I haven't seen any since we got here," said Annie.
"Assuming Sarah couldn't control the rift well enough
to put us somewhere different—which is a big assumption, but it's one that maybe leads to us having a world
tomorrow, so I'm going to make it—she must be somewhere nearby."

"A week would give the other cuckoos time to come
and find her, if they knew this was where she was going
to wind up," I said. "And we have no way of knowing
she came out the same time as we did. Maybe she's
been here the whole time, getting ready. What's so special about Ames?"

"I don't know, but they're all definitely here."

I turned. James was jogging down the street toward
us. He didn't look at all bothered by the chill in the
morning air, despite his lack of a jacket. Stupid sorcerers, with their stupid elemental alignments.

"The people are here, but they're not moving," he
said. "The shops are full. The restaurants, too. I saw a
woman walk through a diner, filling all the water
glasses, then go back to standing perfectly still behind
the counter. I think the cuckoos have put them into a
sort of sleep mode. They'll do what they must to stay
alive, but that's their limit."

"So we know the cuckoos *are* here," said Annie. "That's a start."

"Where is harder," said James.

"Ames," I said. "Ames, Iowa. We're in Ames, Iowa."

"Yes," said Annie. "Look, Artie, this is not a good time for you to fall apart on me. I'm sorry, but I need you to hold it together. Okay?"

"I'm not falling apart," I said. "Your phone. How much battery do you have?"

"Not enough."

"There's a major university here. Cuckoos are math addicts. They'll head for the school if they have any choice in the matter. How far away are we?"

Annie's eyes lit up with sudden understanding. She began poking at the screen of her phone, announcing a minute later, "About three miles."

"Great." I looked back to the mouse. "What else do you know?"

"Only that the Heartless Ones are Not Of This World, and that one day they must Leave it."

"Peachy." I grabbed a rock off the road and started walking toward an old Camaro parked in front of a store that either sold rocks or decorative soaps intentionally made to look like rocks. It can be hard to tell.

"What are you doing?" asked James.

"Getting us to school," I said, and threw the rock through the car window.

The shattering sound was remarkably loud on the quiet, cuckoo-snared street. There was a pressure at the back of my head that I recognized as the cuckoos trying to influence me, whether they knew they were doing it or not. I shunted it aside. I'm a Price. We don't take well to being mentally controlled. Great-Grandma's gift to us, even if we still don't understand it.

"Annie, your cousin is stealing a car," said James, in a carefully neutral tone. I ignored him in favor of reaching through the broken window, unlocking the door, and using a McDonald's bag from the passenger footwell to shovel the glass out into the street.

"My cousin's a genius," said Annie. "You know how to hotwire that thing?"

"I don't need to," I said. "My old Camaro never met a screwdriver it didn't want to be friends with, before you went and torched it. Which is why—ah!" I held up the long, narrow-headed screwdriver that had just dropped from the glove compartment. "Your chariot awaits."

"I'm quite sure this is illegal," muttered James, as he and Annie started toward the car.

"Pretty sure destroying the entire world is worse than a little minor car theft," said Annie.

I slid into the driver's seat, leaning over to unlock the doors on the other side of the car. Annie and James climbed in, and I shoved the tip of the screwdriver into the ignition, wiggling it until I felt that essential, comfortingly familiar catch. When I twisted it, the engine rumbled on.

"Next stop, the end of the goddamn world," I said, and hit the gas.

Nothing moved except for the wind as we drove through Ames. Somehow, the little waves of motion in the grass and the trees made it more obvious how frozen everything else was. There were no cats, no dogs, no squirrels or birds . . . and no people.

"How many cuckoos are we expecting to find here?" asked James.

"Too many," said Annie.

"That's not a number," he said. "I know you think you sound cool when you say things like that, but actual information and tactical plans are much, much cooler. I promise you."

"I'm a big fan of actual information," said Annie.

"Unfortunately, right now, we don't have any. We know Sarah was somehow able to transport us across the country to Iowa. We know there isn't time for backup to get here before we deal with the literally world-destroying cuckoo situation. We know that they've forced Sarah into her fourth instar, which is apparently a big enough deal to make even other cuckoos say 'wait, maybe this is bad.'"

"We know we might have to kill her to make this stop."

My words fell into a sudden silence that yawned like a pit in the middle of our stolen car, seeming to steal away all sound. I glanced at Antimony. She didn't meet my eyes.

"That's what you're not saying, isn't it? We know we have two anti-telepathy charms and the weapons we were carrying when we fell through the hole in space, and we know I just stole a car, and we know that maybe we're about to have to kill our cousin."

"Artie—"

"And you know I've been in love with her since we were kids, and you know she's my best friend, and you know that these last five years have almost literally killed me, so maybe it's only fair that I should *actually* literally kill her."

"You know I don't want to have to do this," she said, and her voice was very small, and very tired.

"I know." It was easier if I didn't look at her. If I treated this like it was . . . like it was the cutscene in a video game, maybe, something distant from me. Something removed. "I do. And I know none of us got to pick who went to Iowa and who stayed home. And the worst part is that I *also* know that I won't be able to shut you out when this is over, because apart from Sarah, you're the person I trust most in the whole world, and I'm going to be pretty messed up for a while. Maybe for a long, long time."

"We gave Sarah five years to put herself back together," said Annie. "We can give you at least that long."

"I've seen Annie achieve the impossible before," said James. "If half the stories she's told me about your family are remotely true, maybe between the two of you, you'll be able to find another way through this. Something that doesn't end with blood."

"Oh, there's gonna be blood," said Annie. "It doesn't matter what else happens, there's *gonna* be blood, because I need to punch some cuckoos until the clear stuff comes out. And then I need to set even more of them on fire. It's going to be a fun, horrifying, violent day."

I kept my eyes on the road. I needed this to end in a way that I knew it wasn't likely to end. I needed it to find the one path that led to me and Sarah walking away, her back in her right mind, the two of us finally able to be together.

I needed us to win, and I didn't see any feasible way for us to be able to do it.

The motionless roads blurred by as I pushed the old Camaro's engine to the absolute limits of what it could handle. It wasn't like there were any other cars to worry about, and seeing a human police officer would almost have been a relief. It would have been proof that there were a few people resistant to the cuckoos' collective thrall, at the very least. But there was nothing. I drove, and the scenery changed, and no one came to stop us, not until we were pulling up in front of the university.

I stopped the engine just in time. The collective weight of the entire hive's cool regard slammed into my brain with all the stress of a wrecking ball, sending sudden, intense pain lancing through my entire body. I shouted, as much in surprise as anything else, and clutched the sides of my head as I tried to make it stop.

Dimly, I could hear Annie shouting for James to grab my head and keep me from slamming it into the steering wheel. That was nice. It was real good of her to look out for me.

There was a flash of something in the collective, bright and sweet and somehow carrying the fruity, acidic taste of Sarah's favorite drink, grenadine and tomato paste mixed with ginger ale. The weight receded. I sat up, gasping, resisting the urge to feel myself to confirm that my body was still there. Of course it was still there. It wouldn't have been in so much pain if it hadn't been there.

"What the *fuck*?" demanded Annie.

"No anti-telepathy charm." I rubbed my temples with both hands. "Nothing to keep the cuckoos out. I still can't hear the hum. Something's wrong with Sarah."

"Yeah, she's gone all Dark Phoenix and started ripping holes in the walls of the world," said Annie. "We knew that."

"But she's still *in* there," I said. "I think . . . I think the hive noticed me and wanted to do something to make me go away. Sarah stopped them. She may not be capable of breaking free of whatever fugue she's in, but she still stopped them from taking me over."

"How are you sure it was her?" asked James.

"She's been in and out of my head since we were ten years old," I said. "I know what her thoughts feel like. They have a taste, almost, like I'm remembering drinking something I never drank."

"One of her disgusting sodas," said Annie, in sudden understanding.

I nodded. "Tomato sauce and ginger ale, and just a little bit of grenadine."

"When we were kids, we used to believe that a drink needed three ingredients to be really fancy," said Annie, as if that would take the bewildered, borderline disbelieving look off of James's face.

"How do you know that it's not some cuckoo cultural drink?" he asked. "Maybe it wasn't Sarah who let you go."

"Maybe," I said. "I have to tell myself it was her, because if there's any chance we can still get her back, I'm going to do my best to take it. I have to believe there's still a chance. It's the only way I can do this."

"If she's gone, I won't make you be the one to kill her," said Annie.

She was trying to be kind. I knew that. I could see it in her face, the soft, weary lines around her eyes, the downturned corners of her mouth. She was trying so hard to be kind, and nothing about this was kind, and nothing about this was fair, and nothing—*nothing*—about this was right, or ever could have been.

I opened the car door.

"Come on," I said. "Let's end this."

James and Annie followed me to the sidewalk, and along it toward the university grounds. Somewhere, the cuckoo hive was gathering, waiting for us to find them. Somewhere, Sarah was working her way through an equation so big and so terrible that completing it would destroy the world.

We were running out of time, and there were no good endings left. So we just kept walking.

We had barely passed the first building when we saw the first cuckoos.

There were five of them, all around my age, standing silently on a patch of grass with their faces turned toward the sky, like they were looking at a particularly interesting cloud. Their eyes were glowing softly white, not as bright as Sarah's had been when she tore a hole in reality, but bright enough that I felt safe assuming they couldn't see us. I motioned Annie and James both to silence and walked faster, until we found a corner we could safely duck around.

"Well, we're in the right place," said Annie.

"Can they not see us when they're like that?" asked James.

"It's . . . complicated," I said. "Their eyes still work, but Sarah used to say it was like trying to watch two shows at the same time on the same screen, and Mark said they were getting sunk in the corona of her metamorphosis before. Things get all jumbled together, and sometimes it's easier to let go of what you *think* you see and focus on what you *know* you see."

"Which means the cuckoos we run across will either be focused on maintaining control over the townspeople or working to help Sarah do her big math problem," said Annie. "As long as we're quiet and don't touch any of them, we should be able to keep moving without much concern that they're going to stop us and ask what we're doing here. They probably won't even notice we're here."

"I'm assuming that by 'ask' you mean 'attack,'" said James.

"See, you're a member of the family," said Annie.

I resisted the urge to snap at them. Sometimes whistling past the proverbial graveyard is the only way to stay sane in the face of seemingly insurmountable odds. Instead, I pushed away from the wall and started walking again, trying to think about the shape of the campus the way a cuckoo would.

Cuckoos were originally insects. Wasps. They were mostly solitary, but when they gathered in a large number, they still fell into the habits of a hive. It would make sense, then, for them to look for the central point of the campus—the point with the heaviest defenses between it and the outside world. Even if those defenses were nothing more than concrete and brick, they'd still be better than nothing to a species that knew, all the way to the bottom of its DNA, that sometimes it was essential to run and hide.

I didn't know Iowa State, but I knew college campuses. They're usually built around some sort of central green space, even in the heart of cities; something that students could use as an informal gathering space. Call it a quad or call it a field, its purpose was the same. I didn't know why the cuckoos had chosen Iowa State—I would have been less surprised by Buckley Township in Michigan, where my family used to live—but if they were at the university, it was because they'd found a space large enough to suit their needs. We just had to do the same.

Annie and James flanked me as we walked, which created the unpleasant sensation of being baked and frozen at the same time. Little flames flickered around Annie's fingers, blue-white in their intensity, while the air surrounding James seemed crystalline and clear, as bright and deadly as a winter morning. It made me feel like I was more than a little outgunned heading into this fight. All I could do was smell really nice and make people want to do things for me, and even that didn't work on cuckoos.

Oh, and I could punch. I could punch pretty damn hard. Maybe punching would be the solution to my problem.

Or maybe it would involve too much physical contact with unfriendly cuckoos and make my problem worse. No one really knows why Great-Grandma Fran was resistant to cuckoo influence. We know it must have been genetic, since she's passed it down to her descendants, but without having a way to study it, we've never been able to learn its exact limitations. James wasn't immune to my pheromones, and the anti-telepathy charm wouldn't stop him from getting enthralled again if one of the cuckoos decided to take me over and use me as a weapon.

"I should never have left my basement," I muttered.

"Wish I didn't agree," said Annie.

Then we came around a bend in the path, leading us to the top of a small ridge. Beyond it stretched a vast green area, large enough to look like some sort of private park. All three of us stopped where we were. My heart felt like it was trying to climb up my throat and run away to someplace friendlier. Someplace where we were less guaranteed to die in the next, say, five minutes.

The green space was filled with cuckoos. Hundreds of cuckoos, maybe even thousands of cuckoos, more than I had ever considered might exist. They were packed in like the crowds at Comic-Con, shoulder to shoulder, seeming to seek skin contact with one another. Their eyes were white, their faces tilted toward the sky.

I saw elderly cuckoos, skin seamed with wrinkles and hair streaked with silver. I saw children, some as young as three or four, still in their pajamas, barefoot in the grass. There weren't any babies. I hoped that meant they'd been left with their unwitting foster parents, and not that they'd all been killed. And then I felt bad for hoping that, since it would mean those families still had ticking time bombs buried in their midst. Which was worse, hoping for dead babies or hoping for family annihilations?

Sometimes there's no good answer to a bad situation. Sometimes there's only trying to find the answer that results in the fewest casualties.

Annie nudged me with her elbow. "Look," she whispered, voice so low that it was like listening to the wind.

I looked.

The cuckoos, tight-packed as they were, had nonetheless arranged themselves in a series of concentric circles, with space between each tier. There was no mingling of one tier into the next: they'd drawn their divisions and they were standing by them. More, most of the tiers seemed to be divided roughly by age. The very youngest and the very oldest were in the outside ring. The tier after that consisted mostly of teenagers, followed by people who looked to be roughly in their early twenties, and so on. The final, central ring was made up of people about my parents' age.

They were dividing themselves according to instar. But that didn't explain why that final ring was so large, or why the elders were with the larval cuckoos, or why there was so much open space between them—

And then one of the older cuckoos opened his mouth and made a pained hissing, clicking sound that hurt my ears, even as his eyes abruptly flashed a blazing supernova white. The light in them died a split second later, and he collapsed forward, nearly landing on the children who had been standing directly front of him. They moved to the side and kept moving until a break had formed in the ring. Several cuckoos approached from the side, entering the break and scooping up the body—and it *was* a body now; he wasn't moving, wasn't breathing, wasn't doing anything at all—before carrying it briskly away. The ring moved back together, closing the gap.

"They're organized by instar," I said softly. "More power the closer in you get to the middle."

"What's at the middle?" asked James.

I was direly afraid I already knew.

More cuckoos fell every few seconds, and when they did, the cleaners were there to scoop them up and carry them away. I moved toward the edge of the nearest ring, gesturing for the others to follow me, and when the next cuckoo fell, I started forward.

What followed was the most stressful game of live-action *Frogger* that I'm ever likely to be a part of. When a cuckoo fell, the rings would shift to make room for the ones who came to remove the body. That would give us the opening we needed to push forward more, without bringing them all down on our heads.

At one point, James stumbled on the uneven ground, and his arm brushed against a cuckoo moving past us with the body of a child slung across her shoulder. She stopped, looking momentarily confused. Then she started walking again, and we all three started breathing again.

I knew what we were going to find at the center of the geometric formation of silent, white-eyed bodies, and even so, it was like a blow when we finally reached the bottom of the hill and I could see into the last ring.

They had arranged themselves to surround a little slice of green, a perfect circle defined by their bodies. And there, at the middle, was Sarah.

She was still wearing her white dress. I hadn't been expecting anything else. There were grass stains on the hem, and somehow that made it even worse. She was barefoot and smeared in green, and her eyes were as bright as stars, while her hands moved through the air like she was conducting a silent symphony of numbers, moving things that only she could see from one place to another.

The skin above her lips was bright with what would have seemed like snot if I hadn't known her biology so intimately. She was bleeding. She was bleeding from the nose and from the ears and even though she wasn't blinking, something that looked like a tear escaped from the corner of her left eye and ran down her cheek, leaving a thick trail behind.

"She can't take much more of this," I whispered. "She's going to break under the weight."

"I'm so sorry," said Antimony. There was a clicking sound, roughly on the level of my ear.

I turned. Antimony had drawn a gun from inside her clothing and had it aimed at Sarah's head, her finger on the trigger. It was a small handgun, the sort of thing that's basically designed to be concealed. It was more than big enough.

"Annie," I said.

"I'm so, *so* sorry," she said.

And then she pulled the trigger.

Twenty-four

$$\pi_2(n) \sim 2C_2 \frac{n}{(\ln n)^2} \sim 2C_2 \int_2^n \frac{dt}{(\ln t)^2}$$

"Some prices are far too dear. And yet we
pay them anyway."

—Jonathan Healy

*Iowa State University, in Ames, Iowa, very far away
from home, incredibly betrayed*

A LL OF US ARE excellent shots.
Verity's the best in our generation, and Alex is
the deadliest—the two things are connected even
though they're not always the same—but we're all excellent shots, because we were never given a choice in
the matter. We learned from our parents, and we
learned from Grandma Alice, and we learned from all
the teachers our family could find for us, because we
had to know. We had to understand what a firearm was
capable of doing, and we had to be able to do it. Punching and stabbing things are all well and good, and they
absolutely have their place, but sometimes, only a bullet will get the job done.

All of us are excellent shots. When Antimony
pulled the trigger, there was no question in my mind
that she'd hit what she was aiming at. Because all of us
are excellent shots. Those words kept ringing through
my head, packing themselves into an impossibly narrow window of time, as I turned in slow horror—as I
whipped around as fast I could—to Sarah.

If she was going to die, I was going to see it happen. I was going to *know* that it had happened. And then I was going to go home to my basement and lock the door and never go outside again.

The sound of the bullet being fired had been impossibly loud from where I was standing, and there was no question in my mind that we were about to be dealing with a whole lot of seriously pissed-off cuckoos. Some of them were already turning toward us, their eyes flashing white, their expressions blank and somehow terrifying in their emotionless coldness.

Sarah didn't turn. Sarah didn't move at all. The bullet was moving too fast for the eye to follow—until suddenly it wasn't moving either. Suddenly it was hanging in the air in front of her, surrounded by a sphere of what looked like water. She had somehow hardened the molecules of the atmosphere enough to stop it before it could reach her.

No, she said inside my mind, loudly enough that it made my eyes water. There was no feeling that she was screaming, or even that she was shouting: her mental voice was just so much bigger than it had ever been before that my brain didn't know how to process it yet.

"Sarah, please," I said.

No, she repeated, and waved her hand dismissively, sending the bullet rocketing back toward us.

Antimony shouted, a wordless sound of panicked warning, and shoved James to the side. The bullet whizzed between them. There was a soft shattering sound. I risked a glance over my shoulder.

The bullet had found a home squarely between the eyes of a large male cuckoo, opening a hole through which clear fluid was already beginning to leak. His eyes went comically wide before he crumpled, motionless, to the ground.

"Artie, I'm sorry, but we need to run," said Antimony, looking frantically around as more and more cuckoos turned in our direction.

"She didn't have to miss."

"What?"

"Sarah didn't have to miss."

"Yes, I'm sure your cousin who's gearing up to un-make reality was being kind to us, now can we go?" demanded James.

I kept my eyes on Antimony. The cuckoos had noticed us, but they weren't moving yet: we had a few seconds. "You've been on the range with Sarah. She's not the best shot, but she doesn't miss at this sort of distance."

"I'm wearing an anti-telepathy charm," said Antimony. "She can't see me."

"She can't *read* you, but she can see you. And I'm right here. She missed us because *she didn't want to hurt us*." I needed her to understand. The words weren't obeying me. No matter how hard I tried to make them, they weren't obeying me. "It's still Sarah in there."

"Artie—"

"I can hear her. It's still Sarah. Let me try."

Antimony looked into my eyes for one long, frozen moment. Then she nodded, mouth twisting into a resigned smile.

"We're surrounded and doomed anyway. If you think you can try—try. We'll hold them off." She shoved the gun into her waistband as her hands burst into flame and she shouted, "All right, you telepathic assholes! You want a piece of this?"

"Oh, joy, this is precisely how I wanted to die," muttered James. The temperature around us dropped precipitously.

I spun on my heel and dove into the nearest ring of cuckoos.

It was hard not to be angry with Annie for shooting at Sarah. No: it was *impossible* not to be angry with Annie. I wanted to shake her and scream and demand to know what she thought she was doing, how she could take that kind of risk with Sarah's life. Except for the part where I knew what she thought she was doing. She was doing what we'd all been taught to do since we'd been old enough to listen to Mr. Rogers and go looking for the helpers: she was trying to minimize the potential loss of life.

If Sarah finished the equation that would tear a hole in the wall of our dimension, that was the ball game. Everyone would die, except for the cuckoos, who would move on to their next target, a fresh new world ready for devastation. I couldn't even try to convince myself that Sarah would find a way to stop them—that she'd be the small, clear voice at the center of the chaos, teaching the rest of her kind how to care—because the equation would have already burned her brain out, leaving her dead if she was lucky, and at the whim of the other cuckoos if she wasn't. They weren't a species of natural caretakers. They wouldn't be good to her.

Antimony had been doing the job we'd all been raised to do. And I . . .

I was following the example that had been set for me by my parents, and by my grandparents, all the way back to the moment when Alexander and Enid Healy had decided to leave the Covenant of St. George behind. I was risking everything I had and everything I knew on the slimmest chance that I could save the woman I loved.

A hand seized my wrist, followed instantly by the crushing pressure of another mind attempting to assert its domination over mine. I turned my head. Even that was difficult, like pushing my way through thick honey. The cuckoo who had hold of me didn't want me to move. Didn't even want me to keep breathing.

Thank you, Great-Grandma Fran, I thought, and looked upon the face of a woman who was so close to identical to Sarah that they could have been twins. Even their eyes were the same shade of blue.

Unlike Heloise, there was no mistaking this woman

for Sarah. She was immensely pregnant, her belly openly declaring her condition to anyone who saw her.

"You're not supposed to be here," she said, in a calm, pleasant voice.

"I'm not supposed to be here," I echoed, despite my best attempts to keep my mouth closed. The thick honey feeling of the air around me was getting stronger. It said that I should listen to what this woman wanted. She was so clever and so beautiful and so much more important than I was; it was really unreasonable that I would dare to interfere with her plans, which I couldn't possibly understand, with as weak and worthless as I was—

I laughed. The woman recoiled, not letting go of my wrist. The feeling of moving through honey receded, enough for me to hear the sweet sound of several cuckoos screaming.

"Second-degree burns or frostbite, which do you think?" My tongue was thick and heavy in my mouth. Every word was an effort. A worthwhile effort, at least: with each one, I could feel her hold on me slipping. She didn't know how to handle a target that could fight back.

Her eyes narrowed, threads of white lashing through the blue of her irises. "Your friends are troublesome," she said. "They'll disrupt our work. That's inappropriate. You have to stop them."

"Oh, they're not my friends. They're my family. We're really big on family where I come from."

The woman blinked, once, before offering me a truly radiant smile, wide and bright and oddly serene. "Ah. Family. That's what matters to you. Well, then, I think you should know that I'm Sarah's biological mother."

I blinked, once. Then, before the air could harden around me again, I slammed my forehead into hers so hard that I heard bone crack. I just hoped it wasn't mine.

The woman cried out, a sharp, startled sound, and staggered a step backward, losing her grasp on my wrist as she raised one hand to her forehead. Her eyes were watering and perfectly blue, with no sign of telepathic activity.

"You don't get to be her *mother* now," I snarled. "You gave birth to her and you *left* her. That wasn't even adoption. That was . . . that was forcing someone else to do the hard work of being a parent for you. And then they died, they *died,* and you didn't come back. You let us take her in. You let us love her. That *was* adoption, that *was* a choice, and we made it, and you don't have any right to take it back. She's not yours. She's *ours.*"

The woman put a hand over her stomach, staring at me with pure loathing. "You have no right to judge us by the laws of your species."

"I don't know." Another cuckoo screamed somewhere behind me. Without their telepathy to help them target Annie and James, they were learning the hard way that sometimes it's a good idea to take a self-defense class. "It sort of feels like you're judging us by the laws of your species, all the time. You gave Sarah up. Not for her benefit. For your own. Also, it's the laws of my species that tell me it's not okay to beat up a pregnant lady, so maybe you should try to be okay with that."

An oak two-by-four slammed into the side of her head. She staggered for a moment and then fell, landing heavily on her side, one arm curled around the vast swell of her belly.

Mark dropped the plank next to her. "My species doesn't have any laws about letting women go unscathed just because they're gestating," he said. "Maybe we should, but I'm not the one who set the standards."

I gaped at him. "You're here. We—"

"You left me in Beaverton. Believe me, I noticed.

But I'm a quick thinker and things got really confused and distracted when you stole the princess; I survived, no thanks to you."

"Um." Something shattered in the distance. Given that James was still in play, I was pretty sure it was one of the cuckoos. "I'm sorry about that."

"I would have done the same thing to you." Mark shoved his hair out of his eyes and glared at me. "You need to end this. We're almost out of time."

He wasn't wrong about that. The air was growing thick again, not like honey this time, but like it had been saturated with electricity. This was the weight of a storm getting ready to descend, and I didn't need to be psychic to know that we didn't have long before whatever was about to happen was too far along to be stopped.

I turned and resumed wading through the cuckoos— what was left of them. Most had rushed off to confront Annie and James, apparently trusting the woman who claimed to be Sarah's biological mother to stop me. There was another scream behind me, followed by a shout of pain. This time, I recognized the voice. Annie was in trouble.

Annie could take care of herself. I kept forcing my way forward until Sarah was right in front of me, her eyes glowing white, her hair floating several inches above her shoulders and belling out around her head like a corona, like she was underwater and no longer subject to the precise rules and regulations of gravity.

Lymph was still leaking from her nose, ears, and eyes, adding a damp slickness to her face. Her eyes were blazing white, so bright I couldn't look directly at them. And still her hands were moving, swiping through the air, moving things I couldn't see into place.

I didn't allow myself to hesitate. Hesitation wasn't going to help us now. I stepped up in front of her and grabbed her wrists, stopping her hands. She turned to stare at me, and I fought the urge to shut my eyes against the brightness.

You are interfering, she said.

"I'm here because I need you to stop before you destroy the world," I said.

The equations must be finished.

"No, Sarah. You need to stop, and let them go, and come home."

The equations will *be finished.*

Her voice was a roar of silent thunder, bouncing back and forth inside my skull, echoing off of everything. It was almost impossible to fight the urge to clap my hands over my ears and stop the headache. I forced myself not to move.

"Sarah. Come on. Come back to me. You're better than this. You've always been better than this. None of these people are worth dying over. None of them are important enough to let them make you a monster."

Let me go.

I took a deep breath. "Make me."

Her eyes flashed white, bright as dying stars, and the air grew even thicker. I dropped her wrists and wrapped my arms around her, pulling her into a tight embrace, creating as much skin contact as possible.

I love you, I thought, as loudly as I could.

She didn't pull away. She didn't put her arms around me, either, and I found myself thinking about Mark, which was stupid. Here I was with my arms around the girl I loved, holding her, maybe for the last time, and I was thinking about Mark.

Mark. Who had managed to come out of his first metamorphosis and into his second instar without killing his parents, because his sister had managed to keep him distracted until his mind had time to assimilate all the information that had been dropped on top of him. All he'd needed was time. Once he had that, everything else had fallen into place. He was still a cuckoo, but he was a new kind of cuckoo, not psychically non-receptive like Grandma, not intentionally modified like Sarah, but . . . new. He might be the closest thing to a real Johrlac we'd ever seen. His sister had, however accidentally, helped him through that transition.

Maybe I could do the same for Sarah.

I pulled back without letting go, just far enough to look into her burning eyes.

"I love you," I said, aloud this time, and leaned forward and kissed her. I felt her take a short, sharp breath, her lips parting against mine. Then she was kissing me back, and everything was white and everything was burning and everything was white and everything was burning and everything

This time, when the endless whiteness formed around me, I was standing in front of Sarah, almost close enough to reach out and touch her. That was nice, considering I knew our bodies were still tangled together back in the real world. I was a little disappointed not to still be kissing her. Kissing her had been nice, even if I wasn't sure how much of it she'd actually been aware of.

She wasn't wearing the white dress here. Instead, she was wearing a long gray skirt and a shapeless green sweater, and her hair was hanging loose around her face, once more subject to the whims of gravity as the rest of us know it, and she had never in her life been more beautiful.

A thin ribbon of clear lymph was running from the corner of her right eye and dripping down her cheek like a viscous tear. I bit my lip. Then I stepped forward and used my thumb to wipe it away, leaving a pearlescent smear behind. It was as thick as human blood, and as warm. It felt wrong. It felt . . . alarming.

"Hey," I said. "You pulled me into your head when

I kissed you. That's good, right? That means you're still in control. Right?"

Sarah shook her head silently, another bead of lymph gathering in the corner of her eye.

"I'm not leaving you."

"Then we'll both die," she whispered.

I hesitated before I asked, "If I stay in here and we both die, does the equation get finished? Do you destroy the world? Because that's what they want you to do, you know. They want you to destroy the world. The whole thing. Movies and comic books and tomato plants and math."

"We'd take the math with us," she whispered.

"Fine. All that other stuff would be gone, though. Wiped right off the map. I mean literally wiped off the map. That's another thing you'd be destroying: the map. No more maps. Seems a little excessive to me."

"Chocolate," she whispered.

"See, most people don't think of destroying chocolate as a good thing. They like chocolate. They think it matters."

"Nasty stuff," she said, with a flicker of humor. The bead of lymph fell, following the track of the last one down her face. "I don't want to kill you."

"So don't." I shrugged. "Don't kill me. Don't finish their homework for them. We've coped with the cuckoos this far. We can put up with them for a while longer."

"I have to. My head . . ." She touched her temple with the tips of her fingers, frowning and wincing at the same time. "My head's so full. It's spinning. I don't know what to do with a head this full. I have to let the numbers out. If I don't, I think I'm going to explode."

"Let them out, then. Don't solve them."

"I don't have a choice." Sarah lowered her hand and looked at me bleakly. "You can't hear them. You can't hear them begging me. This is what I was made for. This is what I was designed to do. I want to do it. I just don't want to . . . I don't want to."

The edges of her irises began to frost over, turning white again.

I didn't stop to think about what my actions would mean. I just stepped forward and grabbed her upper arms, pulling her toward me. Then, not allowing myself to hesitate, I kissed her again.

Sarah's eyes widened, and then she was kissing me back, her hands sliding around to cup the sides of my head, fingers weaving themselves into my hair. She'd never kissed anyone before this trip and neither had I, but she was a quick study and I followed her lead, holding her up as she melted against me, closing my eyes and kissing her like it was the last thing I was ever going to do. Which, if she planned to go ahead with destroying the world, it might be.

It was worth it. Not worth the world being destroyed, but worth dying in Iowa, thousands of miles away from the rest of my family. It was all worth it if it meant that when I died, I was dying with Sarah. Not dying at all would have been better—way better—but I guess I always knew that we couldn't win forever. That's not how the universe works. Sooner or later everyone has to lose. Even the good guys.

Sarah pulled back first, smiling wanly at me. "Why didn't we do that years ago?" she asked.

"You were in Ohio."

"Before Ohio."

"Before Ohio . . ." Maybe we could have changed everything if we'd just gotten around to making out before Ohio. Before Sarah had followed Verity to Manhattan and broken herself against the unmoving wall of family loyalty, opening the door onto metamorphosis and instars and cuckoo women who wore her face like it was some sort of uniform, claiming to have some ownership of her just because they shared the same blood. Maybe.

But maybe never really means anything except for "I have regrets," and all the regrets in the world weren't going to change where we were standing. "I don't know," I said. "I guess we were waiting for the right time."

"Is this the right time?"

"You're sort of about to do the big extra-credit math problem that unmakes the world, so if this isn't the right time, it's the only time we've got." I shook my head. "This sort of sucks."

"I'm sorry." She winced again, putting a hand against her temple. "I feel like I'm going to burst. Artie, I don't think I have a *choice* about doing this equation. Now that it's inside me, it has to come out. No one's supposed to contain it for very long."

I hesitated, thinking of the cuckoos in their concentric rings, their eyes glowing like tiny stars. "Are the rest of the cuckoos helping you do it?"

"I wish." Sarah chuckled darkly. "They're keeping it from getting away from me. It wants to spread itself. It's like a disease. It wants to *infect*, so badly that it burns."

Mark and his accidental avoidance of homicide. The way the process of metamorphosis gave young cuckoos more and more access to their history with each instar, until they understood as much as they could about the structure of Johrlar, back before they'd been exiled, back before they became cuckoos.

"The Johrlac came from a hive mind society," I said, slowly.

"What?"

"The Johrlac came from a hive mind society," I repeated. "Your ancestors, the ones who got kicked out and banished—they were a *hive mind*. I don't know whether they had individual identities or not, but they did everything together. They could balance their data demands across multiple minds. Don't you see? Deleting the information that it wasn't safe to leave in their exiles wasn't just a means of trapping them, it was a way to *protect* them."

Sarah looked at me blankly. "I don't understand anything you just said."

"Oh, crap. You weren't there when we shook Mark down for information. Okay, look. You know how when you want to do something massive, you don't keep it on a single computer?"

"Well, yeah," said Sarah. "SETI needs to be widely distributed or they wouldn't have the processor power necessary to scan as much data as they're receiving."

"That's the problem with this equation! It's too big for one brain, but no one knows that anymore. They won't let it in. You're the queen—"

"I'm the what?"

"—I think that means you have to *direct* the equation, but if you can just put some of the load elsewhere—"

"Seriously, I'm the *what*?"

"Sarah! Don't argue with me about terminology! Just *listen*!" I grabbed her hands. "You need to break the mental connection. You need to throw me out of your head so that I can get Annie and James to ditch their anti-telepathy charms. And then you need to grab every brain you can get your mental hands on and use them like server banks."

Her eyes widened. "I couldn't possibly—Artie, I wouldn't have any idea how to do that, how to control it, how to keep myself from *hurting* you. I could mess up your memories, I could change your personality, I could . . . I could make it so that you're not you anymore."

"Yeah, but the world would still be here. You'd still be here. And you wouldn't be doing it on purpose." I shrugged. "I trust you. I know if anything happens, it's going to be because you couldn't help it. This is the only way we walk out of this with Earth intact, okay? There's not time to find another solution. I'm willing to take the risk. Are you?"

Sarah bit her lip.
Then, slowly, she nodded.
"I think I love you," she said.
"I think I love you, too," I said.
She smiled, and everything went away.

Twenty-five

$$\pi_2(n) \sim 2C_2 \frac{n}{(\ln n)^2} \sim 2C_2 \int_2^n \frac{dt}{(\ln t)^2}$$

"The people who like to sling around words like 'impossible' never consulted with the universe on whether or not it cares."

—Thomas Price

Iowa State University, in Ames, Iowa, about to try a really stupid way of saving the world

THE CAMPUS SNAPPED BACK into focus around me, complete with furious cuckoos and the sound of screaming. Sarah sagged, her eyes still glowing lambent white. Lymph was continuing to trickle from her ears, nose, and eyes. I didn't know how much longer she could deal with the weight of what she was trying to process.

Could I have made things worse by forcing her to split her focus and talk to me? I didn't know, and the question alone was enough to make me feel guilty. I turned, scanning the crowd. There: a flash of reddish-brown amongst the black-and-white bodies of the cuckoos. That was probably Antimony.

One of the cuckoos fell screaming as their hair went up in flames. Yup. Definitely Antimony.

I cupped my hands around my mouth so my voice would carry farther. "Annie!" I shouted. "I need you over here!"

A gun went off. "Little busy!" she shouted back.

"Don't care!" We had a lot of code phrases for moments like this one, where we needed to communicate without tipping our hands. I elbowed a cuckoo in the face as he suddenly seemed to recognize me as a potential target, and yelled, "The fences are down!"

A good *Jurassic Park* reference is universal. Annie swore, and then the commotion she and James had been merrily causing while I tried to get through to Sarah began to shift, moving toward us.

"This is either the best idea I've ever had or the absolute stupidest," I said. Another cuckoo came for me. I punched her in the throat. Cuckoos don't have as many anatomical similarities with humans as they should, based on morphology alone, but lucky for me, they have larynxes. No one with a larynx enjoys being punched in the throat. That's just science.

The cuckoo went down, gurgling and gasping. That was good. There were six more cuckoos behind her, all aiming straight for me. That was bad. That was very, very bad. One of them had figured out that telepathic attacks weren't working and had stopped long enough to pick up a chunk of concrete. That was even worse.

He swung for my head. I dodged, but barely. "Leave my skull out of this," I snapped, and kicked him in the groin.

The screaming was getting closer. I hoped that meant Annie and James would be joining me soon. If they were here, I might be able to turn the tide from "probably fatal" to "eh, you'll walk away from it." Any combat you can walk away from is a good combat, regardless of what's been done to the other guy.

A cuckoo lunged for me. A burning hand grabbed her by the hair and yanked her backward before she could make contact. She screamed. The hand let go. The fire didn't. The burning cuckoo fled into the crowd, carrying more chaos with her.

"What the *actual* fuck, Artie?" demanded Annie,

before kicking a cuckoo in the back of the knee and planting her foot between the fallen man's shoulder blades. He tried to get up. She stomped, once. He stopped trying to get up.

"I need you to take off your anti-telepathy charms." I looked past her to James. "Both of you."

Their eyes widened in comically identical expressions of baffled dismay.

"Uh, *what*?" asked Annie.

"Please. There's no time. We talk too much anyway. Trust me."

Annie took another precious second to stare at me before she nodded stiffly, reached into her front pocket, and pulled out the small glass vial of her personal protective charm. She dropped it. James, who might be confused, but still understood that sometimes it was better to follow instructions from the person who knew what was actually happening and ask penetrating questions later, did the same.

James didn't have our genetic resistance to telepathic influence. We needed to act quickly. I lunged forward and grabbed Annie's wrist, gesturing for her to do the same with James.

"Don't freak out," I said, and grabbed Sarah's wrist with my free hand. "Sarah, *now*."

She turned her head, whiteout eyes focusing on me without seeming to actually *focus*. Her voice echoed inside my skull, saying, *Brace yourselves.*

There wasn't time to brace myself. There wasn't time for anything. There was just the sudden, painful flood of numbers cascading over everything, washing the world away. Not into the comforting whiteness of her mindscape. No; that would have been too familiar, and consequentially, too kind. This was a shifting veil of figures, numbers and letters joined in an unending whirl, each one feeding into the next, none of them making any sense at all.

Someone screamed. It might have been me.

Hold on, said Sarah.

I couldn't hear Annie or James in the mental din: we'd been partitioned off from one another, which meant Sarah was using our brains exactly the way I'd suggested. We were her off-site processors, and she was spinning the pieces of the equation through us as quickly and as efficiently as she could.

Not as quickly or efficiently as she needed to. The tide of numbers grew in both intensity and speed, until it felt like I was actually drowning. My vision blurred around the edges. I blinked hard, looking for clarity, and couldn't find it. It was like the world was being fogged over, wiped away by something I barely had the tools to comprehend.

Sarah, I thought—or tried to think. Her name glitched and shattered in my mind, becoming a series of numbers that were actually letters that were actually images, freeze-frame components of a universe my brain wasn't equipped to hold.

Hold on, she whispered, through everything that still remained around me, every shape and every shadow, every symbol dancing through the endless equation that unspooled through my cells like a disease. *I'm going to try something.*

There was an almost electric jolt through the connection we shared. The equation lightened, lifted, and suddenly rebalanced itself, spreading out across every inch of surface I had and then spreading out to cover the surfaces around me. For the first time since the formation of our chain, I could feel Annie, burning bright and furious just outside the lines of my core. There was another presence beyond her, cold and calculating and confused: James. And beyond him . . .

Mark?

How's it going, Lilu? Looks like I'm one of the good guys after all. The amusement in his mental voice was bright and clear and incredibly self-satisfied. *You found the road. I'm happy to run down it. For Cici.*

Will you all be quiet? Sarah didn't sound amused. Sarah sounded strained, like she was having trouble keeping things together. *This is finicky work. If I mess it up, we're losing Europe.*

Easy there, Dark Phoenix, said Annie. *Take us in nice and gentle, and don't destroy any continents.*

I'm try—

That was as far as Sarah got. Her scream filled the world, and everything went white, then gray, and finally black, as the universe collapsed into nothing, and was still.

Twenty-six

$$\pi_2(n) \sim 2C_2 \frac{n}{(\ln n)^2} \sim 2C_2 \int_2^n \frac{dt}{(\ln t)^2}$$

"The fact that we call being kind, or con-
siderate, or good 'being human' tells you
something about how much of this planet
we have under our thumbs."
—Jane Harrington-Price

*In the whiteness of the infinite void, finally
finishing this*

THE CONNECTION BETWEEN ME and the others—my
offsite processing systems, and bless Artie forever
for suggesting I could even *try* to use their minds that
way—snapped like a stalk of celery, crisp and clean
and horrifyingly loud. I staggered backward, realizing
as I did that I was back in the nothingness of my own
mindscape. My lungs hurt, which seemed silly, since
they weren't real. I still struggled to breathe.

"You *bitch*," hissed a familiar voice.

I raised my head just in time for Ingrid to slap me
across the face. I yelped. She advanced, her eyes blazing white, her clothes streaked with pearlescent lymph.

"All you had to do—*all you had to do*—was accept
the gift any other cuckoo would have been willing to
die for," she spat, pulling her hand back to slap me
again. "All you had to do was gaze on the glory of our
ancestors and use it to steer a path toward our new

home. *Your job was so easy even a lobotomized child could do it.*"

She hit me again. It shouldn't have hurt, but it did. I moaned, low and startled, as I pressed a hand against my cheek and stared at her.

She looked like me. She looked exactly like me. More than Mom did, even, and we'd always looked so much alike that people had no trouble believing we were related. Ingrid was the mold from which I'd been struck.

Three mothers. One who left me, one who lost me, and one who loved me. And now the first of them was back again, fury in her eyes as she drew back to deliver another blow.

"I'll have to start all over," she said.

My eyes flicked to her stomach, which strained against the limits of her clothing. Start all over. She meant abandon another baby with another human family. She meant leave another cuckoo child with no idea who they were supposed to be or how they were supposed to get there, exiled from their species, from everyone who should have known and loved and wanted them.

"You can't do that," I said.

"Yes, I can," she replied. "It's what we do. Or do you mean I can't do to her what I did to you? Leave her with a hapless human couple and then, when she's old enough to have imprinted, take them away and see what happens? You don't think their deaths were an *accident*, do you, Sarah? That they just happened to lose control of their car when there was a suitable replacement family for you in range? The whole thing was planned. A queen must be nurtured."

"No," I said.

"And just look at you. Useless. Weak. Their sacrifice was for nothing. Not that it matters. There are always so many humans to go around."

"You're lying."

"They'd still be alive if it weren't for you."

"You bitch," I snarled.

She slapped me.

I grabbed her wrist before she could pull her hand back, yanking her toward me. "No," I repeated, and punched her in the jaw, the way Verity showed me, so my knuckles slammed into the space where her jawbone connected to itself. She made a startled noise of protest, trying to back away. I didn't let go of her wrist.

"You're not going to do *anything*," I said, and hit her again, and again, until she stopped trying to break away and started trying to claw at me instead, the fingers of her free hand seeking and failing to find purchase in the skin of my face. It was the feeble attempt of someone who had never been forced to fight for herself, and it would have been hilarious, if it hadn't been so damn sad.

"*No.*" This time when I hit her, she stopped trying to scratch me. "That baby isn't a pawn. They aren't a toy. You don't get to decide what they're going to be just because you give birth to them. You don't get to *force* them."

"I get to do whatever I want," she said, eyes glinting white.

I paused.

We were in my head. We were in my space, where everything was up to me; where I controlled the world. The equation was still nibbling at the edges of everything, filling my thoughts with numbers, but it wasn't as bad as it had been before I offloaded a big chunk of it onto Artie and the others. I could think. I could plan.

I could make decisions.

"You called me a queen," I said softly.

Ingrid tried again to pull away from me. My hand around her wrist; the idea of my skin pressing against hers. Things have always been easier with skin contact.

"I'd say I was sorry, except I'm not; not really," I

said. "I wish I could be sorry. I wish I could have all the regrets in the world. But you decided not to be my family, and that was your choice, and that means I'm choosing, here and now, not to be yours."

For the first time, there was true alarm in her expression. I wondered why it had taken me so long to realize that pulling people into this constructed mindscape would let me read their faces as easily as I read their thoughts. I could have been learning nuance and detail this whole time. Except maybe not. I couldn't be sure—not with as little experience as I'd actually had at this—but it felt like the construct was taking a lot of power. Maybe I hadn't been capable of doing this before . . .

Well, before things changed.

"I'll make sure someone takes care of the baby," I said as I gathered as much of the equation as I could hold in my mental hands and shoved it into her mind like a knife being shoved into a wound. I wasn't careful about it. I wasn't kind. I didn't shunt the pieces of her that made her who she was to the side the way I had with the others.

Ingrid screamed. But not for long. She sagged, no longer fighting me. I let go of her wrist. She collapsed to the ground.

I opened my eyes.

Artie, Annie, James, and Mark were standing in a rough circle around me, blocking out the cuckoos who were no longer fighting them, but were instead watching us warily, waiting to see what was going to happen next. That seemed odd—it would have been reasonable for the cuckoos to attack as soon as the others were distracted—until I noticed the bodies littering the ground, their eyes open and still blazing white. They must have touched me, or one of the people who were currently extensions of me, after I'd started offloading the equation. The physical contact would have pulled them into the loop.

The same way I'd pulled Ingrid into the loop. She was on the ground directly in front of me, still twitching, burning white eyes turned upward to the sky. I wanted to feel bad about that. I couldn't. I'd offloaded enough of the equation that I finally had room to spin it properly, to see all its lines and angles. The longer I looked at it, the more I started to understand what trying to complete it on my own would have done to me.

The cuckoos who'd grabbed me without going through the proper chain of metamorphosis and instar weren't going to recover from the equation's incursion into their minds. There wasn't room for them, the history of our people, *and* the equation, and of those three things, the self was what the equation would be most inclined to treat as an invader. It was a living thing. It was hungry. It wanted to expand, to devour . . . and to be completed.

No, I thought, and felt the equation curve and writhe, looking for places to sink its teeth into the chain, for breaks in the processing loop.

I couldn't hold it forever. I wasn't even sure I could hold it long enough to do what needed to be done.

Artie and the others were an echo in the back of my mind, a comforting hum of presence without awareness. There was no room left for awareness, not with the equation sucking up every spare neuron they had. Their core selves were still present, neatly bundled up and tucked away, but that wouldn't be the case forever, not unless I hurried.

Mark was in the most danger. Like the cuckoos who'd touched us without being invited in, he had the history alongside his self, and that meant he had less room for other information than the rest of us. Something was going to give.

Mom—Angela—had been able to go into my head and remove the buried time bombs of cultural history before they had the chance to rupture and spread their poison across my thoughts. I could potentially do the

same for him. Even as I thought about it, I knew how
it could be done, what turns and tweaks I would need
to make to clip those hereditary memories away from
his core self and then excise them, freeing up more
room for the equation to flourish. I could almost feel it
panting with hungry glee at the idea, like all it wanted
in the world was to spread.

Equations shouldn't *want* things. They shouldn't be
big enough or complicated enough to have opinions or
desires. But that's what people are, really. We're equations that have grown large enough and complex
enough to have opinions about the world. To want to
change it.

This equation wanted to change the world. It wanted
to swallow the world alive. And I had to stop it.

I clenched my hands into fists and screwed my eyes
shut, locking myself into the darkness behind them.
Not the flash-white landscape of my mind, no: that
would have been too easy, and would have meant missing variables I needed more than anything else in the
world. Because this *was* the world, every complicated,
complicating inch of it, and it all mattered, and it all
needed to be taken into account.

When working complex math, there are factors that
can be used to cancel things out. If you're adding two
to six and then subtracting five, you're really adding
two and one, at least as far as the end result is concerned. That's so simplistic, so simplified, that any of
the professors I've ever talked to would roll their eyes
and scoff at the idea of explaining things that way, but
it works, it works, it takes the weight out of the final
figures, and I needed to cancel as much of this world-
breaking equation as I possibly could. I needed to cancel things that had never been questioned, to reduce
and refine and prevent it from doing harm.

Even with all these other minds running interfer-
ence, the equation knew I was the one who had to finish and unleash it. It pressed in on me, and I began to

frantically run the numbers, trying to find the answer that did the least damage possible.

The weight of all the lives on Earth, human and non-human and intelligent and nonintelligent. The weight of plants and fungus and bacteria, all the pieces of the biosphere that were so easy to discount, to ignore, to leave behind. They needed to be factored in as precisely as possible, and so I reached through the cuckoos who had been ensnared already and grabbed the next tier of minds, sending their mental fingers questing outward, ever outward, cataloguing and naming and numbering everything we found. There was too much data. I couldn't hold it consciously without starting to delete pieces of myself—and that was what the equation wanted more than anything, I realized numbly. It was willing to let me bargain because it thought I would inevitably overload the processing centers of my mind and need to start choosing what to cut away.

Either I let it run wild and break the things it yearned to break, or I pruned myself down to the cuckoo queen Ingrid had shaped me to be, and the equation would have its freedom regardless of my desires.

I couldn't be the first person who tried to tame this thing. I might not be the last. I still had to do whatever I could.

Quiet, I told it, and kept reaching outward, picking up more and more minds that weren't mine to use, looking for more ways to cancel out the numbers.

The air was growing thick around us, crackling with power that had to come from somewhere, but didn't feel like it was coming from me. I didn't open my eyes. I didn't dare. I grabbed and grabbed and pulled and pulled, refining, reducing, penning the howling demon of the cuckoo's core equation into a cage of subtractions, until there was nothing else to subtract, nothing else to take away, nothing else to do but let it run.

I stared at the equation written on the inside of my eyelids. If I was correct—and I had to be correct, I *had to be*, any error could be the end of everything—then I was still looking at a blast big enough to destroy Iowa, punching a hole into the planet's crust and triggering a chain reaction of destruction that could wipe out the entire continental plate.

There was only one thing left to take away. Only one thing left to lose.

Artie, I'm sorry, I thought, and opened my eyes, tilting my face toward the sky. It was bruised black with clouds, swirling in a slow counterclockwise spiral, like a hurricane getting ready to form. I had never seen a storm so big.

It was mine. It belonged to me. With all these cuckoos yoked to my will, I could do virtually anything, and I didn't understand a thing about what I was doing. We had never belonged here. We had never been intended to be a part of this world.

It was better this way.

I took a deep breath of the ion-charged air and began to speak, babbling polynomials and monomials and terms as quickly as I could, looping them back around one another to prevent errors from creeping in. Numbers merged into letters into operations, stacking one on top of the other, becoming bigger and more difficult to wrangle.

The sky grew darker and darker still. With a vast, furious crack of thunder, it began to rain. The equation rejoiced. Rain would distract me, keep me from finishing it the way I wanted to, leave it with openings to exploit.

I raised a hand and the rain stopped before it could reach me or the people immediately around me. It pattered against an invisible dome instead, sliding down the sides and trickling into the grass. Mark was halfway inside and halfway outside the dome; part of him was getting soaked. That was fine. Other peoples' discomfort didn't—

No. That was a cuckoo thought. I slapped the equation away from the parts of my mind where I stored my carefully learned and hard-won empathy, forcing it back into the box I had drawn for it, and expanded the dome enough to cover Mark completely before I resumed my recitation of the factors to the storm-drenched sky.

Was it enough? Was anything, ever, going to be enough? Because that was a subtraction, too, even if it was only an estimated and hence low-balled figure: the damage the cuckoos had done since arriving in this world, where they had never truly belonged. How many broken families? How many deaths? How many children smothered in their cradles to make room for a cuckoo-child who should never have been there in the first place? The damage was incalculable, and still I did my best to calculate it, and the area of impact shrank, again and again, until it was almost small enough. Until it felt like it might be fair.

I couldn't loosen my grip on the equation for even a second, or I'd lose it. It was furious at what I'd done, thrashing against my mental hands as it tried to break free and restore some of its original scope. This wasn't enough damage to satisfy what it had been built to do . . . but I thought I could see, buried under piles and piles of junk modifiers, the core of what it could have been, if it had been designed by someone kinder. Someone who cared about what it did to the world. The equation the cuckoos remembered forgetting . . . it had been a subtle thing, a scalpel. This was a sledgehammer.

I glanced at Artie, who was standing perfectly still as I used every spare neuron he had to power this ridiculous, impossible attempt. Every spare neuron, and a few he technically didn't have to spare.

"I love you," I whispered, knowing he couldn't hear me. Maybe it was better that way. Maybe he'd have an easier time letting go. I closed my eyes, shutting him out, shutting everything out except for me, what I had to do, and the unfinished equation.

Then I finished it, and the conclusion slammed into me so hard that it was like a bullet to the brain, and I went down hard, with no way of knowing whether I'd done what I set out to do, whether I'd defeated my last and greatest opponent . . . or whether I was going to survive this.

Please let it be okay, I thought. *Please let them walk away. Please.*

Please.

Ple—

Epilogue

$$\pi_2(n) \sim 2C_2 \frac{n}{(\ln n)^2} \sim 2C_2 \int_2^n \frac{dt}{(\ln t)^2}$$

"No one's ever really lost. Sometimes we
don't know where they are, exactly, but
that just means it's time for us to go out
and find them."

—Alice Healy

*. . . well, that's an excellent question, when you
really stop to think about it*

EVERYTHING WAS COMFORTABLE DARKNESS, and
nothing hurt. That was the best part. Maybe I'd allowed a predatory equation from another dimension to
devour the world, but dammit, I'd at least earned the sort
of afterlife where I got to take five minutes to myself. It
would probably suck in a few hours, when I realized I
was going to be alone with my thoughts for eternity, but
whatever. That was a problem for future-Sarah. Present-
Sarah was enjoying the chance to catch her breath without anyone trying to seize control of her mind or force
her to unmake reality. Future-Sarah could suck it.

"I think she's dead."

The voice was Mark's. He sounded remarkably dis-
interested, given that he was reporting on my supposed
death. I already hadn't been his biggest fan, but that
was when I decided to really dislike him.

"Pour water on her. That always works with me."

Annie.

"Because usually if we think you're dead, you're also *on fire*, and it's hard to check someone's pulse when they're burning themselves alive. Has anyone checked her pulse?"

James.

"She's a cuckoo. They don't have hearts, so they don't have pulses, either. A pulse isn't possible without a heart."

Artie.

If I'd had a heart, it would have been racing. Artie was alive. Artie was alive and here—wherever "here" was—and still himself. I hadn't accidentally erased his mind when I'd used him as a way to increase my processing power. I wasn't a monster after all. I wanted to punch the air and scream. I still couldn't move.

Well, that was awkward. If I wasn't dead, I wanted to be able to move. I tried to focus on my body, looking for some sign that it was still there.

I'd never met a cuckoo ghost. Did cuckoos haunt their own bodies when they died, since they were so far away from the dimension that they came from? Was I going to be stuck haunting my corpse? I didn't want to haunt my corpse. I wanted to wake up. I wanted to tell Artie I was okay. I wanted to put my arms around him and press my face against his neck and let him hold me up until I stopped shaking.

"If she's dead, I don't want her in here. Dead things stink. We can't have her attracting predators."

Artie again, but . . . but he was talking about *me*. How could he say something like that while he was talking about *me*? We were supposed to be a team. He was supposed to be on my side, even if it meant he was siding with a corpse.

"If she's not dead, she may know where the hell we are. She was the one leading their stupid ritual. James, grab her chin."

A hand grasped my head and tilted it upward as Annie stopped speaking. The fingers were cold. James.

The next fingers to touch me were anything but cold. They stroked my cheek, almost hot enough to burn.

Then Annie pulled back and slapped me.

I gasped, opening my eyes. A momentary triumph lanced through me—I *could* open my eyes. I had eyes to open. I wasn't dead after all. And then I saw the faces surrounding me, and my triumph died, replaced by confused terror.

Annie, James, Artie, and Mark had formed a loose semicircle in front of the chair where I was sitting. I didn't even need to check to know that I was tied in place. There was no other way I could have stayed upright—and family protocols are very clear. When you have someone captive and you want them to stay that way, you damn well tie them up. We were in some kind of classroom. There was a window behind them. Through it, I could see several more buildings I recognized from the campus . . .

And a slice of sky the color of ripe cantaloupe, sweet and golden and utterly alien. As if to drive that point home, what looked like a centipede the length of a train undulated through it, legs waving like cilia or rudders to keep it aloft. I stared, too stunned to say anything.

"Well?"

Annie's tone was harsh, cold—unforgiving. I turned to face her, eyes wide and shocked.

I couldn't read her face. I didn't need to. The wariness and distrust were radiating off her like the heat from her fingers.

"What did you do, cuckoo?" she demanded. "Where are we?"

"Oh," I said, faintly. "Crap."

Read on for
a brand-new InCryptid novella
by Seanan McGuire:

FOLLOW THE LADY

"Once you make the carnival your home, you'll always belong there. The boneyard remembers your stride. The midway remembers the sound of your laughter. Once a carnie, always a carnie."

—Frances Brown

Passing through Michigan, just crossing the borders into Buckley Township, crammed into the back of a retro travel trailer hitched to a car that's working well above its weight class

WE WERE BARELY OVER the boundary into Buckley when James' car began making a horrifying rattling noise, as if the engine had abruptly been replaced by one of those old-fashioned rock tumblers, the kind they sell to elementary schools to teach kids that pebbles can be beautiful. He yelped and pulled over to the side of the road, taking his feet away from the pedals and leaning back in his seat like he was afraid the car was getting ready to explode.

"Is that a good noise?" I asked, half-hopefully.

Slowly, he swiveled around to stare at me like I had just asked the stupidest question in the world's long history of stupid questions. "No," he said, in a tone that made it clear he wasn't humoring me, the way he sometimes did when he tripped over one of my rich veins of unexpected ignorance. "That is a very, very bad noise. That is a noise that means, potentially, we're not going to be leaving here for quite some time."

"Oh," I said. "Okay, well, that's not great."

James punched the steering wheel.

"I'll just go update the others," I said, and opened my door, unbuckling my belt as I swung my legs out of the car and slid from my seat into the crisp autumn air.

We'd been driving for four days, not quite solid, making worse time than we would have if we hadn't been constantly distracted by the world, and if James had ever been outside the small town where he'd been born. America is a lot bigger than New Gravesend, Maine, and he was seeing it for the first time. If anyone had been primed to actually want to buy tickets to every roadside attraction in existence, it was him.

For the most part, I didn't begrudge him our winding, weaving track across the country. As I'd expected, on our second day on the road, we had run into someone who'd been hunting for a car exactly like Cylia's avocado-colored monstrosity for years. He'd been happy to trade us for our new-old travel trailer, which was actual retro, and not something new designed to look like it wasn't. It was both surprisingly light and surprisingly palatial, with beds for four, a small kitchenette, and a bathroom. He'd thrown in all the accoutrements, and fifteen hundred dollars, all to sweeten the deal. I had no idea what could make a man want the world's ugliest muscle car that badly, but I was glad he had. It made things a lot easier on the rest of us.

It meant that James was doing the bulk of the driving since he didn't entirely trust Cylia with his car, and I didn't drive. Sam *did*, but he was enjoying the chance to lounge around the trailer in full fūri form, rather than forcing himself to look human while he was behind the wheel. Fern didn't drive at all, which made sense. When you belong to a species whose response to being threatened involves shedding most of your personal density, driving isn't the safest activity.

I walked around to the trailer and stepped up onto the bumper, banging three times on the door before swinging it open and letting myself inside. "Knock three times" isn't the best signal I've ever come up with, but since I've been riding in the car with James to keep him from stopping at every fruit stand in the Midwest, I didn't want to institute anything that would slow down getting to the bathroom when we did stop.

Sam was sitting on the trailer's narrow couch, not having bothered to shift back to artificial humanity. I bumped the door shut with my hip, struggling not to smile sappily at him. I didn't really succeed.

Sam Taylor is the best accident I've ever had. His grandmother, Emery Spenser, is the current owner of the Spenser and Smith Family Carnival, which happened to have been the location of my assignment with the Covenant of St. George, a global organization of monster hunters that would have absolutely loathed every single person on our little road trip of the damned. Most of them would have only considered me and James to actually be *people*; we're sorcerers, but that doesn't actually expel us from the human race, even if I might sometimes wish it did. Fern's a sylph, Cylia's a jink, and Sam's a fūri, although his grandmother's a human. By all reports, his mother was, too. Fūri are one of the rare cryptid types to be actually genetically compatible with humans. It's like how sometimes lions and tigers can breed, even though they're very different species.

Sam's default form is sort of "hot monkey guy," although his simian features aren't as pronounced as that implies. His hair is more like fur—dark, dark brown tipped in a slightly lighter shade; his ears are large and rounded, and his hands and feet are equally dexterous and larger than those of a human man. Most noticeable is his long, prehensile tail, which is strong enough for him to swing from, even when he's carrying me. Which happens fairly often. He has more muscle density than a human man of similar height and weight, developed and honed by years spent on the flying trapeze. He hates shoes, bananas, and spending too much time around humans. He loves sweatpants, boring English classics, and me.

That last one has been the hardest for me to adjust to. I was always voted the least likely of my generation to fall in love or settle down—and that includes my cousin Artie the incubus, who seems destined to die alone in the basement of his parents' house, thanks to a near-pathological fear of getting close to any girl he's not related to. It's not healthy, but hey. He's family. Besides, I hadn't been at the carnival looking for a boyfriend. I'd been looking for the source of a string of mysterious deaths and disappearances that had gone on long enough to attract the attention of the Covenant of St. George. I'd been undercover with them, pretending to be a trainee, and since my cover story had involved a carnival background, they had sent me to figure out exactly what was happening.

Carnivals and traveling shows have long been a haven for cryptids who could almost pass as human, but who had needs, attributes, or abilities that would inevitably unmask them to the locals. By hiding behind the mask of the sideshow or pretending to be skilled human athletes, they could keep themselves from becoming targets. They could live happy, functional lives without anyone becoming the wiser. That's the principle by which the Campbell Family Carnival has always operated. I spent my summers there when I was a kid, falling in love with the flying trapeze and setting snares for my cousins, who took too long to learn to respect my need for personal space. Sending me to Spenser and Smith had seemed like the best possible choice.

Maybe it wasn't for the Covenant, but it was for me.

I had found the woman responsible for the murders, a carnival performer named Umeko who had discovered her own true nature as a Jorōgumo relatively late in life, and with no other members of her species around to help her. The transition hadn't been easy. She'd started assaulting, and then eating, people who caught her eye, drawing the Covenant's attention and resulting in my assignment to the show.

Sam had been the first person to find me skulking around the carnival boneyard, and he hadn't liked me being there. Growing up a cryptid in an insular, largely human community left him with a deeply ingrained distrust of strangers, and he'd known almost from the beginning that I was lying to him. Chalk it up to his naturally suspicious nature and move on. I did.

Despite his suspicions, I'd managed to play along for long enough that he'd realized I was smart, funny, and reasonably unflappable, and he'd asked me on a date. I'd already known he was a fūri by that point, thankfully. I don't think our burgeoning relationship would have survived if he'd learned that I was working for the Covenant before I'd known that he wasn't human. But it had, and he'd left his family and the carnival behind to follow me to Florida when the situation forced me to go into hiding for the sake of everyone I'd ever cared about—him included.

Sometimes being a cryptozoologist is even more complicated than it ought to be. Because, see, my family hates the Covenant like nobody's business. We're mostly human, apart from some of my cousins, and my mother's adoptive parents. And sure, I'm a sorcerer, but I get that from my Grandpa Thomas, who was a full-fledged member of the Covenant before he turned on them, so you'd think they'd be used to it. Nope. Magic is "unnatural," so in their eyes, I'm little better than a cryptid myself. Probably worse, since I'm voluntarily banging one, and that makes me a traitor to the human race.

Treachery has amazing abs. I'm just saying.

"Where are Cylia and Fern?" I asked, looking around the small space. The trailer, despite being split into the "living area," "sleeping area," bathroom, and kitchenette, is slightly smaller than my bedroom back in Oregon. There wasn't a lot of space to hide.

"They're taking a nap," said Sam, gesturing toward the closed curtain across the sleeping area. "Are we at another fruit stand?"

"No. The car made a really terrible noise, and James is upset, and we're not moving anymore, and where are you going?"

Sam was standing, reaching for the jacket he had thrown carelessly across the arm of the couch. "I know a few things about engines, thanks to all the maintenance I had to do back at the carnival. I can probably help him out. Where are we?"

"Michigan."

He wrinkled his nose. "Why are we in Michigan? I thought we were cutting down toward Ohio to shave off a few hours."

"My family's originally from Michigan," I said. "We still have a house here."

He perked up. "Great! Maybe we can take real showers before the smell in here gets strong enough to owe us gas money." He grabbed his shoes from the floor and started for the back door, pulling them on and shifting into his human form at the same time as he walked. Unlike a normal person, he was coordinated enough to do all three things without tripping and falling on his face. Oh, the joys of dating a man who breaks all human laws of athletic grace.

The genuine joys, under most circumstances. He wasn't being unreasonable. He just didn't understand what he was getting into, doing essentially anything in Buckley.

My grandparents met there, when the Covenant sent my grandfather to spy on my great-grandparents.

He was a sorcerer, too, so I guess in some ways, his relationship with my Grandma Alice was a nice mirror of my relationship with Sam. He eventually quit the Covenant in order to marry her, but not until after he'd been tricked into making a bargain with the crossroads. Just thinking about them was enough to steal the remnants of my good humor. Sure, they're dead, and they're going to stay that way if the anima mundi has anything to say about it, but they did a lot of damage to my family while they were still around.

We lost Grandpa. Not to death, which would have been understandable and ordinary and something we might have been able to collectively get over. No, I mean we *lost* him, through a hole in the wall of the world that swallowed him down in the middle of the night while Grandma Alice was pregnant with my Aunt Jane, whose impending arrival was the only thing that prevented Grandma from immediately jumping into the hole and going after him. As soon as she'd recovered from labor, she'd dumped both her children on our Aunt Laura, yet another in the string of aunts, uncles, and cousins who aren't actually biologically related to us.

Dad and Aunt Jane grew up essentially as wards of the Campbell Family Carnival, and I know that Aunt Jane at least still considers the carnies more her family than her own mother. Grandma has never been able to regain ground with her biological children, even though all us grandkids love her desperately. So in a way, the crossroads cost us both of them.

Buckley Township, Michigan, is one of those places that gets talked about in hushed tones whenever there's a census, a place where people die young and weirdly. If it wasn't rural and reasonably poor, it would probably be empty by now—or maybe not. People can become surprisingly attached to their homes and don't want to leave them for what they view as silly reasons. "Silly" can mean everything from "bank foreclosure" to "rabid jackalopes ate the neighbors, and now they're coming for us." So Buckley endures, even if it doesn't precisely thrive, and while new people don't often move to town, the ones who already live there don't leave, and neither do their children. If those children die at a rate slightly higher than the national average, well, their deaths are almost always accidental.

Aunt Mary died in Buckley. So did Aunt Rose. So did all my Grandma Alice's biological relatives. She's the last branch of her original family tree, and the existence of some distaff cousins with the Covenant in England won't unbury all the bodies in Buckley.

Somewhat clumsily, I said, "The house isn't the sort of place where people generally go to get naked. Not unless they're local teens doing it on a dare. It's sort of, potentially, I don't know, well, evil."

Sam's eyes widened. "How is a house evil? Is it haunted? Because I thought you had a pretty good relationship with your dead aunts."

"No. If anything, it's the opposite of haunted. Ghosts don't go there if they have any choice in the matter. Aunt Rose won't even cross the threshold. Aunt Mary will sometimes, but it makes her really sad, so we try not to ask her to do that. She knew my grandfather." They were friends, even though they didn't meet until after she was already dead—which means there's a very good chance she was the one who handled the crossroads bargain that eventually claimed him. The crossroads were cruel that way. It's a damn good thing that they're gone and won't have the opportunity to be cruel to anyone else.

"It was your grandfather's house?" Sam stopped in front of the back door, folding his arms and frowning. All his attention was focused on me, to the point that he didn't notice when the curtain behind him twitched aside.

I nodded. "The Covenant bought it for him when they assigned him to Buckley Township to keep an eye on my grandmother and her family. There were four of them when he arrived in Michigan: Grandma, her father, and his parents. Three generations crammed into one big farmhouse. We still own that one, too, but we rent it out to a nice human family, and they don't like it when we show up without warning them first. I guess they're afraid of being evicted."

"Or possibly being shot," said Cylia, voice still groggy with the remnants of her nap. She slid off the top bunk and dropped down to the trailer floor. "We've stopped."

"The engine did an awful thing, and James thinks it might be dead," I said. "Sam was just going out to see whether he could grease monkey his way to a solution." I stopped and grimaced. "Sam, I'm sorry, that wasn't an intentional pun, it just sort of . . . slipped out."

"Uh-huh. See if I wash my hands after replacing the transmission." Sam finally opened the back door and stepped outside.

"You will. You hate being dirty even more than I do," I called back before he could close the door.

The last thing I heard from the outside was his scoff. Then the door slammed shut, and I turned back to Cylia.

"You didn't tell us to be on the lookout for a bad luck event," I said.

"Because we weren't in debt," she countered. "Sometimes things just *happen*, even when you're traveling with a jink."

Cylia Mackie looks perfectly human: tall, blonde, and slender, with cheekbones that could cut glass and freckles on her nose. It's parallel evolution. She's a primate, sure, but her species branched from humanity a long damn time ago. Jinks can sense, see, and manipulate luck, treating it like a pool they use to manipulate the probability of the world around them. Smart jinks, like Cylia, try to keep things as balanced as possible, only spending their good luck when they have enough that the backlash won't be immediate and fatal. Her husband, Tav, died when he got the balance wrong, suffering a massive heart attack right in front of her.

Having Cylia along on our trip had been a godsend so far. Because of her, we'd been able to acquire our precious travel trailer, avoid speed traps, and not get food poisoning from the gas station sushi. All little pieces of good luck that could have happened to anyone, but which had consistently been happening to us since we left Maine.

Of course, that could easily mean that we were due for something catastrophic. Breaking down in Buckley certainly qualified.

"This isn't on me," she said. "If we'd had this much bad luck attached to us, I would have warned you. I wouldn't have done anything to prevent it, but I wouldn't have let it be a surprise, either." She folded her arms and glowered at me. "Antimony Price, I thought we were past the point of mistrusting each other without a damn good reason."

"Sorry, Cylia," I said, shamefaced. She was right. After facing down the evil cabal controlling one of the country's biggest theme parks and going toe-to-toe with the crossroads, we had reached a point where trusting each other needed to be the default, and not some sort of aberration. "It just came out of nowhere."

"And you're used to me controlling the luck, I got it," said Cylia. She turned back to the sleeping nook, tugging the curtains open wider until the light from the rest of the trailer penetrated the artificial gloom. "Fern! Wakey-wakey!"

A small, sleepy sound of protest came from the darkest corner of the bed right before a dainty hand shot out, grabbed the curtain, and yanked it shut again. Cylia laughed. I grinned.

The fifth member of our little expedition, Fern, is a sylph, capable of controlling her personal density to such a degree that she can either float or punch holes in insufficiently solid floors. Despite being a dainty little thing, we've clocked her as weighing up to six hundred pounds when she wants to, all thanks to tweaking her own mass. The laws of physics are not invited to a lot of sylph parties, nor would they attend if they were.

Sylphs are relatively harmless, density parlor tricks notwithstanding. Unlike the fūri and the jinks, they didn't have any way to defend themselves when the Covenant came calling, and so their population took an even greater hit. I don't know how many sylphs are left in the world. I don't think any cryptozoologist does. I've learned more about Fern's species by hanging out with her than I ever could have from book research, and that's only part of why I have almost no human friends.

"Fern," said Cylia, leaning close to the curtain. "Showers, Fern. Hot water. A real kitchen. *Pancakes.*" She drew the last word out until it turned obscene.

Fern yanked the curtains open again. "I'm listening," she said sullenly. Then she blinked. "We're not moving. Why aren't we moving? Are we in Oregon already?"

"We've been making good time, but not bullet train time, so no," I said. "We're in Michigan right now. Near my old family homestead, in fact, which means we're also near one of my grandmother's favorite bars. How do you feel about getting a drink?"

Fern blinked at me, looking confused. Cylia grinned.

"Finally, you're speaking my language," she said. "Let's go."

According to Sam, the engine had thrown a rod and would need to be replaced. James was distraught and unwilling to take the easy way out, which would have involved abandoning his car in Michigan while we grabbed a new junker off of Craigslist. Not even Cylia's reassurances that the new car would prove to be remarkably resilient were enough to sway him. His car was one of the only things he had left in the world, and he was holding onto it.

I could sort of see where he was coming from. During my self-imposed exile from my family, I'd been incredibly protective of the few things I had to call my own. Come to think of it, I still was. I'd just expanded that list to include three cryptids and an untrained sorcerer from Maine. I should learn to pick more portable souvenirs.

Anyway, James had elected to stay with the car and call the local mechanic while the four of us went down to the Red Angel for a frosty glass of whatever was on tap. He'd get towed to the shop down on Lakeside Drive, and we'd join him there once we were done at the Angel.

The fact that I knew it was an easy walk, and that we'd have no trouble finding the place, was our first real piece of evidence that maybe breaking down in Buckley had been a better thing than breaking down in some town big enough to have a Motel 6 to call its own.

I waved to James before turning to lead Cylia, Sam, and Fern across the field between the state highway and Old Orchard Road. I wasn't a Buckley native by any measure—no one in my generation was—but we'd all been visiting since childhood, and I could get myself to the big landmarks without too much trouble. The old Healy house, which we rented out to keep it from sitting empty and falling into disrepair; the old Parrish place, which Grandma Alice maintained mainly for her own use, and which was too cursed and overrun by tailypo to ever fall apart; the police station; the mechanic; the Red Angel. Maybe taking your kids to see the local bar is weird, but my parents did it anyway, the summer I was twelve years old. It was important. My family has a longstanding relationship with the Red Angel, and they weren't going to let a little thing like the legal drinking age get in the way.

"You know I can't actually drink, right?" asked Sam, stepping over a large rock in the field.

"Why not?"

"Because it's hard to stay tense when I'm buzzed," he said, waving a hand to indicate the still apparently human length of his body.

Most therianthropes—shapeshifting cryptids—default to their human forms and have to concentrate to change out of them. Fūri work the other way around. Sam has described the sensation of holding human form as being like fighting to hold in a sneeze that never quite comes.

I grinned at him. "You don't need to worry about that."

"Hold up, hold up," said Cylia, grabbing the back of my shirt and using it to pull herself forward, miraculously not choking me in the process. "Are you telling me that there's a *cryptid bar* in this middle-of-nowhere town?"

"I was hoping to surprise you, but if you really need to know, then yes, I'm telling you precisely that."

"Holy crap," said Cylia, with relish. "I would never have guessed."

"Yeah, well, people take privacy seriously out here. Not like they do on the coasts, where there's enough weirdness in the background radiation of daily life to cover up for a certain amount of slipping." I reached back and twitched my shirt out of her fingers. She laughed and slung her arm around my shoulders.

"Anyway, the Red Angel has been here for more than a hundred years, and apart from one tiny little incident where my great-grandmother used a shotgun to knock when she was looking for her daughter, the owners have always been on good terms with my family."

We had reached the edge of the field, which gave way to the gravelly, dubiously level surface of Old Orchard Road. I still made a small sound of relief as I stepped onto it, causing Fern to shoot me a surprised look.

"Do they not believe in asphalt in Buckley?" she asked.

"Oh, they do, on the roads that are actually inside the town limits, but out here, the rural roads, those are mostly left alone unless they develop bad enough potholes to be legitimately dangerous. And I'd say we have a few more bad rainy seasons before anyone's willing to call the graveler out this way. It keeps municipal taxes low, and it keeps strangers out."

"Not friendly people, your locals?" asked Sam.

"They're friendly enough, to the other locals. They're even reasonably friendly to my siblings and me. Wary, but friendly. Once you come from here, you're from here forever, and that applies to your descendants. Only Dad and Aunt Jane left when they were little, little kids, and Grandpa was from England, which means some people still think of us as outsiders, while others insist that since Grandma was born here, we're locals." I snorted. "She wasn't even born here. Great-Grandma Fran went into labor while she and Great-Grandpa Jonathan were visiting a town of finfolk out in Maine. Gentling isn't that far from New Gravesend. We could have gone there to hide if things had turned out poorly."

"Finfolk?" asked Sam.

"Like mermaids, but less cannibalistic, and more capable of breeding with humans," I replied, and kept walking.

We made a weird little line, working our way along the side of the road, and we didn't see any cars. I pulled out the cellphone I'd signed up for as soon as we were sure that Leonard Cunningham was on his way out of the country, taking the threat of the Covenant of St. George with him. I had a surprisingly good signal, considering our surroundings. I shot a quick text to James, asking whether he'd been able to reach anyone with a tow truck. His reply came just as quickly: the truck was on its way, and he'd been able to confirm with the mechanic that he could tow our trailer wherever we needed it to be.

I responded with the address of the old Parrish place. Maybe spending the night at my family's least haunted house would be more tolerable if we did it in the trailer, and the tailypo probably wouldn't be able to figure out how to get inside. Probably. They have creepy little serial killer hands, like racoons but with longer fingers. For all I knew, they could work locks.

Gradually, the road curved away from the orchards for which it was named, moving toward the lake. The township of Buckley became visible off to the right, a low, ramshackle collection of buildings with no skyline to speak of. Those were for big cities where things happened, not for good, honest places filled with good, honest people doing good, honest work.

I could have told the people of Buckley some stories about the things that could happen even in the absence of a skyline. But they wouldn't have listened, or they would already have known those stories from their own family histories, where they were kept buried, quietly sanitized, or locked away.

The world is stranger than most people admit, and because no one ever wants to talk about it, no one ever seems to realize that they're not unique. Everybody already knows.

The Red Angel was a low-slung building right on the edge of the lake, somehow managing to be two stories and squat at the same time, like it was crouching down and getting ready to pounce. The paint, what little there was, was an unassuming shade of brown that had probably looked sun-bleached even before it had started to peel. There were only a few cars parked in the churned-up mud around the building, each of them looking faintly ashamed of itself, like they knew they didn't belong there.

I sped up. Sam matched me. Fern slowed down.

"I don't want to go into the murder shack," she said, in what would probably have seemed like a perfectly reasonable tone if I hadn't been so eager to get something cold in my stomach and wash away the dust at the back of my throat. I turned and flashed her a smile.

"It's not a murder shack; it's a respectable drinking establishment that profits from being mistaken for a murder shack by most of the locals," I said. "Come on. Don't you want something to drink?"

"I don't want to be murdered," said Fern, uncertainly. "You're sure we won't die?"

"Come on. My family's been going to the Red Angel for generations, and none of us have been—okay, a lot of us have been murdered, but not in the bar, and not by anyone who drinks here. We're good at getting killed." I shrugged broadly, trying not to focus on the sour look on Sam's face. I guess being reminded that his girlfriend had the life expectancy of Bobby's first grade hamster was hard on his nerves. "No one's getting murdered today. Come have a beer."

"I don't drink beer," said Sam.

"Come have a fruity cocktail with too many cherries in the bottom," I said. "I promise they won't offer you banana liqueur unless you ask for it."

He wrinkled his nose but stepped forward and slipped his hand into mine. I resumed my trek toward the Angel, the others trailing along in my wake.

The main door faced the lake, a dazzling view that was fairly wasted on the windowless bar. I pulled the screen open, propping it with my hip before opening the actual door and stepping into the cool, dark confines of the Red Angel for the first time in literally years.

It hadn't changed a bit. That wasn't a surprise. This was the sort of place that viewed bar fights as the moral equivalent of redecorating and had never heard of modernization. The tables were round, scarred, and ancient, covered in thick layers of dark varnish that rendered them all functionally identical. The mingled scents of sour beer and cigarette smoke hung in the air. Technically, smoking indoors had been banned in Michigan since before I was born, but functionally, the health inspectors had a "see no evil, don't get swallowed alive by an unspeakable terror from the dark woods" relationship with the ownership of the Angel.

The woman behind the bar was svelte and pale, with Nordic facial features, shockingly red hair, and an apron tied tightly around her waist. A little too tightly for how wide around she appeared to be; it curved inward at the back, like she didn't have any internal organs to get in the way. That, combined with the swishing lash of her tail, confirmed her species as well as any sort of ID card. Huldrafolk.

Sam, who had entered right behind me, froze and stared at her. Rude. Fern and Cylia stepped around him, heading for the server. Cylia was already relaxed, beaming as she bellied up to the bar.

"Huldra?" she asked. When the woman nodded, she pointed to her chest and said, "Jink."

"No luck bending inside the Angel," said the woman. "We've had a couple of nasty scares."

"Understood, understood," said Cylia. "Can I get a beer? Whatever you have on tap is good."

"Gin and tonic for me, please," said Fern.

I turned my attention to Sam. "Hey, honey. You're allowed to relax now. We're inside, and no one who drinks here is going to rat you out."

"That woman has a tail," he said, in a stiff tone.

"Well, yeah. Cynthia's been running the bar since my grandmother was a little girl," I said. "She's a huldra. They're from Finland, originally, and they can live for hundreds of years before their skins harden and they turn to stone."

"My wife is one of the angel statues out back," said Cynthia, as she slid drinks to Cylia and Fern. "Hi, Annie. Mary stopped by and told me you might be passing through. I admit, I thought she was pulling my tail. Who's your grim-looking friend?"

"This is Sam," I said. "My boyfriend." It felt weird to be introducing him that way to Cynthia, who had been a friend of the family for generations, ever since my great-grandmother had shot her door off its hinges.

"And is there a reason your boyfriend is scowling at me like that?" A note of cautious wariness slipped into her voice.

I couldn't blame her. As both Grandma and Verity prove, my family isn't always clever about picking our romantic partners. One too many Covenant foot soldiers for most cryptids to be really comfortable.

"You don't have any security," he blurted. "Anyone could just come in the door, any time they wanted to! How is this *safe*?"

"We've been here for a long, long time," said Cynthia. "The locals tell lots of scary stories about us, how we cook runaway kids on the weekends, how people will break your jaw just for stepping into the parking lot. We're hiding in plain sight by being part of the landscape. Sometimes that's the safest choice of all."

"But the Covenant—" said Sam.

"They know about the Angel," said a voice from the far end of the bar. Its owner stood, pushing her drink away as she unspooled from her stool. She was short, curvy, and underdressed for the chill generated by the bar's air-conditioning, in cut-off denim shorts and a red tank top. Tattoos covered her left arm, and the left side of her neck, complicated and interlinked. She looked at Sam with all the emotion and sympathy of an alligator assessing a stray dog that had wandered too close to the water. "They've known about the Angel for at least fifty years, and they're smart enough to leave it the hell alone."

"Mary came through, huh?" I said, with a glance at Cynthia.

"Maybe I wasn't her only stop." She shrugged generously. "You want your usual?"

"Please. Sam? This is where you order a drink, so the nice bar doesn't throw us out."

"Um. Hard cider, if you've got it," he said.

Cynthia nodded and moved to start pouring drinks. I approached the woman who was still standing next to her stool, virtually glaring at Sam. She transferred her gaze to me as I got closer. It didn't warm.

"Some of these tattoos are new," I said, gesturing toward her wrist. I didn't touch her. It was never a good idea when she had that absent, unrecognizing look on her face. Maybe she knew who I was and maybe she didn't. If she didn't, unwanted physical contact could get me shot. "Were you traveling again?"

"I've tried a few new dimensions, looking for Thomas, since the last time you came home," she said. The numbness in her expression cracked. "I thought we'd sent you off to die," she said, before sweeping me into her arms and crushing me against her chest. The rules against me touching her didn't run in the opposite direction.

"Hi, Grandma," I wheezed.

Motion out of the corner of my eye alerted me to Sam's approach. When he wanted to be, he was faster than anything human. The fact that he was moving like that told me even without getting a good look at him that he had returned to his more customary fūri form. The true potential of his speed is reserved for when he's moving with the bones and muscles he was born to, and not the human ones he occasionally tries on for size.

"Sam," I managed, despite the lack of oxygen entering my body, "don't hit my grandmother. Grandma, don't attack my boyfriend."

"Grandmother?" said Sam, at the same time as my grandmother said, "Boyfriend?" It was impossible to tell which one of them sounded more confused. But at least Grandma let me go.

I immediately stepped backward, out of easy reach, and started rubbing my sternum with one hand, encouraging the bone to stop aching. "Ow," I said, with as much coherence as I could muster. "Grandma, did you forget that I'm not you?"

No one in our family is in poor physical condition. We've been lucky when it comes to illnesses and injuries, and all of us, even Alex, have chosen extracurricular activities that keep us in excellent physical shape. And then there is my grandmother. She's been moving between dimensions for decades, trying to locate her missing husband, doing a lot of God-knows-what to keep her stomach full and her guns loaded during that time—and honestly, I don't think she puts a priority on food. She could probably bench-press me and Sam both without breaking a sweat.

She looked at me flatly for a moment, and in her faintly confused expression, I could read the answer to my question: yes, she had forgotten, and not for the first time. Whatever function of her dimensional wanderings kept her young, it also left her occasionally bewildered about her own life and family, unable to keep straight whether something had happened to my sister or her mother. It made our relatively rare family dinners exciting.

"Uh, Annie?" said Sam. "This is your *grand-mother*? How is that possible? She looks younger than you do." Then he winced, like I was going to pull some stereotypical "girl in a sitcom" routine and get angry at him for telling the truth.

My grandmother was born in 1938, making her fifty-five years older than me. Despite that reality of our family tree, she looked like she was in her early twenties at the absolute most, and probably a few years younger than I was. That made her collection of tattoos, which completely spanned the left side of her body, all the more impressive; if her apparent age had been accurate, she would have needed to start the process when she was still in her teens, and some skilled tattoo artists were probably going to go to prison.

"It's complicated," I said. "Yes, this is my grandmother, Alice Price-Healy, originally of Buckley Township, Michigan. Grandma, this is my boyfriend, Sam Taylor. He's a fūri."

"I can see that," said Grandma. "Honestly, him being a fūri is a lot less surprising than him existing at all. When you say 'boyfriend,' you mean . . . ?"

"I mean we're dating." I reached over and took Sam's hand. His tail snaked around my ankle a beat later, like me touching him in front of my grandmother was permission for him to touch me back.

"Okay," said Grandma, and took a swig from her beer. "Well, you're a brave man, Sam Taylor. I should buy you a drink. Do you want a drink?"

"I asked for a hard cider," he said. "I think I need a drink at this point, um, Annie's grandmother. The terrifying, infamous, ex-Covenant monster hunter."

"That's a filthy lie," said Grandma. "I was never a member of the Covenant. They wouldn't have had me even if I'd wanted to join, on account of how my grandparents were filthy traitors to their cause and my mother was a carnie brat."

"What a coincidence," said Sam. "So am I!"

"A filthy traitor or a carnie brat?" asked Grandma.

"We met at his family's carnival," I said, desperate to seize control of the conversation back from my grandmother before she could decide that my boyfriend would make a lovely rug. Cynthia slid a bottle of pear cider down the bar. I grabbed it and thrust it at Sam. "He does the flying trapeze. We were partners for a little while before I had to burn the place down so we could get away from the Covenant handlers who thought I was working for them."

"Oh, you *have* had a hard time, haven't you?" Grandma shook her head. "I'm so sorry we sent you into that situation. I should never have agreed to it. But after your sister's little indiscretion, it seemed like the best way to clear things up . . ."

"You mean after Verity declared war on the Covenant of St. George on live television? That 'little indiscretion'?" I asked, not quite able to keep the disbelief out of my voice. My family has always downplayed Verity's errors, leaving me and Alex to clean up her messes. It's never great when it's obvious who the family favorite is, and none of us had ever had any question.

"Everyone makes mistakes, Antimony," said my grandmother. "If we're lucky, they turn out to be mistakes that we can learn from and talk about later. For example, if you burned down a carnival, you've learned a lot about fire since leaving home."

"Yeah," I said. "About that." I extended one hand toward her as balls of flame appeared above my fingertips, each about the size of a marble, ranging in brightness from lambent white to sullen red. "I've learned a *lot* about fire."

For possibly the first time in my life, I beheld the rare sight of my grandmother struck completely speechless. I lowered my hand. She took another swig from her beer.

"Well, I always wondered when that was going to crop up again," she said. "You kids hungry?"

"I could eat," I allowed slowly. "But our friend James is with the car—we're having mechanical problems—and we told him to meet us here. I'll have to call him if we're going somewhere else."

"Oh, there's no need for that," said Grandma. "Cynthia's always happy to have an excuse to fire up the barbeque, aren't you, Cynthia?" She twisted around to look at the bartender, who sighed and reached back to untie her apron.

"For you, Alice, always," she said. "All we've got in the kitchen right now is chicken. That work for everybody?"

"I'm not a vegetarian," said Sam.

"I like chicken," chirped Fern.

Grandma looked at Fern and Cylia like she had just figured out that they were with me—which, if she was having a bad day and hadn't been expecting me to walk in on her, she might not have. She cocked her head slightly to the side.

"Sylph and . . . ?"

"Jink," said Cylia, turning her attention toward our little group. "Annie and I played roller derby together."

"And you didn't bend her luck toward yourself?"

"No, ma'am. Manipulating luck when you have a dozen women on roller skates whipping around a track is a good way to get somebody killed, and I'm not that kind of girl."

Grandma nodded, looking pleased. "You've got a good group here, Annie," she said.

"Wait until you meet James."

"He eat chicken?"

"Yes, ma'am," I said.

"Then he'll fit right in. Come on. We can sit out back."

"I'd rather stay inside if you don't mind," said Sam, gesturing to himself with one long-fingered hand. "It's uncomfortable to play human for too long, and it's harder when I'm trying to eat. It's like trying to hold in a sneeze and swallow at the same time."

"If you need privacy, there's the old pool room," said Cynthia. "As long as you don't mind some cobwebs."

"We're good with spiders," I said. Sam's tail squeezed my ankle, acknowledgment of what was essentially an inside joke. The first hint he'd had that I wasn't just some greenstick girl with no idea about the cryptid world had come when we'd been forced to fight a Jorōgumo—sort of a spider-centaur without arms—to make her stop killing people who just wanted to enjoy the carnival.

Normal people get meet-cutes. I get crime scene cleanup. But I'm used to it, and I wouldn't know what to do with myself if the world decided it didn't want to work this way.

"All right," said Grandma. "Everybody grab your drink."

Cynthia hadn't been kidding about the cobwebs. The "old pool room" clearly got its name from the three pool tables that took up most of the floor space. What remained of their velvet was scratched and torn, making them useless as playing surfaces, although they still did an excellent job of getting in the way. It might as well have been called the "spider storage room." Fern immediately squeaked in delight and launched herself into the air, spinning as she rose into the cobweb-choked rafters.

Grandma and I stared at her, briefly united in our positions as the only humans in the room.

"Well, she's going to get a little dusty," said Grandma.

"No bet," I said, and touched the tip of my index finger to a strand of webbing, which promptly burnt away in a flash of light and crumbled into ash. "I can't do the whole room; I'd burn the place down."

"No need," she said. "Cynthia must be keeping a thousand pounds of cobweb for a reason. I can't imagine what it might be, but it's the only reason I can think of for a health code violation of this magnitude."

"It's delicious," said Cynthia, walking into the room with a Tupperware pan filled with raw chicken and what smelled like barbeque sauce. "So are the spiders."

"Are you on a diet?" asked Sam, using his tail to swipe the cobwebs out of his hair. "Because I can't think of any scenario that results in this *many* spiders where you aren't on a diet."

Cynthia laughed and continued onward to the back door, nudging it open with her foot and stepping out onto the back deck. Cylia followed her. The door banged shut, cutting off the sound of their laughter as they got away from our weird family drama.

Given that Fern was still up in the rafters, I was starting to feel a little bit abandoned by my friends.

"Does your boyfriend not understand sexual reproduction?" Grandma pulled a chair out from the nearest table, kicked it twice to scare off any resident spiders, and whipped it around so she could sit on it. Backward. Of course. If anyone's going to get an emo teen for a grandmother, it's going to be me.

That's not fair. I love my grandmother very much, even if I sometimes worry about her stabbing me because I look too much like someone who's been dead for decades. It's not her fault that she's forgotten how to age. At least, I don't think it's her fault. No one's ever really been able to get her to discuss it.

"He understands sexual reproduction just fine, Grandma," I said, steadfastly not looking at Sam. "He also understands protection, which is why we're not going to be reproducing any time soon. If we ever do at all. 'Boyfriend' doesn't automatically mean 'serious enough that we've been talking about kids.'"

"You have more fun these days than we did when I

was your age," said Grandma, and laughed, while Sam uncomfortably pulled out and dusted off another chair, pausing occasionally to pick cobwebs out of his fur. He looked so monumentally miserable that I joined him, scorching the cobwebs off my own chair before sitting down.

"It's nice to finally meet more of your family," he said, sounding deeply, deeply uncomfortable. He settled next to me, tail once again winding firmly around my ankle. "She seems nice."

"No, she doesn't," I said. "She seems like an unstable old lady who somehow keeps aging backward, and who carries grenades that are older than I am way too frequently for comfort's sake."

Grandma leaned on her elbows and smirked at me across the grimy table. "Please, keep talking about me like I'm not here. It's a *wonderful* idea."

"Um," said Sam.

"Grandma, could you please stop trying to terrify my boyfriend? It took me a long time to find a guy I was interested in dating, and if you scare him away, I'm probably going to be single until I'm dead."

She raised an eyebrow and took a swig from her beer. "That sounds pretty serious, you know. Have you told your parents?"

I deflated. "Not yet. I haven't talked to them yet."

"Why the hell not? They've been as worried about you as I have. More worried, even. You're going to give your poor mother a heart attack if you don't phone home soon."

"Um." I looked down at the dusty tabletop, suddenly deeply interested in the wood. "I wanted to get closer to Oregon before I called."

"Worried she'll be on the first plane to wherever you say you are?"

I took a deep breath. "Worried she won't be."

"Oh, sweetheart." Grandma leaned across the table, putting a hand on my arm. "You know your mother loves you. You know she wants you to be safe and make good choices about your life. Don't ever doubt that she cares."

"It's hard to believe that when she's always been so willing to send me into danger in order to keep Verity out of it." Most younger sisters worry that they'll never live up to the standards set by their siblings. In my case, I have a little more reason to be worried than most. When Verity screwed up by declaring war on the Covenant of St. George live and on television, my family's response had been to ask me if I'd be willing to go undercover, cut off all contact with the people who were supposed to be my backup, leave the *continent*, and place myself in the virtual belly of the beast. Sure, I'd agreed to go, but only because I hadn't been able to imagine saying no and staying with the people who'd considered that to be a reasonable request.

And if I hadn't gone, I would never have met Sam, the crossroads would still have been beguiling people into deals designed to destroy them, and James would probably still have been trapped in New Gravesend, unaware of the deal that bound him there. Me going undercover with the Covenant had turned out to be the best thing that could possibly have happened. But there had been no way of predicting that when I'd agreed to go. My own family had looked at me and decided that I was the expendable one, that out of everyone in my generation, I was the one they could somehow manage to live without.

"I know that look," said Grandma. "You're thinking that your family threw you away. But Annie, everyone's been sick with fright, waiting to hear whether you're okay—and waiting for Rose or Mary to bring you home the only way they know how."

"You know they would have told you if I were dead. The crossroads would have allowed Mary to do that much," I said. "Rose was only keeping her mouth shut because I asked her to. If something had happened to me, she would have broken her word in a heartbeat."

"Maybe so, but that doesn't change a parent's fear. Your father was starting to talk about contacting the bogeyman community. Their whisper network can find almost anything."

True enough, and they would charge dearly for any help they offered. Bogeymen don't work for free. It's one of the things I like about them.

I took a deep breath, trying to shove aside the feelings of resentment and abandonment that almost always accompanied thoughts of my family. Some of them were justified and some weren't, and none of them were useful right now.

"I have something I need to tell you, Grandma," I said.

"You mean apart from your sudden second calling as a flamethrower?" she asked. "Don't think I've forgotten about that. It's a little hard to miss."

"Grandpa Thomas was a sorcerer, too, right?" I snapped my fingers, summoning a tiny ball of flame to balance on the tip of my thumbnail. "Aunt Mary says he was, and this stuff runs in families."

"Yes. Yes, my Thomas could call fire out of nothing when he wanted it." Grandma's gaze went misty, the way it always did when someone brought up my grandfather without mentioning the fact that he was missing and very probably dead. "That man never had cold hands, not even in the very depths of winter."

"Okay, one, too much information and ew, and two, good to know, I'll have to work on that." Being able to keep myself at a decent temperature no matter what was going on with the weather would be useful. "I guess the Price genes won out in my case. That explains the cheekbones."

"It's why I've always had to fight so hard not to let everyone see that you're my favorite," she agreed.

I blinked. "I'm not *anybody's* favorite."

"You're *my* favorite," said Sam mildly.

"Only because you didn't meet my sister first," I said. "Trust me, no one who meets Verity before they meet me chooses the spare."

"Antimony Price, don't you dare talk about yourself like that!" snapped Grandma, sitting up straighter. "You're not the spare anything. You're my grand-daughter."

"Sorry, Grandma," I said, trying to ignore the alarmed look on Sam's face as he stared at me. He didn't like me talking about myself so negatively any more than she did.

The door we'd all come in through banged open, and James stepped inside, looking pale and shaken. "You could have told me this was a cryptid bar," he said, voice dropping as he caught sight of my grand-mother. "Or that you were going to be drinking with friends. Hello, ma'am. I'm James Smith."

"Hello, Jimmy," said Grandma cheerfully. "How'd you know I was a 'ma'am'?"

"Every woman I'm not related to is a 'ma'am' until I'm sure they're not going to eat me," James said. "And I prefer 'James,' if you don't mind."

"Sorry," said Grandma. "Annie, is this the friend you were talking about before?"

"It is," I said. "He's from New Gravesend, in Maine. One of his ancestors made a deal with the crossroads to make sure there would be a sorcerer in every generation. But they didn't word it very care-fully. The crossroads set the bargain to ensure that there would only ever be *one* sorcerer in New Gra-vesend. As soon as the next one was old enough to start manifesting their powers, the old one would die. Freak accidents and illnesses, stretching back genera-tions. James, this is my grandmother, Alice Price-Healy. You'll hear a lot about her from the cryptids you're going to meet."

"I'm sort of an urban legend among the urban legends," said Grandma cheerfully. "People are a little freaked out by humans who live as long as I have."

"Ah," said James. "I mean—you're not really—how are you Annie's grandmother? You look like one of the girls I went to high school with."

"Family mystery," she said, laughing, a bright, cackling sound that seemed to fill every corner of the room.

"She never gives a straight answer to that question," I said. "Whatever she's doing, it's not something she's proud of."

"So *you* age normally, right?" asked Sam. "I'm not going to wake up in bed with a middle schooler one morning?" He sounded genuinely unsettled.

I put a hand on his arm. "Good concern, and one I should have predicted, but no. I age like a normal human, or I always have up until this point; I've only been flinging fire around for about a year, so who knows what that's going to do to me?"

"I've been freezing things for substantially longer than that, and I've been getting older," said James reassuringly. "Don't worry, I think your normal levels of perversion are all you're going to have to deal with."

"Thank the God of carnies and weirdoes," muttered Sam, sinking a little deeper in his seat. Grandma raised an eyebrow. He shook his head and said, slightly louder, "I knew I was signing up for the modern Addams Family when I told Annie I was in love with her. I'm a monkey who pretends to be a man in love with a human flamethrower who's on her way home to a congregation of talking mice, and it turns out there's stuff that's too weird even for me. Aging backward fits the bill."

"Well, dear, it's a good thing I'm not on the market," said Grandma, leaning across the table to pat his hand.

"I'm not really into blondes," he said. "I'd have started dating creepy dead aunt number one if I were, since she seemed a lot less likely to get herself shot in the head."

"He means Mary, and he's the one who got shot in the head," I said, as Fern finally drifted down from the rafters with cobwebs and probably a few live spiders tangled in her hair. "It's been an eventful road trip."

"I should think so," said Grandma. She tilted her head. "But what did you want to tell me that was so important that you keep trying to put it off?"

"The sorcery wasn't enough?"

"I'm your grandmother. I know when you're not telling me something. Now, I know you're not pregnant—"

"Thank *God*," I said, firmly enough that it would probably have been insulting if Sam and I hadn't been so careful.

"—and I know you'd never lead the Covenant to the Angel, or to Buckley. So what's weighing on you, my girl? What have you been up to?"

I took a deep breath. "I told you James' family was laboring under a generational crossroads bargain. What I didn't tell you was that I made a bargain of my own, while I was in Florida. I had to, in order to save myself, and to save Sam. Mary brokered it for me. She tried to talk me out of it, too, but I wouldn't let her. I needed to live. I needed Sam to live."

My grandmother, who had gone very pale somewhere in the middle of all that, stared at me like she had never seen me before. "You know your grandfather sold himself to the crossroads to save me," she said quietly.

"Only because we've all been comparing notes for years. You never wanted to give anyone a straight answer about that."

"Because I didn't want any of you kids to decide that it was okay, or acceptable, or romantic! Saving your lover's life doesn't mean you get to *stay* with them. The crossroads are very clear about that. Mary tried to save my Thomas, bless that poor girl's spectral heart, but they outsmarted her, and they'll outsmart you, too! Oh, Annie. Annie, Annie, my girl . . . I never wanted this for you."

"I'm fine, Grandma," I said. "The crossroads aren't going to hurt me. I killed them."

" . . . what?" The word was barely loud enough to qualify as a whisper.

"They wanted me to murder James in order to fulfill my debt to them and get my sorcery back," I said. "I didn't want to do that."

"And I'm very grateful, but I don't think your grandmother is breathing right now," said James. "You may want to hurry this explanation up a little bit."

"I'm not sure I can," I said. "His best friend from school was a girl named Sally. She'd gone to the crossroads to make a deal when they were about to graduate from high school. The crossroads took her instead of honoring whatever she'd asked for."

"I know Sally went to ask them for my freedom, and I know they didn't grant it," interjected James. "They took her, and they didn't give her anything in return. That's how we were able to get Annie the access she needed to beat the ever-loving shit out of them."

The profanity sounded odd coming from James, who was usually so much more careful about his word choices than the rest of us. I couldn't say that he was wrong.

"Because the crossroads violated their own rules, I was able to get Mary to take me for an arbitration. I bent time in the little pocket dimension where the crossroads 'lived,' and I saw them arrive in this world. They displaced the original force of the living Earth, the anima mundi. The anima mundi wasn't expecting an attack from outside. They weren't prepared to fight off whatever the crossroads actually were. I suspect they were the anima mundi of a dead world, someplace that couldn't sustain them anymore. So they went looking for something new to eat, and they found us.

Or they would have, if I hadn't been waiting there to kick the crap out of them."

Grandma stared at me blankly.

Sam nudged me in the side. "I told you that trying to explain time travel never did anybody any good," he said. "The crossroads existed before you killed them. They did all the things you remember them doing."

"I know," I said wearily. "But because I killed them before they could kill the anima mundi, they never existed in this world. It's a paradox. It sucks, but this is how it is now. We have to live with the repercussions of something that never happened. We have to clean up the messes the crossroads never had the chance to make. Magic is a headache given flesh."

"You can say that again," said Cylia cheerfully as she stepped back inside, leaving the door to slam shut behind her. "Cynthia says the chicken will be done in about ten minutes. Annie, your grandmother looks like she's about to keel over."

"Breathe, Grandma." I leaned across the table to touch her hand. She let me. Under the circumstances, that was probably a good thing, and not a sign of shock. I hoped. "Mary is fine, because of us. As a family, I mean. We're the house she haunts, and so when the crossroads went away, they didn't take her with them."

"Oh," said my grandmother, very faintly. "That's nice."

"Mary thinks so." I took a deep breath. "There were things she couldn't tell you while she still served the crossroads—not unless you were willing to enter into a deal with them."

"I never did it," said Grandma. "I promised Thomas that I wouldn't, no matter how bad things got or how tempted I might be, and I didn't. Not ever."

"I know," I said. "But that's why she couldn't tell you that you were probably right. He might still be alive out there."

Moving with terrifying speed, she grabbed hold of the hand that was touching hers, bearing down on my fingers until I bit my lip and groaned under the pressure. "What do you know?" she demanded. "Whatever it is, you have to tell me, and you have to tell me *right now*."

The temperature of the air to my left dropped by several degrees. "Ma'am, I'm going to need you to let her go," said James.

"So am I," said Sam. "I can't freeze you solid like James here, but I can punch you a lot."

Grandma let go of my hand, settling back in her chair. "Are you boys really going to sit here and threaten me?"

"Yes, ma'am," said James. "We just met you. Annie's our friend."

I shook my hand, trying to make the throbbing stop. "Boys, stand down. Cylia, why didn't you join in the threatening?"

"I love you, but not enough to threaten *Alice Healy* for hurting you," she said. "Unlike the boys, I grew up in the cryptid community. I know what she can do to me."

"Smart," I said. The pain in my hand wasn't as bad as it would have been if she'd actually broken anything. I still pulled it back, resting it in my lap as I said, "We got confirmation that the crossroads sometimes took people and put them somewhere far away, someplace where they couldn't get home. The anima mundi doesn't know exactly where they are, so they can't help us, but the crossroads aren't actively working to keep us away from them anymore."

Grandma stared at me for a long moment, eyes wide and glassy, before she put her hands over her face and said, "Oh."

"Oh?" I echoed.

"Oh." She lowered her hands and smiled beatifically at me. "I told you so. I told you all. He's alive out there."

"Um," I said. "He was. I hope he still is, for my sake as much as yours—I'd really like to have someone who could teach me how to be better at sorcery. Trial and error is resulting in a lot of scorch marks."

"I'd love it if someone could teach her not to set things on fire while she was sleeping," said Sam. "Burning fur smells *terrible*."

"It's worse for the rest of us," said Cylia. "Trust me."

Sam wrinkled his nose at her. The back door banged open, and we all tensed, Grandma reaching for the gun at her hip, Fern bouncing back up into the cobweb-choked rafters and disappearing.

Cynthia, who had just stepped inside with a platter of barbequed chicken in her hands, blinked at us like we were doing something truly ridiculous. "Food's ready," she said, hoisting the platter to show us all before she walked over and dropped it onto the table, adding a handful of plastic forks. "Let me know when you're done, and I'll come pick up the leftovers. If there are any."

The chicken smelled delicious, like sweet hickory sauce and charred meat, and I grabbed a fork and speared a thigh before I could think better of it. "Thank you, Cynthia," I said.

"You kids all right back here?" Something about the way she asked the question made it clear that her question encompassed my grandmother, who was still staring at me, looking like I'd offered her everything she'd ever wanted, but put it on the other side of an impassable lake of molten lava.

"We're great, ma'am," said Sam, his tail tightening around my ankle. "Thank you."

"You're a fūri, right?" she asked, eyes on Sam.

He nodded reluctantly.

"We used to have a fūri living local, back in the

early '70s," said Cynthia, either unaware of the tension in the room or ignoring it. "She was a nice lady. Kept getting in trouble with some of the folk from town, since no one who grows up in Buckley is completely at ease with big, unidentified animals in the trees. You know your troop?"

"Troop?" asked Sam, blankly. "I was raised by my grandmother, ma'am. She's human. So's my mother. I never met my father."

"This modern world." Cynthia shook her head. "My mother was huldrafolk, like I am. My father was a grove of white birch, as is only right and fitting."

"Your dad was a tree?" asked Cylia.

"No," said Cynthia. "My father was about three dozen trees. They each contributed pollen to the making of me, and had any of them been absent, I would have been someone altogether different. My mother was their wife, until they were cut to the ground by humans who wanted the land where they grew. She moved to America with a baby in her arms and a coat on her shoulders to hide the bowing in her back. It was easier in those days to cross international borders without being unmasked as something other than human. No one ever asked her to disrobe, or to unswaddle me. We settled in Michigan, and she built the Red Angel with her own two hands before passing it on to me. She grows behind the building, on a stretch of land the state allows me to pretend I own. As if anyone could *own* land, apart from the trees, and I still have a century or more before I decide to put down roots."

"You were part of what gave me the idea to keep snatching back my youth until I was done with it," said Grandma, warmly. "I grew up and started growing old, and you never did."

"Yes, well, we huldra are made of sterner stuff than you humans—or most of the people who can pass for human. It's like having a fast breeding and birthing cycle made you careless with the way you live your lives." Cynthia made a small scoffing noise. "I love you anyway. Alice, are you and the kids staying in town tonight?"

"We are," I said. "Our vehicle won't be ready until tomorrow at the very earliest. I figured I'd show the gang the old Parrish place, since we don't have any tenants living there." We never did. Renting out the old Parrish place would have upset my grandmother, the family of tailypo living on the property, and inevitably, anyone who thought it was a good idea to live there.

The house had been originally chosen by the Covenant as a way to punish my grandfather for the sin of disagreeing with them. It wasn't haunted; sort of the opposite, as I'd told Sam. No ghost with any common sense was willing to pass its threshold, and no people with any common sense had any business going there either.

"I always stay at home when I'm in town," said Grandma. "It's why the power is still turned on."

Cynthia nodded slowly. "You know I have a room for you if you ever want it," she said. "It'd be healthier than staying there all by yourself."

"I won't be by myself tonight," said Grandma cheerfully. "I'm going to have Annie and her friends with me."

Cynthia sighed, looking briefly disappointed. Then she nodded. "I suppose you will, at that," she said. "Well, if you kids need anything else from me, I'll be at the bar. Enjoy your chicken."

She turned and disappeared then, back out into the slightly cleaner, less cobweb-choked main room of the Red Angel.

As soon as the door closed, Grandma turned her attention back to me. "Where did the crossroads send him?" she asked.

"I don't know," I said. "The anima mundi didn't know either. But they said that the people the crossroads sent away were alive when they went. That means he could still be alive out there. If he's as resourceful as you've always said he was, he could still be hanging on."

Of course, he probably wouldn't have Grandma's little anti-aging trick, and he'd been older than her when he disappeared, all the way back in 1965. He had to be in his nineties by now, and that could make bringing him home difficult. Not that my grandmother gave one good goddamn about difficult. She'd been throwing herself through endless hells since his disappearance, with no goal in mind beyond bringing her lost love home.

It was a little obsessive, sure, but I'd sold my magic and potentially my life to the crossroads to save Sam, and he and I hadn't been together even half as long as my grandparents had. People do stupid things when they're in love. That's sort of what love is *for*.

It would be nice if my family could manage love with a little less disaster, but I guess it's true what they say: people learn from example. And all of our examples are catastrophic ones.

I took another bite of barbequed chicken. Everyone else reached for their forks and speared pieces for themselves, and for a few minutes, there were no sounds but the sound of chewing, and of Fern bouncing about gently in the rafters. Then she drifted serenely down to floor level, stabbed a piece of chicken, and asked, "Are we staying with your grandmother tonight, Annie?"

I looked at Grandma, who nodded. "Yeah," I said. "I guess we are."

Cynthia didn't charge us for the chicken. "It's nice to have proof that Alice has eaten something on this plane of reality more recently than the pie-eating contest we held back in 1992," she said, waving us toward the door. "Now get out of here. This many humans makes the rest of my clientele nervous."

Given that the rest of her clientele appeared to be two bogeymen, a swamp hag, and what might have been a minotaur, I had serious reason to doubt that, but not enough to make me argue with her until she gave us a bill. Instead, I waved and led the rest of our motley group to the exit, where Grandma was waiting.

"We'll have to walk to the house," she said. "I'll leave my motorcycle here for the night. Not the first time, probably not going to be the last, and it's not like I could fit all of you on the seat."

"I know the way," I protested. "We could meet you there."

"Your mother would literally never let me hear the end of it if I lost track of you right now," she said. "Evie's a pretty dab hand with her necromancy, so you know I mean that literally."

I rolled my eyes but didn't argue. People leave ghosts when they die with unfinished business. It's common if undiscussed knowledge among my family that if Grandma Alice dies hunting for her wayward husband, she's going to keep coming to family dinners for the rest of time, because there's no possible way she's going to rest in peace. Again, love sucks, and again, there's a reason I spent so much of my life purposefully not looking for it.

"This way, kids," called Grandma cheerfully, before she started stomping down the road, heading toward the dark, somehow menacing edge of the forest. "Look alive, and don't step on anything you don't recognize."

"She's like a preschool teacher," said James, stepping up next to me, a bemused look on his face. "A heavily-armed, questionably-stable preschool teacher."

"Yeah, but she's not wrong around here," I said. "Buckley is what we like to call a high-weirdness zone.

Sort of like New Gravesend, only your weirdness was artificially imposed. You had the full attention of the crossroads. We don't. We just have the result of generations of cryptozoologists going out of our way to protect some of the weirdest wildlife North America has to offer. The local population is almost entirely human, because only the humans are stupid enough to stay in an area where rock scorpions and dire boars both like to live."

"How does the Red Angel stay open if this is a mostly human town?" The question came from Sam, back in his human form as he stepped up on my other side.

"Cynthia owns most of the lakeside property that isn't actually inside city limits, and this is a popular vacation spot," I said, linking my arm through Sam's as we followed my grandmother toward the woods. "She makes enough in rent from the summer people to pay her power and liquor bills, and while she doesn't gouge, this is the only cryptid bar left in Michigan. Her customers are happy to chip in when she's feeling skint."

"Sounds real community-minded of them," said James.

"She averages a wedding a week during the busy season," I said. "You and me, we're sorcerers, but we're still *human*. You just have to find a girl who's understanding about frostbite when you get frisky, and you'll be fine. Someone like Fern, on the other hand, has to do a lot more work if she wants to find Mr. Right. Cynthia didn't set out to be a matchmaking service, but she provides a safe place in a township the Covenant actively avoids, and plenty of alcohol. That's more than good enough for this modern world."

James flushed red and looked down at his feet, kicking a rock down the road without breaking his stride. Sam frowned.

"Why does the Covenant avoid Buckley?" he asked.

"Because they believe it's haunted by the ghosts of

three generations of Healys, all of whom are pretty pissed off about being murdered," I said blithely. "It's a long story."

"Is *everything* in this family a long story?" he asked reproachfully. "Do you think there's a chance you could make me like, some index cards with the short version on them, so I don't *completely* embarrass myself when I meet your parents?"

"Since you're adopting me, I'd like a set of those cards, too," said James. "Just with the little things I need to know. Like you'd mentioned that your grandmother carries grenades the way most little old ladies carry those funky violent-scented candies, but you never said anything about her being younger than you. No wonder you jumped straight to time travel as a solution."

"When something is normal for you, it doesn't necessarily occur to you to mention it without a good reason," I said. "Isn't there anything you haven't gotten around to telling me?"

"Nope," said Sam. "My life is an open book where you're concerned. Also, I think your grandmother is more dangerous than mine, which is sort of reassuring if you think about it, since my Grandma is pretty pissed off at me right now. If it comes down to Grandma-on-Grandma violence, I think yours will win."

"We are not starting a Grandma fight club!" I said firmly. She was far enough ahead of us that I wasn't worried she'd overhear, although Cylia looked back and smirked at me, clear amusement in her eyes. I did the mature thing and stuck my tongue out at her.

"I might have a few things," said James, ears still red as he kicked his rock around the road.

"It's all right if you have a crush on my girlfriend, my dude, even if she is volunteering to be sort of your sister," said Sam magnanimously. "I don't know whether you've noticed, but she has an absolutely fantastic rack."

"I have honestly not devoted much of my time to contemplating Antimony's breasts," said James.

I smacked Sam on the arm. "Don't say things like that where people might hear you."

"Why not? Your boobs come into a room before you do. People notice them."

"It's a good thing I already love you," I said. "If I didn't, I might shove you into the lake for the blood-worms to swim off with and find myself a boyfriend who doesn't try to make my adopted brother uncomfortable for fun."

"You'd miss me."

"I would," I allowed.

We kept walking. The trees grew closer, dark and tangled and menacing. There was nothing forgiving in the shadow of those trees. I couldn't imagine growing up here in Buckley, in the sight of that forest. The trees in Portland were dense and tangled, but they were forgiving. I had always known that they were on my side.

These trees weren't on anybody's side but their own. These trees had no interest in showing people where the bodies were buried; those bodies belonged to the trees now, and they weren't going to give up what was theirs. I shivered and shifted a little closer to Sam as we walked, creating a tripping hazard. James stole a glance at the tree line and moved closer to me in turn.

"You feel it, too, huh?" I asked. I had never been comfortable in the Buckley woods, but they had never felt this oppressively hostile before.

"The trees are watching me," he said. "I don't like it."

Grandma looked over her shoulder at us, and said, "Your grandfather was the same way about my woods. I think it's a sorcerer thing. They don't like you. I don't know why. Maybe a sorcerer hurt them once. They like *me* just fine."

"Of course the terrifying murder wood likes you," I called. "You're a terrifying murder lady."

She smiled. "Now Annie, don't be jealous. I'm sure there's a nice deciduous forest out there somewhere, just waiting to fall head over heels in love with you."

I snorted, but to be fair, her description wasn't far off. I'd read all the diaries documenting her teen years in Buckley, and her courtship with my grandfather. The trees here genuinely seemed to love her and had saved her life in their immovable way more times than was strictly realistic. She'd had two true loves in her lifetime: my grandfather, and the Buckley woods.

"I'll stick with my monkey, thanks," I said.

Sam preened.

"She just said she'd pick you over a literal forest," said James. "I wouldn't look so smug if I were you."

"Why not? Forests are great. Lots of trees to climb, lots of interesting toads and beetles and stuff to look at. I'm pretty sure that was the nicest thing anyone's ever said about me."

The boys fell to squabbling gently over my head as we walked. I smiled to myself, tuning out their words in favor of listening to their tones. They sounded perfectly relaxed, trusting me and Grandma to keep them safe in this familiar-to-us place. It was comforting, knowing they could trust me that much.

Up ahead of us, Cylia caught Fern's arm as the latter started to fall, having tripped over a rock in the path while her density was dialed down too far to let her recover on her own. I grinned. This was my family now, as much and as concretely as my biological family. We'd been through too much together to be anything else. We might not be together forever—probably wouldn't be, since Fern eventually wanted to meet a nice sylph boy and have babies of her own, and the sylph creche structure didn't really allow for her hanging out with humans and other cryptids while she was trying to reproduce—but we would always be a family, and that was remarkably reassuring.

Something had to be. We followed Grandma around a bend in the road, and a house appeared up ahead of us, tall and narrow and remarkably imposing, painted in an almost gangrenous shade of brownish-green. The shutters on half the windows were actively askew, creating the odd impression that the house was watching us approach. The architecture was somehow subtly *wrong*, like if we took a level and a protractor to the walls and angles, we'd find that they didn't line up and the structure didn't technically exist in this plane of reality.

The tension went out of Grandma's shoulders, and for the first time since I was a child, I actually believed the age she appeared to be. She looked like a teenage girl as she gazed at the house she'd shared with her husband, where my father had been born, where she'd either lost or given up everything she had. Her history wasn't a love story; it was a tragedy still in process. She sped up, heading for the porch. Cylia and Fern hung back. We caught up to them quickly.

"You're *sure* this place isn't haunted?" asked Cylia, voice low.

"According to the ghosts, it's not, and I usually listen to them," I said. "We could call one of them, if you'd like."

"I think it's looking at me," said Fern.

"A bunch of people got murdered here before the house belonged to my family," I said. "Something about a swamp god convincing the last owner that chopping his family into hamburger meat would win him its favor. Never go courting the favor of unspeakable gods of the swamp. They don't have a good track record when it comes to leaving their worshippers alive. Anyway, the ghosts don't like the house because of the whole 'swamp god was here' thing. They respect the territorial claims of the unspeakable."

Grandma had reached the porch. She hopped up the sagging steps, bending to pat something on the porch swing, and turned to wave at the rest of us. "Well, come on!" she called.

We came on.

She had the door unlocked and open by the time we reached her, allowing the distinctive dusty smell of a house that had been sealed off for a while to drift out into the afternoon. A ball of brown-and-black fur chittered at us from the porch swing.

"How cute, a raccoon," said James.

The "raccoon" stood up, uncurling a tail that was easily three times the length of its body, and chittered again before reaching for him with eerily simian hands.

"Not a raccoon," corrected James, a faint edge of panic in his voice.

"Tailypo," I said, reaching down to let it sniff my hand. "The American lemur. They're almost extinct now."

"But your grandfather always liked them, and he encouraged a colony to form around the house," said Grandma, from her place just inside the front door. "Lord love the man, sometimes he made me look like the one with common sense in this relationship."

"I just met her, and I know that's terrifying," muttered Sam. I laughed and elbowed him in the side before taking my hand away from the tailypo and following Grandma inside.

Despite the lingering smell of dust and ancient paper, the house was remarkably clean, with none of the cobwebs that had blazoned the Red Angel. The couch had been turned into a tidy makeshift bed, with two reasonably new-looking pillows under a threadbare patchwork comforter. Grandma's camping supplies were stacked in the corner, out of the room's main walkway. She perched on the arm of the couch as the rest of our group filed in, James at the rear with the tailypo at his heels. It chittered at him as it ran for the kitchen, and he jumped.

"Don't mind them," said Grandma. "There are two

males and three females currently living on the property. They have kits every spring and drive them off as soon as they're properly weaned. We may wind up with the last viable population of tailypo in the country, and all because my husband didn't have the heart to say 'no' when I brought him an injured animal—or when that animal started courting and showing off how nice its situation was."

"Will they bite us while we're sleeping?" asked Fern. "Or touch us with their creepy little hands?"

"They don't bite; we've had plenty of time to reach a compromise on living space here, they and I. Anyone who arrives in the company of a family member is safe and welcome. They don't bite strangers, either. When local teens decide to dare each other to go into the murder house, the tailypo will make a lot of noise and drive them off, but not by biting. They know that biting tends to summon animal control, and any of their children who've been taken away by the dogcatchers don't come back again."

"That's a little smarter than I like my weird woodland creatures to be," commented Cylia. "Are they people-smart?"

"Not quite," said Grandma. "But they're smart enough to know when they've got a good thing going, and I'm here rarely enough that they basically own this house most of the time. They have for years." She smiled wistfully after the tailypo.

"Well, this is all nice and portentful, Annie's Grandma," said Sam, sitting down on the floor and shifting into his monkey form at the same time, so that he could wrap his tail around my ankle again. "Are you going to be in Buckley long?"

"Just as long as you kids are," she said. "I was stopping by between bounties. I'll go when your car's fixed."

That couldn't have been her original plan—my

grandmother's not an oracle, she can't see the future—but Healy luck is a real thing. It's not like jink luck, where they can control the outcomes. It's more like an extreme form of being prone to coincidence. Sometimes it's almost unbelievable, but I've seen it in operation my whole life, and I believe. It would be hard not to. Dad and Aunt Jane have the same thing, in a slightly less extreme form, and then by the time you get to my generation, it's just a higher-than-normal tendency to run into cryptids every time we turn around.

I'd give a lot to know what kind of things my great-grandmother Fran's ancestors got up to behind the woodshed, is what I'm sort of saying here. There's something in our bloodline on that side of the family that's *not* human, and while whatever it is doesn't seem to be hurting anything, it would be nice to know what we're working with.

"And where will you go?" I asked, in a challenging tone.

Grandma sighed, looking around the room at my friends before focusing on me. "You really trust these people."

"They went with me to face the crossroads, so yes, I really do."

"I'm so glad." She smiled so broadly it looked painful. "I was worried you'd never find people you could trust that way. Verity can take up all the air in a room—she gets that from my side of the family—and Alex is good at holding his breath, but you never could. You needed to get out, and you needed to breathe. And now you can go home and keep on breathing. My perfect girl."

"Where are you going, Grandma?"

"Off to talk to Mary, and then to find my husband, and this time, I'm not coming back until I do." She offered me her hand. After only a momentary hesitation,

I took it. "If Mary says he's alive, he's alive. I've known her since I was a baby, and there's no one I trust more where the crossroads are concerned. If he's alive, he's out there somewhere, waiting for me, and I need to go find him before he gives up."

Somehow, I didn't think he was going to hold out all this time only to give up on her now. If he was still out there, he was going to be thrilled when his inexplicably young, hot, emotionally disturbed wife showed up to pull him out of whatever weird oubliette the crossroads had chucked him into. I couldn't imagine my grandmother would be this dedicated to a man who didn't deserve it, although it was difficult to ponder what he might have done so wrong in his life as to deserve *her*.

I made a face. Grandma laughed. "Did you honestly think telling me you'd found and killed the crossroads would get you any other response? Of course, I'm going to go find your grandfather. You know he must be dying to meet you all."

"Um," said James.

"All right, probably not all of you, but he disappeared while I was extremely pregnant, and he probably knows it's been long enough for his children to have had children. I know I would be wondering about my descendants if our positions were reversed."

"I would certainly hope so, since I'm one of them," I said.

Something rustled in the backpack next to the couch. James flinched away from the sound.

"Is it another tailypo?" he asked. "Or worse—rats? Do you put traps down here?"

"I would *never*," said Grandma, and reached into her bag—not with a grasping hand, like a normal person, but with her fingers fully extended and her palm flexed. It was a position I was deeply familiar with, and I smiled even as she pulled her hand free, displaying two mice, one brindle and one pale fawn, sitting in the center of her palm. Both of them were wearing jewelry made from bullet casings, and the brindle had a cloak of stitched-together candy bar wrappers.

"Whoa," said Sam. "More mice."

"More?" asked James. "I wasn't aware that mice were a risk."

"Why are those mice wearing clothes?" asked Fern. "Does this mean that all the other mice I've seen were naked?" She sounded genuinely distressed by the idea.

Cylia nodded toward my grandmother's palm. "S'up, Aeslin buddies?"

Grandma and I both turned to stare at her. She shrugged. "I get around. I've heard the rumors about you people having an intact colony. A lot of jinks get mixed up with the exotic animal trade. Easier to poach when you're guaranteed to find what you're looking for. You know what your friends there would go for on the open market?"

Grandma pulled her hand closer to her body, taking the mice with it. "Our mice are not for sale."

"I never said they were, and that whole gig isn't my thing. I have cousins who work the shows, but I haven't spoken to them in years. I'm not threatening your mice, I swear."

Grandma looked at me. I nodded encouragingly.

"I trust Cylia," I said. "She's saved my ass more than once. She's not going to hurt your mice. Speaking of, hello." I shifted my attention and address to the mice. "Are you the current head clergy of the Pilgrim Priestess?"

"We are," squeaked the brindle, puffing out its chest at the same time. As was often the case with Aeslin mice, I couldn't tell whether it was a boy mouse or a girl mouse, and I wasn't sure it mattered. Not being human, or even humanoid, the mice tend to prefer "it" as a gender-neutral pronoun, and we all go along with that, even as it makes some of us profoundly uncomfortable. Aeslin mice have a casual relationship with human concepts about gender at best. It's not that they don't care about our social norms. It's that once they have an idea in their heads, they don't let it go easily, and they got all their concepts about how humans think about such things from four-times great-grandmother, who found them in her chicken coop on what I'm sure was a very bracing morning.

"I am to be traded to the temple of the Noisy Priestess when this pilgrimage is done," said the fawn mouse.

Grandma Alice is sort of weird within the family because she has two separate temples dedicated to her mysteries. One of them observes the rituals created *before* Grandpa Thomas disappeared, while the other is occupied in chronicling her life as it continues to happen. They'll switch roles if he ever comes back. It makes my temple's structure seem simple and easily understood.

"Annie." James grabbed my arm, white-knuckled. "Annie, the mice are talking."

"Of course they are," I said. "They're Aeslin mice. The hard part is getting them to shut up." I looked at Grandma. "Just the two?"

"I can't take a whole colony with me when I'm moving between dimensions," she said. "It's too dangerous. Size doesn't impact the rituals I use, but the number of living things does."

"Ah." I nodded. "Three is within your limits?"

"I can't use rituals that won't accommodate at least two. What would happen if I found Thomas and didn't have anything on me that would get us both home? Three is a strain sometimes, but it's better than asking one of the mice to travel alone with me the way I used to."

The Aeslin mice are the living history of my family. They remember everything they see and hear, so as long as someone travels with their mice, everything goes into the record. There had been days when I missed the presence of my own mice so badly that it was all I could do to keep from screaming. I'd sent them back to Portland after I burned down the carnival, once it had become clear that it wasn't safe for them to stay with me while I was running from the Covenant. If I'd died while I was in my self-imposed exile, I would have been the first member of the family since great-great-great-great-grandma Beth to be even partially forgotten. Bemoaning the lack of privacy brought on by having a colony of nosy, intelligent rodents living in the walls is practically a family pastime, but I was going to sleep so much better when I was back with my mice.

"Here." Grandma held her hand out to me, mice still on her palm, looking at me with quivering whiskers and bright, curious eyes. "You need to take them home with you."

"Grandma . . ." I raised my hand automatically. The mice transferred from her palm to mine. I pulled them protectively toward my chest as she moved her hand away.

"You *are* going home, aren't you?" She frowned. "Your parents are worried sick. So are your siblings. Alex has asked me to go looking for you, twice. Verity's still in New York, and it's not safe for me to go see her, but I spoke to Dominic, and he asked about you. You need to show them that you're still alive."

"We will Chronicle your journey!" squeaked the brindle mouse, proudly. "We will Recount it to your clergy with precision."

"This is too weird," said James. His face had gone pale, and the temperature of the air around him was still dropping. Poor guy kept thinking he'd hit the threshold of how weird the world could be, and then discovering that once my family got involved, that was a well with no bottom. "Talking mice. And this is normal for you."

"She had two in her backpack when we met," confirmed Sam gravely. "I took them to the airport when she left me. Which she's never allowed to do again—it was very distressing."

"Yes, dear," I said, patting his arm.

The mice cheered. James jumped, obviously startled by the volume. I smirked at him.

"The Aeslin mice are a lot louder than you'd think they could be, sometimes," I said. "And they take a very close interest in the romantic lives of the family. So you'd better get used to it."

"Is a New Relative discovered?" asked the fawn mouse, whiskers quivering with barely contained excitement.

"James here is my brother now," I said. "His old family didn't take proper care of him or appreciate him enough, so I stole him."

"HAIL TO THE COMING OF THE STOLEN GOD!" shouted the mice in unison. Grandma laughed.

"Oh, you're in it now, boy," she said. "Once the mice take to you, you never hear the end of it. Do you like cookies?"

"Yes," he said uncertainly. "Why—"

"I'll bake you a batch when I get home, to say welcome to the family." She rose, spreading her hands to indicate the cluttered living room. "The house is yours, as long as you need it. There's a key under the mat. Lock up when you leave, then give it to the tailypo. They'll take care of things."

"Right," muttered James. "Of course, the tailypo will take care of things. Why would I expect anything different?"

"Why do I need to take your mice, Grandma?" I asked.

"I don't currently have a charm that's strong enough to get four people across a dimensional border," she said. "And I told you, I'm not coming home without Thomas. Not this time."

The numbers didn't add up. "If you don't have a charm that's good for four, how have you been traveling with two mice for this long?"

Her expression sobered. "I've been losing faith, my

lovely. Even I can't keep going without answers forever, and I suppose I was . . . I was starting to believe I'd lost him. Thank you for giving my faith back to me."

"Are you leaving right now?"

She looked at Sam, smiled knowingly, and looked back to me. "Wouldn't you?" she asked.

She grabbed her backpack, which rattled in an ominous way that probably meant it contained more ammunition than any one person needed unless they were planning to challenge an army, and then she was heading for the front door.

She didn't look back.

"Well," said Cylia, once she was gone, leaving the five of us alone. "She seems nice."

"She seems terrifying," said Fern.

"She's both those things," I said, looking down at the mice in my palm. "She's my grandma. I'll go check the kitchen, see if she left us anything to eat."

I transferred the mice to my shoulder as I walked out of the room. They promptly hid themselves in my hair, their claws scratching against my scalp in the soft, reassuring way they had since I was old enough to be considered responsible and capable of caring for my own clergy. No one followed me.

The fridge contained eggs, milk, and half a roast chicken. The cupboard had sugar, coffee, and a loaf of bread. My grandma may be half-feral these days, but part of her still trends more toward Donna Reed than Norma Bates. Lucky for us, although we were going to be pretty sick of chicken by the time we got back on the road.

The tailypo was sitting on the counter, tail wrapped several times around its haunches. It looked at me and chirped. I handed it a raw egg and left the room as it was working to chew through the shell.

"There's breakfast," I said. "Hopefully we'll be on the road pretty soon after we eat. I don't like to stay here longer than I absolutely have to."

James sat up straighter. "Is your grandmother really heading for another dimension?"

I shrugged. "Probably. She doesn't tend to lie about things like that. I think she doesn't see the benefit of lying to her family." She might have had a better relationship with her kids if she'd been a little more dishonest. But then again, they could have gotten the real story any time they wanted it by talking to the mice, and then she would still have deserted them, she would have just lied while she was doing it. Family is difficult sometimes. "We're all used to the fact that none of us matter as much as a man that most of us have never met. Dad was really little when Grandpa Thomas disappeared. Aunt Jane wasn't even born yet. Mary remembers him—they were friends—but she hasn't been able to talk about him for as long as I've been alive."

"The crossroads wouldn't let her?" asked Sam.

I nodded. "They really wanted us to just let him go. I don't think Grandma knows how to do that."

"Maybe she won't have to," said Cylia. "That's a lady with a lot of luck braided all around her. Good and bad mixed together until even I couldn't pull them apart."

"Healy family luck is funky," I said.

"It didn't look entirely human," said Cylia.

"Like I said, it's funky." I shook my head, all too aware of the weight of the mice clinging to my neck. "She'll be fine, or she won't. Either way, I'm not going to be the person who tries to stop her. I like her liking me."

James was looking increasingly alarmed. I flashed him a narrow smile.

"She'd never hurt me. Once the mice formalize your adoption, she'd never hurt you, either. The colony would never forgive her, and she values their good opinion more than she cares about anything human."

"Um," said Sam.

"Anything else intelligent," I corrected. "Now come on, let's all find places to sleep here in the big, creepy house."

Sam and I wound up upstairs, in a bedroom painted the exact color of raw steak. The bed was big enough for both of us, and there wasn't much dust; it was fine.

The mice bedded down in the chest at the foot of the mattress. Sam climbed in next to me, looping an arm around my waist and pulling me close. "When are you going to call your folks?" he asked.

"Tomorrow," I said. "I'll use the phone down at the Red Angel, and I said it in front of the mice. That makes it basically a promise."

A soft cheer rose from the chest. I rolled my eyes, safe in the knowledge that no one could see it.

"You're sure your parents aren't going to be mad?"

"About what? They know why I had to go into hiding. Mork and Mindy will have confirmed everything that happened, and the first rule of the family is that you don't endanger the family. Save yourself, then save everyone else, and that's exactly what I did. I followed the rules."

"I meant about you coming home with a bunch of weirdoes."

"Cylia and Fern are from Portland. They're going to go back to their lives, although they're basically family now—they dropped everything to make sure I was okay, and that's too big a gesture to forget because the road trip is over. Or do you mean 'are they going to be mad that I came home with a boyfriend'?" I rolled over, so that we were facing each other in the bed. Sam was looking at me with sincere worry in his eyes. I reached up and ran my fingers through the fur that crowned his cheek. "A boyfriend who isn't human?"

He nodded silently, biting his lip.

"They're going to love you, because I love you, and they're smart enough to know that I don't give my love away for nothing. I think they'd given up on the idea of me ever falling in love with anything that wasn't a weapon. They're going to *adore* you, and you'd better tread carefully, or the mice will adopt you, too, and once that happens, there's no getting away from this circus act. All right?"

Sam nodded, still looking unsure, so I leaned forward and kissed him. The mice cheered again, louder this time. I grinned. "Or maybe it's too late for you already," I said.

"It's been too late for me for a long time now," he said. This time he kissed me, and we didn't let the cheering of the mice distract us. It had been a long day, after all. We deserved a little time to ourselves.

Fern, Cylia, and James were all asleep downstairs. Tomorrow, we'd be back in a little travel trailer with no privacy, bound for Portland to deliver my grandmother's mice and face the music for my long absence. Tomorrow, I would call my parents.

But tonight, there was nowhere else in the world I'd rather be.

Price Family Field Guide
to the Cryptids of North America
Updated and Expanded Edition

Aeslin mice (Apodemus sapiens). Sapient, rodentlike cryptids which present as near-identical to non-cryptid field mice. Aeslin mice crave religion, and will attach themselves to "divine figures" selected virtually at random when a new colony is created. They possess perfect recall; each colony maintains a detailed oral history going back to its inception. Origins unknown.

Basilisk (Procompsognathus basilisk). Venomous, feathered saurians approximately the size of a large chicken. This would be bad enough, but thanks to a quirk of evolution, the gaze of a basilisk causes petrification, turning living flesh to stone. Basilisks are not native to North America, but were imported as game animals. By idiots.

Bogeyman (Vestiarium sapiens). The thing in your closet is probably a very pleasant individual who simply has issues with direct sunlight. Probably. Bogeymen are close relatives of the human race; they just happen to be almost purely nocturnal, with excellent night vision, and a fondness for enclosed spaces. They rarely grab the ankles of small children, unless it's funny.

Chupacabra (Chupacabra sapiens). True to folklore, chupacabra are blood-suckers, with stomachs that do not handle solids well. They are also therianthrope shapeshifters, capable of transforming themselves into human form, which explains why they have never been captured. When cornered, most chupacabra will assume their bipedal shape in self-defense. A surprising number of chupacabra are involved in ballroom dance.

Dragon (Draconem sapiens). Dragons are essentially winged, fire-breathing dinosaurs the size of Greyhound buses. At least, the males are. The females are attractive humanoids who can blend seamlessly in a crowd of supermodels, and outnumber the males twenty to one. Females are capable of parthenogenic reproduction and can sustain their population for centuries without outside help. All dragons, male and female, require gold to live, and collect it constantly.

Füri (Homo therianthrope). Often proposed as the bridge between humans and therianthropes, the füri is a monkey—specifically, a human—that takes on the attributes of another monkey—specifically, some form of spider monkey. Füri transform instinctively, choosing their human forms for camouflage and their more simian forms for virtually everything else. A transformed füri is faster, stronger, and sturdier than a human being. Offering bananas is not recommended.

Ghoul (Herophilus sapiens). The ghoul is an obligate carnivore, incapable of digesting any but the simplest vegetable solids, and prefers humans because of their wide selection of dietary nutrients. Most ghouls are carrion eaters. Ghouls can be easily identified by their teeth, which will be shed and replaced repeatedly over the course of a lifetime.

Gorgon, Pliny's (Gorgos stheno). The Pliny's gorgon is capable of gaze-based petrifaction only when both their human and serpent eyes are directed toward the same target. They are the most sexually dimorphic of the known gorgons, with the males being as much as four feet taller than the females. They are venomous, as are the snakes atop their heads, and their bites contain a strong petrifying agent. Do not vex.

Hidebehind (Aphanes apokryphos). We don't really know much about the hidebehinds: no one's ever seen them. They're excellent illusionists, and we think they're bipeds, which means they're probably mammals. Probably.

Jackalope (Parcervus antelope). Essentially large jackrabbits with antelope antlers, the jackalope is a staple of the American West, and stuffed examples can be found in junk shops and kitschy restaurants all across the country. Most of the taxidermy is fake. Some, however, is not. The jackalope was once extremely common, and has been shot, stuffed, and harried to near-extinction. They're relatively harmless, and they taste great.

Jink (Tyche iynx). Luck manipulators and masters of disguise, these close relatives of the mara have been known to conceal themselves right under the nose of the Covenant. No small trick. Most jinks are extremely careful about the way they move and manipulate luck, and individuals have been known to sacrifice themselves for the good of the community.

Johrlac (Johrlac psychidolos). Colloquially known as "cuckoos," the Johrlac are telepathic ambush predators. They appear human, but are internally very different, being cold-blooded and possessing a decentralized circulatory system. This quirk of biology means they can be shot repeatedly in the chest without being killed. Extremely dangerous. All Johrlac are interested in mathematics, sometimes to the point of obsession. Origins unknown; possibly insect in nature.

Jorōgumo (Nephilia sapiens). Originally native to Japan, these therianthropes belong to the larger family of cryptids classified as "yōkai." Jorōgumo appear to be attractive women of Japanese descent until they transform, at which point they become massive spidercentaurs whose neurotoxic venom can kill in seconds. No males of the species have ever been seen. It is possible that the species possesses a degree of sexual dimorphism so great that male Jorōgumo are simply not recognized for what they are.

Laidly worm (Draconem laidly). Very little is known about these close relatives of the dragons. They present similar but presumably not identical sexual dimorphism; no currently living males have been located.

Lamia (Python lamia). Semi-hominid cryptids with the upper bodies of humans and the lower bodies of snakes. Lamia are members of order synapsedia, the mammal-like reptiles, and are considered responsible for many of the "great snake" sightings of legend. The sightings not attributed to actual great snakes, that is.

Lesser gorgon (Gorgos euryale). One of three known subspecies of gorgon, the lesser gorgon's gaze causes short-term paralysis followed by death in anything under five pounds. The bite of the snakes atop their heads will cause paralysis followed by death in anything smaller than an elephant if not treated with the appropriate antivenin. Lesser gorgons tend to be very polite, especially to people who like snakes.

Lilu (Lilu sapiens). Due to the striking dissimilarity of their abilities, male and female Lilu are often treated as two individual species: incubi and succubi. Incubi are empathic; succubi are persuasive telepaths. Both exude strong pheromones inspiring feelings of attraction and lust in the opposite sex. This can be a problem for incubi like our cousin Artie, who mostly wants to be left alone, or succubi like our cousin Elsie, who gets very tired of men hitting on her while she's trying to flirt with their girlfriends.

Madhura (Homo madhurata). Humanoid cryptids with an affinity for sugar in all forms. Vegetarian. Their presence slows the decay of organic matter, and is usually viewed as lucky by everyone except the local dentist. Madhura are very family-oriented, and are rarely found living on their own. Originally from the Indian subcontinent.

Manananggal (Tanggal geminus). If the manananggal is proof of anything, it is that Nature abhors a logical classification system. We're reasonably sure the manananggal are mammals; everything else is anyone's guess. They're hermaphroditic and capable of splitting their upper and lower bodies, although they are a single entity, and killing the lower half kills the upper half as well. They prefer fetal tissue, or the flesh of newborn infants. They are also venomous, as we have recently discovered. Do not engage if you can help it.

Oread (Nymphae silica). Humanoid cryptids with the approximate skin density of granite. Their actual biological composition is unknown, as no one has ever been able to successfully dissect one. Oreads are extremely strong, and can be dangerous when angered. They seem to have evolved independently across the globe; their common name is from the Greek.

Sasquatch (Gigantopithecus sesquac). These massive native denizens of North America have learned to embrace depilatories and mail-order shoe catalogs. A surprising number make their living as Bigfoot hunters (Bigfeet and Sasquatches are close relatives, and enjoy tormenting each other). They are predominantly vegetarian, and enjoy Canadian television.

Tanuki (Nyctereutes sapiens). Therianthrope shapeshifters from Japan, the Tanuki are critically endangered due to the efforts of the Covenant. Despite this, they remain friendly, helpful people, with a naturally gregarious nature which makes it virtually impossible for them to avoid human settlements. Tanuki possess three primary forms—human, raccoon dog, and big-ass scary monster. Pray you never see the third form of the Tanuki.

Ukupani (Ukupani sapiens). Aquatic therianthropes native to the warm waters of the Pacific Islands, the Ukupani were believed for centuries to be an all-male species, until Thomas Price sat down with several local fishermen and determined that the abnormally large Great White sharks that were often found near Ukupani males were, in actuality, Ukupani females. Female Ukupani can't shapeshift, but can eat people. Happily. They are as intelligent as their shapeshifting mates, because smart sharks are exactly what the ocean needed.

Wadjet (Naja wadjet). Once worshipped as gods, the male wadjet resembles an enormous cobra, capable of reaching seventeen feet in length when fully mature, while the female wadjet resembles an attractive human female. Wadjet pair-bond young, and must spend extended amounts of time together before puberty in order to become immune to one another's venom and be able to successfully mate as adults.

Waheela (Waheela sapiens). Therianthrope shapeshifters from the upper portion of North America, the waheela are a solitary race, usually claiming large swaths of territory and defending it to the death from others of their species. Waheela mating season is best described with the term "bloodbath." Waheela transform into something that looks like a dire bear on steroids. They're usually not hostile, but it's best not to push it.

PLAYLIST

"Sarah Smiles. . . . . Panic! At the Disco
"Saving the World" . . . . .Brooke Fraser
"Closing Time" . . . . Semisonic
" . . . Ready For It?" . . . . .Taylor Swift
"Just the Other Side of Pain". . . . . Jill Tracy

ACKNOWLEDGMENTS

Here we are again, back with my beloved Price family for another exercise in terrible decision-making and worse self-preservation skills. I've been waiting to tell Sarah's story since the beginning; I hope it was worth the wait for you. It absolutely has been for me. My poor cuckoo-girl, getting everything she's ever wanted and losing it in the same breath. Don't worry, though. She has another book to come, *Calculated Risks*, which will be out next year at the usual time. And as you can see, Alice is up to her old tricks again—we're going to have an eventful few years around the family compound!

I live in the Seattle area. We have not, historically, gotten a lot of snow here. When we do get snow, it's a shock to our infrastructure, and sometimes we all get trapped in our homes. This happened during the writing of this book, and I wound up calling a bunch of snowed-in math nerds to ask them to come up with some utterly bonkers equations for Lee Moyer to use as cover reference. Thanks to Torrey Stenmark, Matthew Dockrey, and Alexis Nast, for giving up some of their snowbound hours to make our math suitably ridiculous. Thanks also to Lee Moyer, for stepping in to do our cover when Aly Fell needed a break. They're both amazing.

My machete squad is one of the best in the world, and I will fight anyone who says they're not. Without them, I would make infinitely more mistakes, and be infinitely sadder. Chris Mangum maintains my website code, while Tara O'Shea maintains my graphics, and they are so good. Thanks to everyone at DAW, the best home my heart could have, and to the wonderful folks in marketing and publicity at Penguin Random House.

Sarah has been with me for a long time, and because of that, I must pause to thank Phil Ames, who can be blamed for this entire series, Martha Hage, and Grant Morrison, who may never know how responsible he is for so many things. I am so incredibly glad to finally be telling you all her story.

Cat update (I know you all live for these): Thomas has adjusted to life without Alice far better than his fictional counterpart. He's still an anxious boy, and has to wear his shirts for the rest of his life to keep him from getting too stressed out, but he's doing okay. Megara is as soft as she is stupid, and she is *very* soft; it's like petting a particularly dim cloud. And our newest problem child, Elsie, has become unquestioned queen of everything, and is sitting on the back of my chair even now, watching me type this. Everyone gets along, which is wonderful, and we had a catio installed in the summer of 2019, so now they get to pretend to be wild beasts whenever they like.

And now, more gratitude. Thank you to the people who've come to see me at bookstores and conventions around the country and the world; to Kate for always being willing and ready to step up when I need her; to Sari, for parties and Ponies; to Michelle Dockrey, for continuing to answer the phone; to Chris Mangum, for daily support; to Steve and Laura, for emergency soup